BEYOND THE DARKNESS

PREDATORS OF DARKNESS SERIES: BOOK TWO

LEONARD HILLEY II

Illustrated by
CHRISTAL A. HILLEY

Again, for my wife, Christal—my love, my life, my inspiration.

CHAPTER 1

*N*ightfall disturbed Daniel. Three years had passed since he and his friends were rescued from the fenced off section of Pittsburgh. Though physically free, the haunting memories plagued his troubled mind. Each night he kept expecting to see the iridescent eyes of bloodthirsty shifters peering from the shadowed crevices along the streets or beneath parked cars.

The majority of the Pittsburgh peninsula had been rebuilt. Most of the inhabitants had returned to their former houses, but Daniel couldn't get beyond the darkness that had tarnished his once optimistic view of life. Buildings could be rebuilt, streets repaved, but healing the inner turmoil that clenched his soul was impossible.

When sunset welcomed the night, he sat in a reclining chair on his apartment balcony, watching shifting shadows, and looking for glowing eyes. The eyes never appeared. Their absence made him more anxious because he sensed they were still out there, somewhere. Waiting.

Julia stood behind his chair and rubbed his tight shoulders. Her brown hair was pulled back in a ponytail. Wearing a silk gown, she hugged herself as a cool breeze swirled around them. She leaned down and whispered her love into Daniel's ear, trying to ease his pained mind, but nothing she said ever calmed him.

The gentle touch of her breath against his ear sent chills down his back.

"

He shivered and glanced over his shoulder to engage her endearing smile. Instantly, his heart warmed. The faint fragrance of her perfume made him want to forget the nightmares, the days when death roamed the streets, but he was trapped inside his own mental vise seeking sanity and survival. Regardless of her gentle touch and her loving words, his anguish remained.

The only thing that alleviated his fears was writing about his ordeals. He fictionalized the details and events, turning his inescapable horrors into best-selling novels. Three, so far.

He hated that he had become an antisocial recluse. Julia offered various suggestions to free him from his prison, but he wasn't interested. He satisfied his depression and fear by sitting on the night-shrouded balcony, writing his next novel. While he wrote, he watched the night streets, always expecting the worst to come, but nothing sinister ever appeared.

Julia loved him, more than ever, and their daughter, Felicia, was a joy to both of them. Felicia was the only ray of light that had emerged from their dark days inside Helmsby's Genetic Research Center. The hours he spent playing with her during the day settled his nerves and gave him purpose. Often he believed he was going to break free of his mental shackles and live a normal life. Then the night set in, the apartment became quiet, and the darkness of night fell.

Daniel's memories of the vicious shifters continually robbed him of his inner peace. He didn't understand why they continued unveiling their presence when he least expected it. Julia insisted that he suffered from post-traumatic stress syndrome and should seek medical treatment, but he shrugged away the idea. He didn't need to pay a doctor to tell him that he was crazy when he already accepted that he was. He insisted that writing was therapeutic. Getting his fears and frustrations onto the page helped him heal. But lately, his qualms increased while his writing greatly *decreased*.

Morton sat on the railing and watched the street. His furry brows rose as if he remembered his own battles against Idris' shifter legion. Perhaps the cat held similar fears that Daniel never knew. Brave and bold, the cat shifter never flinched. There didn't seem to be anything the cat feared.

Julia wrapped her arms around Daniel's shoulders, kissed his lips, and smiled.

"I'm going to bed, honey," she said. "Come hold me?"

Daniel kissed her softly. "Let me write awhile. I'll be in before sunrise."

Sadness claimed her brown eyes. Tears crested and overflowed to form two streaks down her cheeks. "I love you, dear, by please let go of the past.

We survived the worst. Let's enjoy our future together. The shifters are gone forever."

"I don't know about that."

Julia shook her head and squeezed his hand. "Please?"

Morton sat on the balcony rail and watched them from the corner of his eyes while licking his forepaw. Even though in his cat form, the shifter was no more a cat than one of the night creatures that haunted Daniel. But he had befriended the yellow feline and taken him against Helmsby's wishes.

When Helmsby protested, Morton stood in his own defense and told Helmsby he refused to be a lab project and wanted to live with Daniel and Julia. Reluctantly, Helmsby acquiesced but Daniel knew the scientist grieved at the loss of his superior laboratory creation. The scientist's grief outweighed any fear he might have had that the cat would ever turn on Daniel and Julia. The thought never entered their minds that Morton presented any danger to them.

Daniel returned his attention to the streets. "For you, honey, the shifters are gone. But for me, they're still very real. I don't believe they're gone."

Julia closed her eyes tightly, squeezing fresh tears that didn't quench her burning frustration. She silently counted to ten.

Her moist eyes opened. With pain and remorse strained her voice."You're impossible sometimes, Dan. Really, you are. I've begged you to talk to Helmsby, to go see him, but you refuse. Since he works at TransGen-Corp for the government, he can tell you the shifters were completely destroyed. They no longer prowl around. He can prove it to you with documentation."

Daniel folded his arms. "I'll visit him when I feel comfortable about rehashing his betrayal."

"Betrayal?" Julia said with her hands firmly rested on her hips.

Seeing the fire in her eyes, he held no hope of winning this argument, so he looked down at the street.

"*When* did he ever betray us? He's the best friend you have besides Lucas," she said.

Daniel shook his head. "If he were our friend, why'd he let us stay in Pittsburgh when he knew the area was going to be hit by missiles? How many innocent people died because he withheld pertinent information that would have allowed us to leave before they attacked? Do you know how horrible it is to see your best friends killed and there's nothing you can do to prevent it? Hell, you and I almost got killed before General Norhaney intervened."

"I know how horrible it was. I was there."

"And you can forget the pain so easily?"

Julia rolled her eyes and bit her lower lip. "Dan, look at the big picture. Had he not allowed a lot of people to be sacrificed, and I know that was terrible, but hundreds of thousands of others might have died, too. Had the shifter project expanded beyond its Pittsburg territory, God only knows what *that* outcome would have been."

Daniel stared at her. "You would have willingly sacrificed your life to save all the others?"

She nodded. "Yes."

"Even Felicia?"

Julia's eyes narrowed. "That's not fair. She wasn't even born yet."

Daniel stood and gripped the railing tightly. Anger turned his blue eyes icy white. His firm, muscular jaw tightened. "You understand that a lot of children did die before the National Guard could rescue them, don't you? Dozens of college students I knew were trampled to death. I watched some of them dying. There wasn't anything I could do to save them. When I tried to help, Helmsby forced me to keep up with him."

"I know." She wiped away tears. "But it happened, Daniel, and it's over. You can't wallow in remorse over their deaths. Get out and do something with your life. Visit people. Helmsby can help you sort through this, if you'd go see him."

"Helmsby sent me to that warehouse with a killer, not Lucas. What bothers me the most is that he *knew* it was a clone manufactured by Trans-GenCorp."

Julia placed a hand on his shoulder. "He didn't know Lucas had a clone."

Squeezing a tighter grip on the rail, Daniel's knuckles whitened. "If Godfrey knew, Helmsby knew. My life meant nothing to him. All he was interested in was his scientific breakthroughs and discovering things no one else had. It's his euphoria."

"He knew you were capable of handling yourself and that you'd come back safely. He needed you for our survival. We all needed you, and you proved yourself to us."

"Perhaps," he sighed. "But I didn't prove it to myself."

Wrapping her arms around his waist, she said, "Let's not fight. I need you. I love you."

Daniel faced her and stared into her hurting eyes. "I love and need you, too."

"Why not call Helmsby tomorrow and pay him a visit? Work through your past and the bitterness that prevents you from being the man I fell in love with. Or spend some time with Lucas, at least. You should take a weekend trip with him. He's offered many times."

"He's visited us and eaten dinner with us several times in the past few months. He's my closest friend."

"That's not the same thing. You can't hole up in our apartment like a coward for the rest of your life." She folded her arms, shook her head, and turned away. "Well, maybe, *you* can, but I refuse to." She faced him again with a stern glare.

The words bit deeply into his soul. Even when she was angry, she was the most beautiful woman he'd ever seen. Beneath the anger was a fragile woman, his love, who had risked her life to protect him. His heart sank. He placed gentle hands on her cheeks.

"I'm sorry, Julia. You're right. I need to get out more, but I don't know how to handle the pressure. I thought getting out of Pittsburgh would free me, but it hasn't. I never imagined receiving the notoriety that came from surviving incredible odds. If you remember, I did try when we first left Pittsburgh. But I couldn't even go to a coffee shop without being hounded by dozens of people and the media. Everyone wanted to hear about the shifters, wanted my autograph, or to get a selfie of them with me. Always something. I didn't receive freedom. No one allowed me a moment's time alone."

Julia pursed her lips and cocked a brow. "That was three years ago, dear. Certainly your moments of fame have passed. At least give it a chance. Johanna called earlier today. She's coming to town tomorrow and wants to take us both out to lunch. Please come with us."

Daniel had avoided Johanna, too, but for other reasons. He could never forget he had once been intimate with her, and yet, in spite of their former relationship, she and Julia were now close friends. Closer than he imagined two former enemies could be. Each had placed aside their differences and forgotten as much about their confinement in the research center as was possible. They had moved on. He hadn't.

Judging the look on her face, her struggle to smile in spite of aching disappointment, Daniel had to agree to lunch or her growing disappointment in his attitude festered.

Best to surrender than to continue a useless argument, he reasoned.

He nodded. "I will. Get some sleep. I'll be in shortly."

Julia smiled and kissed him. Then, looking at the yellow cat, she said, "Morton, keep an eye on him. Don't let him go back on his word."

Morton scowled. "You really think he'd listen to me better than you? You're talking to a man who flung me off a skyscraper at our first meeting."

Julia laughed, and Daniel shook his head.

"I've apologized about that too many times," Daniel said.

Morton eyed him shrewdly. "Not enough for my satisfaction. Lucky for me the concrete cushioned my fall."

"Okay," Daniel said, waving his hands in surrender. "I'm sorry. Again."

The cat shrugged, unconvinced, and turned his attention to the dark alleys. His tiny eyes seemed as intently as Daniel's, like he, too, expected to see shifters prowling in the darkness.

Julia squeezed Daniel's hand. "Come to bed? I'll make it worth your while."

He pulled her close and kissed her neck. "How can I refuse that offer?"

"You'd best not," Morton said. "You think *my* moods are bad when *I'm* angry? I never want to see her scorned again. If you're wise, neither will you."

Daniel laughed. He embraced Julia tighter, kissed her, and then reached to pat Morton's head.

"Don't *even* go there, pal," Morton said. "I'm an intelligent creation not to be bought with such sentimental gestures. Just ask . . ."

Daniel and Julia stroked the cat's neck. Morton's voice surrendered to a gentle rumble of purrs. "Damn," he said. "Must be those cat genes acting up again."

"I owe you my life," Daniel said.

"We both do." Julia leaned down and kissed the cat's head. "You brought Daniel back to me safely."

Morton rubbed his head into their hands and gave his best Cheshire impersonation. "Don't you ever forget it."

"I never will," Daniel said. "Had Helmsby ever told me about you, I'd have never thrown you off the building."

"I know. I just like giving you a hard time about it, now and then. You two get to bed. I'll keep night patrol until dawn to ease your mind, Daniel. But, as Julia said, the shifters are no more, other than me. You're always safe with me."

Julia took Daniel's hand and led him through the sliding glass doors. They left Morton to the task of watching the streets. Daniel felt foolish allowing Morton to remain on the balcony instead of watching television, but something *was* out there. He sensed it. The strange feeling gnawed at him. It tugged with the familiar uneasiness that he remembered in Pittsburgh. It wouldn't rest until he confronted it face to face. Daniel wondered what new face Death wore now.

CHAPTER 2

After making love to Julia, Daniel slept deeply. No nightmares. No dreams at all. All he felt was the gentle warmth of her hand on his chest while they slept. When he awakened, bright sunlight glared through their bedroom window and stung his eyes. He slid from beneath Julia's arm, careful not to wake her, and swung his legs over the edge of the bed.

Rubbing the tiredness from his eyes, he listened to pattering feet running down the hallway into the living room. He smiled.

Felicia.

Her smile brightened his day.

Damn the shifters, he thought, pulling on his robe. *Except for Morton.*

Daniel entered the hallway, and Felicia squealed with delight. "Cuddles! Cuddles!"

She chased Morton around the living room.

"Come here, Cuddles," she laughed.

Morton caught sight of Daniel and said, "Thank goodness, you're *finally* awake. Get the kid off me. She'll play me to death."

Daniel laughed.

Felicia tugged Morton's tail while the cat lay sprawled on the carpet. He wondered what his daughter would think when she eventually discovered that other cats *didn't* really talk.

Felicia noticed Daniel and ran into his arms. "Daddy!"

"Morning, dear," he said. "You sleep okay?"

"Uh-huh," she said, nodding.

"Turn on the cartoon channel, Cuddles," Daniel said with a smile.

Morton cocked his head and raised an eyebrow. "I believe we've already established that the kid is the only one who can call me that."

"Just find her something to watch while I cook breakfast."

Morton lengthened the digits of his forepaws and sat with the remote in his altered paws. After he typed in the station number, classic cartoons captured Felicia's attention. She sat down on the carpet to watch.

Morton sighed. "I should have thought of that."

Daniel smiled. "You enjoy her rough housing and you know it."

A sly grin stretched across Morton's face.

The bedroom alarm beeped, and Daniel winced. "Meant to turn that damned thing off."

Morton leapt onto the kitchen counter near the stove to watch Daniel.

"You'll be happy to know nothing new prowled our street last night. Just a couple of stray dogs, a few *inferior* cats, and several rodents of various sizes. None had glowing eyes. So, no shifters."

Daniel opened an egg carton and frowned. "Don't patronize me."

"Sorry, but Julia's right, you know."

"What?"

"You need to get past your phobia. I figured by me living with you that you'd forget about them."

"But *you're* different."

"Different how? Different because I look like a pet you had when you were a kid? I could alter my appearance, and still, I don't think you'd be afraid of me."

Daniel shook his head and put several strips of bacon in the frying pan. "No, I wouldn't."

"Why not? Genetically, I'm the same as them. Nothing was altered. I just know how to control what I look like."

Daniel pulled a chair from the table and stared at him. "Helmsby created you. That makes you different."

"Does it? How?"

"He gave you a distinct personality."

Morton smiled evenly. "No. That's something you can't create. He did instill within me the intellect to know the difference between being savage and being affable. The choice, however, is mine."

"I tried to kill you, but you haven't sought revenge."

Morton shrugged and licked his forepaw. "Your actions came from ignorance. You thought I was like other shifters. A brutal, killing predator. Once you learned differently, you never tried again. I may aggravate you about dropping me off the building, but I understand the reason behind your actions. That's another thing. I don't harbor grudges."

"Thankfully. But Helmsby made you more superior than other shifters. You're rational. You're not primal in your instincts. You analyze situations and come to unbiased decisions. That's something Helmsby programmed into your genome and why your presence doesn't disturb me."

"You're still at odds with Helmsby, aren't you?"

"No, not really."

"You've not talked to him since we moved into this apartment."

Daniel sighed and shook his head. "You're beginning to sound like Julia."

"You have a problem with that?"

He shrugged. "No, but if you continue, I'll think you'd make a better badger than a cat."

Morton's eyebrows rose. His eyes became distant in thought. He nodded. "I believe I could manage such a morph. It'd require some input and thinking, but yes, it *could* be done."

"I was joking," Daniel said, taking the bacon from the skillet and then cracking several eggs.

"As was I. Sometimes, Dan, you're just too serious in your thinking. I wouldn't dare alter my appearance around Felicia. You know that. She's a handful, at times, always yanking my tail and ears, but I'd never terrorize or frighten her."

"I appreciate that."

Julia walked up to Daniel with a smile and kissed him. "Something smells great." She took a coffee mug from the cabinet. "Coffee's done. You want a cup?"

"Please."

After breakfast Daniel sat on the couch in front of the television while Julia showered. In a few hours they'd eat lunch with Johanna downtown. He wondered how the day would transpire. It wasn't as if he hadn't seen Johanna during the past few years. Her cable workout program came on each afternoon. Julia often did aerobics to Johanna's routine.

Although Johanna retained her muscularity, she had toned her bulk down quite a lot. Breast implants gave her a more feminine appearance and men swooned over her. Her website inbox was flooded with numerous proposals and requests for autographed photos. In spite of the growing number of men who had taken a keen interest in her, she seldom dated and shied away from anyone who sought a serious relationship. She feared commitment after what she and Daniel had endured. Although she never mentioned it, she was ashamed to have given herself sexually to Lucas' beguiling clone. It showed every time she and Lucas were in the same room. In his presence she never entertained eye contact.

Johanna decided to dedicate herself to her career rather than a man. She kept herself overworked to avoid the inner pain of loneliness.

Daniel thought about her decisions. He understood Johanna had never truly devoted herself to him, either. She never attempted to evolve their relationship to an emotional level. Instead, she only stayed with Daniel to secure the top female position at the research center. Though she had expressed the desire to have a baby, Daniel realized Johanna's true desire was having someone who'd always *need* her.

Johanna's new career and lifestyle demanded her commitment to her cable exercise program without any time to devote to anyone else. Several times she had thanked Julia for slipping her the birth control pills that prevented her from having a baby with Daniel. Daniel was relieved, too. But more than anything else, he was grateful that Julia had come into his life and through their love and devotion for one another, Felicia had been born.

Daniel flipped through the television stations. Two hundred channels with nothing he desired to watch. He skipped news programs altogether because he didn't want to be further depressed by outside strife and turmoil.

He glanced down the hall when the shower stopped. Julia stepped into the hallway wrapped in a towel. She winked and disappeared down the hall.

Felicia was in the playroom when the phone rang.

"Get that, Daniel," Julia said. "It's probably Johanna."

Tension gripped him. He didn't want to talk to Johanna. Reluctantly, he grabbed the phone and put it to his ear. To his surprise and relief, it wasn't her.

Instead, it was a man.

The familiar voice, weak and barely above a whisper, said, "Dan?"

"Yes?" Daniel said. "Lucas?"

Silence.

"Luke, you there? I can barely hear you."

"Yeah, I'm still here. Just making sure no one else is listening."

"Are you okay? You don't sound very well."

Lucas cleared his throat. "I've encountered some problems, Dan. I'm in deep trouble. I need your help."

The desperation in Lucas' voice was not something Daniel expected from the stuntman who feared little. Luke's voice was tired, labored, and filled with pain.

"What's wrong?"

"Is your television on?"

"Yeah, I'll turn it down."

"No, don't. Turn to INS news, quick."

Daniel turned to the news channel and was stunned to see the latest news alert. It showed Lucas handcuffed and being escorted between two police officers. They led him up the stairs of a Washington, D.C. police station. The news caption stated: "Lucas Ridale arrested for the murder of two senate members and two security guards."

The phone slipped from Daniel's hand and dropped into the side of the recliner. He retrieved the phone and placed it to his ear.

"What's going on, Lucas? What did you do?"

"I *didn't* do it, Dan. I just returned home from Denver where they had an early snow. I was skiing at the time the senators were murdered. When I came home, police officers were waiting at my house. I haven't been given a chance to explain my whereabouts. They've only now allowed me to make a call."

Surveillance camera video played. It showed Lucas shoot the two senators outside the courthouse. Then Lucas looked directly into the camera and smiled for several seconds as though he *wanted* the camera to capture every identifying feature of his face. Not something a murderer would intentionally do unless they wanted to be caught.

"The news shows your face, Lucas."

"Not my face. That's my clone."

Daniel swallowed hard. He took a deep breath and cleared his throat. "Helmsby said that your clone or any human clone couldn't survive more than two to three years. The clones shortened telomeres drastically cut their longevity."

"The hell with what he said, Dan," Lucas whispered. "I'm in jail for murdering four people that I know I didn't kill. The police keep showing me the same video over and over, but I can't convince them it's not me. Helmsby's wrong. My clone is still alive. You know I wouldn't do anything like this. Why would I?"

"Easy, friend. I believe you. But this will be difficult to prove without strong evidence. We know the clone escaped and is possibly still alive, but to anyone who wasn't with us, it will sound absurd."

"You have to contact Helmsby. He's the only one capable of proving my clone exists and that I'm innocent."

Julia came into the living room. "Is that Johanna?"

"Lucas," Daniel replied, placing his hand over the phone and nodding to the news story on the television.

She gasped with wide eyes and covered her mouth. The still image of Lucas' face stared directly at her through the screen.

"My God," she said. "Did he?"

Daniel shook his head.

"He called you?"

Daniel nodded. "Yes. He's in jail."

"I should say. But Lucas wouldn't do something like that."

"Dan?" Lucas said. "You still there?"

"I'm here. What exactly do you want me to do?"

"Talk to Helmsby. Find out what the likelihood is that my clone is still alive. Helmsby's my only hope. Believe me, I didn't do this. You've known me long enough to know I wouldn't murder anyone."

"I know."

A new caption scrolled across the screen.

"Damn," Daniel said. "One of the senators was Godfrey."

"Shit. Are you sure?"

"That's the latest update." A tight lump swelled in Daniel's throat. Godfrey had helped rescue them from Pittsburgh and later, after the news settled of the devastation that occurred there, Godfrey had run for the senate and won by a landslide.

Anger rose in Lucas' voice. "You know for certain I'd never kill Godfrey. He is, was, a great friend to all of us."

"I know, Luke. I know."

"I'll have my attorney contact you tomorrow . . . oh, shit."

"What?"

"Armed military police. Shit! They're probably moving me to a more secure lockup. You have to hurry."

"Let me speak to an officer."

"I . . ."

The phone went dead.

Julia stared in horror at the television screen. She turned and faced Daniel. "Are you certain he didn't kill them?"

Daniel shrugged, unable to hide the confused, hopeless expression frozen on his face. He buried his face in his hands and shook his head.

"I'm not certain of anything right now. I've been . . . so out of my mind that I just don't know. I do know he wouldn't do anything like this. But he's under the same stress I am. It's possible for anyone to snap."

"What's his explanation?"

"He says it was his clone. Lucas was in Denver when the murders took place. They arrested him when he got home."

"Then he should have an airline ticket stub and hotel receipts. If he used a credit card, they can easily trace his steps."

"Of course," Daniel said. "That's true, but I'm sure he's attempted to clear himself with those. He wants more to satisfy them."

"Such as?"

"Scientific evidence."

Daniel stood and shoved his hands into his pockets.

"What does he want you to do?"

"He asked me to go talk to Helmsby."

"When?"

"Today, I imagine. I should do it as soon as possible."

"Why?"

Daniel wrapped his arms around her waist and hugged her tightly. "Military police just took him into custody."

"How will you contact him?"

"He said that his attorney will call me tomorrow."

Julia pursed her lips and formed a thin smile. "So you can't keep our lunch date, huh?"

"Sorry to disappoint you."

"Oh, no. That's fine. At least you're getting out of the apartment. Helmsby will be glad to see you. Johanna and I have some catching up to do."

Daniel offered a slight smile. He was happy to *not* have lunch with Johanna, but not under these circumstances. The ghosts of his past were slinking from shallow graves, materializing afresh and possibly stronger than he remembered. He feared what new discoveries would surface and what might happen to destroy the only home he'd known in years.

He didn't know if he could revive the part of him that had allowed him to survive when they were trapped inside Pittsburgh. But somehow, he had to reach deep inside and retrieve the inner strength his depression and self-pity had buried. He wondered if he could resuscitate such dead energy.

CHAPTER 3

*M*orton insisted on going with Daniel to see Dr. Helmsby. Daniel took the cat under his arm and to the apartment elevator. When they reached the car, he placed Morton in the passenger seat.

"Mind if I shift?" Morton asked.

Daniel responded with a puzzled stare.

"Not the gears," Morton said. "Out of this cat suit. Just for a few miles or so. Coughing up fur balls for months on end is one bad side effect of being a cat."

"Backseat and don't let me see."

Morton cocked his head. "I thought you're comfortable around me."

"I am. It's just . . . right now isn't the best time."

"I understand."

Morton hopped over the seat into the rear floorboard.

The half hour drive into Pittsburgh was pleasant. Constant rows of autumn trees made the Appalachian Mountains seem more a painter's land-scape than reality. The low droning of the car eased his mind.

When they reached Pittsburgh, Daniel was surprised at how much improvement had come to the tarnished city where they had been impris-oned three years before. Most of the buildings had been renovated, repainted, or bricked, but a lot remained dismal because hundreds of residents had sold or abandoned their properties and never returned. Hundreds of other residents had never been accounted for, either.

The electrical gates and fences had been torn away, but in some places, remnants of the barriers were still evident. Several cement towers and forgotten fence posts had been missed by the transportation department, but for the most part, Daniel saw the city he hadn't seen in quite some time. A new pioneering city was emerging.

The decayed streets had been repaved, smooth with yellow and white lines. New trees had been planted along sidewalks. Even though many sidewalks weren't repaired, pedestrians stormed the intersections, busy with their lives, hopes, and renewed ambitions.

Along the way the craters where the first strategic missile strikes had been fired were filled with truckloads of gravel to set new foundations for destroyed buildings and parking lots. Total reconstruction was still a year or so away, but the progression flowed smoothly. With time, men, women, and children might again enjoy a time of prosperity in the once dark, shadowed areas that plagued his dreams.

At least the thick fog had dissipated. The shifters were gone, alive only in his memories and his frequent nightmares.

It was frightening to know how evil some people allowed themselves to become. All the horrors he and the other survivors had suffered were invented by a man's desire to manipulate genetics beyond its normal boundaries.

Daniel approached Fort Pitt Bridge that crossed the swollen Monongahela River and held his breath. In that instant, he almost turned the car around. Cars and trucks sped along the refinished bridge as though nothing had ever happened. Apprehension gripped him midway across the bridge. He didn't want to enter TransGenCorp where Dr. Helmsby now worked. His curiosity to what secret experiments the scientists had been performed there wasn't that demanding. He didn't want to know what Helmsby had learned about Idris' sick science.

Some things were best left undiscovered.

Daniel suddenly remembered the desperation in Lucas' plea for help. Only grim circumstances brought such words from Lucas. Never before had he uttered any tone of despair. Lucas faced tribulation unfaltering. *Help* wasn't a word in his vocabulary. Not until today.

Daniel kept driving.

Morton leapt into the front seat and peered out the side window. He then looked at Daniel with genuine curiosity and asked, "Are things back to normal?"

"I don't know that they'll ever be normal, but they have improved."

Once they left the bridge, Daniel veered onto the off ramp and followed the highway until they reached TransGenCorp's security gates. An armed soldier came to Daniel's window and requested identification and purpose. The soldier turned and stepped into a bulletproof-glass office, picked up a phone and conversed with someone while looking at Daniel's driver's license.

While the soldier talked, Daniel looked beyond the chain-linked barriers to see Army jeeps, a helicopter, two tanks, and a line of military officers with their weapons slung over their shoulders. They guarded the perimeter.

Daniel wondered why security was so heightened, and then he noticed the American at half-mast for the dead senators.

Beyond these men and artillery, the office doors of TransGenCorp nestled in the rock face of the mountain. It was difficult to believe this operation was housed inside old coal mining shafts from centuries before. Even if attackers fought their way past the small Army troops, they'd have a hell of a time blasting into the headquarters due to the dense mountain rock.

The officer returned and handed Daniel his license. "Go straight ahead and park in the B lot. You'll see the signs. Another officer will show you to Dr. Helmsby's laboratories."

"Thanks."

He tried to swallow the heavy lump in his throat. Although he had nothing to hide, the brief checkpoint unnerved him. During those few moments when the man was on the phone, he realized a computer glitch could print out incorrect identity information that placed his life into jeopardy. Worse things had happened where men had been shot to death because their social security numbers had been typed incorrectly, and they had been mistaken for someone else.

He looked at Morton. "What could Helmsby be working on that requires the military to protect TransGenCorp?"

"I don't know, but it will be worth the look." Excitement rose in Morton's voice and expressions.

"Perhaps."

After parking in the B lot, Daniel opened the door. Morton pranced from the car and followed Daniel to the front doors. Daniel scooped the yellow tabby into his arms when a guard stepped outside and blocked the entrance.

"Sorry, sir," the officer said. "But no outside animals are allowed inside for sanitary reasons."

Morton's eyes narrowed. He spat at the man. The action was enough to cause the guard step back.

"The cat's with me," Daniel said. "Dr. Helmsby will be interested in seeing him. Call him to verify if you wish."

Morton offered a low, agitated growl and bared teeth. The guard nodded and opened the door for them to pass through.

After the door closed, Daniel said, "Behave yourself, Morton."

The cat leapt to the floor and looked up at Daniel. "I *was* behaving. Imagine what I could have done had I shifted my appearance into something more sinister. Unsanitary? Phhht."

"Just mind your actions, okay?"

"Very well."

The silver halls made the building cold, heartless. The shimmering walls gleamed beneath rows of fluorescent lights. At the information desk, another soldier looked up from several surveillance screens.

"You're here to see Dr. Helmsby?"

"Yes."

"Follow me."

At the end of the center hall, the man pushed the elevator button. When the doors hissed open, he motioned for Daniel to enter. "He's on the second floor. The entire floor has all his laboratories. He knows you're here, so he should meet you in the hall."

"Thanks."

Daniel pushed the button and the doors closed. A few seconds later the doors opened to the second floor, but Helmsby wasn't there.

"Typical," Morton said.

Though Daniel didn't reply, he agreed. Helmsby was never where one expected to find him. His mind operated on his own secret agenda. Only he knew which experiment he needed to attend to first. Like clockwork, Helmsby met his own obligations and answered to no one else. Daniel guessed the same was true with the military personnel surrounding the laboratories.

"Comb the halls?" Morton asked.

"What choice do we have?"

"None."

"Your ears are keener than a normal cat's, right?"

Morton smiled. "Of course."

"Then you should be able to hear him doing his laboratory activities."

"Helmsby? No. He's very meticulous. Quiet. He hates noise. Rarely did he listen to music while doing lab work. He's quite a boring person, if you ask me."

"Then we search the halls."

The echo of a phone ringing and being answered caught Morton's attention. His right ear rose. He said, "Down the left hall, last door on the right."

CHAPTER 4

*D*aniel stopped outside an office door. Helmsby leaned back in a swivel chair with the phone pressed to his ear. He noticed Daniel and waved him to come inside. Helmsby ended the conversation and stood with a broad, nervous smile. He placed the phone into its wall cradle.

Helmsby had gained weight; at least thirty pounds of lean muscle, making his tall frame more imposing than Daniel remembered. His skin was pale, which indicated he still spent all his time inside his laboratories.

"You've bulked up quite a bit," Daniel said. "Are you working out?"

Helmsby shook his head and laughed. "No, I'm afraid I haven't time for that."

"Steroids?"

"Heavens no."

"You've certainly gotten heavier but not fat. How'd you manage that?"

Helmsby shrugged. "I think it's a side-effect from the injection I gave myself after Maria attacked me."

Daniel's studied him. "What injection?"

"I had developed a trial drug that I hoped prevented the patient, in this case, me, from getting infected or tainted blood if we suffered a bite from a shifter. Let's say that I took a gamble after she slashed open my shoulder and used it on myself."

Daniel smiled. "Not a bad side-effect to suffer."

"Not at all."

"It prevented you from changing. Are there any other side-effects?"

"Nothing else that I've discovered. I do self-blood analysis every few months just to keep tabs on myself. None of the results indicate I've been infected. But I have grown stronger and seldom even catch a cold."

Morton leapt onto a stool near Helmsby.

"You still have the feline shifter, I see," Helmsby said, reaching to pat Morton's head.

"*Why* does everyone insist on doing that?" the cat asked. "My appearance isn't *that* adorable."

Helmsby laughed. "I see that I didn't skimp on the sarcastic gene."

"Nowhere near," Daniel replied.

Morton scoffed.

"How long has it been, Dan?" Helmsby asked, clasping Daniel's hand with a fierce grip. "Two years now?"

Daniel looked away. "Closer to three, I think."

Helmsby patted Daniel's arm and pointed to a cushioned chair beside his unkempt desk. "Take a seat and relax. It doesn't look like you're getting enough sleep. Is everything okay?"

"I sleep when I can."

Helmsby stretched back in the swivel chair and folded his hands behind his head. He studied Daniel, and his smile never faded. "I believe the last time I saw you was at the convention when the newspapers and press wanted to have us all together for the photo session and interviews. Oh, and of course, at your wedding two weeks later. How is Julia?"

"She's doing great."

Helmsby rested his feet on the desk. "And Felicia?"

"Growing, talking, and learning everything she can."

"Great. That's fabulous. What brings you here?"

"Lucas."

"Luke?"

Daniel nodded. "He's in some trouble."

"Again? What's he need now? A higher mountain to dive off of?"

Daniel shook his head. "I wish it were that simple. No, I'm afraid it's more serious than that. He's in jail."

The smile drained from Helmsby's face. His hands shook, and he nervously reached for a pen. "Why? What did he do?"

"He's being accused of murder."

Helmsby lowered his feet and sat up. "Murder? Lucas might be guilty of a lot of things, but I think even I know him better than that."

"You didn't hear about it? It was on the news."

Morton rolled his eyes.

"Dan, I don't own a television and certainly wouldn't be tempted to watch one. Internet news can't be trusted, so I don't even read it. The closest device I have to a television is my smart phone. I only use it when Nancy calls. My time is consumed by the government's demand for my research on what experiments TransGenCorp conducted."

"I should've known. How is Nancy?"

Helmsby stood and walked to the coffee maker. "She's fine. She's on sabbatical in Germany right now. Want some coffee or green tea?"

"Sure, coffee," Daniel said. "Black. No sugar."

Helmsby poured coffee into a mug and then he poured green tea from another dispenser into a measuring cup. He handed the mug to Daniel. "Here."

"Thanks. Sabbatical? Where does she teach?"

"Oh, she doesn't. She just finished her nuclear physics doctorate at Stanford." He sipped his tea and stared at a pile of papers on his desk. "NASA's offered her a high scale job, if she decides to bite, but she's more a wild spirit these days than she was at the research center. NASA wants her to help design nuclear propulsion engines."

"She doesn't like the idea of that?"

"She could do it easily enough. But there's another space agency in Germany that's caught her attention. She speaks fluent German, so there's no problem with her fitting in."

Helmsby stared at Daniel, smiled, and shook his head.

"What is it?" Daniel asked.

"After what we all went through together at the research center with you and Lucas killing shifters and scouring the streets for supplies, I never once thought you'd give up biology to become a novelist? How's that treating you?"

"Much quieter. Less dangerous. How'd you learn about my novels?"

"Nancy, of course. She's read all three and can't wait for the next one to hit the stores. She mailed me her copies and asked that if I ever see you to have you autograph them. Could you indulge her that favor?"

"Sure. Where are they?"

"On the bookcase behind you."

Daniel walked to the bookshelf and took a pen from his coat pocket.

"Did you read them? Silly for me to ask. Of course, you wouldn't. Probably not technical enough for you."

"Actually I did read them. They're quite damn good. Delayed three days of work for me though. I couldn't put them down."

Daniel faced Helmsby, half expecting the geneticist to finish his joke. Instead, Helmsby gave a modest nod to reassure Daniel that he did actually read them.

Daniel penned several words for Nancy and signed his name. After he set the books back on the shelf, he noticed a framed photo of Nancy. She had blossomed at an early age and looked more woman than a teenaged lady.

"She's finished her doctorate? She couldn't be more than eighteen."

"Not quite that yet. She'll be eighteen next spring."

Daniel couldn't hide his surprise.

Helmsby smiled. "I told you that her I.Q. is substantially high. Near mine. Possibly well above mine. While we were holed up inside the research center she had nothing else to do except study. I insisted on it, and she obliged. By the time she applied to college, she tested high enough to skip subjects and started her Masters. She finished that inside a year and started on her physics program. She's way ahead of her peers."

Daniel shook his head in disbelief. "Indeed."

"I'm proud of her," Helmsby said, his voice choking. "She's progressed much better than I hoped. With all the bad things that happened our last day inside the research center, I was concerned that the trauma might deter her want to learn and advance in the field of science. She's proven herself to be a very strong, young lady."

"I'm proud of her, too. Envious actually. When you speak to her, tell her congratulations for me."

"I will."

"How is Margaret?" Daniel asked.

The question jolted Helmsby. His face became grim. His grief altered his countenance. Tears formed in his eyes, and he looked away. He cleared his throat. "She's dead, Dan."

The shocking news turned Daniel's stomach. "I'm sorry. I didn't know. When?"

"She died about six months after you and Julia exchanged vows."

"Damn, I'm so sorry."

Helmsby shrugged. "It happens, Dan. There was nothing the doctors could do."

"How did she die?"

Helmsby looked away, hurt by his loss. "Cervical cancer. It's the damnedest thing. By the time we got her to a hospital, which was the day after our liberation from the research center, they took blood and conducted several series of tests. When the report came back, she had less than three weeks to live. Had we gotten out of the research center six months earlier, she would have survived. I'm certain of it."

Daniel remembered the dark bags under Margaret's eyes the last day he had seen her. She appeared weak and frail, but he'd never thought her body was being eaten by cancer.

"But you had patented injections to cure cancer. Didn't you have any in your lab?"

Helmsby shook his head. "For some damned reason, Dan, they just didn't work. We did give her several after her pap smear came back abnormal, but her body rejected the properties of the medicine. She was the first person that the vaccine didn't cure."

The irony was more than Daniel wished to dwell upon. Helmsby had won the Nobel Prize for the cancer vaccine, and yet, the vaccine had proven useless to the very woman he loved.

"Any ideas why?" Morton asked.

"No. I didn't bother investigating further, although I do have cell slides of her tumor to research whenever I can deal with my loss."

Tears formed in Daniel's eyes. "You've not given yourself time to grieve?"

"There isn't time, Dan. I've too many projects that demand my immediate attention."

"Those things can wait. You have to let those locked emotions out."

Helmsby clasped Daniel's shoulder. "The current projects I'm working on cannot wait. If you'll take your seat, we can talk further."

"About what?"

Morton sat on the edge of the desk while Daniel returned to the chair across from Helmsby's desk.

Helmsby sat in his chair and looked toward the closed door. He leaned across the desk and spoke in a low tone. "You see, Dan, all the events that took place the final night we were at the research center might have been part of a front. I don't think the real Idris was taken into custody."

"He cloned himself, too?" Without realizing it, Daniel replied in hushed tones as well. After considering it a moment, he wondered why Helmsby had suddenly acted like he was revealing secrets he didn't want anyone else to discover. Wasn't Helmsby the head of TransGenCorp now?

Helmsby shrugged. "If you had the capability to do so, and you were in his position, wouldn't you? If there were the threat of being captured as a prisoner, you'd send your clone. Not yourself."

"True, but why do you think a clone was taken into custody?"

"I did extensive cellular research on his DNA. The telomeres were far too short for it not to be a clone. Besides, Idris was unusually strong. Few men have the strength to snap handcuffs apart. His clone did."

"Have you questioned him?"

"Can't. He died six weeks after his capture. His body was frozen. We're keeping it in storage until I'm certain I don't have other experiments to perform."

"Are you certain it was a clone? I mean, couldn't it be the real Idris, and after he sustained his injuries, he just died?"

"No, Dan. The injuries Idris' clone Lydia had inflicted and those he received during his apprehension healed too quickly. But it was something else that alarmed me more."

"What?"

"His body had some kind of self-destruction code tacked into his DNA. If he wasn't injected with genetic enhancers within a specific time period, his body underwent biodegradation. Polymers dissolved and cellular functions ceased operation. That's why he died so quickly."

"So you believe Idris is still alive somewhere?"

"Certainly." Helmsby nodded and then peered nervously at the closed office door as if he expected someone to barge in. "And what better way to continue doing his experimentation if everyone else *thinks* he's dead?"

"You think he's still manipulating genetic experiments?"

"I stumbled across some overseas addresses where he has already shipped crates of shifters for large sums of money. To conduct scientific projects like he does, you have to secure outside finances unless you're already wealthy. Genetic engineering is expensive. But somewhere he has another underground laboratory either established or under construction. Within a couple years he'll develop stronger shifters and clones than he already has. His technology was unmatched, which makes it more difficult for him to gather all the materials he needs secretly."

"Lucas wanted me to talk to you about his situation."

The expression on Helmsby's face indicated that he had allowed Lucas to slip from his mind. "About what?"

"He wants to know about his clone. What are the chances that man is still alive? You said before that these clones probably couldn't survive longer than two or three years. Do you still believe that?"

Helmsby rubbed his chin, leaned back in his chair, and stared at the ceiling. "After conducting my research on Idris' clone, I'd say Lucas' clone is very much alive, but only if Idris keeps the genetic enhancer injections on schedule. Without them the clone will die. Why does he want to know about his clone?"

"He believes his clone killed those four men."

"Four?"

Daniel nodded. "Two senators and two guards at a courthouse in D.C. One of the senators was Godfrey."

"Damn." Helmsby scratched the back of his neck. The sudden news made his uncomfortable. "Even if I can show evidence that his clone is still alive, I'd doubt any court would accept the evidence into trial."

"I was afraid of that."

"The only way to prove his innocence is to find his clone and bring him back alive."

Morton stopped licking his forepaw. His eyes narrowed. "And how would you begin such a search?"

"You said that there was coverage on television?"

"Yes," Daniel replied. "Quite detailed and clear."

"Can you get me a DVD copy of the footage? I need to review it to ease my mind."

"What are you suggesting?"

"I haven't seen Lucas since I last saw you, so I'd like to watch the coverage and see if his behavior matches that of Idris' clone."

Daniel's frowned. "Or whether it's actually Lucas?"

Helmsby sighed. "I have to know. Do you realize how foolish I'd look if I try to get the charges dropped and Lucas is lying?"

"I see your point."

"Like I mentioned earlier, I think I know Lucas well enough to say there's no possible way he'd kill anyone, especially anyone of the political agenda. Certainly not Godfrey. Idris has reason to eliminate any political figures that thwart and suppress the genetic reformation."

"So I should find Idris and then I'll find the clone?"

"If the clone committed the murders, yes. Idris would have assigned him to do it so he still controls biotech research laboratories somewhere. But it's unlikely you'll be able to find him alone. Quite frankly, I doubt the CIA or

FBI will buy your theory, either. Hell, they might be involved themselves. It's risky to put your nose where people don't want it."

Daniel shook his head. "I can't let him be executed for something I know he didn't do."

With all seriousness, Helmsby eyed Daniel evenly. "Can you be absolutely certain he *didn't* do it?"

"Yes."

Helmsby looked disappointed. "I wish you'd have said, 'No.'"

"Why?"

"We're still on the top of Idris' chief enemy list. We're a threat to everything he does. If he's still alive, he wants us dead. We know too much."

"So?"

"Don't you see? What better way for him to kill us than by doing what he did before? He placed Lucas' clone right in the midst of us. We didn't discover him until it was nearly too late. Lucas being framed for murder might be his next plot."

Daniel frowned. "How? Why would Idris bring so much media attention to Lucas if he wanted to plant the clone again?"

"Question: Do you know for certain the real Lucas called you? Or is the real Lucas the one they've taken into custody? If it's all staged to appear something it's not, then we're in danger."

"Damn. I never thought about that."

"Nor would they expect you to. If the real Lucas isn't in custody, this is the perfect opportunity for them to send us on a wild hunt, separate us out, and kill each of us unexpectedly. They know how close you and Lucas are. Brothers in everything except blood. You'd give your life for him, and he, you."

"That's true."

Helmsby offered a wry smile. "Seems we're back to where we were in Pittsburgh."

"What do you mean?"

"We cannot trust anyone."

"That's easy for you to say," Daniel replied. "You're inside TransGen-Corp, which is highly protected by the military."

Helmsby laughed nervously. "And *that* guarantees my safety? Daniel, please, since when has the government given a shit about people like us? When my purpose ends here, then what?"

Although Daniel didn't believe Helmsby's life was in any jeopardy, he didn't reply. It was possible for Idris to bribe a guard to have Helmsby shot inside one of his labs, but unlikely. From what Daniel understood, the guards at TGC were assigned bunkers that housed them for six-month periods without leave. The biggest risk for an assassination plot came when the new guards replaced the old ones.

Helmsby changed the subject. "Dan, since we were freed, have you kept in touch with any of the others who lived in the research center with us?"

"No, not everyone."

"Doug is dead."

"Doug?"

Helmsby nodded. "He died outside a bar in Tampa a few days ago. He was stabbed to death for what few dollars he had in his wallet. If I had my guess, he wasn't killed for his money."

Though Daniel remembered Doug mostly for his alcoholic problems, a tinge of remorse stirred inside his mind. Doug had been a good friend during those years of scavenging. As an entrance guard at Helmsby's Research Center, Doug would have died fighting to protect any of the surviving occupants. Daniel was sorry to hear the loss.

"I've wondered why you abandoned us, Dan." Helmsby blew steam off his tea before taking a sip. "It's not something you'd have done when we were trapped in Pittsburgh."

Daniel looked away. "Maybe you didn't know me as well as you thought."

"What are you implying? We all regard you as a hero."

"Don't. I never have. I never placed the obligation to lead on myself. I only took the position because Lucas refused it. The last excursion when I discovered we were fenced in by militants and the world outside the fences still carried on, I almost didn't come back."

Helmsby nodded at Morton. "That's why I sent Morton to keep an eye on you. I realized you were burnt out and might not be alert enough to protect yourself."

"No. I didn't mean I was almost killed. I left the research center and thought about *not* returning. I couldn't handle the pressure and didn't like sorting through all the bickering. Seeing everyone hungry and depressed brought me to the level that I didn't wish to live anymore. Everyone else was better off without me."

Helmsby smiled. "But you *did* come back. That's your instinct. To help others. And yet, you've not once visited me or called to check on Kyle."

Daniel winced at the mention of Kyle's name. In a way, when he had thought Kyle had died during the mock missile attack, he had learned to deal with the loss. But after Julia found Kyle in his maimed and degenerated form, Daniel's level of grief increased. He blamed himself for Kyle's condition. Although he'd never say it aloud, he wished Kyle *had* died to spare his former student of being the humiliating creature he had become. Or was it to spare himself the additional guilt? Somewhere deep within Kyle's devolved mind was the exceptionally intelligent, gifted student Daniel missed. Kyle's dreams and ambitions had been shattered.

"I'm sorry," Daniel said, avoiding eye contact with Helmsby. "You're right. I should have checked on him. I just haven't had the courage. How is he?"

"I understand how difficult it is for you, Dan. Honestly, I do. It's difficult for me to work with him because of how intelligent he used to be."

"But he's better, isn't he?"

"No. I don't believe he'll ever fully recover. Even with all my genetic engineering background, I can't help him evolve back to what he once was. Dementia at his level cannot be reversed. No drugs can repair the holes in his brain tissue once prions have fulfill their course."

"So he has no hope at all?"

Helmsby shook his head. "No, I've done everything I possibly can. But he does mention your name every day. What little memory he retains revolves around you. He doesn't recall saving Julia after he attacked her, but he cannot forget you."

"Do you know what happened to cause his degeneration? Since there wasn't any nuclear fallout from the missiles like the media had speculated, how did he end up like an animal? His DNA shouldn't have altered dramatically."

"No, the bombs dropped on Pittsburgh weren't fully charged. They were a distraction to evacuate the city and leave us there to die. If they had been nuclear, no one outside our fallout shelter would have survived. Hell, most of the shifters probably would have died, too. Since there was no actual fallout, I have to agree with you. Kyle's DNA shouldn't have suffered to the degree it had. Not from those missiles."

Daniel took a sip of coffee and thought for a moment. "Then *what* transformed Kyle?"

"His dementia stems from feasting on dead shifter brains and any humans he preyed upon. That alone is why I have difficulty being in the same room with him. Cannibalistic traits don't easily disappear. The taste for human flesh and blood becomes a need. I keep alert whenever I'm around him. Two armed guards enter his room with me. I never visit him alone."

Morton glanced from Helmsby to Daniel and said, "Surely, something can repress his desires to eat humans. I'm genetically the same as those shifters, but I've never had an appetite for blood or flesh. Of course, my palette doesn't quiver for Purina Cat Chow, either. Don't let the orange fuzzy suit deceive you."

Helmsby rested his elbows on the desk. "It's a desired effect acquired from eating the same food over and over. I assume Idris reared shifters on human blood withdrawn from prisoners. You, on the other hand, I was careful what I allowed you to eat."

"Really?" Morton said. "I don't recall any five-star meals."

Helmsby looked at Daniel. "Anyway, Dan, would you like to see Kyle before you leave?"

Daniel didn't know what to say. He hated seeing Kyle less than the person he had known. However, Daniel's overbearing conscience needed to see what had happened and whether Kyle had recovered even a small fraction since the day when Julia re-introduced Kyle to him. Perhaps refreshing his mind by witnessing Kyle's degeneration, he could replace his guilt with a renewed anger toward Idris. A heated drive to pursue General Idris might enable him to rescue Lucas before it was too late.

Helmsby noticed Daniel's delay in answering. He placed his hand on Daniel's shoulder and said, "You don't have to, Dan, if you don't think you can handle it. He'd be none the wiser should you choose otherwise."

"No, I should talk to him. You said that he's asked about me?"

"Every single day."

Daniel looked at Morton for moral support. The cat offered nothing more than a simple shrug like he did during their chess games, which indicated, "It's *your* move, not mine."

That didn't surprise Daniel. Morton often played the psycho-analyst by placing the decision on the one asking the question rather than giving a definitive answer. He was a cat with a Freudian approach to everything.

"I should see him. Perhaps my presence could unlock other memories for him."

Helmsby stood. "Don't get your hopes up."

"It might help."

"It can't hurt," Morton said.

Helmsby placed the office phone to his ear, pressed two numbers, and said, "Is Kyle awake? He is? Good. I'll be there in a few minutes with some visitors. Yes, make sure he's alert."

He hung up and gave Daniel a serious stare. "He's been sleeping a lot more lately. With dementia, that's generally a sign that he's in the final stage before he dies. So, you've come just in time."

CHAPTER 5

While Julia drove to meet Johanna at the Italian Restaurant in Pittsburgh, she stressed over Daniel. She kept a rigid, stern attitude on the outside, but inside, she was falling to pieces. Her worries about her own mental stability frightened her. His claustrophobic world strangled her because she didn't know how to help him burst through his dismal depressive barrier.

Daniel insisted that writing novels was his therapy, and he did seem to be gaining some progress. But now Lucas was in prison for murder. She feared this dilemma might reverse what little optimism he had recovered and make him even more reclusive.

Perhaps insisting that Daniel visit Helmsby wasn't the best solution. TransGenCorp was the root that fed his deepest fears. His unabated resentment for Helmsby was understandable, but she figured if she had forgiven and made amends with Johanna—her worst enemy while living in the research center—he should be able to cope with what had happened and forgive Helmsby, but bitterness was a hard pill to swallow.

She took a deep breath and shook her head. Why were men so blind and thick skulled? Men held militant grudges that started wars when left unchecked.

Daniel's visit might shed light on beneficial issues for him though. Seeing Pittsburgh's reconstruction after its brief collapse might encourage his desire to overcome past pains and give him hope by letting him know that despite the odds, even the city was willing to become stronger and more fortified. And if so, nothing should hold him back, either.

"Just pick up the pieces and move on," she whispered.

Julia's love for Daniel had intensified, especially after the birth of Felicia and in spite of the emotional wall he shielded himself behind. She also understood why Daniel didn't want to see Johanna. Her affair with Lucas' clone had dissolved any trust he might have held for his former lover. Julia knew that Daniel hadn't really loved Johanna, nor had Johanna loved him. They had simply agreed to be together to birth strong healthy babies, so Julia didn't perceive Johanna a threat to her marriage. She knew neither held affection for the other. And both seemed to possess a great deal of regret for having once been a couple.

Johanna admitted to Julia that Daniel had never expressed any emotional commitment to her, nor had she to him. Johanna confessed that she had wanted to have a baby simply to fill the emptiness in her heart. In retrospect she thanked Julia for secretly slipping birth control pills into her daily vitamins to prevent her from having a baby. With Johanna's television fitness program launching to such a high level of success, a child would have inevitably thwarted her chance to gain the notoriety she now harnessed and craved.

Julia was happy she and Johanna had worked through their differences. Neither of them, however, was able to befriend the real Lydia. Each time they met her, they were apprehensive that she'd suddenly alter into something else and attack or kill them. They tried to reach out to her because Lucas loved her, but Lydia's clone had imprinted such a negative image that no matter how much they wanted to accept Lydia into their circle of friends, they just couldn't get past their mental scars.

When Julia looked at Lydia, she remembered the fear she had felt in Pittsburgh that Lydia's clone would kill Daniel and take him from her forever. Johanna never got over her brush with death after fighting Lydia's clone twice. Although she had gotten best of the Lydia's clone in their second fight, Johanna's pride never recovered. Just viewing Lydia's friendly smile dredged memories of her sinister clone they wished to keep buried.

Their distrust for Lydia had possibly been part of what ended the relationship for Lucas. Their dating relationship barely lasted two years. Soon after their breakup, Lucas continued his daredevil tour with ESPN. He seemed to enjoy the spotlight more than he enjoyed escorting Lydia. At least that was what Julia and Johanna assured one another to prevent their inner guilt from eating them alive.

Julia thought about Lucas. She still found it difficult to believe he had murdered government leaders. But under the same stress Daniel suffered, Lucas might have lost his stability, what little he ever had, and done something stupid. She didn't want to believe that. Maybe Daniel was right. Maybe Lucas' clone was still alive.

Her fingers tightened around the steering wheel. She swallowed hard and looked into the rearview mirror at Felicia seated in her child safety seat behind her.

If the clone is alive, Julia suddenly feared, *our lives are in as much danger as Lucas'.*

Julia watched Felicia staring out the window at the passing trees and houses. Her daughter's bright eyes soaked in the surrounding area with keen curiosity. She was so innocent. So free.

"Thank God you didn't see those horrid things in Pittsburgh," she whispered.

"Mommy, watch out!" Felicia yelled.

Julia stared at the road ahead and slammed the brakes. Rubber squealed and black smoke rose as her van skidded to a dry halt, narrowly missing the stopped car in front of them. Her heart hammered in her chest. For several seconds, she forgot to breathe.

"Are you okay?" Julia asked, looking over her shoulder.

With wide eyes, Felicia replied, "Uh-huh."

Julia took a deep breath, collected herself, and waited for the red light to change. She chided herself, "Get it together, dammit."

"Mama, I wish Cuddles was here."

Julia smiled. "You'll see him later."

"He's with Daddy?"

"Yes, baby."

When Daniel first suggested they take Morton into their home to live, Julia had been hesitant. "We can't have a shifter around our baby," she said. But after three years with Morton she couldn't see them not having the cat as a part of their family. She was fascinated by the cat's intellect and the gentleness he exhibited with Felicia. Morton was better behaved than an ordinary cat or dog would be with a persistent child.

Morton's wit cheered her on days when she couldn't get past Daniel's stubbornness. Even the shifter challenged Daniel into getting out of their apartment. She realized, however eerily, how much they needed the yellow tabby in their lives. She had no doubt he'd protect them at any cost, which allowed her to sleep better at night.

Two more intersections and she turned right. Another block and she pulled into an empty parking spot beside Johanna's sports car at the Italian restaurant.

Julia unfastened Felicia's safety belt and carried her into the restaurant. Johanna was seated at a table near the salad bar. Either Johanna was going to film an exercise program after lunch, or she had just come from her set. She wore a black leotard with a pink tank top. Her long bleach-braided hair was pulled into a tight ponytail, and her makeup was much too dark for social dining. She laughed and nodded while talking into her pink cell phone.

Two tables over, a distracted, pimple-faced busboy cleared a table of dirty plates and glasses without taking his lustful eyes off Johanna. He spilled a glass of ice tea down his apron and cursed.

Julia shook her head and suppressed a laugh. She stood with Felicia in her arms and waited for a waitress to get a booster seat. Johanna disconnected her phone and smiled at Julia and Felicia as they took their seats.

"I know," Johanna said. "I'm early as usual. Got done with the exercise program quicker than normal. Less retakes, so maybe I'm getting better at ignoring the camera."

Julia glanced at her watch. "I'm on time."

"Oh, I know. Hey, Felicia. How's my little girl?"

Felicia smiled shyly. "Okay."

The waitress brought menus and an order pad. "Buffet and salad bar?" she asked.

They nodded.

"Help yourself."

After making two large salads for themselves and a plate of spaghetti for Felicia, they took their seats.

"You'll never guess who called me today," Johanna said, stabbing a fork into a plump cherry tomato.

"Who?"

"Lucas."

Julia's eyebrows rose with surprise. "Today?"

"Yeah, strange, huh?"

"He called Daniel this morning."

Johanna poked at her salad. "He's supposed to meet us here in about fifteen minutes."

"What?" Julia asked, looking around the restaurant nervously. The world shrank in on her. Breathing became painful.

Johanna nodded. "He asked what my plans were today. I told him that you and I were meeting for lunch. He sounded eager to come and catch up."

Julia eyed her shrewdly. "You told him to meet us here?"

"Yes. I invited him to join us. Why? What's wrong?"

Julia leaned across the table. "We've got to get out of here. *Now*."

"Why?"

"Lucas called Daniel this morning."

"So?"

"You didn't see the news this morning?"

Johanna frowned, shook her head, and took a bite of her salad. "No, I didn't have time. Why?"

"Lucas is in jail."

Johanna placed her fork on the table. "Jail? For what?"

"Murder."

Johanna sat stunned with wide eyes. "But he wouldn't . . ."

"No. We don't think he did it. Daniel has gone to talk to Helmsby to see what the possibilities are that Lucas' clone is still alive. Which means, if Lucas told you he was coming here, something's definitely wrong."

Felicia busied herself slurping long strands of saucy pasta noodles through her lips one at a time.

"Wait. Lucas' clone called me?"

Julia nodded. "I'm afraid that's very possible."

"Then we are in serious trouble."

Johanna grabbed her purse and pulled out money for their lunch and a tip.

"Is everything okay?" the waitress asked with a frown.

Johanna said, "I'm sorry. We have an emergency. We are going to need all this to go, please."

The waitress nodded and left. She returned with Styrofoam trays for them to box up their meals.

Julia stood and watched the parking lot while Johanna raked the food into the trays. A black van with mirrored windows pulled into the parking lot and parked on the opposite side of the building from where she and Johanna had parked. The driver's door swung open. Out stepped Lucas. He wore thick black shades. His beard was more silver than Julia remembered, but an odd determination set his jaw while he scanned the parking lot. He wore all black and with boldness he sported a holstered gun for all to see. The real Lucas never did such a thing.

"He's here," Julia whispered, placing a hand on Johanna's shoulder. "Hurry, we have to get out of here."

Julia pulled Felicia from her seat. "But I'm not finished, Mommy."

"It's okay, honey. You can eat in the car."

Johanna fished through her purse and rested her hand on a snub-nosed .38. Julia noted the fear in Johanna's eyes. Something Julia hadn't seen since Johanna's fight with Lydia's clone.

"Let's take my car," Johanna said. "It's faster."

"You don't have room for a child restraint seat in it. We'll take mine."

Johanna frowned. "My Camaro is much faster than your van."

"I know it is, but Felicia's safety is more important than speed. And the way I may have to drive, I cannot afford that mistake."

She tossed her cell phone to Johanna. "Hit number one, quick. Tell Daniel what's going on."

Johanna pressed the number while Julia strapped Felicia in. They slammed the van doors shut. Julia backed out so fast the tires squalled.

"There's no answer."

Julia frowned, fighting tears. For a moment, she wondered if she was overreacting, or did her gut-feeling indicate they were in extreme danger?

"Try again," she said.

Johanna shrugged. "Still nothing."

"Keep trying."

Julia raced into traffic and the black van sped from the parking lot behind them. How had he noticed them so quickly? She pulled into the left turn lane and sped through the yellow light before it turned changed to red. The van ran the light. Several drivers blared their horns as Lucas swerved to miss a pickup.

Johanna pressed number one over and over. "Still nothing."

"Shit!"

"Are you certain this isn't really Lucas?"

Julia gave a sideway glance. "You think he'd pursue us like this?"

Johanna placed her hand against the dash and looked over her shoulder. "No, probably not."

At the next intersection Julia watched a second black van swerve into the lane ahead of them. The van was identical to the one the clone drove. Julia tried to find an emblem on the rear or side of the van, but the van didn't have any identification, not even a tag, which unnerved her even more. TransGenCorp was now under government control. Hell, Helmsby *worked* there. So who sent these vans after them?

"That's not Lucas behind us," Julia said sternly. She nodded at the van ahead of them. "And *that* van's with him."

Johanna took the snub-nosed revolver from her purse. "I was afraid you'd say that. Look, I'm really sorry. I didn't know it wasn't Lucas."

"I know. If Daniel hadn't received the phone call this morning, I wouldn't have known either."

"But still . . ."

"It's okay." Julia faced Johanna. "But whatever happens, don't let them take Felicia."

Johanna flexed her biceps. "They'd have to kill me to get either of you, honey."

"That may be their intention."

"I thought we were through with this bullshit in Pittsburgh."

Julia bit her lower lip. "It's piling up pretty deeply right now. Try Daniel's number again."

"Hon, I keep trying. You said that he's at TransGenCorp?"

Julia nodded, changed lanes, and tried to find a way to turn the van around. Too much traffic. Turning around meant to stop and wait. She didn't have time to risk the attempt. The delay in speed gave the clone and the other driver enough time to box her in. She didn't think Lucas' clone wanted to take them alive. It didn't take much time to kill three trapped people with a gun. She must keep moving. Keep driving and hope, pray, that an avenue for escape opened up.

"If Daniel's there, you realize that civilian cell phones are off limits inside military posts. He probably turned it off or left it in his car."

Julia nodded and swallowed hard. "Or the thick rock walls prevent him from getting our signal. What are we going to do?"

"Drive."

The rear doors of the van in front of them swung open. A man wearing fatigues leveled a gun at them. Julia pressed a button on her door and lowered Johanna's window.

"Do you know how to use that thing?" Julia asked.

Johanna nodded. "I go to the firing range twice a week. You have no idea how many goons wait outside my studio for autographs.

The man fired his gun.

"Shoot him!" Julia screamed.

Johanna leaned out the window and squeezed off two rounds. The first shot hit the pavement, but the second one shattered the tinted window in the rear van door. The gunman dropped to a hunch, making himself a smaller target. He braced himself against the inner van wall and raised his weapon again.

He fired again, but no bullets hit the van. Something metal clinked the grill. The man pulled the rear doors closed.

"What the hell was that?" Julia asked.

The driver ahead of them slammed his brakes, veered sideways, and forced Julia to cut into the center turn lane. Without thinking or planning ahead, she cut the wheel sharply to the left, hit the gas, cut off several angered drivers, and drove the opposite direction.

"Go, girl," Johanna said, uncocking her gun.

Julia frowned, concentrating on the cars and trucks in the lanes ahead of her. Everything was a blur of movement. Cars swerved from their lanes and more angry drivers spoke their protest with their horns.

"Dial 911 and get the police out here."

Johanna dialed the number, and Julia watched the rearview mirror. Both vans approached at high speed. The upcoming intersection was full of parked cars waiting for the light to change. All three lanes were packed bumper to bumper. Felicia was pale with silent fear.

"Get your gun ready," Julia said. "We have to stop. We don't have a choice."

Johanna nodded and told the 911 operator what was happening.

"Police are on their way."

Julia shook her head. Tears burned her eyes. "They won't get here fast enough."

"I told you we should have taken my car."

"Johanna . . ."

"Your van's just too slow."

"Johanna, just let me drive, please!"

"Sorry."

Julia slowed the car, tried to circle around the right lane but several cars blocked the right turn lane. One of the black vans pressed against her rear bumper, revved his motor, and pushed.

The weight of the van popped and dented the rear bumper. The popping sounds frightened Felicia. She teared up and began to cry.

Angered, Julia hit the gas and drove over the sidewalk. She pressed the horn and swung into traffic while other drivers slowed and blared their horns. She made a mad U-turn and drove through the intersection on the opposite side. Confused motorists encircled both of the black vans.

Johanna looked surprised. "Where'd you learn to drive like that?"

Julia shrugged and wiped tears from her eyes. "Did we lose them?"

Johanna glanced over her shoulder. The intersection was congested with cars blocking all angles. No vehicles moved and no one followed them.

"Yeah, for now, but I don't know for how long."

Johanna turned and wiped tears from Felicia's tear-streaked cheeks. "It's okay, honey. They're gone."

Julia typed numbers into the van's console. A flat-screen lowered in front of Felicia's seat. Julia selected one of Felicia's favorite cartoons and hoped it calmed her enough to forget about the chase, at least for now.

"I want Daddy," she sobbed.

"We're going to get him," Julia said.

"And Cuddles."

"Him, too."

"Cuddles?" Johanna asked.

"Our cat," Julia replied. "Damn, I wish he was here with us."

"Daniel?"

"No, the cat."

Johanna pursed her lips and gave Julia a strange side-look.

"I'll explain later. Right now, we have to make sure these people don't follow us home."

"I'm with you on that."

"Watch behind us."

CHAPTER 6

$\mathcal{D}$aniel watched Kyle through the one-sided window and couldn't suppress his guilt. A lump tightened in his throat. He reached for the doorknob and his hand shook. Kyle was so different, nothing like Daniel remembered or imagined except that he was cleaner than the day Kyle had helped save Julia. Daniel closed his eyes and shook his head. Fighting nausea, he turned the knob.

"Are you okay, Dan?" Helmsby asked. He placed a hand on Daniel's shoulder. "You don't have to go in."

"Yes, I do. I'm responsible for this."

Morton looked up at Daniel. Daniel took the cat into his arms and held him against his chest. He stroked the back of Morton's neck. The cat didn't protest.

"I should've fought harder to get Kyle through the fallout door. He didn't deserve this."

"Don't blame yourself," Helmsby said, shaking his head and squeezing Daniel's shoulder. For the first time, he saw remorse in the professor's eyes. "This is my fault more than anyone's. I should have warned you of the possible attack. My ego got the best of me, and everyone else suffered for it. I'm sorry, Dan. I truly am."

Daniel wanted to say it was okay, but his own remorseful fire stoked deep inside. Nothing said or done changed the past. It was too late to make amends. Words meant nothing. What happened had happened. No words undid that.

"He can't see us through the glass, Dan. It's mirrored on his side. It's the best way to evaluate him. We have a hidden camera in the room, too."

Daniel watched Kyle. After a few seconds, Kyle cocked his left brow and faced the window with curiosity. He peered at the window as if he could see through the mirror. His gentle stare turned into a fierce glare. Daniel swallowed hard. He anticipated Kyle bolting toward the glass like a ravenous animal. Daniel knew Kyle sensed his presence.

Morton noticed it, too. "He knows you're here."

"But how?"

Morton purred beneath Daniel's nervous hand. "He's not completely human anymore. His hearing and sense of smell are keener. Like mine, but not as refined. In time, perhaps they will increase."

Helmsby protested the comment with a sharp shake of his head. "At the rate his brain is deteriorating, he'll be dead in weeks. Sooner, if he's lucky."

Kyle lunged at the window. His eyes were dark and crazed like a hungry predator.

Morton hissed. "Perhaps. Being caged like this has probably made him more dangerous. The degradation has stressed his mind and the confusion makes him prone to violence. If he ever escaped, you'd have no choice but to kill him. Otherwise, he'd kill dozens of people."

"What makes you so certain?" Daniel asked.

Morton glanced at Daniel. "It's in his eyes. He's becoming an animal. I calculate he'll be a vicious one."

Helmsby was intrigued. "This is the first time you've seen him, and you can make such an assumption?"

Morton jumped to the floor. "You created my genome, how perfect it is, but what Kyle possesses is from all the various shifters he fed on to survive. Thousands of imperfect, inbred strands of mutant DNA have meshed with his human sequences. Virtual trash. I never fed on other shifters. I did like Daniel and Lucas. I found canned or packaged food to eat. I didn't want to taint my system or accidentally grow extra legs or succumb to other possible side effects."

Helmsby glanced at his watch. "Dan, you need to hurry if you're going to see him. I've other things to show you."

Daniel took a deep breath, twisted the knob, and pushed the door inward.

"Be careful," Helmsby said. "He's not the Kyle you once knew.

"I know. I understand."

"I don't think you do," Helmsby said. "He has violent fits at times worse than an unruly child and his strength is unbelievable. When the mind loses rationality, aggression takes over. Here, take this, just as a precaution."

Helmsby handed him a syringe. "It's a sedative, in case he gets out of control."

"I don't think he will."

Helmsby forced a grim smile. "For your sake, I hope he doesn't. But whatever you do, don't let him see the syringe."

"Why?"

"It sends him into a rage. He put one of my assistants in the emergency room. Broke both of the man's arms, and it only took Kyle a few seconds to do that. Had we not incapacitated him with a dart gun, he'd have killed the man."

Daniel frowned, looking at Kyle's frail, emaciated body. "How's that possible?"

"Extreme fear can turn a weakling into a monster. You know that. You did things on your scavenger trips that you couldn't have done under normal circumstances."

"That's true. But he was outside the research center nearly three years. He had to kill and eat shifters. Why would a syringe frighten him?"

"I wish I had an answer for that, but to be honest, I can't get him to talk to me. He just keeps calling your name. Maybe he can tell you something before it's too late."

Daniel tucked the syringe into his back pocket out of Kyle's sight. He stepped into the room and his knees suddenly weakened. He leaned against the only table in the room for support. Kyle sat on the edge of the bed. At first Kyle deliberately ignored Daniel's presence. His arms were bound together at the elbows with leather restraints. His feet weren't bound, so he did have the freedom to pace around the room.

Helmsby stood at the door.

"Are the restraints necessary?" Daniel asked.

"For your safety, yes."

Kyle's tired eyes blinked slowly.

"Kyle?" Daniel whispered.

The absent look in Kyle's eyes drifted. He cocked his head and studied Daniel's face.

"Do you remember me?" Daniel asked.

Kyle focused a frozen frown at Daniel but gave no reply.

"It's me. Daniel. Remember?"

A wild expression crossed Kyle's face. His lips opened wide, and he gnashed his teeth, emitting a low growl. His hand tightened into a fist.

"Careful," Morton said. The cat leapt onto the table beside Daniel. "He's more animal than human. Don't forget that."

"Why should I fear him if he keeps asking to see me? There must be a reason why he asks."

Morton said, "Revenge could be a possibility, if he believes his condition is your fault."

Daniel fought tears. "Nothing about him resembles the Kyle I once knew."

"He's as feral as the wild shifters. See it in his eyes? I've killed less hungered shifters," Morton said.

Helmsby opened the door. "I'll be down the hall if you need me. One of my guards will be outside the door should Kyle get out of hand."

"Thanks."

CHAPTER 7

Morton glanced at Daniel. "Why is this so important to you?"

"He's like this because of me," Daniel said. "This is my fault."

The cat shook his head. "This? No, *that's* not your doing. You can't blame yourself for what happened. You tried to save him. It was the others that prevented you from pulling him inside."

"I should have tried harder."

"It wouldn't have mattered."

Daniel clenched his jaw tightly. "If I had just been more forceful, or he had come back five minutes earlier. Maybe if I hadn't sent him to the cafeteria . . ."

"You could play the "what if" game for the rest of your life and nothing will change. Face the fact that this was *meant* to happen."

Daniel frowned and ran his hands through his hair. "If he hadn't gotten to the fallout shelter door, he'd have survived and none of this would have happened to him."

Morton sighed. "His condition has nothing to do with being left outside. You heard Helmsby. Hundreds of students were never found in the halls. If the missiles were fully charged, everyone outside would have died or be in the same condition as Kyle. They weren't. There's no proof to show Kyle's degradation was the result of chemical fallout. Think about it."

Daniel's eyebrows rose. "What are you implying?"

"Shifters never evolved on their own. Neither did Kyle. Talk to him. Tell him what you truly want to say. If it's an apology you wish to give, do it now. Helmsby's right. Kyle doesn't have much longer to live."

Tears burned Daniel's eyes. "Kyle, I'm sorry for what happened to you. I really tried . . ."

A tear edged down Kyle's deformed face. His eyes were sunken inside their sockets. The thick cranium reminded Daniel of prehistoric men in biology textbooks.

Kyle's lips quivered. "It . . . Not your fault. You not do this."

Kyle tapped the side of his misshaped head with his maimed arm. The missing hand made Daniel wince. Thick, coarse skin covered the exposed wrist bone. A black layer of thick fur covered his forearm.

"This not your fault."

Daniel looked at Morton.

"It's a start," Morton said.

Daniel stepped closer to Kyle. "What happened to you after the missile struck the ground?"

Kyle looked away and chewed on his lower lip. His eyes indicated he was thinking about the question. Perhaps he even remembered something.

"Something happened. Do you remember?"

Daniel reached into his back pocket and placed his hand on the syringe.

"Daniel, what are you doing?" Morton asked. "Are you actually going to show him that? You heard what Helmsby said."

"Yeah, I know," Daniel replied. "But like you said, the shifters were created by strange science. Maybe there's a reason the syringe frightens him. Maybe showing him will make him remember what happened."

"Or," Morton said. "He'll try to kill you."

"You can stop him if he tries."

"Maybe. Who knows what his reaction will be or how fast he grabs you."

Daniel slid the syringe from his pocket, cupped it inside his closed hand, and slowly showed it to Kyle. "Did someone hurt you with one of these?"

Kyle shook his head as if awakened from a deep trance. His eyes narrowed like an angered monster.

Daniel stepped closer with the syringe. "Did they use one of these on you?"

Kyle resembled a trapped animal. His teeth clenched tightly, making a harsh grading sound. He screamed. "No!"

"Easy, Kyle, I'm not going to hurt you," Daniel said.

Kyle raised his bound arms and rushed at Daniel. He growled. Frothy spit dripped down the sides of his mouth. Daniel stepped to the side and slung Kyle's body across the table. Daniel put his weight against the small of Kyle's back and pinned him down. Kyle's feet dangled several inches above the floor. He had no leverage to push Daniel off.

"No," Kyle pleaded with slurred words. "Don't hurt me. Please don't."

"I won't hurt you. I promise."

The guard pushed the door open with his weapon raised.

"No," Daniel said, waving his hand at the guard. "It's okay. Everything's under control."

"You sure?" the guard asked.

"Yes."

"Okay, but if you need me, I'm right outside. Just yell."

"Thanks."

The guard nodded, stared a moment longer, and closed the door.

"It's apparent," Daniel said to Morton. "Someone injected Kyle with something."

"I agree."

"Hospital," Kyle muttered with a frail voice. "Nurses. A doctor. Gave me shots. Lots of them. They fix bleeding arm, then hurt me."

"Why?" Daniel said aloud.

Morton frowned. "Perhaps to test their genetic enhancers? To see if they could make his hand grow back?"

"And when it didn't?"

"They discarded him as a failed experiment."

Kyle's body eased. His fear subsided to sadness. He whimpered softly.

"It's okay, Kyle. I'll let you up. No one's going to hurt you again. I promise."

Daniel helped Kyle back to the bed.

"This is all strictly speculation," Daniel said.

Morton nodded. "But with Idris, anything was possible, and from the sound of it, still is."

Mentioning Idris' name brought a high-pitched wail from Kyle. He huddled on the floor and hid his face.

"It's no longer speculation, Daniel."

"I see that."

Kyle growled Idris' name.

Daniel placed a hand on Kyle's shoulder. "I can't undo what they did to you, but I promise you one thing. Idris will suffer for what he's done. I'll make him pay. Trust me."

Kyle stared into Daniel's eyes. A childlike smile curled on his lips. "Thank . . . you."

CHAPTER 8

*L*ucas wondered where the military police had taken him. After they disconnected his phone call with Daniel, they cuffed him and placed a black cloth bag over his head. He understood the danger he was in. These *weren't* ordinary officers. They weren't CIA or FBI, either. They were members of a much darker organization. People that governmental officials feared.

When they had placed him inside the transport vehicle, he tried to time the distance they traveled, but two men forced liquid down his throat. In spite of his struggle, enough of the liquid went down his throat to incapacitate him several minutes later. He lost consciousness.

Lucas awakened with the black cloth still covering his face. He lay on a narrow bed with his arms tied to the headboard over his head. He tugged and strained to loosen the leather restraints, but they were secured tightly. Whoever had tied him knew the exact angle to position his arms behind his head to decrease his strength. Had they simply tied his arms to the side of the bed, he could have, in a matter of time, weakened the straps enough to pull free. Rather than wearing down his muscles, he placed himself into a Zen state of relaxation. When the proper opportunity presented itself, he needed all the strength he had left to take down a guard and gain a weapon.

Lucas laughed softly, thinking about his similar confinement inside TransGenCorp. "Nothing more original?"

He thought of Lydia, the *real* Lydia and their two-year relationship. He longed to hold her close, to smell her perfume, and to make love to her again. He missed the music of her laughter and the radiance in her eyes when she smiled. Despite their fiery breakup, her eyes said everything. She loved him. His eyes had told her the same thing, but he couldn't continue the relationship because of how Julia and Johanna acted whenever they were around Lydia. He didn't think it was fair to her.

But Lydia expressed her need to be alone for a while. She struggled with her lapse of family memories. Lucas didn't have the heart to tell her that she never really had parents or a past. She had been created in a laboratory and whatever she recalled were probably things they had programmed her to believe.

Lucas took a deep breath.

God, how he missed her. "I need you."

Before he lost himself to tears, he thought of his circumstances. Daniel didn't have any way to find him. Even if he could contact Daniel, Lucas didn't have a clue where he was or *what* these people planned to do to him.

The door creaked open.

"Comfy?" a man asked. The man took a metal chair and skidded it across the floor, stopping at the edge of the bed.

Lucas tilted his head in the direction of the voice. "What do you want?"

"Your death and the deaths of your friends." The cold statement was followed by a short, heavy chuckle. Cigar smoke drifted in the air.

"Idris?"

"Did you miss me?" Idris asked with amusement.

"I thought you were dead."

Idris released a long, bellowing laugh. "Me? No, not me. My clone."

Lucas tasted blood and realized he had bitten his tongue. "And my clone?"

"Lucian? He's finishing the job he didn't do in Pittsburgh. I believe he is scheduled to have lunch with Johanna and Julia."

Lucas strained against the leather restraints.

"Don't waste your energy. You can't get loose. Besides, even if you did, you're unfamiliar with the outside terrain. You'd just die faster."

"You son-of-a-bitch!"

The chair creaked as Idris' heavy body rose. His hard sole shoes clicked across the floor. "After Lucian kills them, I'll come inform you. If you're a holy man, pray for them now. Because prayer won't help them later."

"Why are you doing this? Everyone believes you're dead. Why pursue us when we didn't even know you're alive?"

"I harbor grudges. This is payback for you being too stubborn to die. And the irony of all this is that Helmsby now works for me."

"He'd never do that."

Idris laughed. "No, not voluntarily he wouldn't. But when you take something he values the most, you can get him to do almost anything."

Lucas frowned as his mind searched. What did Helmsby value more than science? Suddenly, his mouth dropped open. "Nancy?"

"See, even you know his weakness."

"You bastard, you'd best not . . ."

"Easy. She's fine, unless Helmsby refuses to cooperate. When I'm done with my projects . . . well, I can't exactly let them go free."

"You'll still kill them."

"Exactly."

"Not if I kill you first."

"You know I do enjoy challenges," Idris said, pulling open the door. "Oh, and do enjoy your companions."

Metal clicked. A second later, the door closed.

Shifters chattered across the room. Lucas swallowed hard. He never expressed his true fears to Daniel about killing the shifters while scavenging in Pittsburgh. He had nightmares, more now than when they still lived inside the research center. The haunting memories were part of the reason behind his wild, life-endangering stunt shows for ESPN. He did anything to occupy his mind and cage the shifters deeper inside his mind.

A shifter hissed, growled.

"Hungry?" Lucas asked. "Me, too."

More chattering. Toenails clicked along tile floor.

"Come on, get it over with."

The sooner the better.

Lucas thought about what Idris had said about the outside terrain and if he escaped, it would be impossible for him to survive. Where had they taken him?

A shifter moaned from hunger.

Lucas ignored the creatures. In his mind, he tried to map out where they might have imprisoned him. Had he not been sedated, he'd have had a better chance of pinpointing where they had taken him. But he didn't know for certain that the whole trip was by land. He could have been taken to the airport and flown to another location. He could be halfway around the world, for all he knew.

He listened to the shifters. He wondered why none of them crossed the room to attack. From his previous experience with them, he understood their sounds of hunger. The cries on the other side of the room came from shifters that had not eaten in quite some time, but they continued to keep their distance.

Maybe the beasts were caged. Idris was sinister enough to torture some-one's mind. The shifters, as hungry as they sounded, should have charged him by now, especially since he was tied and helpless. Perhaps no shifters were in the room. Idris might have a soundtrack playing in order to break him.

Lucas smiled and allowed his body to relax. "Do your worst," he said. "I'm taking a nap."

CHAPTER 9

*D*aniel didn't feel any better after talking to Kyle, but he certainly didn't feel worse. In fact, the brief interaction reinforced his need to seek revenge against Idris for Kyle's condition. It also heightened his search to find Lucas.

He lingered outside Kyle's door and watched him through the window. Kyle sat on the edge of the bed and hugged himself. This former intelligent student was nothing more than an animal. His mind was a mere shell of the knowledge once stored inside. Kyle's lips moved but no words escaped. Daniel had seen death enough in the past to know this was the last time he'd see Kyle alive.

Dementia claimed the majority of Kyle's memories. Soon, his brain would fail to maintain the capacity to keep body organs functioning. Slowly, one by one, each component of his body was shutting down.

Kyle's weary eyes grew more distant.

Daniel pitied him. Inner anger rose like an inflamed demon. Idris would pay for what Kyle had become.

The guard escorted Daniel and Morton to Helmsby's lab.

Helmsby stood. "How'd it go?"

Daniel shrugged. "About as well as you expected. Although . . ."

"Yes?" Helmsby said.

"Your speculation of what happened after the bombing is quite accurate. The outside survivors were removed from the area."

Helmsby looked puzzled. "He remembered that?"

"The syringe was the key to trigger some of his repressed memories. Kyle's deformities stem from experimentations that Idris made Kyle endure."

Helmsby nodded. "That doesn't surprise me."

Morton leapt onto a stool at the lab table. "It's apparent Idris wanted to test DNA enhancers to see if he could regenerate Kyle's hand," the cat said. "When that failed, they probably discarded him on the streets. I doubt they expected him to live. Of course, there were obvious side effects."

Helmsby scratched his chin. "It goes further than that, I'm afraid."

Morton looked at Daniel then back at Helmsby. "How?"

"If it was only the enhancers," Helmsby said. "I could reverse that. But I'm afraid the dementia and his degeneration come from other things, too. Follow me and I'll explain."

Helmsby led Daniel and Morton deeper into TransGenCorp's facility. Fluorescent lights gleamed off the long narrow, stainless steel halls. The cold air chilled Daniel. Morton pranced ahead of them seemingly intent to explore.

"How far into the mountain do these laboratories go?" Daniel asked.

"A half-mile at my best estimate."

"This place is a lot bigger than I imagined."

Helmsby nodded. "I know. Now, there are things about Kyle I didn't tell you. Large sections of his brain were surgically removed."

"What?"

Helmsby shoved his hands into his pockets. "Yes. If you examine his scalp you'll find the drilled holes where they took portions of his brain."

They entered a darkened hall.

"But why?" Daniel asked.

Helmsby's eyes narrowed. "Perhaps to clone his genius? I'm not certain. You see, Idris is still obsessed with creating super humans, both in body and mental capacity. Kyle's mind was incredibly sharp with the ability to absorb any information presented to him. Much like my own, I should say. A super genius with photographic retention. You see it and simply remember the information. That's the portion of Kyle's brain that Idris extracted. It amazes me that Kyle remembered the syringe after all this time. His further contortions are from eating shifter brains and raw flesh. Prions ate away the remaining healthy brain tissue. That's why I can't reverse what he has become."

They continued walking down the hallway, and the halls grew darker.

Overhead lights were off. A few more steps and there'd be standing with no light at all. Helmsby stopped walking.

Almost hidden in the shadows, Helmsby whispered, "TransGenCorp's operation had more experiments than I had expected."

The hall temperature grew colder. Helmsby pulled his lab coat tightly around his long, narrow waist. "Come with me and I'll show you something. Many of Idris' experiments still remain, too."

"They haven't been destroyed?"

"Government officials don't want anything altered or destroyed before I analyze everything firsthand."

"After three years, you still haven't completed the analyses?"

"Idris had thousands of projects. He was quite prolific with his research during our time inside my research center. Of course, *he* had money and outside help where I didn't. Otherwise . . ."

Morton sighed. "We get it. You'd have done more during the same amount of time if you had equal funding."

"*Twice* the amount . . ."

"So what did you wish to show us?" Daniel asked.

Helmsby smiled and nodded. "Of course. Sorry. I get excited when I think about these experiments. Come on."

The hallway was completely dark for about twenty feet. It was so dark that Daniel couldn't see Helmsby's white lab coat. Large sections of the walls were glass. Black lights glowed behind thick windows.

"Proceed cautiously," Helmsby said. "We don't want to spook them. Not many people visit, so they're not used to humans."

Daniel picked Morton up and stepped to the nearest window. Daniel froze when he saw them.

Black lights glowed from the ceiling. Inside the cage were thick leafy branches. At first, all Daniel could see were bright red eyes. When his eyes adjusted to the lighting, he saw something he wished he couldn't see. One of the shifters fluttered from the cage floor to a branch, ruffled its leathery wings, and stared at him.

"It's just like the one that killed Randy," Daniel said.

"I wondered if they were the same species since I never got to inspect the one that nearly attacked you."

"You have dozens of them. I thought the one Julia killed was the only one."

"I know. The logs indicate one escaped when they were transported to this room. However, *I* believe it was released to see if it could survive in the wild."

Daniel didn't reply. The creatures captivated him. They resembled tiny gargoyles brought to life. Their cold peering eyes made him shudder and resurrected a fear he wished no longer reside in him. But to rescue Lucas these fears Daniel needed to face. Otherwise, he operated with his guard down.

Their eyes indicated a darker evil that sought to torture and kill. More than Idris controlled these creatures. Something more sinister was in the background. The winged creatures appeared to have been molded into existence from the realm of darkness. Whatever fed their desire for blood also handled Idris like a stringed puppet. Daniel wasn't certain he wanted to know who was behind their origin, but these mysteries had to be revealed whether he liked it or not.

Helmsby smiled. His eyes were on the creatures, but his mind seemed far away. "Fascinating, aren't they?"

Daniel remained silent.

"A bit inferior," Morton said, watching several creatures flitter around the tiny enclosed room. One of them made a clumsy grab for a branch and fluttered desperately to hold on without falling backwards. Morton looked at Helmsby and nodded toward it. "*You* could have done better than *this*."

A delighted smile crossed Helmsby's face. His eyes indicated that his mind was piecing together the genetic components necessary to develop a more superior flying creature.

Helmsby nodded. "Yes, had I found the time to develop such a thing. But you were my top priority in the research center. Someone had to protect Daniel."

"And yet, it never occurred to you to give *me* wings?" Morton said. He shook his little head and spat. "Damn! All the fun I've missed!"

Helmsby let out a loud howl of laughter, but Daniel remained solemn. His eyes were still fastened on the winged creatures. Apparently he hadn't heard a word they had said.

A sly smile crossed Morton's face. He glanced at Daniel. "Wings certainly would've been nice when *he* dropped me off that building."

The playful jab didn't faze Daniel.

He remembered the horrendous screech the winged creature squalled when Julia chased it across the rooftop. She had landed one direct swing with the broom handle, crippling it. The injured creature had fallen to the street only to be eaten by shifters.

Her accuracy came too late. Randy's throat had been slashed open by its talons. The bat-like beasts were capable of deadly attacks, in spite of how clumsy these appeared.

"Dan? Are you okay?" Helmsby asked.

Daniel glanced at his watch and nodded. "Yeah. I'm fine. Morton and I should be going, just in case Lucas calls again."

"Oh?" Helmsby said. "Well, do come back. I've missed your company. I wish better circumstances had brought you here."

"So do I." Daniel placed a hand to the glass. "How do you feed these things without getting attacked?"

"There's a separation chamber. It's closed off. We place the food in the other chamber and open a glass door to let them eat. After they return to their perches, we close it. That limits the chance of anyone being attacked or their escape."

Morton jumped from Daniel's arms. "Imagine how I'd look with wings. I could've glided to the floor with elegance."

"Forget about the wings," Helmsby said with a laugh.

Helmsby remained silent while he led them back to the laboratory.

Outside the lab door, Helmsby whispered, "You still have a gun, right?"

Daniel's heart raced. "Yes, packed away, somewhere."

"I hope you've practiced shooting it."

"Why?"

Helmsby rammed his hands into his lab coat pockets. "I know you and Lucas are close friends. There's nothing I can say to prevent you from trying to find him. But there's something you need to think about."

"What?"

"It won't be monsters you have to kill this time, Dan." He paused and looked both directions down the hallway. "Not if you plan to find Lucas. You'll have to kill humans with the minds of monsters. Are you prepared to do that?"

Morton extended his paw. Long jagged claws protruded. "I am. Leave the killing to me."

Daniel frowned. "So you believe what has happened to Lucas is an organized effort?"

Helmsby sighed. "I'm afraid so. I never wanted to think so though. But Lucas' clone is the key clue to answer my questions. You see, six of our Pittsburgh party have died over the past month. Executed with gunshots to the back of their heads. Except for Doug. He was knifed in the back."

"What does this mean?"

"It means our lives are in grave danger. Security here has heightened."

"Why didn't they just kill Lucas?"

"They want to torture him and defame his character before they kill him. Why else? Prepare yourself and your family. They went to a great length to capture him and keep him alive. They'll be coming for you, too."

"What?"

Helmsby nodded. His eyes widened with fear. "And Julia, Johanna, your daughter, and everyone else. Me included, if they get past the guards."

Daniel slid his hand into his jacket pocket and retrieved his cell phone. He had both the ringer and vibration clicked off. He turned on the phone to check for any calls. The entire screen scrolled with Julia's cell number. Chills shot through his body.

"Morton, we have to go. Now."

"What's wrong?" Helmsby said.

"Julia's in trouble."

"Be careful, Dan," Helmsby said. "Don't lose your self-control. You're not caged inside Pittsburgh anymore, but the conditions are the same. The playing field, however, is much larger with a lot more enemies than we had before. Enemies we don't know and may never see, but they're out there, possibly watching our every move. And Morton?"

Morton looked back. "Yes?"

"Protect them." Helmsby's voice crackled, choked with tears.

Morton's eyes narrowed. He sliced the air with long jagged claws. "No need to ask."

"Dan," Helmsby said, raising his voice. "Before you head after Lucas, contact me. I'll get in touch with military higher ups and see if they have any idea where Lucas was taken."

Daniel nodded. He took Morton into his arms and ran down the hall. He felt so helpless. He wasn't sure what had happened, but he had to call Julia the second he left TransGenCorp's protective shield barrier. Had she been attacked or abducted? If so, did he have time to save her?

CHAPTER 10

*J*ulia pulled the van into the parking lot of an abandoned building. Her hands shook as she put the vehicle in park. She wasn't sure if the black vans were still pursuing them, but she hadn't seen any of the vans since she lost them at the intersection. She was thankful Felicia had fallen asleep. Adding a child's terrorized crying would have chiseled her nerves all the more. She didn't need more distractions while she tried to keep them out of danger.

"I don't know what to do, Johanna," Julia said, fighting tears. "Daniel's not answering his phone."

Johanna placed an arm around Julia's shoulder and squeezed. "It will be okay. You did well. We're still alive and you lost them."

"For now, but for how long?"

Johanna clicked the gun's safety on and set the gun in her lap. "I don't know."

Julia wiped tears from her eyes.

"I'm really sorry," Johanna said.

"For what?"

"For inviting Lucas to lunch."

"You had no idea that it wasn't him."

"But still, I put you and Felicia in great danger. I just wish I *had* known."

"I don't hold you responsible, Johanna."

"Thanks."

Julia looked at the van's hood. "What kind of weapon did they fire at us?"

"It looked like some sort of rifle, but I'm not sure."

"I thought so, too. But wouldn't they have shot a hole in the radiator or something?"

Johanna glanced back at Felicia, who was still asleep. "Let's take a look while the little princess is sleeping."

Julia cringed. "I don't know."

"There's no traffic around here. I think we're safe."

Julia closed her eyes tightly and grabbed the door handle. "I feel safer inside. I don't want to get out."

"Okay, dear. I understand. I'll go check."

Julia placed a hand on Johanna's arm. "Be careful."

Johanna frowned and then she forced a smile. "If it's anything, it's not something that's going to attack me."

Julia opened her eyes. Her fear grew stronger as her adrenaline waned. "Hurry. We have to find Daniel."

Swinging open the door, Johanna walked to the front of the van. She shook her head in surprise while running her hand along the grill. Julia lowered her window.

"There's nothing here," Johanna said. "Not a dent or a scratch. Nothing."

Julia opened her door and joined Johanna. "You're sure?"

"Take a look. I can't find anything."

"But they fired *something*. You heard the gun fire, didn't you?"

"Yes, but there's nothing there."

"Maybe they missed us?"

"I suppose."

A strong wind gust blew across the parking lot, bringing with it the sound of crumbled papers and leaves scratching the pavement. Julia looked up and noticed far in the distance, a long line of dark, ominous clouds coming from the west. Soon, thunderstorms would darken the day; much like the threat of death darkened her soul. She wondered if it were a bad omen or a warning that her peaceful life was once again going to plummet into turmoil. A chill pushed through her. The day that had started so warm and refreshing was now cold and dismal.

"Let's go," Julia said, rushing to her open door. "We need to find Daniel. He may be in as much danger as we are."

Johanna got in and fastened her seatbelt. "So the real Lucas called Daniel this morning, and he's in jail for murder?"

Julia nodded and looked both directions before pulling out of the parking lot. "Yes. He said he was framed."

"By his clone?"

"Yeah."

"Then why would the clone be after us?"

"That's what scares me. I really don't know. Maybe he wants to kill us?"

Johanna shook her head. "You know, Lucas has an uncanny sense of humor. You don't suppose . . ."

"That this is one of his jokes? Hell, no. He's not that cruel. He certainly wouldn't go to the trouble of hiring men to drive vans and cut us off on the freeway. I know he'd never frighten Felicia like they did."

"That's true."

"Those vans had no plates, no identification at all. Someone went to a lot of trouble to kill us or take us captive. Plus. they don't want anyone to know who they are."

The cell phone rang. Johanna looked at the caller screen. "It's Daniel."

"Finally. Thank God."

$\mathcal{D}$aniel tucked Morton close to his chest and hurried to the car. He didn't want to appear too anxious in case it drew attention from the guards. He had been told years before that you never run away from the armed tower guards at a prison or a government facility. Guards automatically assume the worst, and they're trained to shoot first and ask questions later. With TransGenCorp's heightened security, they might suspect he had stolen something or assaulted Helmsby.

Once inside the car, he didn't call Julia immediately. He feared Trans-GenCorp had electronic ways to intercept and listen to any calls made on their property. He didn't have anything to hide, but it unnerved him that someone could eavesdrop on a private phone call to the woman he loved.

Besides, he didn't fully know if he trusted Helmsby. Helmsby had changed his story, at first by not believing the clone was still alive, and then by stating that the people responsible for Lucas' frame and arrest were powerfully dangerous individuals. Helmsby had more information than he cared to disclose and that troubled Daniel. He sensed that he was in a similar situation like he underwent at the research center when Helmsby sent him into the streets with Lucas' clone. The dangers hadn't changed, but their enemies had increased.

When Daniel reached the security gate, Morton sat in the front passenger seat. The cat breathed heavily. He was fuming about the possibility of what might have happened to Julia and Felicia. Morton's claws grew thicker, longer. His teeth transformed into sharp fangs. Peering straight ahead, the cat seethed.

"Let's go," Morton said.

"As soon as they lift the gate arm, we're on our way."

Morton's paws swelled. "They'd best not delay our exit. I don't have the patience to stop my transformation."

Daniel stopped for a few seconds at the gate. The guard nodded and the arm rose. As they exited, two black vans entered. Just in a casual glance at the side view mirror, Daniel noticed the rear windows of the second van were shattered. Other minor damage had riveted the doors. The gate guard never stopped the vans. He gave them direct clearance.

Three blocks down the street, Daniel said, "We're going to find them. They'll be okay." The words were more to assure himself than Morton.

"Yeah, but anyone who threatens you or them will suffer."

Daniel hit Julia's number on speed dial. "Damn," he said. "No answer."

"Where are they?"

"She was supposed to meet Johanna for lunch at Luigiana's Italian restaurant."

Morton growled. "Then we go there."

Daniel stopped at the red light. Pedestrians walked calmly while his heart hammered painfully inside his chest. Breathing was difficult. The air seemed thicker. In his mind, he played out several different scenarios with dreadful endings. Without hearing her voice and knowing she was safe, he feared the worst had happened.

He winced, recalling what Helmsby had said, "They will come for you, for Julia, and for your daughter."

Helmsby had *not* said might, but he had said, *will*, which indicated Helmsby knew more than what he was telling. That thought disturbed Daniel. And now his mind raced to the days when he believed Helmsby had used him without warning him of the risks involved.

Daniel's life had seemed as sacrificial as a pawn in a chess game controlled by Helmsby. The geneticist needed to gain more knowledge of Idris' corruption and the scientific manipulations associated with Trans-GenCorp. Daniel had been blind to what he was venturing into. And now, he felt the same betrayal.

Although Helmsby had apologized, Daniel wondered if it was genuine. Helmsby wasn't a man that expressed his emotions, nor was he one to loosely admit fault or error. He certainly wasn't a man to show shame, either. Science was his top priority. He would sacrifice the outrageous cost of friends and family in order to achieve a new genetic breakthrough.

Daniel tried to reach Julia one more time. The phone rang four times before Julia's nervous voice answered. Her voice was clear but tattered with fear.

"Oh, thank God," she said. "I've been trying to get in touch with you for over an hour."

"Are you okay?" Daniel asked.

Morton closed his eyes and slowly regenerated into full cat form.

Julia released a long sigh into Daniel's ear and said, "We are now."

"What happened?"

"We had a run in with Lucas' clone."

"Damn. Are you okay?"

"Yes, we're fine. A bit shaken, but we lost him."

Morton cocked his ear and tilted his head toward Daniel in an obvious attempt to eavesdrop. Daniel put the phone on speaker so Morton could hear. The cat needed to know what was going on.

"Lucas' clone called Johanna this morning," Julia said. "She hadn't heard about Lucas' arrest. She thought it was really him. She invited him to come eat lunch with us. When we tore out of the parking lot, he followed us in a black van. Another van joined the pursuit."

"Wait a minute. Black vans?"

"Yes. Why?"

"They were entering TransGenCorp right as we were leaving. One of them looked like it had had the rear windows busted out. Bullet holes were in the back doors."

"That's them. They tried to run us off the road. They fired some kind of weapon at us. Johanna fired back with her .45. That's why their windows were shattered."

"Where are you right now?" Daniel asked.

"We're headed back to the apartment."

Morton shook his head. "No, don't go there. You won't be safe."

"You think they're waiting for us?"

Daniel nodded. "It's a possibility. Let's meet somewhere else. It's probably not safe for us to go home yet."

"Then where?" Julia asked.

Daniel looked at Morton.

Morton showed sharp teeth. "Make it a very public place."

"How about the donut shop?" Daniel said.
"Why there?" Morton asked.
"Cops. Lots of cops."
Morton grinned shrewdly. "Purr-fect."
"Okay," Julia said. "But please hurry."

CHAPTER 12

When Daniel pulled into the parking lot, Julia ran to meet him. He stepped out of the car, and she embraced him fiercely. Morton leapt to the pavement, sat up, and licked his forepaw while watching their reunion.

"I've not been this scared since . . ." Julia said.

"I know," Daniel whispered in her ear. "It seems to be happening all over again. Perhaps worse this time."

"Your intuitions were right, honey," Julia whispered. "I'm sorry I doubted your fears. How did you—"

"He has a catlike six sense," Morton said.

She pulled back and looked into Daniel's eyes. "Helmsby can't help Lucas?"

Daniel shook his head. "Not really. He believes the clone is probably still alive, but he doesn't believe the courts would buy the argument even if he presented it. I think he knows a lot more than he's willing to share with us."

Johanna brought Felicia to Daniel. Felicia smiled and said, "Hi, Daddy."

"Hi, sweetheart," he replied.

Johanna smiled at Daniel. "Had it not been for Julia's remarkable driving, they'd have gotten us."

"I'm glad you're all safe," Daniel said. "Tell me what happened."

Julia and Johanna explained the details more slowly. Johanna pointed at the van's grill and said, "See, there aren't any marks on it at all."

Morton walked to the grill and stared intently. "It wasn't a bullet they fired. It's a magnetic tracer."

Johanna took a step back. Her mouth dropped open. "It talks?" she asked.

Morton frowned and cocked a brow. "I hope your reference to *it* doesn't mean *me*."

"I'm sorry," she said. "I didn't know you could talk."

Julia smiled. "We've been meaning to tell you."

"But how?" Johanna asked, staring at Morton.

"He's a shifter, created by Dr. Helmsby," Daniel replied.

"A shifter?"

"He's not dangerous," Julia said.

"No, he's safe," Daniel said. "Helmsby created him to protect me during the last few days we were in Pittsburgh. He watches out for all of us now."

"Cuddles," Felicia said, running to the cat. She patted his back and rubbed his ears. Morton nuzzled his face against her tiny hands.

Cars entered and exited the parking lot while they stood at the front of the van. Most patrons used the drive-thru lane and paid no attention to them. Raindrops fell. Softly at first, and then the wind picked up speed. The smell of rain drifted with the breeze. The gloomy clouds covered the sun. Thunder echoed in the distance.

"There's the tracer," Morton said, placing his paw on the lower grill. "It's nearly invisible to the human eye. Lucky for you, I'm here."

The cat extended his paw, lengthening his digits long enough to detach the tracer from the vehicle. He handed the tiny device to Daniel. "They'll use this to find you if we leave it on the vehicle. Perhaps they're watching us right now."

Daniel scanned the parking lot. No one seemed to be parked with their attention on them, but that didn't mean that the clone and his men weren't headed their direction.

Julia leaned closer and looked at the tracer. "What should we do with it?"

Daniel took the tracer and placed it against the curb. "We leave it. At least it will make them think we're still here. Maybe that will allow us to put some distance between them and us. But once they realize our vehicle isn't here, they'll come looking for us."

"Should we go home?" Johanna asked.

Morton huddled under the front van bumper to prevent rain from hitting him. "No. They will want to finish what they started. Our homes will be one of the places they will look first. Dan, you take me back to the apartment. I'll take care of anyone who might show up. You need to find a hotel and stay out of sight. When it's safer, I'll contact you. You'll all be safer if you stick together."

Daniel nodded and looked at Julia. "The vans that pursued you were black?"

"Yes."

He described the vans that had entered TransGenCorp again.

"Our enemies may be more powerful than we realize," Daniel said.

Morton narrowed his eyes. "Perhaps, but tonight, they might be a few men shorter if I have anything to do with it."

CHAPTER 13

*D*aniel drove Morton to the apartment while Julia and Johanna found a hotel.

The rain intensified and visibility lessened. In one sense, Daniel was relieved he was leaving the heart of Pittsburgh, but he regretted being away from Julia and Felicia after the traumatic event they had experienced. But he believed getting a hotel room in Pittsburgh would be the last place where the clone would expect them to be. Morton was probably right. The first place they'd hunt for them was at their homes. He just didn't like the idea of returning to the city without the cat.

He couldn't shake the fact that the black vans were associated with TransGenCorp, and he had been so close to the clone and didn't realize it. Had he known they had just attempted to run Julia off the road, he would've probably slammed his car into the lead van. But such an action inside TransGenCorp was suicidal. The guards would have gunned him down before he had a chance to grab Lucas' clone.

Daniel's anger weighed evenly with his nervousness. The fact that the vans were inside TransGenCorp meant the same people protecting Helmsby were also protecting the clone.

"How much was Helmsby on the level?" Daniel asked.

Morton frowned. "You think he's involved with this?"

"Don't you?"

The cat shrugged.

"You didn't sense any abrupt change in his behavior?" Daniel asked. "Like maybe he was hiding something?"

"I'm a shifter, Daniel, not a psychic."

Daniel watched the road through the rapid rain-sluiced windshield wipers. "I know, but animals do have a keen sense of detecting human emotions."

"Yeah, well, I don't have my Tarot cards with me at the moment."

"This is serious."

"I *am* serious."

Daniel sighed. "I believe he's hiding something."

"A great deal more than we know. I agree with you on that."

"But why put our lives in jeopardy?"

"Who says he has?"

"The vans are there. Lucas' clone is there."

Morton nodded. "Maybe he can't say anything. Maybe *his* life is being threatened."

"I don't trust him. I can't, even though part of me wants to."

"I understand your position."

"Nancy's in Germany. My guess is to keep her out of harm's way while we get stuck in the middle again."

"Remember one thing that he said."

"What?"

"Don't lose your focus. You get preoccupied with nonsense details and you'll put yourself off guard. That's when you'll be the weakest."

"I'm not losing my focus," Daniel said. "I'm just trying to evaluate everything."

"Then you *are* out of focus. Zero in on the key issue here. That's finding Lucas before he's killed or before they find and kill *us*."

Daniel gritted his teeth. "Helmsby seemed certain they are coming after us."

"If so, he's not our enemy. Why warn us if he's involved?"

Daniel didn't reply. There had to be more to what was taking place. Helmsby was involved somehow. What had the military offered him to keep his assistance?"

"You mull it over," Morton said. "My cat genes insist that I take a nap. I'll need to be keenly alert while working the night shift. Wake me when we get there."

CHAPTER 14

Daniel turned onto the street where they lived and nudged Morton. "Almost there."

Daniel slowed to park in their assigned parking spot.

Morton whispered, "No, keep driving. Don't let them *see* you."

"They're here?"

"It's possible. Drive further down the street and let me out at the curb. You go back and protect the women. I'll call you after what's done is done."

"Maybe I should stick around, too."

"No. These men are better trained than you can handle. They will come in the dead of night when our neighbors are asleep. Besides, you saw how frightened Julia and Felicia were. You need to be there to ease their fears."

Daniel turned the car around and parked at the curb. He scratched the back of Morton's ears. "I know, but I don't want you to get hurt."

"Me? I have night eyes. I work best in the dark. And besides that, I'm a shifter. Bullets sting but I heal fast."

"Yeah, maybe so. But be careful. They might have night eyes, too. Who knows what Idris will send?"

Morton nuzzled Daniel's hand. Daniel opened the door and let the cat out. The cool rain soaked his fur. Morton looked up and said, "If it didn't draw too much attention, I'd ask for an umbrella."

Daniel grinned. "Take care of yourself."

Morton ran under a parked car and waited until Daniel drove out of sight. Slinking from car to car, he kept the rain to a minimum on his fur. As best he could tell, no one sat in any of the cars parked along the opposite side of the street. He really didn't think they'd come until after nightfall, but he wasn't taking any chances.

He entered through a side door of the apartment complex and headed upstairs. When he got to their apartment, he popped his head through the cat door.

Silence.

With cat stealth, Morton checked each room and then the windows. No one had broken in yet, but he had the uncanny cat sense they were nearby. With only hours until dusk, he moved through the room, refreshing his mind of each nook where he could hide.

Morton slid open the balcony door. Dark clouds released heavy raindrops. He inhaled the sweet air. The intruders would come this way, he reasoned. It was the quickest, easiest route to enter that lessened the possibility of being seen by other residents.

Morton studied the balcony railing, and he thought it odd that Daniel had worried that the shifters were still out there. He smiled. Just like Morton had mentioned to Julia, Daniel possessed a cat sense of his own. But Morton became uneasy because he hadn't felt what Daniel did. Shifters weren't their greatest danger. It was the people protecting the shifters; armed men who killed and threatened their lives.

He slinked back through the sliding glass door and pushed it shut. He found the television remote and channeled through satellite stations. He stopped at a channel to turn back on later once he made sure their home was safe. He turned off the lights and stared at the sliding glass doors.

Now came the waiting.

Morton sighed.

He wasn't a patient cat.

CHAPTER 15

*D*r. Helmsby wrung his hands under sterilized water at the laboratory sink. He felt contaminated. No amount of washing his hands made them feel any cleaner. The filth clung deeper, to his inner core where soap and water couldn't cleanse. Closing his eyes, he pictured Daniel and Morton leaving TransGenCorp. He feared that was the last time he'd see them alive.

The adjoining room door opened. A man in military fatigues stepped inside. He applauded Helmsby slowly and with a mocking grin.

"Nice work, Dr. Helmsby. Nancy gets to live another day. You have the DNA analysis and the brain tissue we requested?"

Requested? Helmsby thought. *You bastards demanded it at gunpoint.*

The soldier folded his muscled arms. "Well?"

Nervously, Helmsby nodded. "Yes. One second."

He tore a long DNA chain printout from a printer. He picked up a small cooler filled with dry ice and two brain core tissue samples. He handed them to the armed soldier.

"When can I see Nancy?" Helmsby asked.

"Soon. Provided Kyle's brain sample and DNA sequence maps are to Idris' satisfaction."

Angered, Helmsby pointed a finger. "They're *exactly* what he asked for."

"Then you've nothing to worry about."

"At least let me talk to her."

The soldier tucked the cooler under his arm and turned to leave. "Soon."

"What about Daniel and the others?"

"We'll deal with them. We only want the cat. Dead or alive, it doesn't really matter."

"Why the cat?"

"Do you realize how many millions of people would pay thousands of dollars to own a talking cat?"

He's more than just a cat.

"Idris sends his regards."

Helmsby clamped his teeth on the tip of his tongue to refrain a sudden, hostile outburst. He wanted to extend his middle finger and shout, "Give him my regards, too!" But, he didn't. He couldn't. Not with him holding Nancy hostage. Hell, he was a prisoner himself. He couldn't leave the military base or call to warn Daniel. Any action meant Nancy's death and his.

He placed his hands atop a Formica table and leaned forward. For the second time that he ever remembered, he wept uncontrollably. He cursed himself for removing portions of Kyle's brain. Had Idris' soldiers not forced him by abducting Nancy, Helmsby would have died before he performed such an immense and appalling surgery.

After Margaret's death, Nancy was all he had left, except science. He finally understood the importance of human bonding. It was sad that it had taken his wife's death to open his heart and eyes. He had never been an emotionally caring father or husband. It pained him to be denied the opportunity to make up for lost time. For the first time in his life he realized he wasn't worried about his personal welfare. He'd willingly sacrifice his life to save Nancy's.

Redemption wasn't alienated from him, however. Kyle still had some hope. During the surgery, Helmsby saturated the open brain tissue with annealing polymerases in hope of restoring the pocked gray matter the prions had destroyed. Something miraculous had occurred. Not only had Kyle healed faster than normal, but he had also gained some of his lost memories.

Helmsby added shifter-enhanced genetic material as a last effort for tissue regeneration to repair the biopsied sections he had removed. The guards questioned none of his actions since they weren't scientists. It didn't matter what solutions he put inside Kyle's lobotomized brain. They simply viewed the additions as a part of the operational procedure.

In the operating room, Helmsby did whatever he pleased, except that the surgery didn't please him. It crushed and sickened him. But, amazingly, Kyle remembered things he hadn't formally acknowledged like the syringe and Idris doing experiments on him years earlier. Much to Helmsby's satisfaction, the consequences of the surgery were a scientific miracle. What information Kyle might disclose potentially handicapped Idris.

CHAPTER 16

$\mathcal{D}$aniel's cell phone rang. "Yes?"

"Hi, Daniel," Julia said. "Is everything okay?"

"As best I can tell. No one followed me either direction. Where are you?"

"We're at the Holiday Inn. Room 213."

"I'll be there soon."

"Good. Please hurry. We don't want to be alone. Did Morton indicate whether our apartment was being staked out?"

"No, but he acted concerned. He sensed they are coming."

"I hope he's going to be okay."

"He's a shifter, Julia. He'll be fine."

"I hope so."

"He seemed pretty confident in handling himself."

"It's his male cat ego."

"I should be there in a few minutes."

"Okay. We're watching the news, Dan. The clone did kill Godfrey. Lucas could never do that."

"I know. Of course, I knew Godfrey would be targeted since he opposed everything Idris stood for. All the more reason to believe the clone killed him."

"It's sad."

"It just makes matters more urgent. Norhaney died two years ago. Just one year after he freed us from Idris' experimental killing ground. And now, Godfrey. We have fewer allies."

Worry claimed Julia's voice again. "Please hurry."

"I am."

~

A BLACK VAN pulled into the donut shop parking lot. Three men stepped out and scanned the parking lot. Less than five minutes later, they found their tracer at the edge of the curb.

"They're a lot smarter than you anticipated, Lucian," a bulky soldier said.

Lucian, the clone, nodded. "They'll have to be even smarter if they want to stay alive. It won't take too much computer time to discover where they live."

CHAPTER 17

At fifteen past midnight, two metal grapple hooks scraped across the balcony floor, struck the brick inner wall, and resounded with a harsh, solid clink as they anchored against the metal handrail. Inside the apartment, Morton's ears perked. In the darkness, the cat waited.

Three men pulled themselves up the cables quietly. Dressed in black, soaked by icy rain, the men stood outside the sliding glass door. They checked their handguns before they slid infrared goggles over their eyes. Each man wore a bulletproof vest. They slid open the unlocked door. Morton crept deeper into the darkness of the living room.

Morton's eyes narrowed when he noticed the TransGenCorp emblem on their uniforms.

"Where first?" one soldier asked another.

"Find the bedrooms and kill them all."

"Even the child?"

The man nodded. "Yes."

Morton gnashed his teeth and seethed.

The soldiers stepped onto the living room plush carpet. Beads of rain dripped from their skintight clothes, pooling soggy puddles beneath their feet on the carpet. With the aid of night vision, they scanned the room, quietly taking each step, and their fingers tightened on their guns.

"Did you hear that?"

"What?"

"A voice."

"No. Where?"

The man pointed. "Over there. Across the room. Behind the couch, I think."

The other soldier readied his gun and took a step in the indicated direction. He scanned along the edge of the furniture and stopped when his eyes located Morton. The man lowered his handgun.

"It's just the damned cat."

"Grab him. Idris wants him."

"Just a cat?" Morton said.

Stunned, the soldier faced his comrade. "It speaks."

"Oops," Morton said. "I meant to say *meow*."

Morton's eyes glowed red. His jaw changed with rows of sharper teeth. He charged at the soldiers.

Morton attacked the two men before their bewilderment faded. Lengthening his right front claws into wicked jagged talons, he sprang upward and flailed deeply into the softness of one man's throat. The man toppled backwards, and Morton kicked off higher into the air, did a mad cat one-eighty-degree twist, and sank his claws through the second soldier's goggles, piercing through the man's eyes.

The man screamed and swung his hands to yank off the cat. Morton flexed his paw muscles and lengthened his claws into the man's brain. The soldier fell silent.

Both TGC soldiers were dead.

Too simple, Morton thought, but during the scuffle, he had failed to notice the third soldier that stepped inside from the balcony. The silent soldier caught him by surprise. Morton's sensitive ears detected the sudden, solid squeeze of the gun's trigger. He attempted to bolt, but his bloody forepaws slipped on the dead man's wet bulletproof vest.

The bullet ripped through Morton's gut. The impact knocked Morton across the room. The burning pain was instant, and the wound serious.

"Damn cat-hating bastard," Morton snarled in pain.

Morton clawed his way under the couch and closed his eyes. He remained silent and clutched his side where the bullet passed through. He had never experienced such brutal pain. Of the times he'd been shot, none of those wounds had ever hurt like this.

Enhancing his night eyes, he focused on the two dead men. The Trans-GenCorp emblems caught his attention again. Idris still controlled the biotech laboratories, somehow. That explained a lot about Helmsby's strange behavior, Lucas' frame, and why Morton's wound wasn't healing.

Perhaps the bullet was laced with anticoagulants or denaturing agents to slow his genetic ability to knit the hole together.

"Here kitty, kitty," the soldier taunted. "Come out so I can treat you."

"Enticing words, as they are," Morton replied, still holding his wound. "But if you want me, come get me. When you do, you'll be like your two friends sprawled on the floor."

The man laughed. "They were just ordinary men. I'm not."

"And I ain't your normal, everyday kitty cat, either," Morton said, wincing. The pain burned feverishly in his gut. He listened for approaching footsteps, but the man held his ground.

"I know exactly what you are, Morton."

The cat's ears perked.

"I don't want you to die. That's not in either of our best interests."

"I have no immediate pains to die. However, I do plan to kill you. Your presence here is all the threat I need to justify doing it, too."

"Suit yourself," he replied. "I don't have to shoot you with another round. I can simply walk away. Your DNA is tainted with a genetic poison. Without the antidote, you'll die. I have served my purpose. These two men were merely a distraction."

From beneath the dark couch, Morton crouched. "So I kill you and get the antidote I need."

"You're wrong about both theories. You're too weak to kill me. Besides, the antidote isn't on me. So what will it be?"

Morton elongated his claws, sliced foam from the couch cushion and stuffed it into the bullet wound.

He gritted his teeth. "I guess we see how immortal you *think* you are."

Morton was glad Helmsby had made him a cat shifter. He understood that cats' instinctive, cunning behavior made them one of nature's most successful predators. Far more patient as hunters than men, cats out-waited their prey without growing bored. Although injured, Morton still had some impressive gimmicks to quash this opponent.

Morton peered from beneath the couch. The soldier stood across the room, just to the left of the wall-sized HD television. Attached to the television was the studio surround sound, theater quality speakers.

If what the man stated was true, he was one of Idris' genetic soldiers. Unlike the two dead men, this man didn't wear night vision goggles, so a sudden burst of bright light might only affect him for a few seconds.

However, the man's ears were canine shaped. His face was covered with thick, curly black hair. Sharp teeth, not human in appearance, lined his wide mouth. No wonder this soldier came out at night. He was too freakish to be seen during the daylight hours. His wolfish appearance would draw too much attention.

Morton cut more foam from the couch and stuffed his ears. Just inches away, on the floor, lay the universal remote that operated both the stereo and the television. He grinned. He loved the remote so much that Julia often teased him by saying, "I'd think you were a man by the way you hug that controller."

He smiled weakly, remembering her sweet voice whenever she playfully jibbed. His pain flared. He could ignore the pain if he was healing, but the wound remained open, bleeding. Live or die, he was going to protect his family and home.

The armed soldier stood silent with his gun in hand. He waited for Morton to concede or die.

Fashioning his paw to fit the remote, he turned on the television. The bright glare hit the side of the man's face. At the instant the man turned toward the television, Morton clicked the stereo to its highest volume. The speakers blared the hardest heavy metal CD that Daniel owned.

The gun dropped from the soldier's hand. He grabbed his ears to muffle the sound. The sudden, overwhelming thunderous vibrations brought him to his knees. The man's screams turned into a maddened growl. At twelve-thirty in the morning, the neighbors weren't about to be happy.

Morton slinked from the couch with the remote and hobbled to the 9mm. He lengthened his paw further, grabbed the gun and fired three shots into the man's side where the vest didn't cover. The man jerked with each shot, and then he slumped over, holding his side.

Morton killed the stereo volume. His eyes turned crimson red. "Now, let's discuss the antidote."

The soldier shook with spasms. Morton realized the bullets had hit vital organs. Blood soaked the man's teeth and lips.

"I told you that I don't have them on me."

"Where are they?"

The man smiled. He coughed. Blood dripped from the sides of his canine-like mouth. "It's too late. I failed and succeeded at the same time. I will die, but so will you. Our backup team is already on its way."

Minutes later, the man was dead. Options for survival were now fewer.

Morton pulled the foam from his ears and heard, for the first time, the angry neighbors pounding on the walls and the door to protest the loud music even though it was off. He ignored them and limped down the hall to the bathroom.

After leaping to the top of the toilet, he walked across the vanity to the sink and pushed the light switch on. He yanked bloody foam from the bullet wound and inspected it in the light.

The bleeding had stopped but his flesh failed to stitch together. He was lucky the entry and exit wounds were clean. At least the bullet hadn't lodged inside him or struck a vital organ. He took alcohol-soaked Q-tips and swabbed both openings.

He didn't have much time. The deployed backup team could arrive at any second. Perhaps they the antidote? It didn't matter. If he were going to die, he didn't want it to be where these men would find him. But he clung to the hope that death ignored him as it had so many times before.

In the vanity drawer, he found a threaded needle stuck into a thread spool. He stitched the wound. When he finished, he heaved and vomited in the sink.

"That's not good," he whispered, shaking his head. He stared at the thick, bloody hairball. He was in grave danger.

CHAPTER 18

*D*aniel arrived at the hotel where Julia had used an alias to rent a room. He slowly pulled into the parking lot. The thick dark clouds welcomed the night sooner than he expected. Turning into the parking space, the headlights created strange shadows that slinked along the neatly trimmed hedges. Deeper shadows of past horrors surfaced in his mind.

Tired and worried about his family, he understood that the darkness he had experienced in Pittsburgh three years ago didn't compare to what he faced now. He now needed to protect Julia and Felicia, and the threat on their lives was as great as the one on his. Though he'd never mention it to Julia, he wondered if they'd all be alive come morning.

Once inside the hotel room after he was certain no one had followed him, he ordered pizza. After it arrived, Felicia ate and watched cartoons until her eyelids grew heavy and she fell asleep. Julia moved her to the head of the bed and pulled a blanket over her.

She faced Daniel. "So Helmsby doesn't think the clone is dead?"

"He can't deny his existence at this point," Daniel replied. "But he didn't seem too interested in disclosing anything that might help us. Kyle was more helpful in what little information he gave us."

"Kyle actually spoke?" Johanna asked.

Daniel sipped hot coffee from a Styrofoam cup and nodded. "He didn't say much. But we learned that his deformities didn't occur because he was exposed to possible radiation. Idris found him after we had locked ourselves in the fallout shelter. They did experiments on him."

"But he remembers you?" Julia asked.

"Yes. That surprised the hell out of Helmsby."

"Why?"

"For one thing, sections of Kyle's brain have been removed. Helmsby implied that Kyle suffers due to a lobotomy."

Julia placed her hand over her mouth. "My God, seriously?"

Daniel didn't smile. "Would I joke about something like that?"

"No. It's just . . . sick."

"I know. And to make matters worse, Kyle doesn't have much longer to live. Helmsby estimates maybe another month. Probably less. His body is shutting down."

Johanna sat at the edge of her bed. "I always liked Kyle. I didn't know him personally, but I had seen how well he interacted with other students and the professors. He was great. I can't believe he's been reduced to this."

"It's hard for me to accept, too." Daniel looked at Julia. "So these vans didn't have any identification tags?"

She shook her head. "No plates. No markings or emblems. Nothing."

Johanna smiled. "But they're not bulletproof."

"I saw the windows on the one van had been shattered." Daniel set aside his coffee and took a piece of pizza. "But if they're with TransGenCorp, we're in deeper trouble than we realized. Helmsby is involved."

"Directly or indirectly?" Johanna asked.

Daniel shrugged. "Does it really matter? He put my life on the line once before. I suspect he's doing it again."

"Don't hold the prejudices of the past on him," Julia said.

"Excuse me, dear, but I have no choice but to take this personally. This time they came after you, our baby, and one of our best friends, Johanna."

Johanna smiled. "Thanks."

"It's true. And they know who our friends are. It's apparent these people will stop at nothing short of killing us all. Helmsby even said so."

Julia's eyes widened. "He actually said that?"

"Yes. He even asked if I had practiced using my gun lately."

"They know I have," Johanna said with an evil grin.

"Which only means," Daniel said. "They'll come better prepared the next time."

"I'm worried about Morton being at the apartment alone," Julia said.

"He thinks these people will really invade your home?" Johanna asked.

Daniel nodded. "He insists they will. He's to call after he takes care of them."

"Until then, what do we do?" Julia asked.

"You two get some sleep," Daniel said. "I'll keep a lookout through the night. Hell, I can't sleep at night anyway, so I'm better prepared to deal with it."

Julia hugged and kissed him. She slid into bed beside Felicia.

Johanna grabbed her purse. "Should I sleep in the adjoining room?"

"No. It's safer if we stay close together."

She looked surprised. "You're sure you don't mind me sleeping in here?"

Daniel smiled. "No. I insist you stay. For safety."

"Thanks."

Johanna took the other bed. Daniel turned off the lights, left the television on, and sat at a round table near the door. He waited for what the night brought their direction.

CHAPTER 19

*L*ucas didn't know how long he had slept. He awoke to the hungry cries of shifters. The sounds were no closer than when he had fallen to sleep. He believed the cries were nothing more than a recorded soundtrack looped to play continuously in a feeble attempt to frighten him.

The room contained no acrid smells of urine or musky pheromones. He had encountered enough shifters during his scavenger days to know their behavioral patterns. Besides, the room held a disinfectant odor that reminded him of a sterile hospital or a doctor's clinic.

Listening to the shifter choir, his ears noted a distinct tapping rhythm separate from the shifter soundtrack. It was a language he had learned a long time ago. Morse code.

The message was simple: "Help me, Nancy. Help me, Nancy."

Had he not learned how to decipher the code through a website, he'd have missed the message entirely. The tapping was faint, barely audible because of the cyclic playing of the shifter cries.

The rapping noise echoed from beneath his bed, perhaps through an air vent.

Lucas clanged a reply with his handcuffs against the metal headboard. "Nancy Helmsby?"

CHAPTER 20

*N*ancy gasped with both elation and fear at the reply. She thought the past hour of tapping against the air vent on the wall had been vain labor. She was more inclined to think a guard would burst through the door and confiscate the spoon she had hidden after her last meal.

Deep inside she didn't think she'd be heard. She was excited that someone had finally heard her, but she was frightened that the recipient might be one of her captors.

She took the risk and tapped. "Yes."

Her fear subsided. Tears wet her cheeks when she deciphered the next statement.

"Lucas. Here."

"Oh, thank God," she said aloud.

Nancy rested wary eyes on the locked, windowless steel door. She expected to hear the harsh clack of a key turning in the thick lock. No one approached the door, but she still felt watched.

Unlike Lucas, Nancy had the freedom to walk around her eight by ten foot room. They fed her three meals a day and escorted her to a restroom down the hall twice a day. They allowed her a single cot, a welded down metal chair, and a porcelain water basin where she could wash her face.

While she communicated with Lucas, the tapped words didn't come fast enough. This was the only interaction with people she had had in nearly three weeks. The guards never spoke. They set her food tray on the basin and left. Or, they motioned her with their hand when it was time to go to the restroom. Their strange helmets with mirrored visors prevented her from seeing their faces. Knowing some of the bizarre experiments her father had worked on over the past few years, she wondered if the guards were even human. She feared they might be something far worse.

Helmsby had once mentioned that some of the human projects had their genomes mixed with felines and some with canines. Others had both. Perhaps that was why they hid their faces. Not being certain what they were kept her from attempting to flee.

Nancy explained in short, beating phrases that although she wasn't shackled, she didn't know exactly where she was imprisoned inside Trans-GenCorp. She guessed that she might be on the second level.

"Second level?" Lucas tapped.

"Place is larger than you knew."

"Escape."

"Impossible," she replied.

"There must be a way."

CHAPTER 21

*L*ydia sped through the night along rural roads in West Virginia on the Nighthawk motorcycle Lucas had given her. Frustration forced her to push the bike to its limit around sharp, winding roads. As much as she tried to hate Lucas in order to forget him, she still loved and needed him.

The news of Lucas' murders outside the Senate shocked her. She had read the story from new updates on her cell phone earlier in the afternoon. On the CNN evening news she watched the footage of the police taking him into custody. The media constantly replayed the surveillance camera images of his face after the killings. His broad smile at the camera puzzled her. This wasn't the Lucas she had fallen in love with. The man she admired would never commit such a horrendous crime. She refused to believe he had done this. Remembering Lucas' skeptical speculation that his clone was still alive renewed in her mind. If his clone was alive, proving its existence was nearly impossible.

The timing of the unforeseen event couldn't have come at a worse time, especially since her mind continued dwelling on him. She had planned to call him that evening. She wanted to give their relationship another chance, provided he'd even talk to her.

Lydia rounded the next curve less than a mile from her farmhouse. She gunned the engine where the road straightened. Thunder rumbled over-head. She wanted to get home before the rain started.

Her driveway was less than a hundred yards away. Ahead, she noticed a van parked alongside the road. She didn't have a neighbor for miles on either side of her house. Seeing the vehicle disturbed her. She sped past and watched the van in her side view mirror. The headlights didn't come on, nor did it pull from its parked position.

She drove a mile up the road and turned into a rundown church parking lot. She shut off the engine and lights. She wondered why the van was there.

It was more than coincidence for the van to be parked near her house on the same day Lucas had been arrested for murder. After calculating the risks, Lydia understood one thing. If she wanted to exculpate Lucas, she'd have to find out who was watching her house and why. She couldn't take a suicidal straight-in approach. Rather, she'd use the dirt bike training trails she and Lucas had constructed in the huge field behind her house.

CHAPTER 22

*D*aniel sat at the table. He flipped the television station to CNN. Seconds later, his phone rang.

"I took care of them, Dan," Morton said weakly. He coughed and wheezed. "More will come. I have to get out of here. I'm sorry."

"Are you okay?"

"Actually, no. I was shot with some kind of DNA denaturing agent. I'm not healing. My metabolism seems to be degenerating at an alarming rate. It poisoned me. Without the antidote, I'll die."

Tears stung Daniel's eyes. He quickly slipped on his shoes. "I'm on my way. We'll get you to Helmsby."

"No. You don't have enough time. I'll probably be dead before you get here."

"We can't lose you."

"That's comforting, Dan. It really is. Take care of the girls. It's too dangerous for you to come here. More of Idris' men will come. They want you dead. Even Felicia."

"Morton . . ."

Morton ended the call.

Daniel rested his head in his hands and stared at the floor. Without Morton, he wasn't certain they'd survive. Idris was winning, and Daniel felt remorse. He didn't want to fail his family. They had to live.

CHAPTER 23

*M*orton left the bathroom and staggered down the carpeted hallway to Felicia's room. He peered inside. If he were going to die, he wished he could see the little girl one last time. He loved her and she did him.

Sure, she was trying and roughhoused him more than a normal cat could tolerate or survive, but he loved every single minute of it.

Morton looked at her tea table where she dressed him in doll clothes and seated him opposite from her at the tiny plastic table. She served grape Kool-aid as tea, and he learned that he looked pretty darn cute in pink, especially with the bonnet attached to the curly doll wig.

He did what a normal cat couldn't do. He wept. "I miss you, kid."

Morton turned and left her room. He didn't want to die in the apartment where these me would find him. He certainly didn't want Daniel and Julia to find his body. It would upset them. He crept to the balcony, pausing every ten feet or so to rest. When he climbed the railing, he wrapped all four paws around a grapple cable and slid down to the ground. The rain swirled in mists and fog covered the street. Headlights approached from the far end of the street. He slinked into the thorny hedges and crouched. A black ambulance pulled to the curb at the apartment front.

The *pretend* paramedics were there to retrieve the dead soldiers and his little cat body had the three soldiers succeeded with their mission. Morton was glad to disappoint them.

The driver and passenger unloaded the gurney from the rear doors and hurried through the double door entrance.

The cat's eyes widened. A weak smile curled on his lips. In their rush, they failed to shut the rear ambulance doors. He crept cautiously closer. The engine hummed, which indicated they didn't intend to be there long.

Near the I.V. pump were two first aid kits, a plastic tray of rubber vials, syringes, and a preloaded syringe gun labeled, "Retro ANTI."

With the dangerous bio-weapon the soldier had shot into Morton, the TransGenCorp personnel weren't taking any additional chances. As fatigued and strained as Morton was, it required the strength of all four paws to position the needle and squeeze the trigger. When it fired into his gut, he squealed. The medicine eased from the syringe into him. Warmth flushed through him.

Morton kicked away the syringe gun. He sat up on his haunches. His body trembled. He examined the thread-stitched hole on his stomach. After a couple minutes, he worried that he had injected the wrong drug because nothing had changed. Sudden warmth spread around the edges of the wound. The cells in his body accepted the antidote. The wound began healing. His skin tissue pushed out where the hole had been. He smiled, flexed his claws, and arched his back.

He was ready for round two.

CHAPTER 24

*L*ydia turned the Nighthawk around, drove about one hundred fifty yards and stopped. She cut across the ditch onto an old road now covered with thick grass. This road divided her neighbor's cow pasture from her hundred-acre field.

Lightning blazed the sky. The first raindrops streaked her tinted visor. Pounding thunder rattled the night. Violent wind swayed the tops of the trees along the fence.

She drove across the lumpy grass mounds until she located the gate to her property. Giant choke cherry trees towered over each end of the metal gate. She turned off the ignition, took the key to the gate lock, swung off the bike and set the kickstand.

Lydia opened the gate and pushed the motorcycle through. She didn't bother closing the gate in case she needed a quick retreat. She realized she couldn't bullet the entire distance to her house. The roaring engine would alert them that she was coming. Plus, she'd have to take the long trail without the aid of headlights, but that wasn't a problem because she had completely memorized the entire track layout in her mind. Every bump, every dip, every ramp, and every curve she could ride with her eyes closed. The toughest decision was when to ditch the bike and close in on foot.

A spraying mist floated with the night air. Pockets of fog settled in the lower areas along the shallow creek where bullfrogs bellowed and leopard frogs peeped.

Lydia revved the motor and the rear tire slung side to side before propelling forward. Down the steep decline she sped until she came to the ramp that allowed her to jump the creek. The ramp on this side was much higher than the opposite ramp, which made her incoming jump easy, but jumping from the other side required far more speed to rise high enough to clear the second ramp. She and Lucas only practiced jumping from lower to higher right before their stunt shows. Of course, that was when they were still a couple. She hoped that one day she'd make those jumps with him again.

Lydia stopped the bike about three quarters of the way to her farmhouse, which was where she and Lucas had done target practice. She opened the motorcycle saddlebag. She pulled out her 9mm and two clips. She put the clips into her jacket pocket and walked past a human-shaped target. Placing her hand against the splintered wood, she thought about the last time Lucas had practiced with her. As in everything they did together, they were almost equals. But when it came to handguns, she had a keener eye. However, she understood, that was with nonmoving, nonhuman targets.

She wasn't certain how well she'd defend herself against an armed attacker. And she definitely didn't want this to be the day she found out. Perhaps she was overreacting about the van. But something triggered a warning deep inside that its presence wasn't right.

Fifteen minutes passed before she finally stood outside the barn behind her house. She stepped beneath the awning to shield herself from the heavier raindrops. She removed her helmet and listened for movement inside the barn. Since she owned no animals, any rustling noise indicated an intruder was inside. The only sound was the rain pellets striking the metal roof.

After reaching the barn, something else bothered her. The outside security light above the hayloft window was out, and so was the carport light at her house. Of course, the electrical storm might have knocked the power out, but that was doubtful. She figured that whoever came for her had shot out the security light and unscrewed the carport light.

In the center of the barn was her Jeep. The Jeep canopy was removed to allow her easy in and out access whenever she hunted deer in the winter. She eased to the passenger side door, placed her helmet onto the backseat and crept into the front seat. She opened the glove compartment and took out a set of binoculars. Quietly, she pushed the compartment door shut. From where she sat, the entire back of her house was visible.

Adjusting the focus, Lydia zoomed in onto the rear wall. She scanned from the far side of the house and swept to the right. When the carport came into view, she gasped. The tip of a cigarette glowed red. Magnifying the man's image, she whispered, "Shit."

She crouched lower in the seat, got on her knees in the floorboard, and watched while resting the binoculars on the dashboard.

Fear iced through her.

Another man spoke to the one with the cigarette. Both wore all black. Both wore night vision goggles and carried assault rifles. These men were there to kill her. Nothing less. But why?

Lydia only saw these two men, but others might be inside her house or at the front, out of view.

Lydia was thankful these men stood talking and were not on alert. Otherwise, either of them might have seen her. After they turned away, she climbed out of the Jeep. She pressed her back against the vehicle and side-stepped to the rear bumper.

At this distance their rifles were far more accurate than her 9mm. She might succeed in dropping one of them, but the gunfire would immediately give away her position. With the possibility of other men being inside the house or hiding in the dark yard, they'd locate her quickly and possibly surround the barn where she'd be trapped.

With the use of night vision, they'd see her before she got any closer. She needed them to come to her, preferably one at a time.

Lydia wrapped the binoculars strap around her neck, reached into the trunk, and took out her compound bow and several arrows. She hurried to the stairs that led to the barn loft.

Lydia took each step with precision, careful not to stumble and fearful of encountering one of the militants that might be hiding among the antiques stored in the loft. Without night vision, she was at a greater disadvantage should a sniper be positioned upstairs. Looping her left arm through the bow, she slung it over her shoulder. With her right hand she pulled the gun from her belt and clicked off the safety. She sat down on the third step from the top, listened, and waited.

The closest she'd been to the hunter/prey experience was the weekend she and Lucas stalked one another with paintball guns. It was hide-and-wait. The only difference now was the ammo was real. She desperately wished she hadn't broken off the relationship with Lucas. It had been foolish on her part because she knew he loved her, and they had a great deal in common. At least if they were still together, she could be his alibi.

"Or dead," she whispered. "Had I gotten in their way."

Several minutes passed without a sound in the loft other than the steady rainfall bouncing off the metal roof. She stood and climbed the final three steps. Since the men expected her to pull into the driveway at the front side of the house, a sniper hiding in the loft might not maintain the stealth behavior he normally would under different circumstances. Still she took no chances. Gripping the gun tightly with both hands, she positioned it at chest level out in front of her. She thrust her back against the slanted roof and listened. Satisfied with the silence, she crept to the hayloft window when the next flickering wave of strobe lightning brightened the floor.

When she reached the ten-by-ten open window, she crouched to the side and set the gun at her feet. Arming the bow with an arrow, she pulled the string back tightly, and waited for the lightning.

The man was smoking a new cigarette.

"You must be nervous," she whispered.

She lined her sight on the red, glowing ash, but didn't see the other man anywhere nearby. She hoped he had gone inside the house. She had hit bulls-eyes from this distance but under sunny, windless conditions. The wind and rain would affect the trajectory and perhaps throw the shot off entirely.

When lightning flashed, she released the string. The flash of light faded, and so did the man's life. He fell limp to the concrete carport. No scream. No struggle. Just death.

Exchanging the bow for the gun, she retraced her way back to the stairs. Halfway to the bottom, she froze. The other soldier stood face to face with her. He seemed as alarmed to see her, as she was he. Her being in the barn was so unexpected that he was carrying his rifle strapped over his shoulder. He wasn't seeking a victim and didn't expect to become one.

She leveled her gun at his face, but his hands moved swiftly. His left hand grasped her right, and he shoved the gun against the wall. With his left hand turned awkwardly to pin hers, his grip was weak. Lydia locked her elbow and gave a fierce yank. Before he blinked, she spun a sharp, fast one hundred eighty-degree turn. Standing one step higher than her adversary, her elbow sunk into his Adam's apple. The violent impact lifted the man into the air. He plummeted backwards down the stairs. She stood over him in an instant.

"Who sent you?" she demanded with her gun aimed at his face.

He didn't answer. He clutched his throat and fought to breathe. His wheezing made her realize that she had crushed his windpipe. She wouldn't get any answers from him, even if he lived.

Lydia jerked the goggles off his head. She adjusted them to fit her face, put them on, and the night became brighter. The dying man's body shook. When he ceased moving, she claimed his rifle and 9mm.

Walking past the Jeep, she stopped beside another motorcycle. She ran her hand along the vinyl seat. This one was Lucas'. He had promised to return for it. Painted fiery red with orange and yellow flames, the bike matched the heated passion that once burned between them. Their fire hadn't really died, and she'd give everything for him to be there with her. Together, they could take on any obstacle.

Dropping to one knee, she brought the rifle to her shoulder like she did when deer hunting. She peered through the scope to get a better view of her house.

Her hands shook, and she took a deep breath. She had just killed two men.

"Self-defense," she whispered. "They came to kill me. It was self-defense."

She leveled the scope on the kitchen window. Two men sat at the table in the dark. They had yet to discover the dead man on the carport. The two living men were not alarmed.

Lydia could kill one quickly, but not both. The one she chose not to shoot would seek safety and possibly return fire. Then the one who ran out of ammo first, lost.

Weighing her options, she decided to run to the carport. With the men inside confident that the outer perimeter was secured, they wouldn't expect her. A surprise attack was her best chance to get out alive.

It occurred to her that these rash decisions weren't something she thought herself capable of doing. But with Lucas in prison, and these men at her house, she smelled conspiracy. Lucas had told her everything about the dark streets of Pittsburgh, the shifters, and the military plot to destroy everyone that had knowledge of them. However, she never expected that she was also a person the militants wanted dead. Not until tonight.

Knowing TransGenCorp had cloned her did trouble her. She never understood why the laboratories would use her genetic makeup to make clones. At times, she awoke drenched with sweat, after she dreamt that she was trapped inside a glass enclosure filled with fluid. She felt like she was drowning. All she really remembered was what Lucas had told her. He'd found her at the cloning labs.

TransGenCorp had used her DNA to manufacture a clone that became a cold-blooded killing machine. She was perplexed. "What did they know about my psyche?" she wondered.

She was a loving, caring person, but already she had killed two people to prevent them from killing her. And rather than retreat, she prepared to charge in and take out the other two. She pondered how the scientists had discovered something about her that she never suspected before this night.

She could retreat, go back to her motorcycle, and head off into the night. But such an action didn't reveal the truth behind the men responsible for Lucas' imprisonment.

Lydia propped the rifle against the inside barn wall and pulled her 9mm from its snug position behind her belt. She was more comfortable with this weapon because Lucas had spent hours training her how to use it effectively. She had believed his vigorous, devoted training with the gun was nothing more than paranoid behavior on his part.

Fear and paranoia weren't part of his regiment, however. He was a man that wanted to be prepared for anything, and he had told her on several occasions that if she were to be a part of his life, she needed to be as prepared to face his enemies as he was. Of course, she had shrugged it off, at first, but her enjoyment to compete her skills against his made the games more entertaining than her need for survival.

Lydia had tried hard to befriend Lucas' friends. No matter how polite and how much she reached out to Johanna and Julia, they never opened themselves up to her. Her clone, she knew, was the reason behind their mistrust and apprehension to welcome her into their group. Her clone must have been one incredibly wicked bitch.

With the gun in hand, she sprinted through the light, falling rain. She sloshed through mud puddles until she reached the carport.

On the concrete a large pool of blood encircled the dead man's head. The arrow had pierced his goggles straight through his right eye. The razor-tipped arrowhead protruded through the back of the skull. His death had been painlessly quick. She refused to be amused about how smoking cigarettes killed you.

Stepping to the side of the door, Lydia crouched and peered through a slit between the magnolia-patterned curtains. One of the men seated at the table had his back to her. The other was directly across the table from him. Their eyes focused on the tabletop. They were playing cards in the dark.

Lydia curled her left hand around the knob and twisted slowly, quietly. When the knob turned all the way, she held her breath, steadied the gun, and flung the door inward. The door slammed the doorstop so hard that the kitchen windows rattled.

Before the men rose to their feet, she shot the one in the back of the head with such calculated coldness that it frightened her. The other man dove to the floor and rolled. She fired twice, missing both times.

He stood and raised his hands above his head. He yelled, "Lydia, what the hell are you doing?"

The gun shook in her hand.

It was Lucas.

CHAPTER 25

orton meant too much to their family for Daniel not to risk his life to rescue the cat. He was more than an animal or pet. He was family.

Felicia slept with Julia's arms wrapped around her. He leaned over, kissed them, and picked up his cell phone from the nightstand. He walked toward the door.

"You're leaving?" Johanna asked. She rose from her bed and met him at the door.

"I have to. Just for a little while. Morton was shot. It's pretty serious."

She frowned. "I thought shifters healed fast."

"Normally, they do. But he said that he was shot with some kind of DNA denaturing poison. His body isn't healing. Without an antidote, he'll die."

Johanna placed a hand on his arm. She glanced back at Felicia and Julia. "Be careful, Dan. They need you."

Daniel nodded. "I know. I will."

"I'll watch the door until you return."

"Thanks."

"Julia did good today. Real good," Johanna said with a broad smile. "I've never seen better driving."

"I'm proud of her and you, too. In spite of everything that has happened to us over the past six years, I'm thankful we're all still good friends."

Johanna's eyes filled with tears. "Me, too."

"To survive what's happening right now, we have to stick together like never before. Helmsby said that six of the other Pittsburgh survivors were killed recently. So, these people are not going to stop their pursuit. They want us dead. We have to stop them."

Johanna grabbed her purse and set her gun on the table. "Do what you need to do. I'll watch the door. Trust me; I know how to use this."

"Thanks," Daniel said, unlocking the door.

CHAPTER 26

orton sat in the rear of the ambulance. His strength had returned. At first, he thought he'd wait for the two paramedics to return and shoot them with the same biohazard weapon that nearly killed him. But their deaths would bring more men from TransGen-Corp to watch the apartment. No, it was better for Idris to believe Daniel and his family had fled.

The cat placed ten syringes of antidote into a cloth bag. He grabbed the bag with his teeth, and jumped down to the street. The front apartment doors swung open while he pattered to the other side of the wet pavement. He hid under the front of a car and watched the paramedics push and load the gurney carrying the three dead bodies into the back of the ambulance. After the ambulance drove away, another set of headlights came up the street. Morton shook his head in disbelief. He smiled. Never had he been so excited to see Daniel.

THE GUN SHOOK in Lydia's hand. She said, "Don't you dare move. Keep your hands where I can see them."

He smiled. "Baby, it's me."

She shook her head, fighting tears. "No. You're not Lucas. He's in jail. I saw it on the news."

103

He shook his head. "No. I told you about my clone. You remember that?" He slowly lowered his hands.

"I'll shoot you, dammit! I swear to God I will."

"Lydia, *honey*," he said above a whisper. "Do you think I'd murder anyone?"

She tightened her grip on the gun. Her hand shook even harder.

"How'd you get out of jail?" she asked.

"My clone is the one in jail. He's probably still being held without bond."

Tears streamed down her cheeks. She wanted nothing better than to believe him, but Lucas would have no need to bring three armed soldiers. The threat of their presence had forced her to kill in order to defend her life and home. The fact they had night vision gear indicated these men were trained mercenaries. The dead men were enough to make her disbelieve him.

She removed the goggles from her face but kept the gun firmly aimed at Lucas' head. She swallowed hard and took a deep breath. Reaching inward, she grasped the coldness that had allowed her to kill and her hands stopped shaking.

Lydia took a step back and flipped on the kitchen light. Backing up two more steps, she checked the man slumped over the table for a pulse. Nothing. He was dead. His head lay on a pile of blood-soaked poker cards.

"If your clone is in jail, why the hell did they send these three men to kill me? And why are *you* with them?"

He laughed. "To kill you? They were assigned to protect me. Besides, if that was their reason, they wouldn't need to send three . . ."

Her eyes narrowed. "I killed them all."

He looked surprised. "They'd need more than a dozen then."

Guilt lowered her weapon. Remorse fought against her. She was consumed by the questions she had no answers to.

"What do I do?" She shook her head. Her sudden confusion overcame her. "I killed them."

"Just put down the gun. Everything will be okay."

Lydia shook her head. "I can't."

"Please."

She wanted to. She really did. But she needed conclusive proof that the man standing in front of her was the real Lucas. She had been angry earlier in the night because Lucas' imprisonment left no hope of mending their relationship. And him, here and now, was too good to be true. She worried that maybe the wrong Lucas was in jail. If so, the clone had come with these men to kill her.

The more she thought about it, the more she realized the real Lucas wasn't someone that allowed others to guard him. Such an idea was insulting. He'd refuse to have others act on his behalf. She just didn't know how to prove which man this was. Or perhaps she did.

"Look," he said, still smiling. "Either put down the gun or shoot me. My arms are tired."

Her hand trembled. "I don't trust you."

"It's me. You don't want to shoot me. You can't shoot me. Not if you ever loved me at all."

Lydia squeezed her eyes shut and shook her head. She lowered the gun. Even if he was the clone, she couldn't shoot him. It was almost the same as shooting the man she loved. She wasn't sure how that might affect her. She needed to know who he was.

He let his hands fall to his sides.

"I've missed you," he said. "Come to me. Let me hold you close again."

Her hand tightened on the gun. "Sure."

He put his arms tightly around her. She placed her free arm around his neck and embraced him while pinning the gun tightly against her upper thigh so he couldn't easily pry it away. She gently lifted his hair off his collar. Her knees weakened. The tattoo she had inscribed on his neck for a birthday gift wasn't there. This *wasn't* Lucas. He had come for one purpose —to kill her.

CHAPTER 27

*D*aniel parked the car. Morton scurried from hiding with the bag gripped tightly in his mouth. Daniel opened the passenger door.

"We'll get you to Helmsby quickly," Daniel said.

Morton shook his head. "No. I'm fine. Look in the bag."

Daniel took the cloth bag from Morton and opened it. He inspected the syringes.

"What are these?"

Morton smiled. "Those are antidotes."

"How'd you get these?"

"From the back of the ambulance that just left. They took the dead assassins away."

"So you're okay?"

Morton patted his stomach. "Yes, but next time, I'll be more observant."

"Good."

"I want to see Felicia," Morton said. "Take me to her."

"Okay, but she's asleep."

"I'd think you less of a parent if she wasn't. I need to know she's safe. I'll sleep at the foot of her bed."

Daniel started the car and pulled away from the curb. Maybe Idris wasn't as strong as he believed.

"Keep your focus," Daniel thought to himself.

CHAPTER 28

The clone could easily have snapped her neck during their embrace, but he didn't. Instead, he said, "I was us to go back to what we had. What we had was something special. We can have that again."

The offer wasn't something she expected so soon. Since Lucas had achieved celebrity status with ESPN as one of the top daredevils, the tabloids heavily publicized their split. That turned out to be far more painful and damaging to them than had they parted privately. So the good and the bad in their relationship was public knowledge and the media hyped up the coverage needlessly.

What did his clone gain by coming to her? And it dawned on her. He might be seeking a normal life by replacing the real Lucas and assuming his identity. Declining his offer to be with him was inevitably a death warrant.

His strong hands cupped at the small of her back. A few seconds later, he squeezed her buttocks and pulled her firmly against him.

"I've missed you so much. I need you. Now."

She pushed him away. She couldn't believe that he'd even insinuate intimacy only minutes after she had a gun pointed at his head. "Not right now. Not after all that's happened here tonight. I'm not in the mood for sex."

"Come on," he said with a sudden heat of anger in his voice. His eyes darkened.

"I killed three men, Lucas. *Three*. I'll be held accountable for my crimes.

This isn't a time for me to consider romance. The authorities will come for me. No amount of foreplay could get me stimulated."

"We leave. No one will suspect you're responsible for their deaths."

Lydia placed a hand to his cheek. "They'll hunt for you, too."

"No. We can make them believe someone else killed these men and forced us into hiding."

Lydia tucked her gun behind her belt. She stared into his eyes and coldness returned to her voice. "It's best we leave soon. I need you to drive me to my motorcycle. Mine is in the field behind the barn."

He shook his head. "We can take the van."

"That's not a good idea. It probably has a GPS locator device. We leave it so they can find the bodies."

"Both of us riding on one motorcycle? That will slow us down."

Lydia eyed him evenly. "*Your* bike's still in the barn."

He looked away and walked to the door. "Let's go."

Outside, the rain had stopped. The night air was cooler. Fog settled, making the barn appear sinister. They tromped and splashed through the mud puddles, hurrying to the barn.

He swung his leg over the motorcycle and turned the key.

"One sec," she said, grabbing her helmet from the Jeep.

"Where's mine?"

"You never wear one. Except when it's required in your stunt tournaments."

She climbed on behind him. He drove through the field. The fog grew thicker the deeper into the field they traveled. The bike trail wasn't easy to see with the headlights reflecting off the fog. Once they found her bike, she'd have to find a way to lose him. Too many factors clued her to the fact that he was the clone. The longer she stayed with him, the more she jeopardized her own life.

He drove slower than she would have driven in the fog. The gold and white reflectors were the only reason they found her Nighthawk. Otherwise, they'd have better luck finding a slinking ghost in the drifting fog.

Lydia climbed off. "You remember the trail, don't you?"

"Of course," he lied.

"Then you'll have no problem leading the way out."

His confidence faded with his reply, "Well, it's been a while."

Lydia was thankful her black visor hid the broad, gleaming smile on her face because he'd kill her right then.

"Fine," she said, starting her bike. "You follow me. Try to keep up."

She spun the Nighthawk around in the mud and took off. She tried to remember the strange qualities Lucas had told her the human shifters possessed. She wondered what similarities the clone had. Then she remembered the clone had killed Vicki during sex, not out of violence, but from the immensely strong pheromones his body secreted. Was that also his intention when he pressed her in the kitchen? He wanted her, regardless of the dead man on the table and other two dead men outside. His sexual urges seemed to control him.

"Dear God," she whispered.

Lydia sped the Nighthawk along the slick mud trail until she couldn't see him behind her. Suddenly, his headlight burned through the fog, and he was at her rear tire. His bike bumped into hers. She skidded to the side but straightened out without losing control of the motorcycle. Losing him in the fog must have angered him, or he was simply trying to keep her in view. She wasn't certain if he had a gun or not. He had not pulled one in the kitchen, but it wasn't out of reason for him to be armed and use it if she provoked him. She had to race away and escape immediately.

Speeding ahead, she rode out two small dips then careened up a medium-sized hill. The clone matched her without error. She feared she wouldn't be able to shake him. Ahead, she noticed the long tire mark she had made on her way to the house. She accelerated and flipped off her headlight. She took the ramp and soared across the creek and stuck a perfect landing. Behind her echoed the most horrendous clamor of mangled metal. The clone crashed.

With the headlight back on, she eased to the edge of the creek. She positioned the light so she could see the wreckage.

Not anticipating the jump distance, Lucas' clone crashed into the wall of the other ramp. A normal man without a helmet would have died instantly. Not him. He was exactly what she feared him to be. Perhaps worse.

Lucas' clone moved in the shallow water. A weak hand rose from the water and grasped the side of the motorcycle. Bloody, battered and bruised, he pulled himself over the handlebars and moaned. His head hung limply. He struggled to breathe. The bike was in shambles. He was too injured to pursue her on foot.

Lydia aimed the gun at his forehead and tightened her finger on the trigger, but she was unable to make herself squeeze off a single round. Closing her eyes, she took a deep breath and lowered the gun. Killing him, if that were possible, didn't end the ordeal. She had no idea how many others were leagued against her. By herself she wasn't a match for newfound enemies.

She needed help. The only person she knew she could trust was Daniel. She hoped he believed her story.

She drove back to the blacktop and sped to the parked van across the road from her house. Pulling her gun, she shot out three of the van's tires. Should Lucas' clone manage to make it back to her house, which was highly doubtful, the van offered him no quick escape. The keys to her Jeep were on the Nighthawk key ring. If he wanted the Jeep, he'd have to hot-wire it.

Lydia needed Daniel's phone number, but she wasn't about to set foot inside her house again. Not alone and certainly, not in the dark. She revved the engine and sped off into the night. Not having Daniel's phone number memorized, she decided to drive to the only other place she could find it—Lucas' house. That was almost an hour's drive from her home.

Normally, she'd have been sound asleep at this hour, but had she been, she'd be dead. Lucas' arrest had troubled and angered her. She had thought the long motorcycle ride would drive it from her mind. It never occurred to her that she was in danger.

The fuel gauge needle favored the E, so she pulled into a gas station near the interstate. She filled the tank but never bothered to remove her helmet, which was another decision that saved her life. In the bay beside her was a black unmarked van, which suddenly caught her interest.

Lydia locked the gas cap, placed the nozzle into its holster, and waited for her credit card receipt. Not certain how long she could run on adrenaline, she walked across the parking lot to a vending room. She purchased two highly caffeinated energy drinks. She carried the drinks to her motorcycle and placed them inside the saddlebag to drink later. She wasn't foolish enough to remove her helmet in front of the van.

Two muscled men stepped out of the van. Crimson TGC letters were stitched on their jacket sleeves. They stretched and rubbed their eyes but didn't pay any attention to her. She climbed onto her motorcycle and sped out of the parking lot in the direction of the interstate. If those men weren't looking for her, they soon would be.

Driving the near empty interstate cut twenty minutes off her trip, but she wasn't mentally prepared for what she found at Lucas' house.

The front door was splintered in half. Books and papers were strewn across the floor. Couch cushions were slit open. His computers were missing. In his bedroom, she burst into tears. The mattresses had been slashed open. The dresser drawers were emptied onto the floor, and the entire closet contents were tossed on the floor. The only thing not damaged or moved was her picture on the nightstand. Her heart ached for him because he hadn't gotten over her, either. If she had only known.

Lydia returned her attention to the mess and whispered, "What do you have that they want?"

She hurried back to the living room and searched for his home phone. She found the rechargeable cradle and pushed the locater button. The phone beeped from beneath one of the slashed cushions. She picked it up.

A scratching sound came from the kitchen. She turned with her 9mm instinctively drawn without realizing she had pulled it. The clawing grew more desperate, urgent. Fear gnawed at her. She thought of the shifter stories Lucas had told her. The tales brought chills up her arms. She shuddered and approached the kitchen warily.

All the cabinet contents and drawers had been spilled across the floor. She slid boxed food and cans aside with her foot while she moved through the kitchen. The noise intensified behind the pantry door. A whining cry came through the bottom door slit. Then it yelped and barked.

Lydia eased the door open to find an eager-eyed, pink tongued, German shepherd pup. It wagged its tail in appreciation. On its collar was a green cloverleaf dog tag. "Rex II" was inscribed on it. She smiled. He had named this pup after the dog he lost in Pittsburgh.

"You poor little thing," she said, kneeling to scratch behind its ears.

She marveled that the men hadn't killed little Rex. They weren't compassionate people. Of course, letting an animal starve to death was more heartless than instant death.

Lydia took a bowl off the floor and filled it with tap water. She set it on the floor for the thirsty dog. It lapped the water and wagged its tail.

"How long have you been in there?"

She pressed "1" on the phone auto dial. Daniel's phone number appeared on the glowing phone screen. She wrote down the number and called from her cell phone. Daniel answered on the second ring.

"Daniel," she said, relieved to hear his voice. "It's Lydia. I need your help. Some men just tried to kill me."

CHAPTER 29

*D*aniel listened intently while Lydia explained all the events at her home and what she had discovered at Lucas' ransacked house. She mentioned Lucas' clone and why she was certain it wasn't really Lucas. She then mentioned the pup.

"Lucas bought another German shepherd?" Daniel asked.

Morton sat up in the passenger seat. "Tell her to bring the pup. He might provide me with crucial information that will help us."

Daniel placed his hand over the phone. "I wasn't aware that you could communicate with other animals."

"I speak German." Morton smiled and stuck out his tongue.

Daniel rolled his eyes and patted the cat's head. "Glad to see you made a full recovery."

"Hey, it's hard to kill a cat with twenty-nine thousand, two hundred, and twenty-six lives."

"That many, huh?"

Morton shrugged. "Maybe more."

"Okay, funny bones. Lydia's life is in danger. Let me tell her where we're staying."

Daniel gave Lydia directions to their hotel and the room number.

Lydia sighed. "Daniel, that's several hours away. I'm exhausted."

"You're still at Lucas' house?"

"Yes."

"Unless things have changed, he still has that single engine plane in the hanger down near the woods. I know he taught you how to fly it."

"No. The fog's too thick for that."

"Oh."

"Listen. I'll find a place where I can sleep a few hours and then I'll meet you at the hotel. Will you still be there?"

"If our plans change, I'll call you. Give me your number."

He wrote down her number.

"One last thing, Daniel," Lydia said.

"What?"

"They really tore Luke's place apart. Any idea what they're looking for?"

"No."

"They took his computers, but I don't think they found what they wanted."

"Why's that?"

"Their search was desperate. The computers seemed like their last hope to find whatever he has that they want."

"Luke is a complex person. You'd have a much better chance of knowing than I do. But you can take one thing to heart."

"What?"

"If what Lucas has is that important, it's more likely he's still alive. At least until they find it. But, if I were you, I wouldn't stick around there any longer than necessary. They might be watching or set the house to explode. I'd get out of there."

"I'm on my way out."

"Good. Get some sleep. You're going to need it."

"I know," she replied. Her voice quivered. "Answer one question for me. How do you deal with murder? I killed three men tonight."

Daniel sighed. "It's not murder during a time of war. And that's what you've stepped into. A war. Those men were there to kill you, and the scary part is—it's far from over. Consider yourself very lucky to be alive."

Lydia wiped tears from her eyes. "I know. Thanks."

"Don't mention it. Now, just stay alive."

"I will."

She disconnected the call and stared at the pup. Little Rex wagged his tail and barked.

"Well, Rex," she said. "You can't stay here. I hope you're not afraid of motorcycles."

Lydia picked the dog up and carried him outside to the Nighthawk.

The hell with sleeping, she thought.

After she placed Rex on the seat, she grabbed one of the energy drinks, popped the top, and gulped it down. Even though she was tired and her adrenaline had waned, her active mind prevented her from sleeping. All the scenes of the night would haunt her if she had to lay and think about them.

Lydia climbed onto the bike and placed Rex across her lap. From the saddlebag, she took a tie hook cable, ran it through the dog harness, and strapped him to the seat. With the speed she'd have to use, a sharp curve might sling the pup into a ditch. She couldn't live with herself if Rex died because of her.

She took a moment to let her eyes survey the surrounding thick pine forest. She wished she had kept the night goggles. The woods were a sniper's paradise. Daniel was right. She had unknowingly walked into a war with enemies that could be anywhere. Enemies she didn't know.

"Well, Rex. Let's get to a safer place," she whispered.

With Lucas in jail, it seemed highly improbable for a sniper to remain behind, but that didn't mean the house wasn't being watched.

From the thick fog-covered, serpentine road that ran through the forest behind Lucas' cabin came the rumbling of an approaching truck. A huge explosion bellowed deeper down the valley where his plane was stored. She'd have been killed had she decided to take his plane.

Lydia started the Nighthawk. The rear tire spun momentarily before pulling forward. The crack of gunfire blasted from the truck. The bullet flicked a chunk of mud and gravel into the air where she had been parked. The second shot sliced a small pine branch from a tree ten feet ahead of her.

Rex whined.

Lydia leaned forward and sped through several twists along the long drive back to the main road. The truck roared and stuttered as its gears were shifted. The hill impeded its progress. She assumed the vehicle was a military flatbed, and an old one at that. Whoever pursued her was farther down the slope now. She reached the blacktop and turned right. She didn't plan to stop driving until she found Daniel.

CHAPTER 30

r. Helmsby hoped Daniel could look past his hostility and discover all the subtle clues Helmsby had intentionally looped into their conversation. Nancy was the biggest clue.

Sitting on the edge of the bed, he stared at the wall and thought about Morton's welfare. The cat was resourceful, but even he couldn't survive the new denaturing weapon Idris' men carried unless he had the antidote.

The DNA denaturer was the product Helmsby formulated after six intense years of scientific research and development. He never thought it might be something used to kill his beloved cat. The first three years of research were done while he lived inside the research center basement trying to figure out how to eradicate the shifters. Had he completed it then, they could have wiped out the shifter packs in a matter of months.

Before General Norhaney's unfortunate death due to congested heart failure, he persuaded Congress to grant several million dollars to Trans-GenCorp to ensure the completion of Helmsby's DNA denaturing serum. After receiving the grants and better lab equipment, Helmsby succeeded.

Three months earlier, Helmsby remembered, the power shifted in both Congress and the military. Each greeted Idris secretly with open arms, pardoned the charges against him, and gave him back a prominent role at TransGenCorp, which sadly gave him authority over Helmsby.

When knowledge of the corrupt changeover reached Helmsby, he stormed out of the facility, outraged. Three days later, Nancy vanished. Her disappearance was followed by a series of threats on her life should he refuse to return to TransGenCorp. At first he thought the threats were a sick prank until the digital pictures of Nancy arrived in his inbox. His return to TransGenCorp didn't free *her*. It *imprisoned* him.

Helmsby had not seen her during the past three months. He wasn't sure she was still alive. After repeated denials for them to fulfill their promise to release her, he decided it was time to botch the shifter data or somehow leak to the media that the man responsible for the Pittsburgh missile attack was again the man presiding over TransGenCorp. Idris. Once he figured out a way to do it without getting caught, he would. Until then, he was nothing less than a puppet. Cutting their strings required more creative thinking, but his mind was drained. He hoped Daniel or Morton understood the implications he hinted at. Otherwise, all of them were doomed.

CHAPTER 31

*L*ucas' clone crawled up the creek bank and collapsed in the mud. Rain chilled him. Pain pulsed through his entire body. Blood oozed from his nose and mouth. He coughed and winced in agony. Worse than the pain, he discovered an inner pain that ached even more—the feeling of betrayal.

The injuries he suffered would have killed an ordinary man instantly, and it almost killed him. His near death experience did something else. It forced his body to succumb a near sleep stage so his body could heal. But the abrupt crash also jarred recent memories to play inside his mind. It was like he had stepped out of his body and back through time to his last meeting in General Idris' office earlier in the day.

Idris sat behind the desk and puffed a cigar. He didn't bother looking up. "What is it, Lucian?"

"I did as you ordered, sir," Lucian replied. "I killed Senator Godfrey and his associate. The two security guards who tried to stop me are dead, too. I need my enhancer shots now."

Idris tapped cigar ash into a ceramic tray on the desk. He leveled a harsh stare at Lucian. "Very well, son. You did well. Go see Dr. Brockton. He'll give you an injection."

Lucian clenched his teeth with a harsh grating sound. "No, sir. That's *not* good enough. I want enough injections to last me several weeks."

"I'm afraid that's out of the question."

117

"You promised." The veins in Lucian's neck swelled and his face reddened.

Idris shrugged. "Perhaps you misunderstood our agreement."

Lucian formed tight fists and stepped beside the desk. His outrage was evident, and his eyes narrowed. "No misunderstanding. You promised if I disposed of Godfrey that I could have enough injections to last a couple months so I could take leave."

"Impossible," Idris spat. "I've need of you on these facility grounds at all times. Don't forget you brought you to life."

"How can I?" he replied. "But this is *my* life."

"And I control it. Don't forget that."

Before Idris blinked, Lucian stood behind the general with his gun pressed to the heavy man's throat. "Don't forget that if you're dead, you control nothing."

Idris took in a sharp breath. "Easy, son."

Lucian pressed the gun harder and released the safety. "Never call me that again."

"Okay. Look, we can work something out. Just put your gun away."

He kept the gun against Idris' throat but lessened the pressure. "What deal now?"

Idris said, "An injection today, and after you fulfill one more assignment, I'll give you three months leave with enough injections to sustain you. You can travel wherever you wish."

Lucian pressed the gun against Idris' neck. "You lie."

"No, I swear it."

"Put it in writing. If you don't keep your end of the agreement this time, I'll come back to kill you. You know I will."

Idris grabbed a pen with his shaking hand. He wrote out a promise on white copy paper, signed it, and stamped it. Lucian snatched the paper and read it.

"Okay," Lucian said. "What's the assignment?"

"Kill Julia and Daniel's daughter. Daniel is scheduled to meet Helmsby here later today. Kill them while he's here, and he's a broken man. Much easier to kill him then."

Shock shot through Lucian's body at the request. He forced his hand to remain steady.

"Why?" he asked.

"You weren't programmed to ask questions, just to carry out orders."

Lucian shrugged. "I have the gun and you don't. So tell me."

Idris' face flushed red. "I want them out of the way. Every survivor from Helmsby's Research Center must be killed. With what's about to occur, only they can finger all the projects back to me. Dead, they cannot. So do as you're commanded if you want your enhancers. Kill me and your death will be painful. Without those enhancers the pain becomes unbearable. Your body will eat itself into nothing."

Lucian contemplated pulling the trigger, but already his body suffered. He was only one day late for his injection, but his brain felt like waves of fire rolling against his temples.

"Ah, yes. You feel it, don't you?" Idris asked. "It's eating at you inside. Your body chemistry is decomposing. Soon, you will have severe shakes. Your vision will darken. Best hurry to Dr. Brockton."

Lucian squeezed his eyes shut. "Shut the hell up! I'll do the damn assignment, but I have no idea how to find them."

Idris took a printout paper off the desk. "Here, we got access to Johanna's cell phone records. She talks to Julia quite often. Call Johanna. Use your charm. Find a time when she'll meet with Julia. If we're lucky, you'll get a chance at her, too. A bonus kill."

Lucian holstered his 9mm and took the paper.

Idris smiled. "Go see Dr. Brockton. He'll give you your meds. When you finish the assignment, come back for the rest. I'll keep my word."

"You'd best."

Lucian stormed out the door and slammed it.

Blackmail and betrayal. That's all Idris had done since the Pittsburgh Release. Lucian hadn't wanted to kill Godfrey, but he had no choice if he wanted to stay alive. He hated that he had to do that, but the new order was for him to kill Julia and Felicia. No, he couldn't carry out such an atrocity. Not intentionally. He was a pawn, nothing more, but he needed his enhancers or he'd die.

It was madness what Idris demanded, but he didn't see any other way out.

His jaw tightened. His head throbbed so badly his eyes hurt. How much worse would he suffer before he died? Could he become desperate enough to kill a child? He closed his eyes and massaged his temples. He didn't want to carry out the order. He didn't have any other choice. No choice at all.

Lucian entered Dr. Brockton's office. The doctor nervously set down his phone when he saw Lucian.

Brockton was short, stocky with silvery blonde hair. Lucian had always liked him because his eyes reflected a gentleness that he had seldom seen.

"Ahh, Lucian. I didn't expect you here so quickly."

Lucian stared at the cell phone on the table. "Idris, correct?"

Brockton nodded. "Yes. He told me you were coming. You looked tired, feverish. How do you feel?"

"Like my brain is on fire."

"That'll fade soon enough after the injection."

Lucian wiped sweat from his brow. He felt dizzy. He grabbed the back of a chair to steady himself.

"Sit. Sit," Brockton said. He walked to a hanging cabinet and unlocked it by pressing a series of numbers into a security panel while pressing his right thumb against a scanner. The cabinet door popped open. Inside the cabinet were dozens of enhancer vials.

Lucian's heart raced and his mouth watered. The cabinet contained several years' supply of his needed drug and it was only a few feet away from where he sat. If he had some way to steal those, he'd have a life of freedom. He could flee the country and not have to worry about following Idris' orders ever again. His hand slid to his gun and he contemplated stealing the vials. But Brockton grabbed a vial and quickly shut the cabinet.

Lucian resisted the urge to pull the gun. Even with the code, he couldn't get inside the locked cabinet. Each number required the fingerprint signature of one person—Brockton, in this case.

He decided to carry out the assignment and worry about stealing the locked contents later should Idris not keep his word.

Dr. Brockton injected the viscous solution into Lucian's hip. It stung, burning like liquid flame, but he felt, in spite of the irritating pain, a sense of relief pass through him. A brief euphoria.

The doctor smiled. "That should take care of your pain. You're good for another week. Try not to be late next time to avoid those nasty headaches. Any longer and it grows more severe."

Lucian nodded. He regarded Brockton for the better part of a minute. The man's kindness seemed genuine, rare.

"Good luck with your assignment, whatever it may be," Brockton said. "And be careful."

"Thanks," Lucian said, walking to the door.

"Lucian?" Brockton said suddenly.

Lucian stopped and turned.

Brockton handed him a metal box and winked. "More enhancers, just in case you need them. Not everyone here agrees with how Idris treats you."

Tears moistened Lucian's eyes. He swallowed at the lump in his throat.

Such an overwhelming emotion had never possessed him. He struggled to speak.

"Thanks."

"Don't mention it."

A BOLT of furious pain blazed through Lucian's back, shaking him from his dream-state. His body was healing, but the damage was possibly more than he could recover from, especially without medical attention.

With his eyes closed, his mind located the areas with the most damage. He had at least four, maybe five, broken ribs. The head-on collision with the ramp wall had fractured his skull. His right shoulder was dislocated, and he suffered from internal bleeding.

Grabbing handfuls of mud, he crawled several feet further. The pain was too intense. He lost consciousness. Healing came with sleep. His high metabolism operated at an alarming speed. When he awoke, his body would be rid of the broken bones and torn muscles. But other unknown dangers awaited him when he awakened. Dangers he had not yet been exposed to with symptoms he was blind to understand.

CHAPTER 32

*L*ydia arrived at the hotel at 7:30 a.m. Daniel lay asleep with his arm draped over Julia. Morton rested at the foot of the bed where he sat catty-cornered to keep his eyes on the door and Felicia at the same time. Since he didn't require much sleep, he convinced Daniel to sleep while he guarded them. He'd alert them should anyone attempt to come through the door.

Lydia's abrupt knock brought Morton to all fours. He jumped to the floor, ran to the window, and peered through the slit where the curtains met. A woman, dressed in full black leather, stood holding her black helmet in one hand and the pup in the other. Morton hurried to Daniel, placed his paws on Daniel's cheek, gently shaking him awake.

When Daniel opened his eyes, Morton said, "Lydia's here."

Daniel rubbed his eyes. "It's noon already?"

"No, it's still early."

Julia rolled over and looked at Morton. "Lydia's here? Why?"

Daniel sat up. "She called me last night. Three men and Lucas' clone tried to kill her."

"Oh, dear God. Why are they after her, too?"

Daniel walked to the door. "I'm under the impression that anyone who has a close friendship with Lucas is being targeted by these people."

When Daniel opened the door, Lydia nervously stepped inside. He scanned the parking lot before closing the door. Other than a few people packing luggage into their cars, it didn't appear that anyone had followed her.

The morning sky remained hidden behind gloomy gray clouds. A slight mist drifted with the breeze. He shut the door and locked it.

Lydia collapsed in the nearest chair. She forced a weak, tired smile and placed Rex on the floor. She set her helmet on the table. Her red, puffy eyes revealed her exhaustion. Her blonde, short hair was matted flat from sweat. Hiking up her muddy jeans, she leaned over and unzipped her mud-caked boots. Daniel knew she'd been through Hell getting to them.

"Are you okay?" he asked.

She nodded. "My nerves are frayed, and I've probably picked up a lot of bruises along the way. Other than that and being hungry, I'm fine. Just minutes after I talked to you, I think they blew up Lucas' plane with explosives. A huge explosion occurred where his kept the plane."

"Shit. Are you serious?"

"They were still on his property when I left," she replied in a whisper.

Julia handed her bottled water and a pack of cheese crackers. "Here," Julia said. "It's not much. Dan can get us breakfast soon. I'll go fill the tub with hot water. You'll feel much better after you bathe and get some sleep."

"Thanks."

She opened the crackers and gave Daniel a grim smile. "I never had taken Lucas seriously about his clone. That was almost a dangerous mistake."

"When we were living at the research center, his clone fooled me, too."

Rex walked a circle under the table before lying down. He placed his head on his forepaws before closing his eyes. The dog was as tired as Lydia.

"How well did he take to the bike ride?"

Lydia took a sip of water to wash down a mouthful of dry crackers. "I strapped him to my lap. He was nervous at first, but after ten miles, he seemed to enjoy it."

Daniel smiled.

"Why are you guys staying in a hotel?" she asked.

"Like you and Lucas, our place was attacked."

"*Why* is this all happening?"

"I'm not quite sure what it's all about," Daniel said with a sigh. "But whoever set Lucas up wants all of us dead. Sweeper teams were sent to kill us. They attacked Julia, Johanna, and Felicia yesterday. In broad daylight, too."

"So they're not worried about being seen."

"No. That makes me wonder how deeply this conspiracy lies."

Johanna's cell phone rang. She reached from the blanket and patted the nightstand until she found it.

"Hello?" she said. "What? Hell no! Are you freaking serious?"

Johanna kicked off her blanket, swung her feet over the side of the bed, and ran a hand through her wild hair. Stunned and shocked, she disconnected the call.

"What's wrong?" Daniel asked.

"That was one of my producers. My studio was set ablaze during the night. One of my directors and another producer was found this morning. Both had been shot to death. Apparently *before* the fire was set."

"I'm so sorry," Daniel said, shaking his head. "They can't find us, so they're going after those closest to us."

Julia opened the bathroom door. Steam drifted out like a cloud.

Lydia," Julia said. "Your bath water's ready."

Lydia used the chair armrests to push herself to her feet. Johanna's eyes narrowed when she noticed Lydia. Lydia exchanged a feeble smile for the glare and said, "I'm not your enemy, Johanna. I never have been. I wish you'd get over whatever my clone did to you. You can't live in the past, and if we don't work together, we may *not* have a future."

Lydia went into the bathroom, shut the door, and locked it.

Johanna looked at Daniel. "What is *she* doing here?" she whispered. "*Why* is she here?"

"She's here to help keep us alive."

CHAPTER 33

The morning sun burned through the layered, drifting fog at Lydia's dirt bike trails. Lucian stood and then staggered a few more steps before resting. He was a little less than one hundred years from reaching her barn.

His injuries had been severe enough that he had nearly died during his healing process. Healing required energy. Energy required calories. A lot of calories. Because he didn't have any source of food, his body fed on his muscles. He was weak and nearing starvation. He needed food soon or he'd die.

He had crawled the first fifty feet from the creek until the pounding pain in his head subsided enough for him to stand. He hobbled to where he now stood, but his shaky legs warned him that his muscle tissue had emaciated to the point that he could collapse any moment.

Walking stiff-legged, he reached the side of the barn and pressed himself against the wall, keeping his knees locked. Should he bend his legs slightly, he knew he'd fall. If he did, he doubted he'd be able to stand again. Less than thirty yards separated him from the kitchen door, but it was impossible to walk that far.

Intense hunger gnawed through him and involuntary groans escaped his lips.

With his body digesting itself, he fought step by step to keep from falling. Finally, he reached the Jeep. He didn't have time to hot-wire the vehicle or hunt for a key, provided Lydia had one hidden in it.

The sunlight filtered through the fog, and he noticed a black tarp at the front of the Jeep near the spot where Lucas had parked his motorcycle. He propped against the Jeep for balance.

Gasping for air and mentally fighting the pain, he slid himself along the side of the Jeep until he was at the front grill. He grabbed the tarp and yanked. Beneath the dusty tarp was a riding mower. Falling forward, he hugged the seat.

Convulsions undulated through his body. He figured swallowing a large metal meat hook and having his insides tugged slowly out his throat would have been less painful. His hamstrings tightened from fierce unrelenting contractions. He dropped to his knees. His shaking arms clung to the lawnmower seat like it was the only life preserver in his sea of misery.

The severe cramps bent his legs behind him, but he managed, after three attempts to roll into the narrow space between the seat and steering wheel.

Lucian turned the ignition key. The engine rolled, whined, rolled. He tried again. One long whine. Again. The engine awakened, roared. Blue smoke streamed from the muffler.

With his left hand he pressed down on the clutch and pushed the gearshift into low with his right. The riding mower kicked forward, slowly rolling down the slight gradient toward the house.

When he reached the carport and killed the motor, he was parked beside the kitchen door. The door stood slightly ajar. After prying his curled, aching fingers from the steering wheel, he crawled up the stairs and shoved his weight and shoulder against the door. The door swung inward, and he collapsed to the floor.

His body already ached so much that he didn't feel the impact. He welcomed the coolness of the linoleum.

On the floor beside the table was his dead comrade's spilled beer. He pulled himself across the floor on his elbows to the puddle of beer. He lapped the Coors like a dog drank water. His injuries demanded he forsake his dignity.

An unopened Coors lay on the floor beside the dead man's boot. Lucian took the can and popped the tab open. He downed it in one long gulp. His body ached from hunger and desperate need. The leg cramps subsided enough to gain minor mobility, but he relied more on using his elbows to move. He crawled to the refrigerator.

On the lower refrigerator shelf, he found a bottle of pure grape juice. He drank what remained in the bottle to boost his energy. He ate cheese, yogurt, and raw eggs. After a few more minutes, he moved to the pantry. He opened a jar of peanut butter and scooped out a thick handful and licked it from his dirty fingers.

After a half hour of gorging himself, he became invigorated. His energy renewed somewhat. To heal from all the damage his body suffered he needed more than just food. He needed his genetic enhancer injections. Severe injuries required he receive more than one injection per week. Brockton had warned him weeks earlier. Without the enhancers and because he was a clone, his shortened telomeres reverted to their aged state preventing further mitosis from taking place. At that stage, death was inevitable and expedient.

"Damn you, Idris," Lucian whispered.

The extra enhancers Brockton had given him were in the van. They were the only reason he had lived longer than the typical three-year clone life span. And this was the first time he'd administer the injection to himself. Without the courtesy Brockton had shown by giving him extras, Lucian would probably die before he could return to TransGenCorp. Idris certainly wouldn't have allowed Lucian another shot until his assignment was completed. That was the tradeoff. Assignment first or no injection.

Genetic blackmail.

But not anymore.

Because of Brockton, Lucian didn't intend to return to TransGenCorp. He hated Idris, and he wanted to live his own life. He no longer wanted to be an assassin. He didn't like being a piece of discardable property, either.

Lucian had come for Lydia, not to kill her like he was assigned or like she had expected, but he wanted to win her heart. He'd planned to kill the soldiers with him to prove that he'd protect her from danger, only she killed them, proving she was capable of protecting herself and didn't need a bodyguard.

But then she deceived him and damn near killed him, which left one thing on his agenda: Finish the assignment and kill Lydia.

Lucian walked to Lydia's bedroom and undressed. He stepped inside her shower and turned on the hot water. Plunging his face into the water, he let his mind drift. He pictured how he'd torture Lydia and how he'd kill her.

He smiled.

After turning off the shower, he wrapped a towel around his waist. He needed fresh clothes, so he searched her closet. He found what he hoped she still possessed—some of Lucas' old clothes.

He dressed and looked into the mirror. Another smile curled beneath his grayish black beard. He still had surprises of his own that even Idris was unaware of.

With deep concentration and focus, he extended his chin, widened his nose, and changed his hair and eye color. He had trained himself to shape shift his facial components during the last two years. The process was becoming easier since he had tainted his genome with shifter DNA.

"Hell," he thought to himself, "With a high enough dosage of estrogen, I could grow breasts and disguise myself as a woman."

He hurried to the kitchen, took the dead man's 9mm, tucked it behind his belt, and then picked up another 9mm off the concrete carport. He walked briskly to the van. When he noticed the three flat tires, he cursed and slammed his hands on the hood.

Opening the door, he reached under the driver's seat and retrieved the metal box. He extracted a syringe and injected it into his hip.

Storm clouds on the horizon turned darker, vanquishing the sun. Lucian inhaled the humid air and sighed. Walking down the highway, he pictured what it would be like to simply set at the side of the road and enjoy the elements around him. He could relax and soak in his surroundings.

Knowing his life was destined to consist of only a few years, he never experienced the chance to see what lie outside the laboratories. He never had been so close to death, either. He wondered what religion a soulless man claimed. Death had no meaning to him. Life was what he made it or what he took from others. That's why he sought to take a leave from Idris' duties, only that bastard refused to let him. Idris knew that if he allowed Lucian such luxury, Lucian would never return.

Lucian didn't bother wasting time to take Lydia's Jeep. Even if he found a way to start it, he'd never get near her. She'd recognize the vehicle as hers the instant she saw it. But opportunities presented themselves in unusual ways.

Half a mile down the road, a car approaching from behind slowed. An elderly man stopped his car and lowered the window.

"Hey there, neighbor," the old man said. "You need a ride?"

Lucian smiled. "As a matter of fact, mister, I do."

He raised the pistol and squeezed the trigger.

CHAPTER 34

$\mathcal{P}$ittsburgh FBI Office: 8:00 a.m.

FBI Director Mike Carpenter entered the conference room with a grim expression on his face. He stepped to the end of the long rectangular table and his dark eyes pierced into each of his agent's eyes. Five of his best agents sat with manila files in their hands.

Eugene Michaels, a ten-year field investigator, stood at the head of the table and turned off the flat screen television.

"You've shown them the surveillance video, Agent Michaels?" Carpenter asked.

"Yes, sir. We've reviewed it at least ten times."

"Good. Then perhaps some of you probably have drawn the same conclusion to this as I have. It makes no sense to me at all. I've watched dozens of murders captured on digital discs for years, but this one still doesn't follow profile."

"How's that?" Agent Kat Gaddis asked. She sipped her coffee, brushed her light brown hair from her eyes, and said, "What's so different about this one?"

Michaels nodded. "It's an open and shut case, sir, if you don't mind me saying. The gun was found at the scene. Ballistics show this is the same weapon that killed both Senator Godfrey and Senator Jenkins. The finger-prints on the weapon are an identical match to Lucas Ridale—the man in D.C. police custody—so it's an open and shut case."

"I agree with Michaels," Gil Matherson said, folding his hands over his manila folder.

Carpenter offered a narrow, tight smile. "It ought to be an easy, open and shut case, but some things surrounding this case don't set well for me."

Kat frowned. "Like what?"

Carpenter took the DVD remote from Michaels. "Like I stated earlier, I've seen a lot of murders captured by surveillance cameras. I've never seen one where the killer deliberately makes his face so easily identified. Most go out of their way *not* to be seen. This man wanted the whole world to see his face. And why leave behind the gun?"

Gil shrugged. "Maybe he wanted to get caught."

Carpenter shook his head. His piercing glare indicated that he didn't see anything amusing by the suggestion.

"Why?" Carpenter asked. "Why would he leave his gun?"

Michaels flipped open his folder and said, "It's no secret Lucas and his fiancée suffered a major split."

"That doesn't necessarily drive a man to murder." Carpenter flipped through his notes. "It's no secret that Senator Godfrey was one of the pilots that helped rescue Lucas and the other survivors from Pittsburgh when the city was under quarantine. Lucas even used his celebrity status to gain votes for Godfrey's Senate campaign. Why kill a man in such a seat of power? You'd gain more through blackmail if there was something you truly wanted or needed."

Gil folded his arms. "But even celebrities have been known to murder."

"True," Kat said, glancing from Gil to Carpenter. "But I have to agree with Carpenter on this. Most jilted people tend to murder an ex spouse or lover. Not political figures. It has happened in the past, but it's outside of the norm."

Carpenter teased a broader smile. "Let me show you something else."

He clicked the scene selection button and brought up a part of the film no one had yet witnessed. He hit the play button. "Okay, this is film footage from inside the Congressional Hall that was never released to the press. You see here, Lucas is simply talking with the two senators in what appears to be a joking, relaxed manner. Once they step outside, his demeanor totally shifts. They keep talking, but he stops. And here is where I believe he gets his gun. Watch the approaching man in the brown suit. Right . . . there. See? He bumps Lucas. Lucas turns, and suddenly, he has the gun in hand."

Kat gasped. "Wait, hold it."

"What is it?" Carpenter asked.

"Back it up and freeze it."

Carpenter backed the film frame by frame.

"There!" she said. "Right there."

Carpenter and the other agents stared at the screen with great interest. "What do you see, Kat?"

"His eyes. They're not normal."

Carpenter laughed. "Kat, what is it with you and people's eyes?"

She cocked a brow. "You learn a lot from a person's eyes. It's always the eyes. The looking glass to the soul."

"Shit!" Gil said, spilling hot coffee into his lap and standing to wipe his slacks. "His eyes are green where there should be white."

"What the hell?" Agent Denton said. He rubbed his eyes and leaned on his elbows to look closer.

"My point exactly," Kat said.

"Which leads to the point I want to make," Carpenter said.

Agent Tyler shrugged. "But it's still Lucas."

"Don't be so certain," Carpenter said.

"But the fingerprints."

"From his *clone*," Carpenter said, his eyes narrow, serious. He shoved his hands into his pants pockets.

"A clone?" Denton asked with such disbelief that the other agents chuckled.

Carpenter nodded. "Kat, I believe you worked in the Seattle office when the missile attack occurred in Pittsburgh?"

"Yes."

"I've added the files into your folder so you can read about the post investigation when the military rescued the occupants of Helmsby's Research Center."

"But a clone?" Gil asked with a laugh.

"As in the reports before you, all the survivors from the research center were debriefed by us before the press got a chance to get their stories. The clone is also responsible for the death of one female at the research center."

"Cloning is illegal," Gil said. "Besides the survivors' testimonials, what proof do we have?"

Carpenter nodded at the paused screen. "Note the time of the murder on the screen. 10:50 a.m."

"So?"

"Lucas Ridale was aboard a plane out of Denver at that exact time."

"You can prove this?" Denton asked. His thick hand wrapped around his coffee mug so tightly that the ceramic mug cracked. He set it down quickly before it shattered in his grip.

Carpenter lifted a printed page. "Here's Lucas' credit card receipt. I've requested the surveillance video from the airport. It should be here within a few minutes."

Tyler said, "If the clone committed the murders, don't the police have him in custody?"

"No. Lucas, the real Lucas, was arrested when his plane landed in West Virginia. The clone is still out there somewhere. And here's the part I don't find funny at all. Lucas was tested for gun residue. They found none."

"Okay," Kat said. "Where did the clone come from?"

"TransGenCorp. That's the reason D.C. has handed this over to us. We're closer to the science facility, so they want us to do the investigation."

Silence filled the room. They all exchanged glances.

Carpenter eyed each one of them. "Nothing discussed here leaves this room. Is that clear?"

"Yes."

"The man who was in charge of TGC, General Idris, was also the person behind the Pittsburgh bombing. Although no actual nukes were used, a small dirty bomb released enough radiation to cause a panic. The area was then fenced off from the public."

"Why would he do that?" Kat asked.

"To keep his secret experiments secret. Not only did he clone humans, he created super human assassins and bloodthirsty animals. Both had incredibly rapid healing metabolisms. Some of the animals had the ability to morph from normal creatures, like dogs or cats, and turn into hideous killing monsters. The clone was programmed to be a cold-blooded killer."

"Then what do we do?" Tyler asked.

"We bring Lucas here so we can talk to him."

"And then?"

"We find the clone and Idris."

Carpenter pressed the intercom button on the table phone. He said to his secretary, "Lucille, get me Police Commissioner Harris on the line, please."

A couple minutes later, she connected the Commissioner to the intercom phone.

"Director Carpenter, what can I do for you?"

"I need to borrow one of your prisoners."

"Which one?"

"Lucas Ridale."

"Lucas? I'm afraid that's not possible. Military brass took him into their custody."

"I have jurisdiction on this case. They don't have the right . . ."

"You signed the waiver, sir."

"What? I never signed any such order."

"I'm sorry. He's gone. The paperwork was in order."

Anger grew in Carpenter's voice, "I never authorized his transfer."

"It *looked* like your signature."

"Who took him?"

"High Military Personnel. Way up the chain of command, but I have no idea where they transported him."

Carpenter tapped the disconnect button with a hard, stiff finger. "Dammit, I told you something didn't set well for me on this case. We have to find him. We start by talking to his friends."

They nodded.

"Kat, you and Tyler go to Daniel Hutchinson's apartment. See if they've heard anything from Lucas."

"The author?" Kat asked.

Carpenter nodded. "You a fan?"

She smiled and blushed. "I've only read his first novel. Pretty dark stuff."

"Okay. Gil, you and Denton take a chopper out to Lydia Parker's house. I know they've split from one another, but if he's in trouble; he may have tried to contact her. Find out what she knows."

"Eugene, you work the computers. Find out what kind of vehicles they drive and trace their GPS trackers so we can pinpoint their locations if necessary. Also, I'll need their cell phone numbers. It's imperative that we find them in case their lives are in danger."

"You think they are?" Denton asked.

Carpenter shrugged. "I don't know. Anything's possible. Contact me with any information you obtain. Be careful."

CHAPTER 35

The more Nancy thought about escaping, the less she liked the idea. Or perhaps it was that she feared the consequences of what might happen should she try and fail. Not necessarily what happened to her, but what they'd do to her father.

And yet, she gambled. Using the flat end of the spoon handle like a screwdriver, she had removed one of the four screws that fastened the air vent screen to the wall. The process had only taken her six hours to accomplish. Five of those hours were spent simply trying to bust the screw loose so she could unscrew it.

With three more screws to remove and an abundance of time, she was comforted by the knowledge that Lucas was nearby. Where exactly, she didn't know. She had no idea how'd she find him once she freed herself, but she'd diligently keep working until she pried off the cover.

A key turned in the locked door. Nancy ran to the bed and stuffed the spoon and screw under the mattress. She lay on the bed and pretended the opening door had awakened her.

A female guard stepped into the room.

"Come on, girl," the woman said. Her voice was deep, cold. "Time for you to shower."

The woman was husky, almost manly in size and muscled width. Had it not been for the feminine qualities of her face and light makeup, Nancy would've assumed she was a man.

The guard didn't carry a gun. She had a wooden baton strapped to her belt. Even without the club, Nancy knew she wasn't a match for this woman. She could hurl Nancy across the room with less effort than a windstorm knocked down a tree.

Nancy humbled a quick nod and stared at the floor. She walked past the guard and into the hall. She might outrun the woman, she thought, but she didn't know which doors were locked or if she could even gain access to an elevator without a retina scan.

CHAPTER 36

*K*at and Tyler's drive to the Hutchinson apartment was quiet and filled with tension. Neither looked at the other and each seemed afraid to break the silence by uttering a single word. They had stopped at the vending room to get coffee before heading to the apartment.

Tyler had slugged coins into the coffee machine and smiled. "You sure you don't want to go to the concert tonight?"

Kat blushed and looked away. "Sorry, but I have errands to run."

"Maybe tomorrow night?" he asked with a tinge of disappointment.

"Tyler," she said softly. "I don't think we should date since we work together."

"Why?"

"It's unprofessional."

"I thought you had a good time."

"I did."

He took his coffee from the machine. "We hit it off well."

"I know."

"It was the carriage ride, wasn't it? I'm sorry. That was a premature move. Too romantic."

"No, Tyler. That was sweet. Under different circumstances, maybe different fields of work, we could chance dating. But we enter dangerous situations in our line of work. Emotions tend to allow people to make mistakes, and it's something I cannot risk."

Tyler was crushed. His shoulders slumped. Tears dampened his eyes, so he walked to the condiment counter. He poured creamer into his coffee and stirred it.

Kat had wanted to reach for him, embrace him, but if she did, she counteracted everything she had said to him. He'd know immediately that what she had said was a lie. She took a deep breath and walked to the door.

She turned and said, "I'm sorry, Tyler."

Kat stood a second longer, but he didn't reply. And now, she was stuck riding in the car with him. She chided herself for not being able to open up. Deep inside she really wanted to, but growing up without a father had made her sorely independent.

Because she had never depended on her father for emotional or financial support, she found it difficult time accepting affection. She feared giving Tyler access to her inner feelings and her trust, because eventually, she believed, he'd abandon her, too.

Kat was safer being alone and single. But living a solitary life held emptiness and was unrewarding. She delved into investigative work to make a difference by helping others.

Tyler stopped the car about a block from Daniel's apartment building around nine o'clock. City police had squared off the apartment front with yellow tape to prevent onlookers from stepping onto the sidewalk.

Without saying anything, Tyler put on sunglasses and stepped out. With the heavy cloud cover, Kat understood *why* he wore the shades, and she was to blame. She wanted to kick herself, but she had a job to do.

Kat sprinted to catch up with Tyler.

"What the hell happened here?" Kat asked him.

"Beats me," he replied with a shrug.

Detective Donald Seals greeted her at the yellow tape barrier. "Hi, Kat. You here for this?"

"Actually," she said, pushing her windblown hair from her eyes. "We're here to talk to Daniel Hutchinson, the author."

Detective Seals lowered his eyes and stared at the pavement. "Then you're here for *this*."

She scanned the side of the building. Two black cables hung from the balcony rail.

"That's his apartment where the cables are fastened?"

Seals nodded. "Afraid so."

Kat stared at the black grapple cables. "Forced entry?"

The detective looked up. "They scaled the walls with the cables, but the balcony door was apparently unlocked." He sighed. "But that's normal for a third floor apartment. Most people feel a certain security that high up, like no one's going to barge in. At least not from the balcony door."

Tyler gave a grim smile and shoved his hands into his pockets. "Not too many people use grapple hooks, either."

Kat looked at Seals. "What about the Hutchinson family? Are they okay?"

Seals shook his head. "We don't know yet. There's lot of blood, but no bodies."

Tyler's eyebrows rose. "No bodies?"

"No, Todd Webster from the state forensics is collecting evidence right now."

"Then he's the man we need to talk to," she said, walking past Seals, but then she stopped. "Did any of the neighbors report hearing gunfire?"

"No," Seals replied. "No gunfire. But several did mention an abrupt blast of hard rock music around one-thirty last night. Maybe lasted two minutes."

Kat frowned. "Okay . . . thanks."

CHAPTER 37

Daniel's apartment door was open. Kat and Tyler entered carefully, pulling on latex gloves so not to disturb or destroy any physical evidence. Todd was crouched in the center of the living room gathering blood samples. His lab assistant busied herself snapping photos of each smear, drop, and pool of blood.

"Any idea what happened here, Todd?" Kat asked, picking up Daniel's latest novel from the desk.

"Kat woman!" Todd said, not looking up.

Kat woman was the nickname Todd had given her after she had climbed across the catwalk in a condemned theater to rescue a lost runaway. They had looked for the teenage girl for two days before one of the girl's friends finally revealed where the girl was hiding. She had gone into the theater to keep the police from finding her. When the FBI agents arrived to help, none of them dared to cross the rusted catwalk to help the girl. Most implied that they weighed too much to cross, which was probably true, but Kat never hesitated. With the nimbleness of a cat she made her way quickly across. After Todd read her heroic actions in the paper the next morning, he teased her and called her Kat woman. Since her name was Kat, and he loved comics, he tagged her with the name.

"Best as I can tell right now," Todd said. "Three people died here last night."

Kat took a deep breath and flipped the book over to study the back dust

139

cover. A photo of Daniel and Morton at his desk covered the entire back jacket. Her eyes were instantly drawn to Morton.

"You think the Hutchinson family was killed?" she asked.

"Can't be certain of anything until the DNA results come back. What brings you here anyway? This murder investigation being taken by the Feds?"

"Not yet," she replied. "But probably. We wanted to ask him a few questions about Lucas Ridale and the senate murders. We're speculating that Lucas might not be the person responsible."

"No shit?"

"No shit."

She looked at Morton's picture again. She sensed something different about the cat. The eyes. Definitely the eyes. They weren't *catlike*. They were almost human in how they regarded the camera. The cat sat poised in an elegant, regal posture. She almost dropped the book when she noticed an oddity even more baffling. The cat was smiling.

"Aww, now. I don't know about dat. That video was pretty damning evidence against him."

"You can't always believe everything you see."

Todd nodded. "Well, now, that's true."

"Neighbors say they never heard any gunfire."

"Yeah. At least two of the victims weren't shot. The third one is questionable."

"What makes you believe that?"

"Without the bodies, I can't be one hundred percent certain." He pointed at the thick pool of blood. "To lose that amount of blood is consistent with the throat being slashed."

Tyler stood at the balcony door. Wind ruffled the curtains. "Isn't it odd," he said. "That whoever came here left the hooks behind?"

"Yeah," Todd said. "They came and left in a hurry. They used a gurney to take out the bodies, too."

Kat followed a small trail of blood from the larger pool to the couch. "Are those paw prints?" she asked.

"Yeah, they had a cat."

"Did you find a cat body?"

"No, but he was injured, possibly shot because there are blood spots under the sofa."

Kat stared at the cat's picture again. "Why shoot a cat?"

"No clue, Kat woman. No clue at all."

"When you get the DNA results in, Todd, please fax them to me as soon as possible."

"I sure will."

Kat looked at Morton's picture and thought, "What do you know about what happened here? It's a shame you can't talk."

The cat's smile held a mocking gleam.

On the elevator she told Tyler, "Judging by what's happened here, the theory of a clone doesn't sound unreasonable."

Tyler shrugged. "So you buy it then? The idea of a clone?"

"Something major is happening. Whoever wants Lucas framed also wanted the Hutchinson family dead."

"You think they're dead?"

"God, I hope not," she replied. "But it's possible. We won't know until the results come in."

CHAPTER 38

*E*ven though the large muscled female guard turned her back while Nancy undressed, Nancy felt more vulnerable than ever. After she had reached puberty, she never liked to undress in front of her mother, but being in front of a complete stranger was much worse. She covered her breasts with one arm and her pubic area with the other.

Nancy slipped around the corner into the open shower room.

"I'm Yvonne," the stern, rock-jawed guard told her from outside the door.

Self-conscious, Nancy glanced back to make certain the woman was out of view. Yvonne made no attempt to look at her. In a sense that comforted Nancy, but she still didn't like the idea of showering out in the open. She was thankful this guard was a female. All the others had been male, but they never allowed her to shower. They gave her a cloth and a bowl of hot soapy water to use in her room.

Yvonne stood outside of Nancy's view and washed her hands at one of the six white porcelain sinks. Bright fluorescent light glared off the white-tiled floor and walls. The light spilled into the dark, cold shower room.

"I suppose you already know who I am, don't you, Yvonne?"

The sink water stopped and the automatic hand dryer came on.

"Yes, Nancy. I know."

The cold concrete numbed Nancy's feet. She turned the hot water knob and huddled beneath its warmth. As the hot water met the floor, thick steam pillars formed a curtain around her. She lathered a soap bar between her hands and then washed herself.

"Is my father okay?"

"Other than constantly worrying about you, he's doing okay. Of course," she said, "I'd worry, too, if you were my daughter."

"Do you have children, Yvonne?"

"No. I . . ." her voice trembled. "I'm unable. I've always wanted them. Especially a daughter."

Nancy scrubbed her underarms. "I miss my mother."

"I imagine so. Her death was such a tragedy."

"You knew her?"

"No. Your father talks about her all the time. He's a good friend to me."

Nancy pressed her back into the hot water and folded her arms across her breasts, absorbing the warmth. "Then why are you keeping us apart?"

"I'm not. Those are Idris' orders. If we don't follow them, we die."

"Idris?"

"He's in command of TransGenCorp again. You need to get dressed. I have to take you back to your room."

Yvonne held a towel around the corner without looking in. Nancy accepted the towel and said, "This is the first shower they've let me have."

"I know. I hope you enjoyed it."

"Oh, I did."

"Because it will probably be your last one here. Now hurry."

Nancy dressed quickly. She was alarmed by the abrupt tone change in Yvonne's voice—from meek and caring to cold and almost hostile. Although steam rose from her reddened skin, Nancy suddenly felt chilled to the core.

CHAPTER 39

*L*ydia's house: 10:00 a.m.

THE HELICOPTER LANDED in the field across the road from Lydia's house. Swirls of lingering fog drifted away from the pilot's view as the whirling blades spun through the air. Denton and Gil stepped from the chopper with their guns drawn and approached the black van parked in the ditch.

They never took their eyes off the van. Kat and Tyler's findings at the Hutchinson apartment had reached them via radio transmission. They were placed on high alert. The helicopter pilot shut off the blades, which whined and spun slower until they stopped rotating. He, too, was wary of the surroundings. The fog was still thick in patches and weather radar showed more approaching storms due to hit the area within the next hour.

Denton reached the van first. He ignored the mud and grass seeds stuck to his Devon wingtip shoes. Reaching for the van's rear door handle, he held the gun to the side of his face. He eased the lever down slowly. Gil positioned his gun out before him, ready to shoot a possibly armed perpetrator in the rear of the van.

Denton yanked the door open. Seconds later, they lowered their weapons and holstered them.

"It's empty," Gil said.

Denton seemed relieved. "I'll check the glove box. See if you can find anything here."

"No problem, but other than these empty assault rifle casings, I don't think there'll be anything more."

Denton opened the passenger door and popped open the glove compartment. Empty. Not one scrap of paper. It didn't appear as if anything had been stored inside. He looked under the seats. Nothing. He shook his head.

"These people are going to a lot of trouble not letting themselves be traced. There's no vehicle registration up here. Not anything to identify this vehicle or the owner."

Gil said. "I noticed. There's no tag either."

Denton checked the driver's door for manufacturing information. The sticker had been scraped off with a razor blade. He looked on the dash panel for the VIN number. "Dammit! They even filed off the VIN number."

"Commissioner Harris said that it was a high branch of the military. Top secret group, I suppose."

"Must be. Or a militant group operating under illegal status."

"Always a possibility," Gil said, pulling his gun. "Let's check the house."

Denton stepped to the side of the van and noticed something on the ground. "Wait. Look. An empty syringe?"

"Odd."

"Yeah," Denton said, taking his handkerchief, picking it up, and dropping it into a Ziplock bag. He placed the wrapped syringe in the driver's seat. "We need to have this analyzed. It may be the only mistake they made."

"If we're lucky, they made more inside the house."

"I wouldn't bank on it. These people seem professional."

They walked slowly up the driveway, and the late morning breeze pushed through the fog. Both men held their guns tightly, afraid to tell the other of his fear, and afraid of what they might find in the house. With the van parked across the road, finding a victim or perpetrator was a strong likelihood, but neither man was prepared for what they found.

Crows cawed from the Virginia pines beyond the fog-shaded barn. No lights reflected through the windows at the front of the house. Nearing the carport, they noticed the kitchen light gleaming through a partially opened door. Three quarters of the way up the drive, they noticed a body sprawled on the concrete. The dead man wore black fatigues.

"One victim down," Denton said with his hand tightly on the gun.

They stood over the body. Gil noticed the arrow shaft protruding through the man's night vision goggles. "Damn," he said.

Denton stepped around the riding mower and peered into the kitchen. Another man dressed in black lay facedown on the table. Coagulating blood spilled from the hole in the back of his head and covered the poker cards.

"Another dead man in the kitchen."

Gil punched HQ's number into his cell phone while he watched the barn. "We need a forensics team out here ASAP. We've got dead bodies."

They eased into the kitchen with their guns drawn. Tension constrained their chests. The refrigerator door stood wide open. Food and condiment jars were scattered across the floor. Empty food boxes and drink containers were strewn all over the floor and countertops. Bits of food, wrappers, and blood covered the floor.

Denton crushed a half empty bag of pretzels underfoot while looking through the clutter. "Someone made one hell of a mess."

"One angry, violent raccoon?"

"Never seen a raccoon on a military tactical squad," Denton replied.

"Tactical?"

"With the precision of the arrow through that man's eye on the porch, and this man at the table being shot execution-style through the back of the head, we're dealing with a professional."

"The home owner, maybe?"

Denton shook his head. "Lydia? Highly unlikely. Carpenter said that TGC had made killing machines. It would have had to be the clone."

"You believe the clone exists then?"

"Not totally, but we can't ignore that possibility. When has Carpenter ever BS-ed us?

"Never."

"Why would he start now?"

Denton nodded toward the next room. "Let's check out the rest of the house. Someone may still be here."

They went room to room, and the only thing they found Lucian's discarded clothes on Lydia's bed. Water dripped from the shower-head. The scent of soap and shampoo lingered in the air.

They returned to the carport.

"There's no sign of Lydia," Denton said. "Their van was still here but three of the tires are flat."

"Perhaps they had another vehicle," Gil said.

"Why is this lawnmower here?" Denton asked. He looked at the muddy indentions in the grass where the mower had been driven from the barn. Blood smears were on the steering wheel and a bloody handprint was also on the kitchen door. Fainter handprints trailed to the refrigerator. "Whoever drove the mower to the carport is probably the same person who made the mess with all the food. He was severely injured."

"Or she?"

Denton shrugged. "Let forensics sort it out."

"Let's check the barn."

"Might as well."

They stepped to the edge of the concrete but before they took a step into the wet grass, Denton thrust an arm out in front of Gil, stopping him mid-stride.

"What?" Gil asked.

"Look at the footprints," he said, pointing. "There's our woman. That set is unquestionably a woman's. She came to the house from the barn. It looks like she headed back to the barn with a man. Let's steer clear of that path. That's good evidence."

After walking around the far side of the path, they entered the barn and discovered a third dead body. Gil knelt beside the dead man at the foot of the stairs. A large bruise covered the man's throat. He pressed softly on the man's throat.

"Damn," he said. "This man's throat was crushed."

Denton nodded toward the stairs. "Do you think he's still here?"

"I don't know. But with what we're up against, I'd rather find him before he finds us."

They took the creaking stairs and the outside wind intensified, whistling through the rafters. Denton stood one step above Gil. They aimed their guns at the top stair. A long tree branch scratched the tin roof. Denton paused. Wind howled through the center of the loft like a banshee's shearing cry. Denton eyed Gil. Both eased one more step up.

Denton motioned Gil to check the left side of the loft while he took the right. Numerous antique chests and wardrobes were visible in the gray morning light. What might linger within those shadows concerned them both. They stepped light-footed from chest to wardrobe to chest, but no matter how softly they stepped, the floorboards creaked. After ten minutes of searching, they still found no one.

The loft had no hidden perpetrator but Gil found Lydia's compound bow.

"I'm curious whose prints will be on that," Denton said. Then, he noticed on the dusty edge of the loft near the window. "Those boot prints have to be a woman's."

Gil nodded. "Then maybe she stopped the three men before one of them got her."

Denton shook his head. "I still don't see her being capable of doing this."

"But if the clone came after her, he certainly wouldn't kill his own men."

Denton closed his eyes. "I have no idea what to believe right now. Not until the forensics evidence comes back in and we find her."

"So what do we do now?"

"We wait for the forensics team."

CHAPTER 40

*B*y the time Lydia finished bathing, Daniel had returned with fast food breakfast and coffee. The scent of fresh coffee was pleasant to Lydia's tired mind. She didn't know how long she had dozed off in the tub, but the warm water eased her tight, tense muscles.

Johanna stood when Lydia came out of the bathroom. "I'm sorry," Johanna said. "For my rude behavior earlier. You're right. You've never been my enemy. I've had a lot of stress."

Lydia winked and gave Johanna a friendly squeeze on the arm. "Right now, we're all under a great deal of stress. That's why we have to stay together."

When Lydia reached the table where Julia sat, Julia's eyes widened. She quickly rose to her feet. "Were you shot, Lydia?"

"No. Why?"

"Your jacket. There's a bullet hole on its right shoulder."

"And one on the back of the jacket, too," Daniel said. Looking closer, he said, "But there's no wound."

"I told you. I haven't been shot."

Julia inspected the hole on the front of the jacket. Singe marks were fresh with dried blood. Other than no wound, one could immediately conclude that a bullet had passed straight through her shoulder.

Julia crooked a finger into the front hole and pulled back the material. She couldn't find a wound, scar, or any bruising.

"See?" Lydia said. "I'm fine. I've not been shot. If I had been, I'd have felt the pain and gone to the hospital."

Rex stood at her feet and begged for food. He whined and wagged his tail. Lydia crumbled a sausage biscuit on the floor. The pup gulped it down.

Morton sat at the foot of the bed and with sarcasm said, "Meow, meow." He didn't even attempt to make it sound like a real cat's cry. He enunciated the words just like a human pronounced *meow*.

Lydia stared at the cat with genuine concern. "What's wrong with your cat? He sounds sick."

Morton rolled his eyes.

Daniel laughed. "I think he wants me to tell you something."

"You can understand him?"

"We all do, actually. He can talk."

"Dan, you're putting me on, right? I'm totally exhausted and don't have time for mind games."

"I speak quite well," Morton said.

"Oh my God," Lydia said, taking a step back. "How'd you do that? I know people can throw their voices, but to get his mouth to move in time with the words . . ."

Morton puffed his mouth with air, and then released it, making a popping sound. "It's no trick. Dr. Helmsby aligned the sequences in my genome to make talking possible for me."

Rex's mesmerized eyes watched Morton. His curiosity prevented him from barking.

Daniel took his vibrating cell phone from his pocket. "I wish I knew who keeps calling me. The number doesn't show any identification. This makes the tenth time it has rang."

"Maybe you should answer it," Julia said.

Daniel shook his head. "I don't think it's a good idea yet. Not if we're going to stay at this hotel. If I answer it, they might locate us faster."

Morton leapt to the floor, then to an empty chair at the table. "They can zoom in on your phone anyway, Daniel. You know that. You should do as Julia suggests. Answer it."

"Not until we know our next move," Daniel said. "We might have to move quickly."

Daniel peered out the hotel window and sighed. Nothing outside seemed out of the ordinary, but that was always when the vilest things happened. Or at least, that's how events unfolded in his life. He hoped this time would be different, but the tension in his gut alerted him to prepare for the worst.

CHAPTER 41

Yvonne marched silently behind Nancy. The woman hadn't spoken one word since they left the showers. Nancy worried that Idris might demand her death before too much longer, or perhaps he had already, and Yvonne was her assigned killer.

The comment about her taking her last shower troubled her. Should her father no longer be useful to Idris, nothing prevented the general from killing them both. She needed to work harder and faster to remove the last three screws on the air vent. But even then, she wasn't sure she had a way to escape.

Nancy stood to the side of the door and Yvonne unlocked it. Once inside, Yvonne gave a stern, threatening glare.

"Give me the spoon, Nancy," she said, holding out her muscled hand.

Nancy swallowed hard. Her voice trembled. "What?"

"The spoon you've been using to loosen the screws on the air vent. They know you have it. Now hand it here."

Nancy fought her urge to cry. She lifted the mattress and, like her spirit, she surrendered the spoon to Yvonne.

Yvonne walked to the vent and knelt before it. "You're smart enough to know that they'd count the utensils. You're resourceful though; I'll give you that. Not many people would have thought to use the end of a spoon as a screwdriver. Now, where's the missing screw?"

Nancy handed her the long screw. After Yvonne took the screw, Nancy noticed the door was still open. She looked for a weapon, anything, that she could use to incapacitate the large woman, but nothing presented itself of use.

Yvonne placed the screw on the floor between her knees while pulling a flathead screwdriver from her back pocket. To Nancy's surprise, Yvonne twisted out the other three screws in matter of seconds. She set the vent cover aside and motioned Nancy to her.

Yvonne placed a tight grip on Nancy's shoulder, leaned near her ear, and whispered, "This room is bugged. Now *hurry*. They're coming for you later today. Here's a rough map I've drawn of the ventilation system. It will get you to Lucas. Here, use this key to unlock his restraints. Once you leave the duct system, be careful. Shape shifters patrol the lowest levels, but that's the route you need to take. It's the only way so the outside guards do not see you. I let you shower to help mask your feminine scent from the shifters."

Perplexed, Nancy asked, "Why are you doing this?"

"For you and your father. And for me."

"I don't understand."

Yvonne smiled. "Your father promised to pay for my fertility treatments once I rescued you."

Nancy embraced her and whispered, "Come with me then."

Yvonne shook her head. "I stay to protect your father. Besides, I could never squeeze inside there. Now go."

Nancy crouched and crawled into the air duct. Yvonne placed the cover back over the vent. She quickly fastened the screws into place.

"Thank you," Nancy whispered. She crawled farther into the dark vent and thought, "I think."

CHAPTER 42

$\mathcal{L}$ucas lay blindfolded on the bunk with his eyes closed. The door opened and closed. The sound of footsteps eased closer.

Idris stood at the side of Lucas' bed. "Like your accommodations so far?"

Lucas yawned and didn't turn in the direction of Idris' voice. He said, "You might find a market for this shifter soundtrack you've been playing. Perhaps you have another volume? I'm rather bored with this one."

Idris snorted his contempt. "How'd you figure it out?"

"Shifters have a nasty musk odor, kind of like you. Besides, this room smells too clean for even one shifter to be caged here."

"I can have the handlers bring a couple of the beasts in here and turn them loose on your smart ass."

"You won't do that," Lucas said with a broad smile. "I have something of yours that you want. Something valuable. With me dead, you'll never get it back."

"I know what you have, and believe me, you're going to give it back. Everyone has a pain threshold. Everyone has a breaking point."

Lucas chuckled and said, "How'd that work for you last time? Howard paid a heavy price for the torture he inflicted upon me, and I never surrendered any information to you."

Idris' eyes narrowed. "You will this time."

Lucas shook his head. "Doubtful. I can't see how you ever reached the rank of general. You have no leadership qualities. You rely simply on bullying tactics, which might work on some people, but it doesn't work with me."

"Reputation means everything in this world. Like it or not, I'm capable of taking advantage of other people's weaknesses. That's how I got my status, and how I reclaimed TransGenCorp as my own. Congress respects me."

"Money doesn't buy respect. I imagine you lined a lot of political pockets with your money. That might get them to look the other direction, but it doesn't buy you loyalty. As far as I'm concerned few politicians have worthy reputations. Besides, I don't see how this has anything to do with me or what I stole from you."

"That's why Godfrey is dead. I will destroy everything you treasure. I started by framing the two senators murders on you, which ruined your credibility with your fans."

"Godfrey and the other senator were innocent. Neither possessed what you're looking for," Lucas said.

"But they would have eventually, right? You were going to give the information to them."

Lucas chuckled. "They're the reason why I stole it. They needed it as evidence to put your ass in prison. They didn't take your bribe, and because so many others did, they decided to shut you down again."

Idris ground his teeth hard. The scraping was audible. "Just tell me where it is, you bastard."

Lucas laughed. "You'd have better luck finding a buried needle in the Sahara on a moonless night. Think about it. I never revealed anything to you when you captured me years ago. You might as well count your losses and forget about it. Howard never got me to talk."

"Torture is an art I've seasoned since our previous exchange. Hell, in other countries where I've hidden, torture is now encouraged as sport."

"Fine. Torture me. I won't talk."

"You're a fool. I'll punish you by torturing and killing the people you love most. Four extermination teams were dispatched last night. They're due to report in any time."

Lucas didn't reply. Maybe Idris wasn't aware of the phone call Lucas had made to Daniel. Daniel was a great fact gatherer. He'd warn the rest of their group. They'd be on alert. Daniel was paranoid enough to overreact to protect his family and friends.

"Struck a nerve, didn't I?" Idris asked.

Lucas despised the smugness in the general's voice. "No. Not really."

"You're not the least bit worried about them?"

"I figure it like this. If your teams haven't reported back to you yet, your men are dead. *Not* my friends."

"You overestimate your friends."

"You forget the mental conditioning we endured while caged like animals inside Pittsburgh. You may have trained men to kill, but we've already survived a war. We know how to react to our environment. We kill those who come after us."

"Perhaps," Idris said with a tired voice, which indicated he had grown weary of their verbal chess match. So he targeted a checkmate by saying, "And what about Lydia? She wasn't part of your group."

Lucas fought to maintain his composure and not to tense any muscles in reaction to the threat. He was thankful for the blindfold. His eyes were unable to conceal the sudden shock and loss that stabbed his heart.

While Lucas and Lydia's relationship had blossomed, he warned her about his clone many times. Too many times. When he thought she had sickened of his story, he decided on a new tactic. He'd make her as good with weapons as he was. As it turned out, she became better. She could defend herself, but he feared she wasn't convinced about his clone's existence. If she didn't believe, she was vulnerable. That vulnerability could cause her death.

Lucas sighed and offered his best lie. "We haven't been lovers for a long time. If you've kept up with us like the media has, you'd know that, asshole. It wouldn't bother her if I burned in Hell. In fact, that would probably amuse her. Why should I care what you do to her?"

"You care," Idris said. "Because it will be your clone that'll kill her. And, in every detail except the mind, you will be the one who killed her. But death is too easy. It's what he does to her *before* he kills her that pleasures me."

Idris walked across the tile floor to the door and opened it.

He paused at the open door and said, "I also have Nancy Helmsby prisoner. If what happens to all the others doesn't get you to talk, can you handle watching shifters eat her alive while we make her father watch? Think about it. I can prevent any of this from happening. Talk."

"Go to Hell," Lucas replied.

Idris slammed the door and strode down the hall. In his anger, he had forgotten to do one important thing—he failed to lock the door.

Lucas' tired arms yanked and tugged at the restraints, but he didn't have enough strength to loosen them. The awkward overhead angle in which they had tied Lucas' wrists made his shoulders ache and burn. He tried to adjust himself into more comfortable positions to lessen the strain, but he was unable to find one. He hoped Nancy found a way to get free. If lady luck still charmed his favor, perhaps she'd find him before Idris returned.

CHAPTER 43

 ancy crawled through the dark air duct. The cold, galvanized tin that formed the walls, floor, and ceiling of the air ventilation system numbed her fingers. The flimsy material popped and buckled between the duct supports with each movement forward advance she made. She was thankful that she was tall and slender and didn't weigh any more than what she did. Another ten pounds or so, and the duct floor might not support her.

She was relieved that she had not encountered any spider webs. Should sticky web mesh cling to her face, she'd probably scream. She hated spiders and the thought of one spindling into her hair or running across her body brought chills up her back and down her arms. The cool air of the ventilation system was a deterrent for arachnids, at least so far.

The map Yvonne had given her was useless in the lightless sections of the air tunnels. Beyond the darkness where faint light filtered through side vents, she paused to study the crude map. Although the distance between her cell and the room where they held Lucas wasn't that far, uncertainty washed her confidence of succeeding away.

Nancy knew about the various shifters caged inside TransGenCorp. Her father hadn't kept that a secret from her. Pausing at each side vent, she peered into the rooms with great curiosity, hoping to see one of the uniquely intelligent but hideous creatures. The rooms, however, were boring and looked like medical examination rooms with white tables, weight scales, and various wall charts. No shifters.

She did fear the possibility of encountering an escaped shifter in the dark tunnel. Where various ducts intersected with her path, a hidden shifter would hold the advantage by striking from the darkness. She pushed aside that fear and focused on the one danger she did have to face.

Lucas was being held on the floor beneath hers, which meant that somewhere she'd have to drop down to the floor. Not certain how far she'd fall, she didn't like the idea at all.

The map indicated she'd pass two more rooms before it was necessary to make that drop. On her hands and knees she crawled past two side vents before the path turned left into total darkness again. If the map Yvonne had given her was accurate, the path divided to form a T directly ahead of her position. To rescue Lucas, she must descend the T's leg.

She slid her arms all the way out in front of herself, then arched her back, bringing her knees forward in the same manner an inchworm crawls.

Faint voices carried from a room beneath her. Nancy held her breath. Two men argued. One she recognized immediately as Lucas. She identified Idris after he made his threat, "I also have Nancy Helmsby prisoner, too. If what happens to all the others doesn't get you to talk, can you handle watching shifters eat her alive while we make her father watch? Think about it. I can prevent any of this from happening. Talk."

Scooting forward, she looked down the airshaft. The slits of the vent cover revealed a poorly lit room. She estimated the T leg to be roughly six feet deep. Being tall like her father, that distance could be easily managed by lowering herself down into the shaft while supporting her weight with her elbows. However, the distance from the vent cover to the floor could be another eight to ten feet. After breaking the vent cover loose, if she landed incorrectly on the floor, she could easily break an ankle or knock herself unconscious.

The dimly lit room below prevented her from seeing the floor and what obstructions lay in her path. All she knew was she had no other options. No other way out. Eventually, sooner or later, they'd discover her room was empty. Should Yvonne prove to be a true ally, the female guard couldn't prevent Idris from eventually coming to her room. Once other guards were alerted, escaping became more difficult.

Sliding her legs over the edge, she pressed her stomach against the cold duct floor and eased down slowly. Her feet touched the vent cover without having to stretch. For the first time she was proud of her five-foot, eight inch height.

Nancy thought her one hundred fifteen pounds was enough to dislodge the screws from their hold, but the metal cover sustained her without sagging. She flexed up and down on her tiptoes, allowing her weight to fall heavily on her heels several times. The cover bent slightly. She repeated the motion, but this time nothing more happened. She decided to make a small jump of five to six inches and prayed she landed properly once the cover broke free.

Nancy thrust herself upward, and the vent cover shifted and creaked. Her full weight came down on the cover and she plummeted through. In two blurred seconds, she realized where she'd land. Right on top of Lucas. She widened her stance so her feet landed to each side of his crossed legs.

When Nancy's feet hit the mattress, she was unable to keep her balance. Falling forward, she pivoted to her right to avoid a head-to-head collision with Lucas.

"What the hell?" Lucas asked, a second before her elbow struck his stomach. He sucked in a deep breath and groaned.

"I'm so sorry, Lucas."

"Nancy?" he whispered, still wincing.

She pulled up his blindfold and smiled apologetically. Standing on her knees, she dug in her pocket to remove the key to the restraints. She quickly unlocked them.

Lucas' stiff arms dropped. He moved his aching arms to his sides still in obvious pain. She didn't know which hurt more—his arms from being stretched above his head for hours or her elbow to his stomach. She was afraid to ask.

"Glad you dropped in," he said with his trademark wide grin. He looked at the vent cover that hung by two screws. "How'd you manage to get into the ventilation system?"

Nancy helped Lucas sit at the edge of the bed. She rubbed his shoulders while he stretched and flexed his arms.

"One of Dad's friends. She helped me. But how do we get out of here? No way we can get back up there."

"Even if I could get up there, there's no way I'd fit. My shoulders are too broad. But, Idris didn't lock the door when he left."

"What about the guards?"

"There are never more than six guards inside TransGenCorp at any given time. The majority is posted along the outside perimeter." Lucas massaged his right biceps. "But I need to find one, though."

"Why?"

Lucas smiled and winked. "We need a weapon."

CHAPTER 44

$\mathcal{I}$dris fumed when he reached the morgue, not realizing his anger was tame compared to how much it was about to escalate. He expected to see the dead bodies of the Hutchinson family on the autopsy tables. Instead, he found the three bodies of the soldiers he had sent to kill them.

Idris eyed his chief medical examiner, Jacob Benson. "How the hell did this happen? How did they survive and my men died? Daniel couldn't possibly have outwitted them."

"Daniel didn't, sir. He wasn't home."

"Then who?"

Jacob shrugged. "I'd say the cat."

Idris clinched his jaw tightly. "Impossible."

Benson showed the deep lacerations through one soldier's throat and the pierced hole through the other's eye into the brain.

Idris nodded toward the third dead soldier with the canine ears and jaw. "And him? Cat claws couldn't have stopped him. He's like Lucian. He could heal himself."

"He was shot three times with denaturers."

"By a cat?"

"A shifter cat, sir."

"Damn Helmsby! You're certain of this? I know the cat talks, but it's also a shifter?"

Benson smiled. "Sir, it's all caught on film."

Idris followed Jacob to the computer. A cable linked a pair of night vision goggles to the laptop computer. Idris watched the video playback in disbelief. "Spectacular agility, this cat. Far greater than any shifter I created."

"Keep watching."

"The cat was shot? Where's its body?"

"That's the problem. They didn't find it."

"There's no way he survived the denaturer. Dammit, I need that cat's body."

Benson offered a defeated shrug. "There's nothing I can do. The authorities have scoured the apartment by now. If the cat was there, I'm sure they've disposed of it."

Idris shook his head. "What about the other teams? Have they reported in?"

"Lucian's team hasn't been heard from. The one that was sent to Johanna's aerobics studio did kill two individuals, but not Johanna. They set the place ablaze to destroy any evidence. Lucas' airplane and barn were destroyed, but there was an altercation at his estate."

"With whom?"

"Lydia, if their guess is correct."

"Lydia? What about the team sent to get her? Do you think they're dead, too?"

Benson shook his head. "I can't say what happened to them. It's highly unlikely she could manage that."

Idris returned a shrewd stare. "Nothing surprises me anymore. Especially when it involves Lydia." He shook his head and turned away, suppressing a sudden urge to smile.

CHAPTER 45

Carpenter reached Senator Godfrey's office at eleven-thirty with warrants in hand. He was surprised to find the information he needed within minutes.

On Godfrey's desk was a folder labeled: "Operation Meltdown."

Carpenter flipped through the file and discovered that Lucas had been entering TransGenCorp for weeks, pretending to be his clone in order to obtain information for Godfrey. Godfrey had planned to use the detailed information to pass new legislation to shut down TransGenCorp forever. What better way to infiltrate a facility, and ironically, what better way to get even than to mimic the clone in order to kill Idris?"

Carpenter called Kat's cell phone. When she answered, he said, "Kat, where are you?"

"We're heading back to Pittsburgh. Why? What do you need?"

"I think I know where Lucas is."

"Where?"

"TGC."

"How certain are you?"

"High upper ninety percentile."

"I've received some good information myself."

"What?"

"The blood at the Hutchinson apartment wasn't theirs. It apparently belonged to three men—the intruders—and a cat."

"A cat?"

"The Hutchinsons owned a cat. The strange thing is that one of the three men had similarities in their blood to those of the shifters and the cat does, too."

Carpenter frowned. "What do you mean?"

"From what Todd's report reads, this cat's DNA components are the same pattern as the shifters found in Pittsburgh after the Helmsby Research Center residents were rescued. And one of the men has the same kind of components."

"There has to be some kind of error."

"No," Kat replied. "I had Todd re-analyze the cat's blood. It's a match for shifter tags."

Carpenter ran a hand through his hair. "Okay. And the one human's blood sample has those shifter markers, too?"

"Yes, I'm afraid so."

"Damn, so there are still super humans out there?"

"It looks that way."

"Then it's best we have a good strategy before we raid TGC."

"Well, some good news though."

"What?"

"I believe we've located the Hutchinson family. Not only them, but Lydia and Johanna, too."

"Really? Where?"

"We've traced their cell phones and GPS trackers. They're at the Burnside Hotel."

Carpenter said, "You need to get there quickly. With all of them holed up in one location, they're an easy target for TGC."

"I know, but none of them are answering their phones."

"I don't particularly blame them. When you get there, call me. I'll send a team out to meet you. In the meantime I have to figure out how we can get inside TGC safely."

"I'll contact you soon," Kat said. She disconnected the call and watched the rolling fog billow.

CHAPTER 46

Tyler drove, staring straight ahead. Giving him a side-glance, Kat could see that hurt still lingered in his eyes. She wanted to say something to ease the silence but nothing came to mind. Perhaps after they got the Hutchinson family to safety, she'd soul search and tell Tyler that she'd give their relationship a chance after all.

Trying to be a hero kept her in constant isolation. Standing alone prevented others from becoming collateral damage. She kept people at a distance and suffered loneliness to protect others. Denying herself intimate relationships deceived her into believing she could make life's twisted journey alone.

She considered Tyler an attractive man, and one, if she wasn't so apprehensive, she'd become intimate with. Another fear resonated. Her rejection might bring tension between them. She hoped he wouldn't turn bitter, and they'd always be friends. But such things in life could never be predicted accurately.

CHAPTER 47

*L*ucas had stretched and rolled his shoulders several minutes before he finally stood. Stiffness and pain lessened his agility, which concerned him. He expected their escape required desperate speed. Otherwise, they'd never get out of TransGenCorp alive.

Lucas looked up at the open vent. "How'd you know where to find me?"

Nancy pulled the crumpled map from her pocket.

Lucas studied the map. "Which floor are we on?"

"Sublevel three."

He frowned. "I've been here a lot over the past couple months. I thought there were only two floors."

Nancy shook her head. "Four, I believe. That's what my father said."

Lucas walked to the door. He grabbed the doorknob and faced her. "I can get us out of the building, but the perimeter guards won't be easy to get past."

"Yvonne advised we go down, not up."

"Yvonne?"

"She drew the map."

"She can be trusted?"

Nancy nodded. "Yes. I don't think she'd have warned me about the shifters on the lowest sublevel if she didn't want me safe. Besides, I don't think we have too many choices."

"No, we don't. Damn. Shifters are on the lower levels?"

"Yes."

"Then I definitely need a weapon. Come with me and stay close," he said, taking her hand and opening the door.

The poorly lit hall wasn't what Lucas had expected. The temperature couldn't be warmer than sixty degrees Fahrenheit. No visible security cameras scanned the hall, but that didn't mean they weren't being watched. At the far end of the hall an exit sign glowed. No guards stood between them and that door.

Halfway down the hall large windows lined the right wall. They approached cautiously.

Lucas peered through the windows first. Rows of glass tanks housed nude, muscular men. Feeding tubes and monitors snaked from the genetic soldiers to individual life support computers.

"I'll be damned," Lucas said, glancing into the room. "Idris wasted no time getting his cloning project running again."

Nancy looked over his shoulder and gasped.

"Cover your eyes!" Lucas said. "You really shouldn't see this."

She smiled. "I don't mind. I'm *not* a little girl anymore."

"Well, you still are to me."

"Why are they inside those glass cylinders?"

"Your father never told you about them?"

"No."

"They're clones manufactured to become militant assassins."

Nancy frowned with concern. "Shouldn't we disconnect them or something?"

The idea was tempting, but these metamorphic glass cocoons were armed with sensory detectors. Their alarm sensitive triggers were like those on Lydia's incubation chamber years earlier. When vital signs dropped into the failure zone, not only would doctors rush into the room, armed guards would come as well.

"No. We get out of here. I'll take care of these later."

At the exit he pushed the door inward and let her enter the stairwell ahead of him. The stairs led downward into a dark, spiral catacomb. Cool, stagnant air hung with the strong scent of mildew.

"You're certain we're on sublevel three?"

Nancy nodded. "Yes, when I went to shower, all the rooms were in the two hundreds, and I had to drop a floor to get to you."

"Well, the thing that puzzles the hell out of me is how do you get up to level two from here? There are no stairs that go up."

She shrugged. "I don't know."

"And why keep going down to leave when the entrances is three floors above us?"

"I wish I knew, but Yvonne didn't tell me anything more. I'm sorry."

Lucas shook his head. "Don't be. It just doesn't make sense, but it's also hard for me to trust people."

"Here lately, I'm the same way," she said.

No lights glowed down the descending stairs. He ran his hand along the wall, hoping, but never found a light switch. The cold, wet air smelled of death.

Lucas placed a hand on her arm and turned her toward him. "We don't have a weapon, so if you see shifters, run."

Her face showed creases from fear. She swallowed hard and nodded.

NANCY DIDN'T WANT to believe Yvonne had betrayed them, but the dark stairwell, carved out of limestone, didn't look promising. Water dripped from the sweating walls into overflowing pools that trickled and meandered down the slick, mossy steps.

The further down the spiral steps they descended, the nastier the smell became. She covered her nose and mouth with the top of her shirt.

A couple of times she slipped on the stairs and grabbed the cold, iron rail that ran along the outer wall to keep from falling. Then, in the darkness, she placed her foot on a broken step. The limestone chunk dislodged, tipped forward, and she fell headfirst. Had Lucas not been standing directly in front of her and caught her, she'd have injured herself.

Nancy placed a gentle hand against Lucas' back so she knew where he was in the darkness. At any moment the stairs might end and they'd plummet endlessly into a bottomless pit.

Lucas stopped walking when strange sloshing sounds drifted up the stairs. An instant later, a blinding, searing light vanquished the pitch darkness.

The glare temporally disoriented them. They pressed their backs against the cold, wet column the stairs spiraled around. They shielded their eyes with their hands.

"Damn, the light switch must have been at the bottom of the stairs," Lucas said. "Who'd have thought?"

CHAPTER 48

*L*ucas wiped stinging tears from his eyes with his thumbs and blinked several times to clear his vision.

A scraping sound ascended the stairs. He motioned for Nancy to press tightly against the wall like he was doing. She did so without hesitation.

The cold water on the wall soaked the back of his shirt. The sudden shock made him take in a sharp breath. His arms and shoulders tightened.

As the sound moved closer, Lucas realized someone, most likely a guard, was coming up the stairs toward them. He and Nancy could run, but they risked falling and injuring themselves on the slippery stairs.

Since no alarms had sounded and their escape had not been discovered yet, the guard wouldn't be on high alert, which meant he'd be at ease, making his rounds, and his gun was probably holstered.

When the man's combat boot stepped into view on the step below, Lucas swung around with his right fist, full force, and shoved all his weight behind it. The blow struck the man square in the chest, lifted him into the air, and sent him tumbling down the stairs.

Lucas rushed his opponent, hoping to reach the man before he drew his gun. But the guard didn't go for his gun. He didn't stay down, either. The man was fast. Incredibly fast. Before Lucas closed the distance between them, the man thrust himself to his feet and bowed low. He wrapped his arms around Lucas' thighs and carried Lucas up three stairs before jack-hammering Lucas against the steps.

The crushing pressure drove the air from Lucas' lungs. Pain rattled down his spine.

Nancy screamed.

Lucas opened his eyes in time to see a flash of silver arcing downward at his face. He shoved his head to the right. The knife struck the step, barely missing his left ear. The guard brought the blade up again.

Lucas fought to get out from beneath the man, but the guard straddled him and pressed his knees tightly against Lucas' ribs. Lucas moaned in pain.

The guard brought the knife down again. Lucas caught the guard's wrist. The blade froze an inch above his face. His fatigued shoulders and arms grew weaker. He couldn't hold the man much longer.

The soldier placed his left hand behind his right wrist and pressed his weight against the knife to bear down and plunge the blade into Lucas' eye. Suddenly, the guard's strength lessened. He collapsed and fell beside Lucas.

Lucas looked up to see Nancy holding the broken limestone step she had hit the guard with. He smiled.

"Thanks," he said.

Nancy shrugged.

Lucas took the guard's gun. "Go around the corner, Nancy. Not far. Just out of sight."

She nodded. She understood.

When she rounded the stairs, Lucas rolled the guard over. Dark blood oozed from the head injury. This soldier wasn't human. Not fully human, at least. He was genetically enhanced like those in the incubation chambers. No ordinary human possessed strength, agility, and speed like that.

Lucas sighed. Pulsating pain ached through his joints. He didn't want to fire the gun in the stairwell because the echo would carry up and down the stairs. But this man was a genetic soldier. He couldn't chance the possibility of leaving the man alive. He'd recover. Then he'd follow and kill them from behind.

He aimed the gun at the man's head. The guard's eyes opened. His arms bolted upward, reaching for the gun. Lucas took a quick step back and fired. The bullet struck the man between the eyes.

The soldier collapsed. His body shook with violent, involuntary spasms. Lucas lowered the gun and leaned against the wall. He shook, looking at the dead man.

"What the hell?"

The flesh around the entry wound was darkening. A black gooey depression sank into the center of his forehead. Flesh melted, dissolving like acid poured directly onto the skin.

Lucas caught up with Nancy four stairs down.

"Are you okay?" she asked.

"Yeah, I'll live, but we need to find our way out. Fast."

They hurried down the remaining stairs and the sloshing, splashing rhythm grew louder. A foghorn sounded in the distance. The stairwell exit opened into a large cave. An inlet of one of the two rivers divided the chasm. Docks were on both sides of the narrow stretch of water.

A guard marched along the far side dock. A speedboat was tied to the dock on their side. No other guards stood on patrol. Lucas wondered why.

Lucas and Nancy crouched lower and headed to a row of large wooden crates and hid behind them.

"I know this will look like murder," Lucas said. "But the soldier that nearly killed me wasn't exactly human. I don't think that man is either."

"What do you mean?"

"They're like the men upstairs."

"In the glass containers?"

"Yes. This will seem brutal, but he's not going to just let us take that boat."

She shrugged. "I've been held her against my will for nearly three months. If I knew how to shoot a gun, I'd shoot him myself."

Lucas arched his back and winced. His eyes squinted tightly from obvious pain. He braced himself against a wooden crate and let out a long sigh.

"He roughed you up pretty badly."

"I'm bruised up, but at least I'm alive. Thanks to you."

Nancy blushed. "I didn't know what else to do. I nearly lost my balance on that step on the way down. It was the only thing I could find. I've heard that broken steps are dangerous and can kill you."

"Well, it didn't kill him."

"Really?" She looked relieved that her strike hadn't ended the man's life.

Lucas nodded, sensing her regret. He rubbed his ribs. "Yeah, he recovered fast. I had no choice but to kill him. A few more seconds and he'd have attacked again and probably killed us."

The stagnant stench that filled the stairwell was even more nauseating near the water. Rotten clams and dead fish littered both inlet banks. Fly swarms buzzed and crawled over the decaying carcasses. They laid their eggs while lapping up putrid juices with their sticky tongues.

A bell rang. Lucas searched nervously for the arrival of new guards. Instead, a barrage of chattering reverberated from the inclined, tiled corridor across the water.

Nancy gave Lucas a questioning, frightened look.

A scuttling shifter pack tapped their clawed paws down the tiled floor. They had thick bodies like short bulldogs and broad mouths with long pointy teeth. Their eyes glowed green and narrowed when they neared the water's edge. The guard regarded them without fear, and they, in turn, ignored him until Lucas shot the man through the back of the knee.

The guard fell to his side, clutching his shattered knee. Half of the shifters stood at the edge of the water, ripping and chewing the heads off of dead fish. The other half of the pack, when they smelled the fresh blood, turned on the injured man with crazed hunger.

"Come on," Lucas said.

Lucas ran the best he could to the dock with Nancy following close behind. The fallen guard was too busy fighting hungry shifters to notice them step into the boat. He fought two shifters off, but four more rushed him—two on each of his arms while the others tore into the man's bloody leg. Soft sounds of torn flesh were masked by screams and cracking bones.

Lucas turned the ignition switch and fired the boat engine. He turned the boat around in the inlet and steered toward the cave mouth. The river was covered with a layer of smoky white fog. A mist of rain sprayed over them. Due to the fog and chilling weather, boat traffic was at a minimum, but that didn't make navigation any faster.

After getting the boat to the safest, fastest speed possible with such poor visibility, Lucas hunted for a dock close to a busy highway where they could hitch a ride to safety. He wasn't certain where they could hide safely, but he wanted to find a place where TransGenCorp couldn't capture them again. Their best bet was to find Daniel. In order to stop Idris and TGC, it would take a lot of outside help to bring down the corrupt facility.

CHAPTER 49

Kat studied the back dust jacket of Daniel's book while Tyler drove. She was relieved, yet confused, that the Hutchinson family hadn't been victims in their own home. Except the cat had either been killed or injured and somehow escaped. The analysis of the cat's blood disturbed her. The Pittsburgh Lockdown File that Carpenter had given her showed the cat's DNA also had the same gene markers the shape shifters possessed. That information troubled her, but it explained why the cat didn't look or act like a normal feline.

"Carpenter wants us to go to their hotel and see if we can make contact with the Hutchinson's," she said.

Kat typed the hotel address into the console computer.

Tyler nodded but didn't reply. He kept his attention on the road. Occasional fog patches drifted across the roadway. The steady rain refused to lessen and the window defroster failed to keep the windshield from fogging up.

Kat glanced out the side window. A thick fog canopy hid the river from sight. "He also believes TGC has Lucas. The real Lucas."

"Really?" Tyler asked, looking her direction for the first time. "Why?"

"He didn't say. He's on his way back. I'm sure he'll tell us more when he returns."

Tyler slammed the brakes. He narrowly missed the tail end of the car in

174

the road ahead of them. A line of red taillights blazed for as far as they could see.

"Dammit," he said. "Must be a wreck up ahead."

"It's always something."

CHAPTER 50

$\mathcal{N}$ancy shivered when Lucas tied the boat at the marina. Her clothes were drenched with icy rain. Her fingers were shriveled like raisins.

Lucas hid the gun inside a storage compartment behind the boat driver's seat. They hurried past house and fishing boats until they came to a nearly vacant parking lot. Due to the weather, no fishermen stood outside their vehicles telling exaggerated stories about the fish that got away.

Emergency lights flashed on the highway. A police cruiser, an ambulance, and a wrecker set at the middle of the roadway. Several people pushed heavy-duty contractor brooms and rushed to clean up broken glass while paramedics tended to the injured.

Lucas cringed, seeing all the law enforcers nearby. The last thing he needed was a police officer recognizing him. Getting arrested would definitely make the evening news, and once again, he'd be handed over the TransGenCorp. But this time, he knew Idris would kill him without any worry about finding the device Lucas had stolen.

Lucas stared at the line of stalled vehicles. He nodded toward the far end parking lot exit about one hundred yards away. Nancy glanced in the direction he indicated. Policemen stood filling out their accident reports. A few others motioned one lane of traffic to maneuver around the wrecked vehicles.

"We have to be careful," Lucas said. "If they see me, they won't hesitate to arrest me."

"Why?"

"My clone framed me for murder this morning, so we need to avoid the police officers as best we can."

"What do we do?"

"Since the police are there, let's head to the other exit near the overpass bridge."

"How is that going to help us?"

"Let's see if we can gain charity from someone else stuck in traffic. If we're lucky someone will give us a ride."

CHAPTER 51

Johanna sat on the edge of the bed and wiped her eyes. Sadness and anger rushed through her. Everything she had worked her ass off to achieve since she had been freed from Pittsburgh was being destroyed and taken from her. The longer she sat inside the hotel room, the more she stood to lose.

"I have to get out of here," she said, rising to her feet and grabbing her purse. She unzipped it, saw the gun, and tucked the purse under her arm.

Julia placed her hands on Johanna's shoulders. "No, you can't go out there alone."

"I have to. Don't you understand? Two of my workers were killed. One was a friend who believed in everything I am doing."

"Honey," Lydia said. "They're after *all* of us."

"I have to go to the studio."

Daniel shook his head. "No, Johanna. You go there and they'll kill you, too. They've attacked our homes and your workplace in order to flush us out. They want to shake us up and make us vulnerable. The closer we stay together , the better a threat we are to them."

"I'm too mad to be vulnerable," she said.

Julia and Lydia wrapped their arms around Johanna in a tight embrace.

"Don't guys," Johanna said. "You'll make me cry."

"Crying's okay," Julia said, brushing Johanna's hair from her eyes.

"Not for me."

Daniel gave her a gentle stare. "If you die, we'll all mourn. Stay with us. We'll get them for what they've done."

"I guarantee that," Morton said.

"It's difficult losing the people close to you," Daniel said. "I lost so many when we were trapped in Pittsburgh. I eventually stopped allowing myself to get close to anyone. You're the only circle of friends I have left. I'll be damned if I let anyone attempt to take you away."

Johanna wiped tears from her eyes. "What do we do now?"

Daniel sighed. "I've been thinking about that. We can't stay here much longer. Eventually, they'll locate our vehicles and when they do, we'll be pinned inside this room. We might hold them off for a while, but a strong enough force will overtake us in the end. We can't sit with our backs to the wall, but we can't take foolish chances, either. I don't know if Lucas is still alive. I only hope that he is. However, we do know his clone is very much alive."

Lydia nodded. "Unless his injuries killed him. That's highly unlikely."

"Very unlikely the crash killed him," Morton said.

"He was in horrible shape when I left him," she said with a slight smile.

"But he's also not a normal human," Daniel said.

"I know," she replied.

"Why didn't you kill him when you had the chance?" Morton asked.

Lydia sighed. "I almost pulled the trigger and killed him, but I simply couldn't."

"Why not?" Johanna asked.

"Because in a sense, he's Lucas. I thought if I killed him, I could never mend my relationship with the real Lucas. I doubt that makes any sense at all."

"It does, actually," Julia said.

Lydia shook her head. "But leaving him alive will keep us guessing where he's at. I was too weak."

"Nonsense," Daniel said. "I don't know anyone in this room that would have shot and killed the twin of the one we loved the most."

"But he'll keep coming."

Morton flexed his claws. "Then we'll be ready when he shows up."

CHAPTER 52

Fifteen minutes of sitting in traffic unnerved Kat. She needed to get to the hotel as quickly as possible. Every minute they lost waiting was a minute TGC gained to find Daniel and his friends before she did.

"I'll be damned," she said.

Tyler looked at her. "What's wrong?"

Kat pointed toward the vehicles parked ahead of them. "That's the clone."

Tyler rose in his seat. Three cars ahead, Lucas rested his hands on the passenger door of a gray SUV and talked to the occupants through their lowered window. Although he seemed cordial and polite, in the end he gave a sad, understanding nod and then he moved to the next car.

Kat lowered her window a couple of inches to hear what Lucas said to the people in the car ahead of them. In spite of his friendly smile, his nervous demeanor made him look like a fugitive.

"What's he doing?" Tyler asked.

Kat shrugged. "I'm not sure. Looks like he's trying to get a ride."

"Who's the girl?"

"I don't know."

"Excuse me, sir," Lucas said to the driver of the car in front of Kat and Tyler. "Our car is broke down. Could you possibly give us a ride? No? I understand. Well, thank you anyway."

The teenage girl walking with him didn't seem frightened or that he was forcing her to stay with him. She had a genuine childlike trust.

Kat pulled her gun and held it between the seat and her door when Lucas approached their vehicle.

"Get ready," she said to Tyler.

Tyler looped his fingers through the door handle. Lucas smiled at Kat through the tinted glass. Kat lowered her window and smiled. Lucas opened his mouth to speak. One second later, her gun was pointed at Lucas' face.

Tyler shoved open his door, rested his elbows on the roof with his gun aimed at Lucas. He said, "FBI. Put your hands behind your head and don't move."

Lucas did as instructed without any argument. Kat stepped from the car and handcuffed him.

"Who are you?" she asked Nancy.

Tyler lowered Lucas into the backseat of the car.

"Nancy Helmsby."

"Dr. Helmsby's daughter?"

"Yes."

Kat frowned. "Why are you with him?"

"Lucas?"

"His clone."

"That's not his clone," Nancy said, shivering and hugging herself for warmth. More rain beaded through the white fog. Moisture dripped from her slicked down hair. "Look. May I get inside the car, too? I'm very cold."

Kat nodded in spite of her bewildered stare. "Of course. I'm sorry."

Once inside, Kat asked, "How can we be absolutely certain you aren't the clone?"

Lucas smiled. His teeth chattered. He shuddered from the cold, too. Streams of water formed lines down his face. "For starters, you're both still alive. The clone would have taken your gun before you saw his hand move. He'd have killed you both. Even if you had shot him, he heals rapidly. Besides that, when I was up ahead asking for a ride, he wouldn't have taken no for an answer. He'd have pulled the driver through the window and stolen the car."

"Guns don't intimidate him?" Tyler asked.

"Few things frighten him."

Kat dialed Carpenter on the car phone. "Sir, we just picked Lucas up."

Carpenter's voice filled with surprise. "The clone, you mean?"

"No, I believe we have the real Lucas in custody."

"How? Lucas?"

"Yes, sir?"

"It was our understanding," Carpenter said. "That TGC had somehow transferred you into their custody."

Lucas nodded at Kat. "Yes, they did."

"And you simply escaped?"

"Not simply, sir."

Nancy spoke up. "Actually we both escaped."

"Who is that?" Carpenter asked.

Kat smiled. "Dr. Helmsby's daughter, Nancy."

"TGC was holding you, too?" he asked.

"Yes." Nancy explained the circumstances surrounding her capture and how she escaped to free Lucas.

Traffic ahead of them began to move.

"So," Carpenter said. "You're saying TGC held you prisoner? Why?"

Lucas replied, "To get her father to do experiments he'd never do under normal circumstances."

"Like what? Cloning techniques?"

"Yes. Exactly."

"That makes no sense. Idris had already made clones," Carpenter said. "He didn't need Helmsby to make more."

"Why dirty your own hands when you can force someone else to do the job for you?"

"True," Carpenter said. "Kat, did you handcuffed him?"

"Yes."

Carpenter replied, "You can remove them if you're like me and believe him."

Kat looked deeply into Lucas' eyes and read his inner pain. The hurt also showed in the gentle creases around the edge of his eyes. Pain had worn those crows' feet. But so much innocence beamed that she couldn't stop herself from smiling. She turned the key and unlocked the cuffs.

"It's a strange story," she said. "But not too strange to be true."

Carpenter said, "I have Godfrey's Operation Meltdown File. I understand why Idris had both senators killed. But what I don't understand is why they kept you alive, Lucas. You care to elaborate?"

Lucas rubbed his wrists and shrugged his shoulders to loosen the tightness. "I have something that can destroy TransGenCorp and everything Idris holds sacred. But I have to get it back inside TransGenCorp in order for it to work."

"What exactly do you have? I can't find anything in the file about it."

"Trust me," Lucas said. "You're safer not knowing should I fail. Two dead senators and two guards are enough proof for that."

"Okay. I'll take your word for that right now. At least until we decide the best way to stage an attack on TGC."

Lucas popped his neck and interlocked his fingers, stretching them. "Idris threatened the lives of all my friends. He sent sweeper teams to kill them. I don't know that he did but that's what he claimed he did."

Kat nodded. "He did send teams, but from our evidence they all failed. We believe they're all alive at a hotel."

"If that's true, they need warned of the danger. Idris won't call off his hunt until they're all dead."

"We know," Kat said. "That's where we're going. Our biggest concern is that they won't answer their cell phones so we can help them."

Lucas grinned. "In times of crisis, Daniel becomes very paranoid. He never fully recovered from our ordeals at the research center. If he doesn't recognize the number, he's not going to answer."

"Lucas?" Carpenter said.

"Yes?"

"According to the Meltdown file, you've infiltrated TGC several times. Is this correct?"

"Yes, sir."

"So you know the guard detail and the facility's ground layout fairly well?"

"I'd say I know the outside as well as their guards."

"How about the inside of TGC?"

"I know the first two floors really well. And what I don't know about the lower levels, Nancy probably does. Hell, she even has a partial map."

"Okay," Carpenter said. "So you're telling me if we get you back inside TGC, you can shut it down?"

"I can."

"How many perimeter guards are there?"

"Twenty-four."

"That's it?"

"There's four more at the gate and six that patrol inside."

"I would have expected more. A lot more."

"The guards are hired ex-military, top elite mercenaries. Only the gate guards are American."

"Let me make a few phone calls," Carpenter said. "If you're able, we'll get you back inside TGC today. I want it shutdown immediately before more innocent people get killed by what experiments Idris has created."

"I can handle it. The sooner we stop him, the better. I know Idris is there right now. This time he won't get away."

"Kat," Carpenter said. "Reunite Lucas and Nancy with their friends. I'll get everything into motion on this end and call you back. Be careful."

CHAPTER 53

ex sat at the foot of the bed and barked incessantly at Morton.

"I told you dogs are stupid," Morton said. "Can't understand its mindless prattle."

"I thought you said that you could communicate with it," Daniel said.

Morton gave Daniel a shrewd, stern glare. He nodded at the dog. "You hear anything *German* coming out of its mouth? At least if it was part shifter, it would have enough brainwaves for me to have a halfway decent conversation with it."

Daniel frowned. "So he's not a shifter at all?"

"It's *just* a dog," Morton said with disgust.

"You're certain?"

Rex wagged his tail and barked.

"Well, you could kill him and do an autopsy to find out," Morton replied with a beaming smile.

"No. That's never an option."

Morton stared into the dog's eyes with grim determination. He stared long and hard until the dog whimpered and lay down, burying its eyes beneath its oversized paws.

***

LUCIAN TRIED to shunt his need for vengeance but his violent lust to shed blood became more than he could control at times. After Lucian had stolen the car, he left the frightened old man at the edge of the road. Lucian had managed not to shoot the man, but instead fired the gun into the air and pointed at the old man a second time. While Lucian held the gun on the man, the old fellow cautiously stepped from his vehicle, pleading for his life. It took everything inside Lucian to resist the urge to kill. Yet, he still fought with an inward need for vengeance.

Something had kept him from shooting the man, and he pondered for a reason. Then it occurred to him that the man had done him no harm and was innocent.

But Lucian still sought to find Lydia and make her suffer for his heartache and for nearly dragging him across the threshold of death. But finding her wasn't going to be an easy task.

With all the elimination teams sent to kill Lucas' friends, Lydia had no one she could run to. All she could do was run, but with a world full of hiding places, he guessed he'd never see her again. To quench his burning hatred, his desire to kill had become momentarily misplaced upon the elderly man. Now he realized whom he needed to kill—the man that created him into a life filled without hope, no eternity.

Idris.

❧

AFTER TYLER PULLED into the hotel parking lot, Lucas said to Kat, "Daniel may not answer your calls but forward a call to him through my cell number."

CHAPTER 54

Daniel's phone rang. He read Lucas' name and number on the message screen with a great deal of skepticism. He understood the danger of staying at the hotel much longer. He was also out of fresh ideas for what to do next. He decided to take the call. If it were somehow Lucas, that was welcomed news. But if not, and it was something sinister, they'd be forced to make a move.

"Lucas?" Daniel asked quietly.

"Yeah, Dan. It's me."

"Are you okay?"

"Now that I've escaped, I'm doing a lot better."

Lydia stepped closer to Daniel to listen. She shook her head and spoke in a whisper. "It could be his clone."

Daniel placed his hand over the phone. "I know. I'll be careful."

He placed the call on speaker and said to Lucas, "You've escaped? Where are you?"

"In your hotel parking lot."

"You're outside? How'd you find us?"

Johanna and Morton peered through the slit in the curtains. "If he's out there, I don't see him," Johanna said.

"I do," Morton said. "He's in the car with the tinted windows."

Lucas said, "I had some help. Nancy's with me. She's the only reason I got out of TransGenCorp alive."

"Nancy's in Germany, Luke. Helmsby told me that yesterday."

"That may be what he told you, but the truth is they were holding her prisoner to blackmail him."

"He's not lying," Morton said. "She's in the backseat with him."

Johanna looked at Morton. "How can you see them? The glass is tinted."

Morton smiled. "Just something this cat can do."

Rex barked. Morton glared at the dog. With sad eyes, it lowered its head to the carpet and sighed.

"Is that Rex?" Lucas asked. "You have my pup?"

"Lydia brought him here," Daniel said. Julia wrapped her arms around Daniel's waist and like Lydia; she was trying to hear what Lucas said. Felicia sat engrossed with the cartoons on the television.

"Really? Why was she at my house?"

"It's a long story. Let's put it this way. We're all fortunate to be alive at this point. Who are the people with you?"

"The FBI."

"FBI?"

"Yes. They're going to help me shut down TransGenCorp for good."

"How?"

"I'll explain that to you later. Right now, can we come inside?"

Daniel looked at Lydia. She put her hand on her gun and nodded.

"I'll know if it's really him," she said. "The clone has one thing less than Lucas. And only I would know that. Let him in, alone. If it's Lucas, we can allow the others in afterwards."

"You hear that?" Daniel asked.

"Loud and clear. Why the distrust in her voice?"

"Your clone tried to kill her last night."

"Damn, I'm sorry Lydia. I'm glad you managed to escape."

"Come alone," Daniel said. "So she can look you over."

Lucas laughed. "It's been awhile, but okay."

Johanna took her gun from her purse and stood at the window as Lucas crossed the parking lot. Julia took Felicia to the bathroom and locked the door. Daniel never thought he'd be this nervous again. Memories of the clone's past betrayal made him fear that this might not be Lucas and their lives were all in immense danger. He tried to reassure himself that it was Lucas because Nancy wouldn't be with the clone. But how far had Trans-GenCorp gone? Had they cloned her, too?

The room filled with tension. Only Morton remained calm. He sat on the table and watched the door. Did he have a sense that revealed to him that Lucas was Lucas? He hadn't expressed any warning when he saw Lucas through the window.

Lucas knocked on the door. When Daniel opened the door, Lydia and Johanna had their guns aimed at him.

Lucas raised his hands. "Nice to see you all again, too."

Daniel pushed the door closed. "Sorry, but we really have no choice."

"I understand. Believe me, I do. What do you want me to do? How can I prove to you that I'm who I am?"

Lydia motioned with her gun. "Put your hands against the wall and spread your legs."

Lucas obeyed without offering the slightest snide comment.

Lydia approached him cautiously. "Don't make any sudden moves."

Lucas stared at the floor. "I won't."

Rex padded across the floor and sat at Lucas' feet. His tail wagged from recognizing his master.

Lydia placed her left hand on the collar of Lucas' shirt and lifted the hair off the nape of his neck. The gun shook in her hand, and she holstered the weapon. Her eyes moistened with tears. The tattoo was there. She grabbed his arm and turned him toward her. With a fierce embrace, she wrapped her arms around him and buried her face against his chest.

"Oh, thank God," she whispered. "It's you. I was so worried about you."

Lucas hugged her tightly. "I've been worried sick over you, too. All of you."

Daniel shook his head and stared at Lydia. "I don't understand. How do you know it's him?"

Lydia turned her face toward Daniel but didn't loosen her hold on Lucas. "Lucas has a tattoo on his neck that I bought him for a present. That's how I knew the clone wasn't Lucas. He doesn't have it. And most people don't know it's there because Lucas always wears his hair down over his collar."

"Well, you have me there. I certainly had no knowledge about it," Daniel said.

Johanna put her gun back inside her purse. "I'll get Julia and Felicia."

Daniel nodded. "Nancy's with you?"

"Yes," Lucas replied. Lydia looked at him with a wide smile, and he kissed her. To Lydia, he said, "I've never wanted to be apart from you."

She took a deep breath. "I was ready to call you and tell you I wanted to try dating again. Then I saw the murders on television and your arrest. I was crushed."

"I told you about my clone."

"Continually."

"I didn't think you believed me."

"Not completely, but . . . I don't think I would have had you not been arrested. I knew you couldn't murder anyone in cold blood. But, I killed three men last night."

"They were trying to kill you. That's self-defense."

Lydia shook her head. "Yes, but it doesn't make me feel any less guilty. They're still dead."

"And you're alive," Lucas said with a smile. "I wouldn't want it the other way around. Those men were monsters assigned to kill you. Idris sent them. If they had succeeded, I'd have no reason left to live."

She smiled through her tears. "The same goes for me. Without you, there'd be no me."

"Guys, I hate to break this up," Daniel said. "But we need to figure out what we must do. Get Nancy and those agents up here. I'm interested in knowing how they plan to help us."

～

LUCIAN CALLED Idris from the car phone.

"We've had no report from you," Idris said. "Where's the team?"

"Dead."

"Dead? What happened?"

"Lydia's what happened. She picked them off one by one."

"Lydia?" Idris sounded amused.

"She almost killed me."

"Any idea where she went?"

"No."

"Don't worry, son. We'll find her soon enough. You can count on that. Report back to headquarters."

"I'm on my way," Lucian said, patting the gun on the seat beside him. He smiled a devilish grin.

CHAPTER 55

Carpenter arrived at the hotel less than fifteen minutes after Lucas entered the hotel room. Gil was with him.

"So everyone's here, Kat?" Carpenter asked, slipping out of his black trench coat. His shoulder holster secured his 9mm Beretta.

"Yes."

"Good. I'm relieved to see all of you alive. You've been under a great deal of stress. Not as much as the last time we all met, but I want you to know we're here to ensure your safety and protect you." He set a briefcase beside the table.

Kat looked surprised to see Morton sitting on the bed beside Felicia. "Daniel? That's your cat, correct?"

Daniel nodded. "Sure. Why?"

She blushed and handed him the book she had taken off his desk. "I'm sorry. I picked that up at your apartment."

"I see."

Kat folded her arms and stared intently at Morton. "I only took it because of the picture on the back cover. Your cat is of great interest to me."

"Why?"

She sighed. "When we went into your apartment we found three different pools of blood on your carpet. A fourth blood sample was found under the sofa that belongs to your cat."

Daniel shrugged. "And? I'm not certain what you're getting at."

"Well, the blood analysis our lab tech, Todd, worked up is a bit odd. Your cat doesn't seem to be a typical cat."

Daniel frowned. Julia stepped beside him and placed her arm around his waist. He said, "He doesn't behave like a typical cat, but what are you implying?"

"Forensic tests came back. Your cat seems to have the same blood markers as the shifters mentioned in your debriefing with the FBI three years ago. I take it, although I don't know why, this cat is like those blood-thirsty animals."

Morton's eyes perked. He turned and faced Kat. "I never thirst for blood. That's beyond repulsive."

Daniel shook his head. Kat and Carpenter stared at the cat. Bewilderment claimed their gazes.

"Yes," Daniel said. "He possesses some shifter genes that make him, well, very unique. Dr. Helmsby created him in the lab when we lived in the research center. He's one of a kind. Without him, none of my family would be alive."

"But he talks?" Kat smiled. "Helmsby did this?"

Carpenter frowned and stepped closer. His curiosity overwhelmed him. "How is that even possible?"

"The scientific explanation is beyond my comprehension. You'd have to ask Helmsby for more specifics, but I doubt he'd tell you."

Morton's lips curled into a smile. "I can explain it. Though it's over all your heads, but I know the systematics and the DNA anneals he used to align my sequences so I can talk and heal at remarkable speeds."

Kat laughed. "I see he doesn't just possess the ability to speak, but he has a high intellect, too. This definitely explains why I was so captivated by his picture on your book."

Daniel said, "I know. I told him to act normal, but . . ."

"I *did* act normal," Morton insisted.

"But," Kat said, facing Daniel. "Why would you bring a shifter into your home with your child?"

"He's the best pet and friend you could ask for," Julia said.

"But he should be dead, judging by the amount of blood he lost at your apartment."

"I heal fast," Morton said.

Kat nodded, suppressing a smile. "I see. I suppose you killed the three attackers in the house? Or were you there, Daniel?"

"No, I wasn't." Daniel said.

"I merely did what was expected of me," Morton said. "I defended our home. Daniel was here with Julia and Felicia."

Carpenter studied the cat with great interest. "You're telling us that you took out three men? A cat?"

"And *that* surprises you?" Morton asked, rising on all four legs. "I'm a shifter cat. They were humans. Well, except for one of them. He was a super human. His genes were tainted with canine DNA. One dog-ugly individual."

"But a cat?" Tyler asked.

Morton offered an even smile. "I'm not always a cat. What I become I don't like to bring out, but to protect my family, I go to necessary lengths. Felicia has never seen what I truly am. It would frighten her too much."

"Helmsby created Morton to protect me when I roamed the streets for food and supplies. Of course, I never knew he had made Morton in the lab. Not until Morton explained it all to me. He's been with me, us, ever since."

"Okay," Carpenter said. He looked at Lydia and said, "Lydia?"

"Yes?" she replied, still gripping Lucas tightly around the waist.

"There was quite a disturbance at your estate last night. Three men died there. From the report my men sent, and Gil can confirm the report, it seems someone who possesses the skills of a tactical soldier killed them. Did the clone turn on his own men?"

Lydia closed her eyes tightly. Tears etched down her cheeks. Lucas squeezed her and said, "It's okay. Tell them what happened."

Kat, with her arms still folded, looked from the cat to Lydia.

Lydia shook as she retold the incident.

"So you killed all three men?" Gil asked.

"In self-defense," she said defensively.

"We're not questioning your motive, Lydia," Carpenter said. "I know it was self-defense. They were there to kill you. But what I don't understand is how you countered their attacks with the professionalism you used. They were soldiers with sniper rifles and possibly had mercenary ties. They were very dangerous, highly trained men."

"I really don't understand how I did what I did. I just . . . reacted. I don't remember killing them. I do remember seeing their bodies afterwards." Her eyes were distant as she thought. "I felt threatened and I took action. Lucas and I trained with weapons a lot on my property. Guns, archery, knife throwing, and martial arts."

Carpenter grinned. "Really? All that? Like you were preparing for an attack?"

"She had to be prepared for anything," Lucas said. "I trained her because

I knew my clone was probably still out there. Even though she didn't really believe me, she went along with it."

Kat smiled. "That's definitely good for her."

"And me," Lucas said.

"Did you kill the clone?" Carpenter asked.

Lydia shook her head and lowered her gaze. "No, I had the opportunity, but I couldn't."

"Why not?"

"I couldn't pull the trigger because it would be like shooting Lucas. At least in my mind it would have been. I couldn't live with that. For some reason, I second-guessed myself, too. Just in case it was really him."

Carpenter nodded and grabbed his briefcase. "I can understand that. If my wife had had a clone, I'd feel the same way even if her clone were evil. How could you be absolutely certain?"

"Yes, exactly," Lydia said. "But he never tried to kill me. He acted like he wanted to protect me."

"That's his deception," Daniel said. "He did the same thing to us in Pittsburgh."

Lucas nodded. "That's how they programmed him. Gain peoples' trust and then kill them."

"But you figured out he was Lucas' clone?" Kat asked. "How?"

She explained the tattoo and then said, "Little things he should have known, he didn't. These were things Lucas wouldn't have forgotten."

Johanna stepped closer. "Have you found out anything new about my studio?"

"Nothing new," Kat said. "I'm sorry. They killed two of your employees and torched the place. I believe they knew you'd figure out their intent."

Julia nodded. "Of course we'd know. They sent men after us not long after the news reported Lucas' arrest. We were the first attacked. In broad daylight, too."

"I'm not familiar with this," Kat said.

Carpenter frowned. "No. I've not heard about this, either."

Julia explained the car chase in fast detail.

"The police never gave us a report of your call," Kat said. "It may have been overlooked by the dispatch as not being related to this, but we can find the report if necessary."

"But," Carpenter said. "If what Lucas told us earlier is true, I don't believe we have much longer to worry about TGC. Once we shut down that facility for good, all these problems should end."

Carpenter cleared the hotel table and rolled out a map. "This is an aerial map of TGC. Any idea, Lucas, how many perimeter guards are posted and their positions?"

Lucas ran his finger along the L path of the fence line. "Their main concentration is on these two strips of the fence. The fence line that runs alongside the river is the least guarded due to the steep, rocky embankment. That section of fence is also electrified."

Carpenter eyed Lucas. "At your best estimate, how many men are posted along the river?"

"No more than two."

"Okay," Carpenter said. "Besides Dr. Helmsby, do we have anyone else we should take the precaution to protect once we reach the inside?"

"A female guard named Yvonne," Nancy said.

"Yvonne? The one who helped you escape?" Kat asked.

"Yes."

"Anyone else?" Carpenter asked, looking from person to person. They shook their heads.

"Well," Daniel said. "Kyle's still there, but Helmsby insists that Kyle's not going to live much longer."

"How bad is he?" Lucas asked.

"Deteriorating rapidly, but he'd never be the same even if he did live."

Carpenter nodded. "We'll try to get him out, too, but if his condition is that severe, I can't guarantee it."

"I understand."

Carpenter rolled up the map. "Lucas, get whatever gear you need or tell us where you need to go and we'll take you to get it."

Lucas picked up Rex and tucked him under his arm. "This is all I need."

Kat and Carpenter exchanged glances. In unison they said, "A dog?"

"It's a long story. When this is over, I'll give you a detailed report."

Carpenter smiled. "Fair enough. The rest of you sit tightly. I have a lot of agents posted outside to protect you."

Daniel shook his head. "No, I go with Lucas."

Lydia tightened her hug on Lucas. "Me, too."

"Count me in," Johanna said, grabbing her purse. "It's the least I can do for my producer and friend."

Morton jumped from the bed to the table and said, "No one goes anywhere without me."

In exasperation, Carpenter shook his head. "I appreciate that all of you want to help, but the FBI needs to handle this. I'll have a sniper team in position within the hour and the National Guard is on standby."

"Don't you understand?" Daniel said. "You try to take TransGenCorp by force and Helmsby is dead. Idris will kill him without hesitation."

"What do you suggest?" Carpenter said.

"I'm going back," Nancy said.

Kat shook her head in protest. "No, dear, you can't."

"I have to," she replied. "He's my father."

"She'll be okay," Lucas said. "She'll be with us."

"How do you plan to get inside?" Carpenter asked. "They'll shoot you on sight."

Daniel's cell phone rang. He waved a finger at Carpenter. "Let me answer this and then I'll tell you. It's Dr. Helmsby."

"Dad?" Nancy whispered.

~

"Hello?" Daniel said.

"Thank God, you're alive," Helmsby said. "I heard about the attack on your home and Johanna's studio. Have you heard from her or Lydia?"

"They're okay. They're with us."

Carpenter frowned and shook his head at Daniel for giving out too much information.

"I warned you, Dan. I told you they'd come after you."

Helmsby's voice was shaky, nervous. He could hear Helmsby swallow hard. Daniel detected someone breathing heavily near Helmsby.

"Yes, you did," Daniel said.

"I know where Lucas is."

"Where?"

"I can't discuss it over the phone, in case it's bugged. Come here like you did yesterday, and . . ." Helmsby's voice stopped short. In a choked whisper, he said, "Then I can tell you."

"I'm afraid I'm not in the most trusting mood right now."

There was a long silence. Helmsby gasped and took in several large gulps of air. Someone had forced him to make the call. That someone was probably Idris.

"You'll be safe here with me. I promise. I'd like to see Lydia and Johanna again."

"Have you heard from Nancy lately?"

"No, Dan. It's been a long time." He sounded near tears. "You're coming, though, aren't you?"

"We'll be there. But there's something else you should know."

"What?"

"The sabbatical is over."

Daniel disconnected the call.

~

HELMSBY HUNG up the phone with a shaking hand. Idris removed the gun from Helmsby's temple.

Idris holstered the gun and smiled at Yvonne. "I have a meeting that requires my immediate attention. Notify me when they enter the gate. Until then, Yvonne, watch his every move."

"Yes, sir," she replied. She waited until Idris marched through the door and down the hall before she whispered, "Are you okay, Bob?"

A nervous smile crept across his pale face. "Actually, I'm better than you might expect. Daniel told me that the sabbatical is over, so that means Nancy must be with him. You did it, didn't you? You freed her?"

She smiled. "A promise is a promise."

"Indeed. If it costs me every penny . . ."

Yvonne took his arm, looked caringly into his eyes, and shook her head. "Don't promise me your fortune, Bob. You promised you'd help. That's all I expect. Nothing more. It may be I'm a woman who cannot bear children. If so, I have to accept it. Besides, we need to get out of this place alive. I'll be damned if Idris hurts you or your friends."

"Once they arrive, Idris plans nothing less than to kill them right in front of me. He wants me to suffer before he ends my life."

"Why does he hate you?"

Helmsby released a sound so pitiful she couldn't tell if it was an attempt to laugh or cry. "Let's just say that we have a horrid history and leave it at that. When he discovered the military placed me in charge of his experiments, he planned to take it back at the cost of my life and my friends as well. A few of the other Pittsburgh survivors were killed recently. They died in suspicious ways. I believe Idris had a hand in it."

Yvonne flashed a bold, determined smiled. "I have a few plans of my own. He'll be the last to expect them, too."

CHAPTER 56

*A*gent Denton arrived at the hotel and set a box of Kevlar bulletproof vests down on the table. He left the room and returned to the parking lot.

Carpenter reluctantly handed a bulletproof vest to Daniel, Lydia, Johanna, and Lucas. "I suppose there's nothing I can do to talk any of you out of this?"

"No," Daniel said. "We survived worse in Pittsburgh. We worked best as a team."

Carpenter shook his head and finally, he handed the last vest to Nancy. "I still don't see the point in taking Nancy along with you. She's still a child in my eyes."

Lucas slipped his vest on. "She'll go with me by boat. We'll re-enter the cave. When we find Helmsby, she can lead him back to the dock. I want them safely out of TransGenCorp before the meltdown process begins."

Carpenter looked at his watch. "The sniper team is already in position. We should reach the gates in thirty minutes."

"Good." Daniel said. "Make sure we get through the front doors before the snipers fire a single shot. And by all means, *don't* let the outside guards circle in behind us."

"I'll definitely alert the SWAT commander. National Guard units are positioned two blocks away. They'll move on my signal."

Denton entered the room with another box. He placed it on the table.

"Kat," Carpenter said. "Distribute the ear mike receivers to them. You're automatically linked to us with these. We can hear you and give you instructions, if necessary."

Kat took Julia aside. "Gil will stay here with you and Felicia to make sure no one comes through the door. We'll have more agents posted outside. Use the radio to contact us if necessary."

Julia nodded. "Thanks."

Carpenter looked at Tyler. "Tyler, you and Kat can drive Nancy and Lucas back to the marina."

"Sir," Tyler said. "If you don't mind, I'd like to ride with Agent Denton."

Carpenter glanced at Kat. She looked shaken about his request. He nodded. "Okay, fine by me. Kat, you and I will drive them."

Kat forced a smile. "Okay, sure."

CHAPTER 57

*I*dris met Benson at the genetic soldier incubation chambers. Idris stared at one of the glass cases. "How about we put these soldiers to the test?"

Benson's eyebrows rose in question. "What do you mean?"

"I have arranged for Daniel and the others to meet with Dr. Helmsby. I need some of these men brought out of incubation so we can test their prowess."

"I'm afraid that's impossible."

Idris' eyes narrowed. "Why? They're fully developed."

Benson sighed, shaking his head. "Their bodies are fully developed. Not their brains. Not their minds. You can't rush the development of a neurological organ like the brain without risking cataclysmic malfunctions or abnormalities that could induce permanent comatose victims. It takes weeks, perhaps months, of mental conditioning to program their memories, instincts, and military tactics."

"So out of all the men we've created, you're telling me that none of the one hundred forty men are usable yet?"

"We have six out of chamber that are currently undergoing Phase III mental expansion."

"Good. Suit them up and tell me when they're ready."

"Sir, I must warn you. They're far less prepared than the one the cat killed."

"The cat was a shifter."

"True, but it was also an animal he'd never seen before. His curiosity probably helped get him killed. Why not bring in some outside guards to comb the halls?"

"Can the six men fire a weapon?"

Benson nodded. "Yes, of course. With remarkable accuracy."

"Then that's all I'm interested in. It's enough."

"But why?"

Idris smiled. "They're Helmsby's co-creation. Before he and his daughter die, I want to make certain he did his job properly and didn't skimp on the science. If he did it correctly, I don't have any more use for him."

Benson grimaced. "Without them being fully developed and if they fail, you'll never know."

"Just have them ready."

Idris turned and walked away.

A PATROL GUARD stopped Idris in the hallway and told him that Nancy had escaped.

"That's impossible!" He shook his head and bit down on his cigar. "Was the door locked?"

"Yes. Still closed and locked."

"What about the ventilation system? Did you check the screen?"

"Yes. The screws are bolted tight. The door lock hasn't been manipulated."

"What about Lucas? Have you checked his room?"

"I'm headed that direction right now, sir."

"I'll walk with you."

When Idris noticed the door to Lucas' room was ajar, he stopped mid-stride and pulled his 9mm. The guard beside him did the same. Although he expected the room to be empty like Nancy's he also remembered how Lucas had used guerrilla tactics when he escaped TGC the first time. In desperate circumstances, Lucas was cunning and had even killed some of Idris' best men, which was a reason he treasured having Lucian—a spawn with similar talents.

Had Lucas not stolen the most valuable possession in TGC, Idris would have killed him days ago. Now that opportunity might have passed him by.

The guard pushed the door inward with his boot and aimed the gun across the room as the door gap widened. The door thudded softly against the doorstop. Idris stepped into the room. Seeing no one, he holstered his weapon.

His eyes surveyed the room. On the bed lay the metal cuffs and a key. Above the bed, the battered vent cover teetered by a couple of bent screws.

Idris fumed. His seething anger flushed his face red. A swollen vein pulsed in the center of his forehead. He faced the guard with a narrowed glare. "I thought her air vent was sealed shut."

"It is, sir. I swear."

Idris thrust a finger toward the vent. "How do you explain that? That's the point of entry soldier. Only she would have been narrow enough to come through the ventilation system."

"The vent in her room is sealed."

Idris took a deep breath and then exhaled cigar smoke. "Very well. If that's true, someone has turned on me and helped her escape. Review the surveillance tapes. Find out who visited her room last and report back to me. I want that person dead."

"Yes, sir." The guard turned and ran down the hall.

Idris dialed an extension number on his cell phone. "Benson, are those men suited up and ready? Dammit, get a move on then. There's a change in plan. Instead of positioning them on the ground floor, here's what I want you to do . . . "

CHAPTER 58

*L*ucian drove through TransGenCorp's security gate and parked in the lot closest to the front entrance. He wondered if the old man he had stolen the car from had gotten home safely. Remorse gripped him. He hoped that when he had fired the gun above the man's head that nothing serious had happened to harm him. The man might have been frightened into a panic attack or worse—a heart attack. But car theft had been Lucian's only option to get back to TransGenCorp quickly.

He sat in the car for several seconds. It dawned upon him that this was the first time he was actually concerned about the safety of another human. This new emotion was something he'd never felt before, but still, his urge to rid his vengeance by killing Idris seemed justified. He understood that he must prevent further torment from his superior. Not just for him, but for any others in the future. Death was the only way to stop Idris.

Lucian put one gun behind his belt and tucked the other in the front. He grabbed a paper bag and tucked it under his arm before getting out of the car and entering TGC.

The seated guard at the front desk entertained a brief conversation before Lucian crept into the neighboring silent hallway. He paused outside a door midway down the hall and looked both directions before he entered.

Once inside, Lucian hurried across the room and pulled a key ring from his pocket. He inserted a key into the door and turned. The lock clicked. He twisted the knob and stepped inside.

Lucian smiled. "Remember me? It's me, Lucas. You remember?"

"Yes. You . . . shot me."

"No, that was my clone. I'd never hurt you," he lied.

He opened the bag and took out a foil-wrapped chocolate bar. "I bet they don't let you have these, do they?"

The timid hand snatched the bar from Lucian and bit a large chunk and chewed.

"That's good, isn't it? It's okay. Idris won't know."

"I . . . hate . . . Idris."

"I know and I understand why."

"I *hate* him."

"I know, Kyle. That's why I'm getting you out of here."

CHAPTER 59

Kat and Carpenter drove Lucas and Nancy back to the marina. Kat worried over how badly she had hurt Tyler. His request to ride with Denton certainly raised Carpenter's curiosity, but he hadn't questioned her about the situation yet. However, she couldn't forget the look in Tyler's eyes. Of course, she didn't know if there ever was a way to let someone down easily when they held affection and interest in you.

Lucas pointed to the dock where they had left the boat. Carpenter stopped the car and said, "Are you certain you want to use the back entrance into TGC?"

Lucas picked Rex up off the seat and shrugged. "There's really nothing else we can do. As long as they believe we're in their custody, it's best not to show ourselves at the front gate."

"And if they've discovered your escape?" Kat asked with worried eyes.

Lucas smiled. "Then it's going to be one hell of a game of hide-and-seek."

"Keep your ear mikes in place. If anything dangerous occurs, I'll contact you."

Lucas nodded. "Much appreciated."

"Keep a close eye on Nancy," Kat said.

"I'll protect her with my life."

$\mathcal{D}$aniel pulled to the TransGenCorp security gate. Tyler and Denton drove past and parked across the street. They were to wait for Carpenter and Kat to return from the marina. And then, under Carpenter's command, all chaos ensued.

Johanna wiped her sweaty, restless hands on her pants. The confidence she had wielded at the hotel room faded. Fear tainted her eyes.

"There's still time for you to back out, Johanna," Daniel said. "You don't have to go inside."

She stared through the gate with narrowed eyes. "Yeah, I do. For Mike and Clint. They died because Idris wanted me dead. I have to do this."

"You're sure?"

She nodded. "I'll be okay."

Lydia, however, showed no emotion whatsoever. Her solemn eyes studied TransGenCorp's gate guards, then, without turning her head, she located the closest perimeter guards. Her right hand was hidden inside her jacket pocket. Daniel knew she was holding her gun.

Lydia's eyes reflected a coldness that brought chills up his spine. She looked nothing like the tired lady that had arrived at the hotel room. Never had he seen her like this. She appeared more sinister than her clone that had bested Johanna three years earlier. She meant business, and he was truly glad she was on his side.

An armed guard approached the driver side door, so Daniel lowered his window.

"Daniel Hutchinson?" he asked.

"Yes."

The guard motioned his comrade inside the glass booth. "Dr. Helmsby is expecting you. Head right in."

The gate arm lifted and Daniel drove through. He looked at Lydia in the rearview mirror. When her eyes met his, he said, "That was a little too easy."

She gave a single nod. "I agree."

Perhaps Daniel was more apprehensive on this visit than the previous, but all the guards focused their attention on his vehicle as he drove through the parking lot. Their glares indicated their inner hunger to kill. They didn't possess a macho guard attitude. Harsh coldness reflected in their angered eyes. All they needed was a signal to fire and without any hesitation they would carry out the order. Daniel began to doubt they'd leave TransGen-Corp alive.

"They're watching us, Dan," Johanna said nervously.

"You noticed that, too?"

"Yes. I'm not very comfortable."

"Yeah, but we can't turn back now."

Johanna nodded. "I know."

Morton crawled out from beneath Daniel's seat and hopped up beside Lydia.

"Did I miss anything?" he asked.

"Not yet, my little friend," Daniel said. "But if you want to see a lot of heated action, I believe we stepped into the right playing field. We're dead in the middle of it."

"I'm up for that," Morton said.

Johanna cringed. "Did you have to use the word, *dead*."

"Sorry," Daniel replied.

"I'm too uptight right now," she said.

"I understand."

Morton grinned. "The only dead will be those who attack."

"Let's hope so," Daniel whispered. But, for some reason, he didn't think that would be the case.

CHAPTER 61

$\mathcal{Y}$vonne checked the ammo clip in her 9mm. She smiled at Helmsby. "There's something more about Nancy's escape that I didn't tell you."

"What?"

"When I sent her through the ventilation system, I gave her directions to where Lucas was being held. I also gave her a key to unlock his restraints. So if Nancy is with Daniel, Lucas is too."

Helmsby was stunned. "Then why the hell are they coming back here?"

"My guess is to rescue you."

He shook his head. "Why?"

She smiled. "Why wouldn't they?"

Helmsby shrugged, obviously at a loss for words.

"Do you think they'll bring guns?" she asked.

"Definitely. Why?"

"Come with me. They might get through the gate with them, but they will never get past the metal detectors down on the ground floor."

Helmsby took brisk steps to keep up with her. She turned into the main hall that led to the front entrance, and the seated guard spotted Helmsby behind her. The guard rose and aimed his gun at Helmsby.

"Put down the gun, Henry," Yvonne demanded. Her voice was steady, and the gun in her hand was even steadier. She had a clear shot at the man's forehead.

"Yvonne! What the hell is he doing out here? You know he's not supposed to come anywhere near the front doors."

Helmsby stopped walking.

"He's with me, Henry, so put your gun down."

Henry didn't flinch at her order. Thick veins bulged in his neck. "I have my orders, Yvonne."

"I have mine, too. Back down now, or I swear I'll kill you without another warning. I outrank you so holster your weapon."

Frustration built and flushed Henry's face red. His brow furrowed and his lower lip trembled. Tears welled at the corners of his eyes.

"Do what you have to do, ma'am," Henry said. "But my orders are to shoot Dr. Helmsby on sight if he comes anywhere near the front desk. You know what happens if I don't carry out that order?"

Yvonne's jaw tightened. "I know what *will* happen if you attempt to carry it out. Think about it."

Tears streaked his face. "Damned if I do, and damned if I don't. It's that kind of decision you cannot win."

Henry's hand shook. For a moment, he looked as though he might comply, but then his jaw tightened. His trigger finger moved.

She fired without another word of warning.

Henry collapsed to the floor, dead.

"Yvonne?" Helmsby said with surprise. "You . . . killed him."

She turned and shook her head. Her voice lowered with remorse. "Don't question it. He wouldn't have backed down. He was going to kill you. Besides that, he was right. Idris would have killed him for not carrying out the order. He took the quicker route by having me kill him. I'm not proud that I had to, either."

"I know," Helmsby said. "But now, Idris will . . ."

"Kill me?" she laughed. "I don't plan on staying here. Whenever your friends arrive, I'm leaving with you. I don't know what their plan is, but I do know one thing."

"What?"

"They aren't going to march you out the front door. If Henry was willing to die, you can bet the perimeter guards will fire without question. The only reason we came this direction was so I could shut off the metal detectors. While I'm at it, I'll turn off the surveillance cameras, too."

Yvonne squatted down behind the desk and flipped off two long rows of switches on a control panel. She popped open the circuit box on another panel and pried two breakers from their connections. She slid them into her pocket.

"Let's go," she said.

"What about him? Won't the outside guards come inside?"

"Fortunately, the outside glass is mirror tinted. No one saw him fall. The sound of the gunshot probably wasn't even heard outdoors. His body should also keep your friends more cautious when they enter."

Helmsby noticed movement outside the front door. He pointed, at first in fear, and a couple seconds later, he smiled. Daniel pulled the door open, letting Johanna and Lydia step inside, and Morton pattered in behind them.

Once the door closed behind Daniel, Yvonne locked the doors. "This will buy some additional time," she said. "Should anyone inside set off alarms, I don't think the outside guards will stay out there long."

Helmsby rushed to Daniel, shook his hand, and then he embraced him. "Is Nancy okay? Where is she?"

"She's with Lucas. They're coming by boat."

He frowned. "Boat?"

"They're going to enter through the docks on the lowest level."

"She's coming *back* here? Why?"

"For you. We couldn't talk her out of it."

"But why? I can leave with you. That doesn't require her to be here."

"She's going to lead you two back to the docks while the rest of us stop Idris." Daniel looked at Yvonne. "There's only one problem."

"What?" she asked.

"Lucas doesn't know how to get from sublevel 3 to sublevel 2."

Yvonne smiled. "Easy enough. At least we know where to meet him."

Johanna cringed when she saw the dead guard behind the desk. "What happened?"

"Insubordination," she replied.

"I see. Pretty strict repercussions," Daniel said.

Yvonne shrugged. "It seems I'm the only one here willing to die to protect Bob. The rest are willing to die trying to kill him."

Morton sat and licked his forepaw. His eyes glowed crimson red. "We're here now, so let's even the odds."

CHAPTER 62

The fog lifted from the river, but the thick gray sky brought a new threat of intense thunderstorms. Lightning forked the distant sky and the subtle echo of angry thunder shrouded the hope of sunshine.

Rex placed his paws on the side of the boat and watched the choppy water. Lucas kept the engine at a moderate speed. The afternoon wind blew mist over them. Nancy huddled under a plastic tarp while Lucas steered the boat.

Her teeth chattered. "Did your father ever spend a lot of time with you when you were young?"

"We hunted and fished a lot. Why?"

"Just curious. My father has never spent any real quality time with me. He kept my nose buried in books all the time. Scientific books. Nothing else. We never really did much together outside of him tutoring me. I wish he was more compassionate with me than to his scientific discoveries."

Lucas glanced at her from the corner of his eye. "After the past three months of being kept away from you, I believe he'll be more than ready to spend time with you."

"Maybe."

"Separation and isolation changes people. It makes you realize how important certain people are in your life and how much you value them once they're gone."

"Like Lydia?"

Lucas grinned. "Exactly. I'm speaking from my own personal experience."

When they approached the mouth of the cave, he killed the engine. The boat maintained enough speed to coast to the docks without the aid of paddling. Had they not exited from the cave earlier, he'd never known the open rock crevice was there. The huge tree pine branches along the edge hung like curtains and concealed the opening.

Before they reached the dock, Lucas turned the boat around so Nancy wouldn't have to whenever she and Helmsby departed. He gave her a quick rundown on how to start the engine and how much to push the throttle.

Lucas took the gun from behind the boat seat. After their earlier confrontations, he expected the docks to have more guards posted. But apparently, no one had patrolled since he and Nancy escaped. All that remained of the dead, mauled guard was his clothes and a few bones. The shifters had returned to wherever they had come from.

Lucas placed Rex on the dock. He climbed out and helped Nancy step up.

Lucas lightly tapped his earpiece. "We're inside, Carpenter. All's clear at the docks, so we're heading up."

"Good. Keep us posted."

Lucas pointed. "We take the stairs. I don't know where the sloped corridor goes, but we both know that's where the shifters came from."

The stairwell lights were still on as they headed up. When they reached the dead soldier, his remains horrified them. His forehead was a sunken pool of pinkish brown goop. His skin was leathery and shriveled like a raisin.

Nancy looked at Lucas. "What caused that?"

"I don't know. Let's go find your father."

"Is it contagious?"

"I hope not."

CHAPTER 63

*L*ucian led Kyle to the chemical storage center. The shelves were lined with glass bottles. Some contained dry chemicals. Others liquid. Vials and flasks covered the tables and countertops. Several Bunsen burners were set up for use, but none were lit.

Kyle's weak deep-set eyes studied the room with great interest. Dark circles puffed beneath his otherwise bright eyes. Walking was difficult for him, almost painful. What little energy he possessed was expended by the time they reached this room. Even with his clothes on, anyone could tell how emaciated his body had become. He wasn't anything more than a skin-covered skeleton.

A door slammed farther down the hall. Lucian placed his hand on his gun and headed for the door. "Stay here, Kyle. I'll be back in a few minutes. I promise."

Kyle didn't reply. He leaned against a table and struggled to keep his balance. The second sublevel had a nine-room floor grid. The blueprint for this floor looked like a tic-tac-toe board because of how the two sets of double halls intersected.

Lucian had left Kyle in the south center room. The slamming door sounded from the far north end of the hall. The north central room was the main computer center—the brain of TGC—where all the research data was stored.

The door directly south of the computer room was one of Dr. Benson's labs. If the door that slammed was the main computer room, it meant Idris was possibly there.

Lucian pulled his gun and headed to the north end of the hall. Before he reached the first intersecting hall, an armed man stepped into view. Lucian sensed immediately that this wasn't a regular hall patrol, but a genetic soldier like himself.

The soldier was armed with a military assault rifle. Lucian didn't understand why this man was stationed in the hall. These soldiers were engineered for assassination squads. Why waste their value using them for patrollers? Having one in the hall signified that TransGenCorp was under attack.

Lucian wondered if Idris considered him a threat now that he had returned, especially since he had not reported his failure at Lydia's house. Had word gotten back to Idris about Brockton supplying Lucian with the small case of enhancers? If so, that was enough to infuriate Idris and send him further over the edge. Total disregard for a direct order made Lucian an enemy. Idris wasn't one to forgive offenses, and any enemy must be killed.

Lucian suddenly found himself worrying about Brockton's welfare and how far Idris' punishment might have gone for the scientist and Lucian's only friend. He realized that Brockton was the only person in his life that he could esteem as a positive parental role model. Idris never held those qualities. Before Lucian could dwell on that thought, or how to find Brockton, the soldier in the hallway must be eliminated.

Lucian wished he had a better weapon, but he wasn't one to turn and run. Instead, he crouched and slid his back against the wall. The soldier never noticed him.

The more he thought about the soldier, the more he believed it possible that this man was placed here to stop Lucian from finding Idris. Idris overreacted with heavy-handed threats. However, Lucian had discovered that Idris was also hasty in his thinking processes. He never mapped out his plans or goals. He acted with rash decisions, which caused Idris to reap more failure than success.

Lucian didn't have time to ponder over the soldier. For a moment he thought he might sneak by the assassin without being seen. Something crashed in the room where he had left Kyle. The noise caught the soldier's attention, and the man quickly turned. He noticed Lucian, raised his rifle, and without question or word, he squeezed the trigger.

Instinct had taught Lucian a lot during his six years of life. The man shooting was an infant compared to Lucian. When the trigger tightened, Lucian dropped flat to the floor on his stomach. He rolled quickly, came to his feet, and fired. The bullet struck the man in the side of the head. His assailant collapsed, and three more soldiers rushed into the cross section of the halls.

Two rounds hit the floor, flaking bits of tile into the air. Lucian turned and bolted toward the chemical storage room. He dove for the open door threshold and slid out of the line of fire. He spun around and slammed the door shut.

Kyle lay on the floor beside the table. He wasn't moving. He didn't seem to be breathing. His condition was much worse than Lucian had anticipated. Apparently before Kyle had fallen he had grabbed a stainless steel tray of utensils for support. The contents were spilled across the floor. Lucian hurried to him and placed two fingers against Kyle's throat to check for a pulse.

"Dammit!" Lucian closed his eyes and shook his head. "I'm sorry. I should have gotten to you sooner."

A rush of anger and remorse flooded through him.

The thudding rhythm of heavy boots marched down the hall and stopped outside the door. Lucian didn't have a key to lock the door, and even if he possessed one, the thick wooden door wasn't enough to stop gunfire from splintering through.

He rummaged through drawers and the cabinets. He found a glass gallon bottle of ether alcohol. He took the bottle and a cloth towel. After twisting off the lid, he tucked one corner of the towel into the mouth of the bottle until only one-third of the cloth remained exposed.

The doorknob turned. He lit the towel. When the door burst open, he heaved the bottle across the room. The glass shattered against the wall, igniting the alcohol, and splashing liquid flame down the soldier's body.

The man recoiled, screaming in pain. He batted at the licking flames. Lucian raised his 9mm and fired a round through the man's forehead. His flaming body dropped backward and fire leapt off him onto the second soldier's legs. This man ignored the fire and raised his rifle. Lucian dropped behind a table.

As the soldier approached, Lucian slid to the edge of the table and fired two shots into the man's leg. The soldier dropped to one knee. Realizing his pants were burning and melting into his flesh, his eyes. He dropped his rifle and patted at the flames.

Before the third soldier entered the room, Lucian made his attack. The man fought to extinguish the flames without any success. Lucian kicked the man in the chest, knocking the man backwards onto the floor. Lucian grabbed the rifle. With only seconds to spare, he pulled his knife from his ankle sheath before the next man entered the room.

Lucian flung the knife, fast and hard, and it lodged in the man's heart. The man's eyes grew larger, and he fired three rounds into the ceiling before collapsing to the floor.

Lucian took his handgun and fired a round into each soldier's head. It was the only method he knew that killed a genetic soldier like himself. Severe head trauma was the most difficult injury to heal. Most often, it proved fatal.

These soldiers guarding the hallway were neophytes. Their forced maturity made them incapable of quick thinking. It didn't guarantee that they couldn't kill him though. Lucky accidents could happen. He had to keep his wits keen. Any distractions meant death.

With rifle in hand, Lucian slipped to the edge of the door and peered into the hallway. Another man fired. The bullet grazed the wall just inches about Lucian's head. Bits of concrete block exploded. He ducked back into the room and a second shot struck where his head had been. He propped the rifle against a table, pulled his handgun, and heaved one of the dead soldiers up, carrying the man's corpse to the door. Using the man's body for a shield, he stepped into the hallway.

Three rounds lodged into the dead man's chest, which gave Lucian enough time to fire four rounds of his own. Two hit the assailant's stomach while the last two went through his forehead. He dropped the dead body shield to the floor.

"Time for you, Idris," Lucian whispered through clenched teeth. "It's time you die."

He stepped into the hallway intersection, and another soldier struck him in the jaw with the butt of a rifle. Lucian staggered backwards, seeing flashes of light beneath his closed eyes. He blinked several times to clear his vision and steadied himself on one knee to keep from falling. His adversary kicked him in the face. Blood splattered into the air from his mouth and nose.

Lucian growled and gnashed his teeth. The soldier came straight at him again. For a moment, it seemed the room spun in strange colors

This soldier was different from the others. He didn't want to use his gun for a quick kill. Instead, he lusted to inflict as much pain as possible. While Lucian's vision continued to dim, the man kicked him again.

Lucian toppled backwards. He rolled, tried to gather himself, but he wasn't given enough time to get to his feet. The soldier grabbed Lucian's hair and slammed his face onto the floor several times. The hallway grew darker.

Lucian shook his head, rolled, but instead of getting to his feet, he mule-kicked the man with both feet, striking the man's sternum. Ribs cracked. The impact lifted the man into the air. He landed on his back and his head struck the side of the doorframe. His rifle skidded down the hall. He paid no attention to his loss of weapon and was back on his feet in an instant.

Lucian struggled to stand, but before he attained his balance, the man pulled a long blade from his belt sheath and smiled.

Lucian reached down and yanked his knife from the dead soldier's chest. A sick, sucking sound smacked as the flesh released the blade. Blood dripped on the floor from the tip of the knife. With a firm grip on the handle, Lucian faced the genetic soldier. The man showed no fear, but then, neither did Lucian. They faced one another and paced in a circle.

The man made a wild swing. A flash of silver glistened beneath the fluorescent lights. He lunged for Lucian's face, but Lucian parried the attack, slashing his enemy's forearm. Dark blood pooled in the deep laceration. Small streams of crimson spilled from the wound. Beads of blood dripped and splattered on the floor.

The soldier's face revealed no pain, no concern. He gritted his teeth and stepped forward, making another advance. Metal cut through the air. The blade split Lucian's shirt but missed flesh. The soldier came again, with an overhead slice. Lucian sidestepped and flayed open a deep gash in the man's gut. He didn't wince. He simply smiled.

The man should have been in serious pain, but he seemed to be enjoying the fight and challenge.

Lucian attacked with another solid thrust, and then back-slashed a sharp cut that peeled a thin line down the soldier's forearm. The soldier countered with a swift kick to Lucian's stomach. Lucian doubled over, and the man attempted to slash Lucian's throat.

The blade came in an instant, moving rapidly, but Lucian pulled back. The knife swooshed through the air. For a brief second, he wondered if he could kill this man. Again, he moved on the offensive, slashed forward, and metal scraped metal as the soldier parried his attack.

Lucian aimed high, and then slashed low on a quick retreat. He gashed a deep laceration across the man's left thigh. Blood came quicker from the gaping wound. The soldier paused to inspect the damage with wide eyes.

Even though the severed tissue was repairing, the blood flow was faster than the flesh regenerated.

Panic finally claimed the man's face. His inferior training proved that he wasn't a seasoned warrior.

Lucian wiped blood from his nose with the back of his hand. He inhaled through his mouth.

Blood flowed heavily down the man's leg. The cut had gashed through his femoral artery. In spite of the damage, the man still moved forward, but weaker, slower, and more cautious than before, which allowed Lucian to block oncoming attacks easily. Another five minutes and the soldier was dead anyway. Without blood, even a genetic soldier couldn't survive.

Lucian smiled.

The soldier's face paled. His strength vanished. A pool of blood covered the floor beneath their feet. The soldier stared narrowly ahead—blankly, absently. His knife dropped from his hand and clanged on the floor. Another minute and he fell face forward. Lifeless.

Lucian leaned over to catch his breath. He wiped blood on his shirt and sheathed his knife. If this was the best Idris could do, Idris was dead.

CHAPTER 64

*Y*vonne led Helmsby, Daniel, Johanna, Lydia, and Morton down the front stairwell. The gunfire on the second floor made them pause outside the floor entrance doors. Lydia held her gun at her side.

Daniel peered through the door's square window. Four dead bodies were sprawled in the hallway. Dark crimson pools spread beneath them. No gunman was visible, but someone had killed these men. The problem was for them to figure out where the killer was hiding. In the darker halls or in one of the stairwells, the person could be anywhere.

Lydia opened the door wider, but Daniel gently tugged her back. He shook his head. Her eyes were cold, in a trance, and her fingers tightened around the trigger. He placed his hand beneath her chin and turned her face toward his. She blinked and looked into his eyes.

"Lydia? Are you okay?" he asked.

She shook her head, blinked, and nodded. "Yes. I'm fine."

Yvonne placed a hand on Daniel's arm. She stared at Lydia. "Let's go. We don't have much time to get to Lucas. Sublevel three may have more soldiers waiting."

"What's happening on this floor?" he asked.

"Idris forced Dr. Helmsby to call you. It's his intention to kill all of you. I'm here to prevent that if I can. But, Idris has brought out some of his super humans from their incubation chambers. They're as bad as Lucas' clone, if not, in some respects, worse."

"How?" Johanna asked.

Yvonne talked quietly as they descended to the third floor entrance. She held her gun slightly in front of her waist in case she needed to use it quickly. "Unlike, Lucas' clone, they don't have any conscience at all. No rational thinking. They follow orders to the detail. You cannot reason with them. They'll shoot you for trying."

"How many soldiers like that exist?" Daniel asked.

"I believe there are one hundred and forty still in the incubation chambers. They are months away from maturation development before they can be brought out of hibernation. I overheard Idris demand Dr. Benson to have six prepped. The good thing is their minds aren't educated enough for them to be the super humans they could be. That doesn't mean they're not a threat to us. They're capable of great marksmanship skills. It's instilled into them."

"The four dead men in the hallway wore fatigues," Daniel said. "Not sure which soldiers they were or who killed them."

Yvonne pulled the hall door open but saw no one. She motioned everyone to follow. "Come on. Lucas will be coming up the stairwell on the other end of this hall."

Helmsby faced Daniel. "Are you sure Nancy will be okay?"

"She's with Lucas. I've trusted my life with him many times. He and I were the only ones to scavenge the streets for supplies during the last two years in streets of Pittsburgh. You know he's capable of protecting her."

"Yes," Helmsby said, nodding. "But I still have my fears. It's been three months since I last saw her. I miss her terribly."

Johanna squeezed his shoulder. "She'll be fine. I feel it."

Lydia raised her gun. She whispered. "Listen. Up ahead, look."

Halfway down the hall Dr. Benson stood. Yvonne raised her gun and pointed.

Dr. Benson dropped his clipboard and threw his hands above his head. "Don't shoot! All that upstairs is Idris' doing, not mine!"

Lydia had her gun trained on him, too.

Yvonne nodded. "Yes, we know. You're nothing but his little puppet. Today your strings have been cut. You want to live?"

Benson nodded.

"Then you do what we tell you to."

Benson lowered his hands. "No problem with that."

Helmsby came closer. Without any thought, he swung a hard right into Benson's jaw. The doctor spiraled from the blow and dropped hard to the floor. Helmsby grabbed Benson's lab coat and tightened the collar around the man's neck.

Daniel had to grab Helmsby and pull him back.

"You bastard!" Helmsby spat. "You did far more than follow orders. You sent someone after my daughter."

"I'm sorry . . ."

"Oh, you'll be sorry." Helmsby faced Daniel. "And Daniel, he wanted Morton for his own."

Morton's eyebrows rose. "Why?"

Helmsby kicked Benson in the stomach and towered over him. "For money. He figured he could clone you and market talking cats to the world for large sums of money."

Morton seemed amused. "Afraid that mold was broken by me."

Helmsby grinned. "You're so secret that I never filed a patent for you."

Benson clutched his stomach and lay on the floor shaking his head.

The hallway door opened. Nancy ran to her father and hugged him. Lucas placed Rex on the floor.

Daniel tapped his earpiece. "Carpenter, we're all together. We're ready to send Helmsby and Nancy back down to the boat."

"Okay," Carpenter replied. "We're waiting for SWAT to set position. We should be through the gate in about fifteen minutes. Make certain Lucas gets to his destination."

"You got it."

Benson rose slowly to his feet. Yvonne motioned the doctor back into the room where the glass incubation chambers were.

Johanna smiled when she noticed all the muscled sleeping men in the liquid filled chambers. She nudged Lydia. "Now, *this* is how we should choose a man. Saves on that hit and miss dating shit."

Lydia didn't smile. She kept her gun and eyes aimed at Dr. Benson. An uncertainty shrouded Lydia's face. She was obviously uncomfortable being in the room and Johanna didn't understand why.

Benson was frightened, paranoid. He kept looking around the room cautiously. His pale face grew rigid with pain. A bullet ripped through his chest. He stood momentarily before dropping to his knees. Idris stood beyond him with a gun in his hand.

Lydia fired a round, but Idris fled up a hidden stairwell. Two incubation chambers were positioned in such a fashion that the stairway was nearly impossible to see in the dim lighting. Helmsby rushed up the stairs after him.

"Bob!" Yvonne yelled. She ran up the stairs to catch him.

Nancy headed for the stairs, but Lydia pulled her aside and sprinted past. She clicked off her gun's safety. Nancy followed.

Yvonne reached for Helmsby's lab coat to stop him before he made the next landing, but he moved far faster than she expected. She holstered her gun and sprinted up two stairs at a time, but Helmsby had already shoved open the door and entered the hall.

When she pushed open the door, Idris held a gun on Helmsby.

Idris smiled. "I've waited a damn long time to do this. Now, you've given me the perfect opportunity."

Before Idris fired, Yvonne slung her nightstick. It careened off Idris' right elbow, knocking his aim off when the gun fired. The bullet struck Helmsby in the right shin.

Idris clutched his elbow but didn't bother to retrieve his gun. He stumbled and ran down the hall. He looked over his shoulder and disappeared in another room.

Helmsby screamed, fell to the floor, and grabbed his shin.

"Dad," Nancy sobbed, quickly kneeling beside him. "Are you okay?"

"It's my leg," he said. "I'll live."

Yvonne rushed over to help. She failed to see the armed guard that entered the hallway behind them. Lydia fired one shot and claimed the man as another statistic. He died without firing a single round.

Helmsby braced himself against Nancy, using her like a human crutch. The bullet had gone through the front of his shin and exited through his calf, barely missing the bone. His face creased when he attempted to place weight on it.

Nancy leaned against the wall with him. "How bad is it, Dad?"

He winced. "It hurts like hell."

"You'd be dead if not for Yvonne. We both would."

"I know."

Taking her thin belt, Nancy knelt and tied a tight tourniquet around his calf to stop the bleeding. He growled from the fiery pain. "I can't say *that* made it feel any better." He took in a sharp, deep breath. A tear streaked down his cheek.

"It will stop the bleeding," she said, looking into his eyes.

Helmsby smiled through the pain. "You look every bit as beautiful as your mother. God knows I've missed you."

She wrapped her arms around his neck and squeezed. His lab coat reeked of sweat and formaldehyde. Nancy held her breath. "Cologne, Dad. Promise me you'll start wearing cologne soon. And get a new lab coat."

He laughed hard and placed a hand to her cheek. "Okay, I will."

Yvonne's broad shoulders blocked the patrols from getting a clear line of fire on Helmsby and Nancy. Yvonne fired two rounds, dropping the guards. Idris peered from the doorway down the hall. She fired and missed by inches. He retreated further into the room.

"Nancy," she said. "Get your father downstairs now. More troops will be called soon. I'll secure the door while you get him to safety."

Nancy nodded and draped her father's arm around her shoulder. They headed slowly down the spiral stairs. The door opened behind Nancy. Yvonne kept her gun aimed at the door as they descended. Instead of stopping at the floor with Daniel and the others, Yvonne led Nancy and Helmsby to the next floor. She opened a side door to a hidden hallway. The door closed tightly behind them. On the other side, no handle was available that allowed them to pass back from where they came.

Should TGC's guards follow them through the door, she knew only a fool flung open a windowless door into a hallway of the unknown. But TGC soldiers weren't recruited for their high intellect. Most were hired for their ruthless, cold-blooded spirit.

Yvonne stayed close to Nancy and Helmsby. She constantly watched each direction for movement. When she was confident no one was coming through the door, she insisted Nancy support Helmsby's left shoulder while she lifted his right so she could keep her gun in her right hand. With her strength she wrapped her arm around his waist and hefted him up so neither of his feet touched the floor.

The hall grew dimmer. The floor sloped downward at a forty-five degree angle, which meant they weren't far from the docks. The air smelled of dead fish. Nancy became apprehensive, thinking about the shifters that had killed the guard earlier. They were standing in the hallway where the shifters had been. But where were they hiding?

The few fluorescent lights that lined the ceiling flickered. The bulbs needed changed. Halfway down the corridor a clicking noise echoed, followed by what sounded like the rhythm of a crisp deck of cards being shuffled—only, much, much louder.

More than a dozen panels—about the size of dog doors—dropped open on each side of the hall. Bright iridescent green eyes peered from the manmade dens. Hungry, chattering cries rattled from the tiny openings. Seconds later, shifters swarmed into the hallway.

These shifters, slightly larger than house cats, had little fur and hard red exoskeletons. Their small mouths gleamed with two prominent rows of sharp teeth. Their wide, clawed feet pattered across the floor swiftly. The creatures surrounded their human prey and blocked the hall from both directions. The only visible door was the one that had sealed shut. Getting it opened was impossible.

The shifters sniffed the air, smelling the blood on Helmsby's leg. They drooled and lusted for his blood. Crazed hunger enveloped their eyes. Primal urges increased the threat of their guttural growls. Their eyes widened, as did their hungry mouths.

Yvonne stopped moving. She gently lowered Helmsby. She aimed at the nearest shifter and fired. The hellish beast yelped and rolled into a ball. Then it sprang to its feet and snarled. The bullet only increased its anger. The circle of shifters moved closer in a tight semicircle.

"I'm sorry, guys," she said. A stunned, frightened expression paralyzed her face. "I don't think we're going to out of here alive."

CHAPTER 65

$\mathcal{D}$aniel and Johanna kept their attention on the doorway while Lydia stood guard at the stairwell. Lucas put Rex on an examination table near the last row of incubation chambers. Morton sat on the tall stool and watched.

"What exactly are you going to do with the dog? I don't understand why he's important to the destruction of TransGenCorp," Daniel said.

"You'll see in a minute," Lucas replied.

"Should I go after Idris?" Lydia asked, leaning out the door into the hall.

"No," Lucas said. "Not yet. This is more important. Hold Rex for a second, Lydia."

She stepped to the table and held the dog with one hand. She watched the door while Lucas rummaged through drawers and cabinets. He returned with a syringe, a scalpel, and some gauze. A few minutes later he found alcohol, bandages, and a pair of tweezers.

Daniel glanced over his shoulder. "What are you doing?"

Lucas pinched the nape of Rex's neck and inserted a syringe fill with Novocain to deaden the pain. "This is where TransGenCorp implants their tracers into clones."

"And you're taking one out of the dog?"

"Not exactly. I'm removing a computer chip I had a veterinarian friend of mine implant. This is what they were looking for and why they trashed my house, kidnapped me, and killed the senators. Only they never suspected my dog had all the information."

"What's on it?"

Lucas grinned. "Every vile, corrupt experiment TransGenCorp has ever concocted."

"How will this help us?" Lydia asked, patting the pup's head.

Lucas laughed. "This chip's corrupted with a viral worm that will delete every data file in TransGenCorp's networking system. The computer meltdown is code encrypted. By the time Idris hires techs to decode it, if there is a way, all his genetic soldiers and his shifter pets will be dead. The shifter cages will have all the oxygen sucked out through the ventilation system. The life support systems for the incubation chambers will shut off. The information files, even the ones Helmsby documented will be scrambled and encrypted. TransGenCorp is finished."

"How'd you get the chip?" Johanna asked.

"I stole it."

"From where?" Lydia asked, holding the dog still.

"Here. About two weeks ago."

Lucas massaged Rex's neck until he felt the chip. He made a small incision with the scalpel and pushed the chip out.

"Why would Idris keep a chip here when it can destroy their database?"

"Its original format has nothing more than backup files for the genetic codes on shifter biochemistry," Lucas said. "Let's just say I had the files modified. Once I replace the file data chip with the contaminated one, the malfunction meltdown begins."

Daniel shook his head. "Since when have you been big on computer programs?"

"I'm not," he replied. "But I have a couple of friends I met on the motocross circuit who are hackers and owed me a favor. You meet all kinds on that tour."

Lydia nodded. "Tell me about it."

The outer dark hallway was quiet. No guards patrolled since the majority of them were now dead. Morton looked bored sitting on the stool, watching Lucas stitch the incision.

"You'd have saved yourself a lot of time if you had gotten a shifter pup," Morton said. "No sewing required."

"That's true," Lucas said with a broad smile. "But sometimes you have to settle for second best."

"You see, Daniel?" Morton said with one brow raised. "I told you dogs are inferior to cats."

Lucas chuckled and examined the microchip encased in a protective plastic shell. He washed it in alcohol, dried it, and then he removed the plastic cover with a scalpel.

"What do we do now?" Daniel asked.

"We take this to the computer main drive in the records room."

CHAPTER 66

Fourteen snipers were positioned atop high-rise buildings across the street from TGC. They awaited orders to fire. As soon as the security checkpoint gate arm lifted, Kat and Carpenter drove through. Two blocks away the National Guard's jeeps and a tank were parked, waiting for Carpenter's signal.

Kat hoped the plan worked because if Lucas failed, she feared what monstrosities might escape the facility. She didn't believe the National Guard's weapons could stop them like they had in the past. Surely, Idris had upgraded and strengthened his creations.

After the gate arm lowered, Carpenter gave the order to fire. Whispered bullets pierced the air. Like a wind gust leveled dominoes, fourteen TGC soldiers collapsed—dead. A few seconds later, another fourteen dropped.

The National Guard tank rumbled down the street and burst through the gate, followed by a small Jeep convoy. After the outside soldiers were disposed, the inside TGC soldiers remained. Troops needed to gain entrance to kill those soldiers before they killed Daniel and his friends.

FROM THE CORNER of her eye, Yvonne glimpsed a lunging shifter coming right at her. She thwacked it in the face with her 9mm. She struck it hard enough to slam the creature against the wall. However, its suckered toes fastened to the wall. Suspended, it turned its wicked face at her and chattered. Wide, black pupils peered in the center of its green eyes. She feared staring too long in case the creature could somehow read her thoughts or lull her into its gaze.

Helmsby adjusted his footing and eased his hand into his lab coat pocket. He pulled out two ammo clips.

"Use these," he said.

She took them and shrugged. "What's the difference?"

"They're denaturers. They'll do what ordinary bullets won't. They'll kill them."

Yvonne looked surprised. "Where'd you get them?"

"I stole them from Benson's lab."

"How'd you ever get past the guards?"

Helmsby smiled. "I find ways around that even Idris never suspected. Knowledge is power."

Yvonne squeezed the gun's release. The gun clip dropped to the floor. She kicked it and the clip scraped down the sloped corridor. Their little green eyes followed its movement, which gave her enough time to slam a denaturer clip into the gun.

She shot the shifter that clung to the wall. It stiffened. Blood leaked from its body in a steady stream, forming a long thin line down the sloped floor. The hungrier shifters ignored their potential human prey and scuttled to lap up the fresh blood.

The life in the clinging shifter's eyes faded. Its body trembled. Spasms riveted through its muscles. Slowly, one by one, the suckered toes lost grip. The dead shifter fell crumpled to the floor.

Yvonne fired at the feeding shifters. Her accuracy didn't seem to matter, just as long as the bullet penetrated their skin. After the bullet ripped and tore through the shifters' flesh, the bullet exploded, sending denaturing agents through their bodies like a cancerous, gangrene acid.. The pile of shifter carnage fed the widening pool of thick dark blood. The living shifters scurried to drink the blood.

She raised the gun to fire again, but Helmsby placed his hand on her arm. He shook his head. "No. Let them be. We might need the rounds further down the corridor."

The feeding shifters no longer regarded them with any interest at all. Their offered feast satiated their appetites. Yvonne motioned for Nancy to help Helmsby walk.

Nancy's eyes were wide with fear. Her face was pale. She held her father's arm and looked at Yvonne for assurance that they were safe.

"Won't they come after us?" Nancy asked.

"The blood's a free meal and there's plenty of it. That should buy us enough time to reach the boat."

Yvonne wrapped her arm around Helmsby's waist and lifted him. "Okay. Let's get you out of here, Bob."

CHAPTER 67

*L*ucas and Lydia met Daniel and Johanna at the door.

Daniel faced Lucas. "So you knew the clone was still alive when you called me?"

Lucas nodded. "Of course, but I had to warn you."

"Why not just tell me rather than making me come to TransGenCorp? You know how much I hate this place."

"Yeah, I know," he replied, smiling. "But me simply telling you wasn't enough. You wouldn't have believed me. I needed your help and the only way to achieve that was for me to stoke your paranoia. Otherwise, you'd have never been prepared for their attack. You'd all be dead, and I couldn't live with that on my conscience. I value you too much."

"You'll never know how much I appreciate that, but you know that Helmsby betrayed us in Pittsburgh, don't you? He put our lives in grave danger. You and me."

Lucas shook his head. "A lot of bad things happened on those dark streets, Dan. A lot of bad things. But Helmsby was never directly involved in them. Not intentionally. Sometimes we askew our memories so the blame rests on others in order to lessen our own inner turmoil. Without enduring those dark, treacherous times, Felicia wouldn't be here. You wouldn't be with Julia." He squeezed Daniel's shoulder. "Now, let's get our revenge by destroying what Idris holds dearest. That ought to give us both a great deal of satisfaction."

Daniel smiled. "That it will, my friend."

CHAPTER 68

Kat and Carpenter parked in the center lot and got out of the car. No one moved along the fence line, so SWAT had been successful. Carpenter radioed the National Guard to move in.

Carpenter studied the parked TGC military vehicles along the riverside fence. He wondered how many corrupt people in Washington and the military had aligned themselves with TGC and secretly pooled money into the facility in hopes of greater future gains.

Carpenter and Kat holstered their guns.

He said, "It looks like everything is about wrapped up."

Kat sighed. "I hope so."

A BLACK JAGUAR slowed outside TGC's broken gate. Both men wore camouflage uniforms. The driver, tan skinned with a muscled face looked through dark shades. "You're sure Lucian's in there, Donovan?"

His blonde, fair-skinned passenger pointed his finger on the laptop screen. "Yes, Magnus. His tracer chip shows he's here on the map."

"Dammit!" Magnus said. He surveyed the National Guard activity inside TGC's fences. Dead guards were all along the fence line. "We're never going to get to him with all this shit going on."

"It's a million dollar bounty, Magnus. We cannot let that pass through our hands."

"Are you seeing what I am?"

"I see it. I know."

Magnus looked through binoculars. "Damn, what the hell is going on here?"

"Idris' shop is being closed."

"That's good. Good for us."

Donovan smiled. "In a sense, but without the bounty for Lucian, we're hurting."

"There's no way past all these soldiers and the FBI agents. They'll see us."

"Lucian knows too much. We must dispose of him so he doesn't inform the FBI or CIA."

Magnus sighed and pulled the car into a parking spot two blocks away where they could keep an eye on the activity at TGC. "He was the best of us. He trained us. I don't see why he's considered expendable now."

"According to Idris, he's turned against our foundation and sister labs. It's just a matter of time, and he'll turn on us. He's changed, grown soft. TGC must continue. They might shut down the operations here, but they don't know about the other laboratories. Lucian does. That makes him dangerous if he turns."

Magnus frowned. Even through the dark shades, Donovan felt his glare. "You think he's here to kill Idris?"

"At the very least."

Magnus shook his head in disbelief. "That would be foolish. Without Idris he'll die. Unlike us, he has to have enhancer injections."

"Surveillance shows that Brockton has sided with Lucian. He gave Lucian a box of injections, so he wouldn't be at Idris' mercy."

"So Brockton has to die, too?"

Donovan nodded. "We have to get inside and kill them. With our fatigues, we shouldn't have much problem blending in."

"No, not here. There's too much fire power should we be discovered. Even being what we are, we do have our limitations."

"So we kill the guards, too."

Magnus shook his head. "That kind of eagerness will get us both killed."

With several keystrokes on the laptop, Donovan smiled and pointed. "Watch."

CHAPTER 69

*A*loud squelching alarm cried from speaker poles around the perimeter. In front of one of the military flatbed trucks, two metal doors pushed upward from the asphalt, revealing a set of descending stairs. Armed soldiers swarmed from the bunker like an angry swarm of disturbed ants.

If Kat had not already been looking in that general direction, she would never have heard the doors strike the pavement due to the harsh sirens.

Bullets from three firing soldiers sent Carpenter scrambling across the parking lot toward Kat. She was in mid-stride when the bullet hit her right shoulder. Carpenter lunged, caught her around the waist, and pulled her behind the car, out of the line of gunfire.

"Are you okay?" he asked.

She nodded. "I think so."

Carpenter inspected her shirt for blood. "Looks like the vest stopped the bullet."

Kat closed her eyes and sighed. "It still hurts like hell."

Carpenter pulled his gun. Kat kept a weak grip on hers. Her arm was numb and she found it difficult to keep her fingers curled around the gun. She massaged her forearm, hoping to gain back control of her hand.

Soldiers approached, firing their weapons. Bullets chinked and ate at the other side of the car. Tyler drove through the gate and swung his car to the front of Carpenter's. The two cars formed an L, which allowed them protection from two different angles.

The soldiers turned their attention toward Tyler and fired. Denton swung open the passenger door and dove to the pavement. Tyler fumbled with his seatbelt. He tugged and pushed the button, but it wouldn't release.

Gunfire chiseled the glass. One round burst through Tyler's forehead, spraying a stream of blood across the roof upholstery. His head slammed back against the headrest and dropped limp against the steering wheel. The car horn blared.

"Tyler! No!" Kat yelled, fighting to stand.

Carpenter shook his head and placed a firm grip on her shoulder to hold her down. "He's dead, Kat."

Kat weakened beneath his hold. Tears burned her eyes.

Carpenter said to Denton, "How many soldiers are approaching our position?"

"At least a dozen," Denton replied through clenched teeth. "Maybe more and wearing full body armor, too."

"Shit," Carpenter sighed. "No way our bullets can penetrate their armor."

Kat squinted to squeeze away tears. She didn't want to cry. She couldn't with the present danger they faced. She took a couple of quick breaths. Bullets flaked chunks of metal from the car hood.

"They're closing in fast. Can we run for it?" she asked.

"No," Carpenter replied. "We have nowhere to run."

Kat put her gun in her left hand and rose to her feet. Carpenter reached for her, but she moved too quickly to grab. She fired two rounds, but the bullets bounced off the body armor. She fired again. It was a futile effort. She prepared to fire again, but a bullet hit dead center of her chest. She fell backwards.

"Kat! Dammit!" Carpenter yelled, crawling toward her. "Are you on a suicide mission?"

She winced. "Damn, that hurt!"

"Our weapons are useless against them, Kat," Carpenter said. "We have to get out of here. Let the Guard do their duty."

Denton shook his head. "There's no way we can pile into a car without getting killed. They're right on us now."

They were helpless the longer they stayed seated behind the cars. Carpenter judged the distance to the front doors of TGC. He shook his head. "We'd never be fast enough to get to those doors. Just hunker down."

The bullets battered the sides of the cars. Bits of glass showered to the pavement. The heavy gunfire ate and punctured the car bodies. The tires sank. The noise became unbearable.

Kat closed her eyes. "The best we can hope is that Lucas has succeeded."

Carpenter nodded. "True. Where the hell did all these soldiers come from?"

"Underground bunkers," Kat said. "The alarms must have triggered their opening."

Denton sat low against the car tire. "What set off the alarms?"

"No idea," Carpenter said, squinting as more glass rained down.

"I guess Lucas didn't know about them?" Denton asked.

"I guess not," Carpenter said. "But what worries me more is what else he might not know about TGC."

Bullets sprayed in the heated battle. Several cars were blazing slowly. Occasional bullets chipped off the pavement, barely missing them. A metal object clanked on the ground near them. It rolled and spun. Right in the midst of them was an unpinned grenade. Carpenter hugged Kat closely before he flung his body over her. Denton grabbed the grenade and lopped it back over the car. The explosion sent chunks of asphalt and soldiers into the air, but the roaring blast didn't stop their assault.

The only thing that saved Carpenter, Kat, and Denton was the Guard intercepted the gunfire. However, the TGC mercenaries were better equipped and trained to kill without second thought. The Guard was being picked off one by one.

Kat looked up at Carpenter. She forced a smile. "I think you've invaded my personal space."

He smiled. "Sorry. Please don't file a formal complaint."

Several TGC soldiers made their way around the Guard and were approaching the agents' position. They raised their rifles. Kat's breath caught in her throat. She couldn't swallow. It was then she realized it was over.

CHAPTER 70

*M*agnus' cell phone rang. "You found where Daniel's wife and daughter are? Where? The Burnside Hotel. Thanks."

"What's that all about?" Donovan asked.

"I put out a credit card trace to find where Daniel's family was staying. Idris' attempt to kill them failed and made the news. We won't make the same mistake as the other team did."

"We don't have to worry about them. They were a thorn in Idris' side, not ours."

"Maybe not, but if we want a shot at killing Lucian, we need the FBI out of here. I have a way to get them out of here and eliminated at the same time."

"How?"

"We send Bane to the hotel. I have no doubt that agents are posted there to protect Daniel's family. Once Bane attacks, the agents will contact Carpenter to help rescue them."

Donovan frowned. "Don't be foolish. Typhis will never allow that."

"Typhis doesn't need to know."

"Dr. Helmsby has had access to all of Idris' data for three years. He can prove that Idris has never had much success splicing canine DNA with his super humans, especially nothing like Bane."

Magnus laughed. "Idris would be pissed to know that Typhis beat him to the achievement."

"True."

"After Bane kills the agents at the hotel, Daniel and the others will come out into the open. They'll be vulnerable. Bane will kill them all."

"But if he fails and is killed, his DNA will lead the FBI right to us."

"If, Donovan, *if*. Bane is practically invincible."

Donovan shrugged. "Make the call."

A LOUD ROAR of engines revved. Crumbled chain-linked fence crashed to the pavement. Another tank entered the parking lot. It fired into the remaining twenty or so mercenaries. The blast killed half of them.

The last dozen soldiers turned away from Carpenter, Kat, and Denton to fire at the tank. Armed Guardsmen sent a barrage of armor-piercing bullets through the TGC soldiers. All except five fell victim to attack and died. The last five men dropped their weapons and raised their hands in surrender.

After the gunfire ceased, Carpenter helped Kat to her feet. "Come on," he said. "We have to help Lucas."

"Wait," she said. She wiped away tears and opened Tyler's car door. She gently moved his head off the steering wheel. The car horn ceased, but the blaring sirens still split the air.

A chunk of the back of Tyler's head was missing. Blood soaked the seat. His eyes were wide and his skin cold. Her hands shook. She closed his eyes with the gentle sweep of her hand. Her insides quaked. No words described the inner turmoil twisting through her stomach and mind.

She looked across the asphalt at all the carnage Idris was responsible for. Her anger boiled. Although she was a full eight inches shorter than Carpenter, the heated anger in her eyes made him uneasy when she confronted him. "According to the files you gave me, *all* of this was supposed to have been over three years ago. What the hell happened?"

Carpenter shrugged. "It beats me. Until the Senate murders, Kat, I believed it was over."

"Well," Kat said. "It's time to finish it for good."

The National Guard cuffed the remaining five soldiers. Denton checked his gun clip while Carpenter motioned her to follow.

"We'll make certain it's over this time," he said, staring at the pavement while he walked. "Lucas holds the power to shut it down."

"So he believes," she said. "But what if what he does *isn't* enough? What then?"

"We'll sail that ocean when we reach it."

"By God, this has to end today. Too many have died already for one man's corrupt science."

Carpenter offered a grim smile. "Yes. The sad thing is that we all thought Idris was dead, too. The fact he is still alive was news to me. Some higher ups made damn sure they kept that information a secret."

Kat shook her head. "Someone knew he was still alive. Someone put him back in the control seat. The question is who?"

"I wish I knew, Kat. Honestly, I do. We'll find the answer somehow. But we must first make sure he's dead this time."

"Even if it's done illegally?"

He whispered. "Whatever it takes, it will be final this time."

She stopped and faced him. "I'll hold you to that."

Carpenter nodded and walked past her. "Please do."

CHAPTER 71

*L*ucas took the computer chip and placed it inside a Ziplock bag before stuffing it into his jacket pocket. He looked at Daniel. "I'll take Lydia with me. The computer room is down the hall. Once I get this chip into place, our time is limited. You need to get out of this building as soon as possible."

"I know. I'll go find Kyle. We can't leave him here. Provided he's still alive."

"Hurry," Lucas said. "And be careful."

"Always," Daniel said. To Johanna and Morton, he said, "You two come with me."

Johanna forced a smile.

Lydia held her handgun low and peered into the hall. "Idris went in that direction."

"Damn," Lucas said. "That means he's gone to the computer room."

Lydia released the safety and smiled. "Then we'll take care of two things at once."

Lucas pulled his gun. Daniel, Johanna, and Morton headed for the stairwell while Lucas and Lydia eased down the hall. Rex padded cautiously behind them.

Lucas kept his back against the left wall in the hallway while Lydia did the same on the right. With catlike stealth they moved toward the computer room. The empty hall was silent. He wondered if all the interior guards were dead or if another one or two might be patrolling. Anything was possible in this madhouse, he reasoned. Hell, shifters might have been released by now.

Lydia swung her back against the wall beside the closed door. Lucas lowered his stance and moved beneath the window to the other side of the door.

"You ready?" he whispered.

She nodded.

Lucas turned the knob slowly before shoving the door open. The heavy gunfire slammed the doorstop, but no gunfire erupted in the room. Idris stood in the center of the room without a weapon in hand. He clutched his elbow tightly.

"Name your price," Idris said. "Anything at all."

Lydia and Lucas leveled their guns at his chest.

Idris took a deep breath and closed his eyes. "This is my life's work," he said with pure sincerity. He panted and sweat trickled down his face. "Name your price. Don't destroy what I've worked so long to achieve."

Lucas' eyes narrowed. "At the cost of how many lives?"

"It's science. With science, there's always a cost."

Lucas kept his gun aimed on Idris. He walked to the main computer panel. "Oh? You killed two senators and then you attempted to kill all my friends in order to achieve your accomplishments? You call that science?"

Idris smiled weakly. "Believe me, it wasn't personal."

"To me," Lucas said. "It's very personal."

Lucas dropped to one knee. "If he moves, Lydia, shoot him."

"Please," Idris said. He took a step back and Lydia tightened her finger on the trigger. "No, I'm not going to run. Please, let me lean against the wall. I feel faint."

"It'll pass," Lucas replied.

Idris gasped for breath. He wiped sweat from his brow. "Are you certain, Lucas, that what you're doing is in your best interests?"

Lucas pulled off a rectangular metal door on the central computer. Lying on his back, he pulled himself into the small opening. "Destroying TransGenCorp is in everyone's best interest."

A thin smile parted Idris' lips. His yellow teeth were lined like neat kernels of corn. "By destroying one thing, you'll unleash numerous other dangers you're not aware of."

"Bluffing again?"

Idris' heavy eyelids opened wider. His yellowing eyes peered angrily.

"Call me on it then, if you think I'm bluffing. But be forewarned . . . there are experiments here that even Dr. Helmsby has no knowledge of."

"I supposed you've backed them with your lifeless shifter soundtrack?"

Idris took another step backwards. Lydia took a step closer. Her eyes never moved off him, and she never lessened her grip on the trigger. He leaned back against the wall, panting for air. He was pale. Sweat dotted his fevered brow. He held his elbow tightly and closed his eyes. He licked his lips. When he opened his eyes, Lydia stood less than ten feet away from him. He smiled.

"I always knew you were the best," he said. "My strongest."

Lydia frowned. "What the hell are you talking about?"

"You mean Lucas never told you?"

She glanced at Lucas, but she couldn't make eye contact. He was under the computer main drive fumbling with the chip. She looked at Idris. "Told me what?"

Idris licked his lips again and swallowed. He took another deep breath. "Where you really came from? What you really are? He didn't tell you?"

Lydia took a step toward Lucas. "What the hell is he talking about?"

Lucas squinted, trying to align the chip where he had removed the other. Without looking at her, he said, "Don't listen to him. He's trying to distract you and get you to drop your guard."

"Lucas," Idris said in a raspy voice. "It'd be best if you told her, don't you think? After all, you *stole* her from me."

Idris slid his back down the wall and seated himself on the floor. His arms fell to his sides. He released a long, hissing laugh. "You tell her or I will."

"Pay no attention to him, Lydia. Can't you see he's delusional?"

Idris chuckled. His throat made rough sounds like he needed water. His eyes were yellow and wider. "You're the absolute best I ever created."

She leveled the gun at his head and tightened her finger on the trigger. "You're telling me that I'm one of your clones? That's bullshit! I was held here and you made clones from me."

"No, dear, no," he said. "You're much more than that. You're a flawless, genetically enhanced assassin."

"What?"

Lucas finally clicked the microchip into the slot and whispered, "Gotcha."

"Tell her, Lucas," Idris panted. His tongue was narrowing like a serpent.

"Tell her how you persuaded one of my best scientists to get her out of her incubation chamber."

Lucas wiped his hands on his pants and stood. He pulled his gun and aimed at Idris' head. "I've wanted to put a bullet in your brain for a long time."

Lydia stepped between his gun and Idris but kept her gun trained on the general. "No."

"What are you doing, Lydia?" Lucas asked. "Please move."

She shook her head. "Not until you tell me the truth. Did I come out of one of those chambers like the men downstairs? Am I like them?"

Lucas lowered his gun and sighed. "No, you're not like them. After all, he made a clone from you. Your clone had no childhood memories, but you do."

Idris snorted. His facial skin was dry and scaly, almost leathery. "Lydia's memories were fabricated, and you're fully aware of that. What she remembers is nothing more than subliminal implants. But Lydia, your clone had flaws, impure DNA, unlike you. The shifter DNA in you is pure, but hers was damaged. You are the prototype. You could never imagine what kind of progeny I'd have gotten had I succeeded in breeding you with Lucas' clone."

Her eyes narrowed. She pointed the gun firmly at Idris. A tear of anger trickled down her cheek. "Am I nothing more than an animal to you?"

"Hey! I'm all for it," Lucian said, stepping into the room behind them. He held one 9mm on Lucas and the other on Idris. "It sounds like a pleasurable way to spend the rest of this hellacious day."

CHAPTER 72

*D*aniel cautiously stepped into the second floor hallway. Pools of thickening blood spread beneath dead soldiers. He held his gun tightly and took a slow step forward. The smell of burning flesh lingered in the air. A thin line of smoke filtered from the chemical storage room.

"What happened here?" Johanna asked.

Daniel shook his head. "I have no idea. Maybe one of the clone assassins malfunctioned and went on a killing spree."

"They'd do that?"

Daniel frowned. "Have you been away from the research center too long to remember the hell we faced back then?"

"No. Of course not. But God knows, I'd like to forget it."

Daniel walked to the nearest soldier and stared in disbelief. "Damn."

"What?" she asked.

"This man is one of the soldiers in the glass chambers. Idris must have released some of them."

"How can you tell?"

"Their faces are all the same. Apparently, they're all from the same prototype."

Morton huffed. "And yet, they're all dead."

"Only one person could have been good enough to bring them down," Daniel sighed.

"The clone?" Johanna said with wide eyes. "Then he's probably still here, somewhere."

Daniel nodded. He glanced at the far end of the hall. "Let's check out the storage room. It's too risky to go any farther in that direction."

Johanna clicked off the gun safety and followed Daniel. Morton sprinted ahead and peered into the room.

"No one is alive in there," he said with a serious tone. "Uh, Dan, I don't think you should go inside."

"Why not?" he asked. "What's in there?"

Morton sat on his haunches outside the door and shook his head. "It's Kyle. He's dead."

Daniel holstered his gun and stepped past the cat. He hurried over a smoldering soldier and knelt beside Kyle's emaciated body. Kyle's face was sunken; his dead eyes stared straight ahead. Brown smudges encircled his bluing lips. Morton came closer and placed an ear near Kyle's mouth.

"What's on his face?" Daniel asked.

Morton sniffed the brown substance and his eyebrows rose in surprise. "Chocolate."

"Chocolate?"

"Strange, but yes."

"You think the chocolate killed him? In his condition?"

Morton shook his head. "No, Dan. You saw how poor his health was when we visited him yesterday. He only had a few hours before he'd die anyway."

"How'd he get in here?" Daniel asked.

"No idea," Morton replied. "But he doesn't appear to have been forced here against his will."

Daniel noticed a brown paper bag on the table. He opened it. "There are candy bars in here."

Johanna turned toward the door. "Someone was feeding his sweet tooth."

"But why?" Daniel asked. "That doesn't make any sense."

Morton said, "We may never know. But let's get out of here. The Meltdown should start soon."

Daniel knelt and put an arm behind Kyle's neck. He scooped Kyle into his arms like a rag doll.

"What are you doing?" Morton asked.

"Getting him out of here."

"No, Dan. Don't," Morton said evenly.

"Why not?"

"His parents already believe he died in Pittsburgh three years ago. Let's leave it at that. You don't want them to see him in his present condition. They've had their grief and adjusted to life without him. Don't add to it by letting them see what Idris did to their son."

Daniel lowered Kyle's body and gave a grim nod. Daniel closed Kyle's eyes. Johanna wiped tears from her cheeks.

Daniel sighed. "You're right. His parents suffered enough without having to see him now. I wish there had been more I could have done for him."

"We all do."

They headed back into the hallway and went to the stairs. Ascending one flight, they returned to the front desk. Daniel took the dead receptionist's key ring from his belt. He tried half a dozen keys before he found the one to unlock the front door.

When they opened the door, Carpenter and Kat stepped inside. Outside, the gunfire had ceased. Two dozen Guardsmen marched through the doors with assault rifles in hand.

"Where's Idris?" Carpenter asked.

"Sublevel three," Daniel said. "I think Lydia and Lucas have cornered him in one of the computer labs."

Carpenter attempted to contact Lucas via transmitter but he didn't receive a reply. "What about the clone? Did you find him?"

Daniel shook his head. "With all the dead bodies strewn down there, he has to still be here somewhere. But we've not seen him."

"Okay," Carpenter said with frustration. He extended his hand to Daniel. "You do make a great team. I'm glad you're all safe. Now, it's time for you to get the hell out of here while we clean up. Your job is over."

Daniel nodded. "Thanks."

Carpenter turned to the Guardsmen. "Scour the halls and find the clone."

CHAPTER 73

Gil stood at the hotel window, peering through the blinds. He had been overly quiet since Carpenter and everyone else had left. His eyes were shifty. Although he stood at the window, he shuffled his feet a lot, but never spoke a word. His silence made Julia uncomfortable.

Julia sat with her back against the headboard, holding Felicia in her lap while they watched cartoons.

Without directly watching Gil, she kept him in view. Occasionally, he glanced in her direction, cleared his throat as if he was going to start a conversation, but in the end, he maintained his intimidating silence. She disliked being locked in a room with a stranger. It didn't matter that he was an FBI agent. She was apprehensive and distrusting since Lucas' clone had tried to run them off the road. At least with her arms wrapped around Felicia, she could mask some of her discomfort.

The last few times he had looked toward her, uneasiness creased his brow. If something outside troubled him, she feared what dangers might have made their presence known. But, she wondered if his careful gaze through the window and his suspicious behavior were more to make certain none of the other agents came inside. Darkness loomed around him, making her fear him. She wished Morton were in the room.

Gil turned away from the window and faced her with a grave expression on his face. His hands shook. Swallowing hard and loosening his tie, he approached the bed. Sweat cropped his brow.

"We need to talk. Alone," he said. He nodded toward the open bathroom door. "In there."

Julia's heart raced. She wrapped her arms tighter around Felicia. "You can say what you need right here."

Gil licked his lips and shook his head. "No, we need to go in there. It won't take long."

She glared at him. "We talk here or not at all."

He glanced nervously at the door and then at her. He placed his hand on the butt of his gun. "You come with me, or you're really going to regret it."

Lydia held her gun on Lucian and seethed. "I knew I should've killed you."

"Hell, sweetheart, you almost did. I never cleared that last landing. Of course, you *knew* that. Pretty calloused of you to leave me out there to die."

Idris laughed. "Told you she's an assassin."

The gun shook in her hand. She looked at Lucas. "It's true, Luke. I'm like your clone."

Lucas shook his head. "No, you aren't."

"I killed three men last night."

"You defended yourself. The law's on your side."

"No," she said, shaking her head. "I attacked them first. I stalked and killed each one without question or warning. Like a predator."

"They came to kill you."

"So?" she replied. Tears burned her eyes. "I didn't know why they were there."

Lucian studied her jacket and smiled. "And somewhere during the night, you took a bullet. How'd that treat you? Looks like it went all the way through."

Lydia frowned, deep in thought. Her words came slowly. "I don't remember being shot. I don't have a scar."

Idris wheezed a feeble laugh. His facial bones contorted, making his nose and mouth meld closer together. His skin was graying. His yellow, bloodshot eyes flicked her direction. He was changing. Into what, they didn't know. Long, thick claws protruded from his widened, scale-covered hands.

"Of course, there's no scar," Idris said. "Your metabolism allows you to heal at a rapid rate. In fact, you heal faster than my best shifters."

"I never felt a bullet," she said.

"You wouldn't have," Idris said with a smile. "You're engineered *not* to feel pain."

Lucian gave a tight, grim smile. "Must be nice not knowing pain."

Idris coughed. "Pain distracts in battle. Without pain, an injured soldier keeps advancing, keeps fighting until his mortal wounds overtake him. What more proof do you need to know that you're one of mine?"

Lucas stepped beside her. His gun was aimed at his mirror image. His clone, in turn, kept a gun on Lucas and the other on Idris.

"You see, Lucas," Idris said. "You should have left her with me. Lydia needed my guidance, and my instruction. You'd have been better equipped to face the world. I never would've kept you in ignorance of your true potential."

"That's bullshit," Lucas said. "Lydia, what happened at your farm doesn't make you like them. You didn't do anything wrong defending your home. Even the FBI told you that."

Lydia didn't reply.

Idris ignored his statement and lifted his lizard-like hands toward Lucian. "Son. Get my genetic enhancers to stop my transformation. If you hurry, we can reverse what's happening to me."

Lucian's eyes narrowed. "I warned you to never call me your son. I hate when you call me that. Besides, I never returned to help you. I came to kill you."

No surprise filled Idris' reptilian eyes, only a sick sense of relief. He growled a deep, bellowing laugh. "If that's your plan, you'd best do it before what I become takes over. Once that happens, the three of you together cannot stop me. I'll eat your hearts out."

"Enough said," Lucian said, firing three denaturing rounds into Idris' forehead. His head slumped to the side. Blood leaked from the holes.

Lydia and Lucas pointed their guns at Lucian.

Lucian aimed both his weapons at Lucas. "I don't want to kill you, Lucas. I really don't. I'm thankful to keep you alive and that you're destroying TransGenCorp. I exist because of you. I'd hate to kill the template that birthed me."

"We can't let you walk away," Lucas said. "You murdered two guards and two senators. One was my personal friend."

"I know," Lucian said. His eyes weakened with sorrow. "I regret my actions, but Idris blackmailed me. Without genetic enhancers I'd be dead in less than a week. I followed Idris' orders only to survive."

"And what about Vicki at the research center? How do you justify her death?"

Lucian sighed and stared at Lucas' feet. Genuine pain filled his eyes. "That was an accident. I never meant her any harm. I really liked her. I had no idea that Idris had incorporated chemicals that released excessive stimuli during sex. Hell, I have no idea how he even did it. Had I known, I would've restrained myself from having sex with her."

"And now?" Lucas asked. "How many more women have you killed during sex?"

"None," Lucian said, shaking his head. "I've had some … adjustments made. Genetic interventions were weaved into my genome that prevents those chemicals from being formulated during sex. Being intimate with women no longer presents any danger."

Lucas shrugged and tightened his finger on the trigger. "You want us to forget all you've done and believe that you're innocent and trustworthy? That you've changed?"

He met Lucas' firm, angered gaze. "Idris sent me to kill Daniel, Lucas. That's what they programmed me to do. But the bond of friendship you have with him is stronger than what they subliminally programmed me to carry out. I sensed your bond every time I was around him. It ran so deeply that I couldn't kill him. It would have been like cutting off my right arm had I obeyed."

"You cannot justified yourself to me."

"I won't beg you to believe me, but know this . . . had I not wanted to protect Daniel, I'd have let the TGC soldiers kill him in the tunnel. I didn't have to kill him. They would have. But instead, I killed the soldiers. I tried to rescue Julia, too."

Lucas nodded. "Yeah. Julia told us how you shot Kyle without hesitation."

Impatience filled Lucian's voice. "Only because I didn't recognize him to be Kyle. He looked like a filthy animal. I shot him because I perceived him to be a threat to Julia. My apologies. I don't have time to argue with you, so tell me what I can do to convince you that I'm not your enemy? I've made a lot of mistakes. I understand that, and I'm willing to correct the wrongs of my past."

Lydia shook her head. "What about Johanna? And Julia and Felicia? You tried to kill them. You personally. You expect us to ignore that, too?"

"It's true I went after them. But I went to warn them about what Idris was doing, *not* to kill them. I gave my men orders not to use live rounds.

The only weapon they used was a magnetic tracer chip fired from a rifle. Nothing more."

Lydia's angry eyes pierced with fiery hatred. Her finger tightened on the trigger. All her built up fury ended if she squeezed the trigger. "You told us you felt Lucas' loyalty to Daniel. Trying to kill Julia and her daughter is certainly not reassuring."

"If I had intended to kill them, they'd be dead."

"You tried to run her off the road. You rammed her vehicle with yours."

"That's true. I did that to scare her into hiding so Idris wouldn't find them. I meant her no harm. There wasn't anything else I could do to convince her to trust me. My plan had been to sit with them at the restaurant and explain the situation. I had no knowledge that Lucas had called Daniel earlier that morning from jail, which left me no choice but to further frighten her. She already believed I was an enemy, so all my actions strengthened her fear."

"And what about me? Lydia asked. "You were at my home with soldiers lying in wait to kill me."

"No," Lucian replied, shaking his head slightly. "No, I came to take you with me. I wanted to prove my devotion to you."

"Devotion? With armed guards?"

"Those men were loyal to Idris. I'd have had to kill them to save you, but you have abilities I never imagined. I wasn't informed that you were Idris' female prototype. I thought you were another clone like the one I accompanied to the research center. I learned about what you really are at the same time you did."

Lydia scowled.

"I'm serious, Lydia. I didn't know, but Lucas *did*."

Lucian glanced toward the door. "We don't have much time. We need to get out of here."

Lucas shook his head. "There's nothing you can do that will convince me that it's safe for you to be out in the world. You're not leaving."

Lucian sighed. "Lucas, you're in no position to make threats."

Lydia stepped between them. "No, but I am."

The clone smiled. "After what you did to me, I wanted to hunt you down and make you suffer a long, agonizing death. But, I've reconsidered. Besides if that were the route I still wanted to take, there'd be no fun in it since you can't feel pain. So, just let me go live my own life."

"Your own life?" Lucas laughed. "Hell, you look just like me."

"I don't want to look like you. I don't *have* to look like you. Watch."

The muscles in Lucian's face tightened, stretched, twisted. Minutes later, he stood before them with a new mask made of flesh. "Are you satisfied? I don't want to be *you*. I want my own life away from these laboratories, which is something I've never had."

Coldness rang in Lydia's voice. "If he says you're not leaving, then you're not going."

Lucian's eyebrows tightened with desperate anger. He nodded toward Idris' decaying corpse. "Really? You might want to reconsider since I have more denaturers. Look at what's left of Idris. His face has melted like plastic. You can shoot me, and I'll heal. But if I shoot you, you might not feel the pain and anguish as your DNA dissolves, but you will still die a gory death."

She shrugged. Her arm stretched toward him, her finger tightening on the trigger. "I'm not too fond of living right now anyway."

"Suit yourself. I gave you an offer even though I didn't have to. You let me live my life, and you'll never see or hear from me again." He turned his other gun from Lucas and trained both guns on her. "That's a guaranteed promise I intend to keep."

"Wait," Lucas said. He tucked his 9mm behind his back. He slipped his arm around Lydia and lowered her gun. He looked into the eyes behind Lucian's new face and nodded. The reflection of his eyes was hauntingly the only thing that had not changed.

"Go," Lucas whispered through clenched teeth.

Lucian backed out of the room. "Thank you." Before he left, he set a box of ammo on the filing cabinet. "You may need these to get out of here."

"What are they?" Lucas asked.

"More denaturing rounds."

Lucas opened his mouth to reply, but Lucian turned and ran.

Lydia faced him with sad eyes. "Why'd you let him go?"

Lucas shrugged. "He'd have killed you. And as strange as it sounds, I do believe he wants his own life. I'll let him be. For now."

"How can you? He killed Godfrey."

"I know." Lucas glared at the door.

She grew still and quiet.

"I can't afford to lose you again," Lucas said.

He reached to pull her to him, but she stepped back and put her gun to her right temple. "I'm sorry. I cannot live knowing what I am and what I've done."

"No Lydia, don't. You're not like them."

"I'm everything they are, Lucas. I don't want people to know I'm like those men in the incubation chambers."

"They don't know and they won't."

Her finger tightened on the trigger. "I'll always know."

"Please put the gun down."

"I can't. I have to stop what I'll become. I don't want to kill again."

"Lydia, you're not a killer. You aren't going to do that again."

"How can you be certain?"

"Because that's not what you are inside."

She shook her head. "We don't *know* what I am inside. Neither of us."

Tears welled in her eyes. She refused to make eye contact. She focused on the wall without blinking. Her hand shook.

"You just don't understand," she whispered. "I think I actually enjoyed hunting those men down. When it ended, I had wished there had been more of them to kill."

"Lydia, I'm absolutely certain you're not like them."

"How?"

"You have a conscience. You have remorse. It shows in your face. But you also hold the ability to love and be loved. Those are not qualities Idris instilled into his super human soldiers. And those are the reasons why I love you."

Lydia blinked and two large tears streaked down her face. Her lips trembled. "You can love me, knowing what I am?"

Lucas smiled. "What you are, is the most beautiful woman in the world. How you came to exist and what your genetic codes are, those aren't important to me. What is important is who you are and what you are inside my heart."

She lowered the gun. He pulled her close and kissed her. Then he wrapped his arms around her and whispered, "If I lost you here today, I'd have to put a gun to my head, too. Because my world ends without you."

"I'm sorry."

Hot tears fell on his collar.

He took her hand. "Let's get out of this hellhole. The Meltdown should begin in less than twenty minutes."

"The place will explode?"

"No, the air will be sucked out of here. All the caged shifters and humans will die."

Lucas tapped his earpiece and reactivated it. "Carpenter, this is Lucas."

"Go ahead."

"Meltdown will begin shortly. Get everyone out of the building. All exits will be vapor locked in about twenty minutes. Anyone left inside will die."

"What about Idris? Is he with you?"

"No. He's dead. My clone killed him."

"Where is your clone?"

"He escaped and he's armed. We're on our way back to you."

"Hurry. I'll call back the troops now."

Gil motioned toward the bathroom door again.

Julia adamantly shook her head. "No. I'm not leaving Felicia alone."

CHAPTER 74

Gil exhaled slowly. "Fine. Bring her with you, but hurry."

She sat in disbelief, wondering how perverted his man was, but she misunderstood what he meant and what his intentions truly were.

Something struck the hotel door hard. Gil pulled his gun. "Get to the bathroom, now!"

Julia slid off the side of the bed with Felicia in her arms. She ran to the bathroom when the door rattled again. When she turned to close the door, Gil handed her a 9mm butt first.

"Here," he said. "You might need this. Do you know how to use it?"

Julia clasped her hand around the gun and clicked off the safety.

"Yes," she replied.

Gil removed another gun from the back of his belt. "Lock the door. I'll try to stop him from getting to you. But if I can't, use the gun."

Julia nodded. "Who's out there?"

"I don't know," he replied. Sweat cropped his brow and upper lip. "He's dangerous and fast. He killed the agents parked outside before they ever noticed him. They're still seated inside their vehicles."

Another weighted thud bombarded the door. Wood splintered. The metal hinges bent. Gil pulled the door closed, and Julia quickly locked it. She huddled with Felicia in the bathtub. She flung the curtain back as if it were a magical barrier that evil couldn't penetrate, but she knew that wasn't true. She wondered what was beating its way through the door. If the outside agents had been unable to kill him and now were dead, she doubted Gil stood a chance to protect them. He was coming for them.

"Momma," Felicia whispered. "I'm scared."

Julia hugged Felicia closer and rested her chin on top of her daughter's head to keep her from seeing her Momma cry. "I know, baby. Me, too."

It was okay to tell her fears but not show them.

"You are? Really?" Felicia asked.

"Yes."

"I don't like guns."

"Me, either."

"Will you shoot someone?" Felicia asked.

"Not unless I have to."

Felicia pulled back with wide eyes. "You would?"

Julia embraced her closer, tighter. "To protect you, honey, yes. Yes, I will."

The beating on the hotel door became louder, less patient. The weak, battered door crashed to the floor. Gil had moved near the center of the room. His voice was frantic as he addressed Carpenter via his transmitter. Five rounds fired from his gun before a high-pitched scream abruptly dropped to silence.

Julia didn't question whether or not Gil was dead or alive. Whatever had come inside had killed him, and if he discovered them hiding in the bathroom, the same fate was theirs.

The bathroom was tiny, almost making her feel claustrophobic. Her fear of what might be in the other room made breathing even more difficult. She hated being separated from Daniel and Morton. She had a great sense of security when she was with them. They were the solid foundation that drove her inner fears away. She suddenly realized that she had unduly criticized Daniel for his phobias when she had similar fears of her own. And, to make matters worse, Daniel had been right. Something inside him had warned him about the ensuing danger. Instinct? Premonition? She wasn't sure, but she could no longer argue that he was being paranoid.

Julia had shrugged off her fears because he and Morton's presence allowed her to ignore danger. She knew they'd protect her. But now, being alone, with death creeping outside the door, Felicia's only hope lay with her mother. Julia hated knowing that their fate relied on how she handled the situation.

When she had entered the streets to follow Daniel and keep an eye on

Lydia's clone, she had feared losing him. But entering the shadowed realm of shifters introduced her to fears she could never have imagined. With her heart hammering in her chest, she managed to find him but ended up getting separated and having to fend for herself. But, at this moment, she wasn't worried about her own life. She had to protect Felicia. If that meant killing the invader on the other side of the door, she'd do it. There wasn't anyone else to rely on.

Perhaps Julia had been at ease the past three years because she trusted Helmsby to oversee TransGenCorp safely, but the sleeping giant was heavily armed and relentlessly roaring with its sharp fangs exposed. If Lucas failed to stop the facility, it stood to destroy any who dared oppose the outrageous experimentation.

Julia held the gun at her side. She suddenly feared that what killed Gil and the other agents might be one of Idris' creations. She worried that her gun wouldn't be enough to kill it. Deep in her soul, she knew it wouldn't. After all, Gil had fired several shots without stopping it. The outer silence indicated he was dead. Otherwise, he'd have opened the door by now.

Felicia sobbed against Julia's chest. Julia held her tightly with one arm while aiming the gun at the door. Heavy breathing panted outside the door. The locked doorknob rattled as someone or something turned it from the other side. Julia closed her eyes and whispered a prayer.

Lucian ran down the hall. Little time remained before the Meltdown enacted. He hurried to the lab where Kyle's body lay. With two fingers, he checked for a pulse again, hoping that something miraculous had revived him. But there was nothing but death's coldness.

"Dammit." He lifted Kyle's limp body and placed him over his shoulder. He headed out the door and down the hall. "Perhaps there's still time."

Yvonne and Nancy carried Helmsby down the corridor and paused where the tile floor ended and the limestone slab began. After Lucas inserted the Meltdown chip, emergency-warning lights flashed along the hall and at each emergency exit sign. The breeze thickened with the heavy scent of rotten fish and stagnant water, and Yvonne noticed movement on the dock.

Without a word spoken, Yvonne motioned Nancy to pull Helmsby against the wall. Two uniformed guards untied the motorboat and started the engine. Their sleek black uniforms made them look like life-filled shadows. They climbed into the boat and started the engine.

"That's the only boat," Nancy whispered.

Yvonne nodded. "Yes, I see that."

Helmsby winced and lifted weight off his injured leg. "They aren't human," he said.

Yvonne cocked an eyebrow and faced him. "What?"

"Those areas of the laboratories where you said that we don't have access or know what's in them?"

"Yes?"

Helmsby cleared his throat. "I know what's there. Well, not exactly, but I know they aren't quite human. They're genetic monsters. If they see us, we're dead. I don't know that the denaturers can kill them."

"And you know this *how?*"

Helmsby blushed. "I did a little investigating in the hidden chambers a few months ago. I never got a close enough look to discern exactly what they were. No files about them are accessible to me, so I'm not aware of their genetic makeup. The Meltdown has started, and these two are free. It means Lucas was too late."

Yvonne shook her head. "It means we're dead. That boat's the only way we had out of here."

Sadness shadowed Helmsby's eyes. "That, too."

Yvonne radioed Carpenter. "We have a problem at the docks."

"What's wrong?"

"Two soldiers just left in the boat. We cannot leave by the river now."

"We'll send a boat to retrieve you, but it will take some time."

"Time isn't something we have to spare."

"I know. Do you have any other way out?"

"I don't know," Yvonne replied. "The door we came through locked after it closed. We can't go that direction. Shifters were released in the corridor, too."

"Damn," Carpenter said. "We'll find some way to get to you."

"Well, you need to stop the soldiers that took the boat. Helmsby says that they aren't human."

"What?"

"They're like the clone."

Helmsby squeezed her arm and shook his head. "No, they're *worse.*"

"Correction," she said. "They're worse than Lucas' clone."

"In what way?"

Yvonne looked at Helmsby. He shrugged. "Stronger. Perhaps indestructible."

"I thought everything was under control," Carpenter said bitterly.

"Apparently not," Yvonne answered.

Nancy rested her head against her father's shoulder.

The shifters farther up the corridor chattered softly. Their hard toenails clicked on the floor, slowly moving toward them. Helmsby glanced back to a glowing mob of eyes. Some shifters staggered and fell down because the toxic blood they had eaten poisoned them. But the stronger ones approached bravely. Either the toxin had not affected them, or they were smart enough to detect the danger of ingesting tainted blood.

"We have to get you to the other side of the water," Yvonne said. "The other stairwell leads up, so maybe we have enough time to get to the front doors."

"But," Nancy said. "Lucas was attacked in that stairwell when we escaped. What if more soldiers are up there?"

Yvonne pulled her gun. "Then we'd best hope these bullets kill them."

CHAPTER 75

*L*ydia pulled away from Lucas' embrace and wiped away her tears. "I still don't understand why you let your clone escape. There's no telling what he'll do after he leaves TransGenCorp or how many more people he might kill."

"I know," Lucas replied. "And since he won't look like me anymore, it won't be easy to track him. But I believe in Karma. His will come. Should I cross paths with him again, I'll kill him. If he wants to live, he'd best stay far away from me. It matters more to me that you're alive."

Gil's voice came over Lucas' earpiece. "Carpenter, it's in the room," he said, frantically. "It burst through the door. I ... the bullets aren't affecting it. Outside agents are all dead. Dear God!"

Lucas looked at Lydia. Her wide eyes revealed she had heard the same through her earpiece.

"Gil!" Carpenter said. "Gil?"

Grave concern overshadowed Lydia face. "He's guarding Julia and Felicia. We need to get there to help them."

Lucas lowered his head. "Even if we leave now, we won't have enough time to get there."

Lucian carried Kyle down the hall and stopped at another lab. He rested

Kyle's body on top of a Formica tabletop. Once more he checked for a pulse. Nothing.

Kyle's lips and skin held a bluish tint. The already dark circles around his closed eyes had darkened. Lucian sighed.

"Death can't be victorious here today," he thought. "Not today."

Lucian sprinted to Idris' office and opened a side drawer of the desk where Idris kept his personal stash of enhancers. Other vials must have been inside, too, because of what Idris had started evolving into. He pulled out a small steel box that was buried beneath sterile syringe packets. Setting the box on the desktop, he opened it and removed a vial. Inserting a needle into the yellow serum, he withdrew 3ccs of the shifter enhancer reagent.

Lucian hurried back to Kyle and injected the serum. After several minutes, he checked for a pulse.

Nothing.

"Dammit!" he seethed.

He clasped his hands on Kyle's chest and administered CPR. He counted the pumps he made with his hands and paused. After the third set of thrusts, Kyle's eyelids fluttered.

Lucian performed another set and Kyle coughed.

Lucian smiled. Even though Kyle had suffered a lot of genetic damage and might never achieve complete regeneration, the chances were increased that he'd have some renewed progress once the solution passed through his bloodstream.

The virulent shifter DNA might restore Kyle's suppressed memories. And if Kyle was fortunate, the chances for his brain lesions to heal had increased. Lucian doubted Kyle's maimed arm could ever completely regenerate, but recovering lost motor functions was more important than an arm. Kyle had been too brilliant to lose all his brain data.

Kyle's eyes lulled back. Only the whites were visible. Strange, gurgling sounds creaked in his throat. His labored breathing became gentle, more stable.

Kyle's pulse grew stronger. He gulped for air and his chest rose higher and higher. He'd survive. This might not undo Lucian shooting Kyle, but at least, Lucian had proven that he had attempted to make amends.

Lucian looked at Kyle and smiled. Kyle stared back.

"I've never had a brother before," Lucian said. "Until now."

Brockton entered the room and Lucian turned with his gun steadied at the doctor's head. Brockton stared closely. "Are you the real Lucas or his clone?"

During the struggle to revive Kyle, Lucian's facial muscles had relaxed back to their former state. "Lucian."

"Don't kill me, and I'll help you with Kyle."

Lucian lowered the gun. "Why would I kill you? You've been nothing except kind to me."

Brockton wiped sweat from his brow. "In this establishment, you've no guarantee who's your friend one day and your enemy the next."

"How can you help him?"

"There are ways. Some injections of d-amphetamines might help restore his locomotion capabilities somewhat. And other things. But, it looks like I got here in time. He's not dead, so that's good."

"Well, he was. I revived him. Does that make any difference?"

"No," Brockton said. "I don't think so. I was just afraid that if he had died, you might not know how to revive him. You did good. Where's Idris?"

Lucian looked away. "I had to kill him."

"Oh?"

"Yes. He was undergoing some strange transformation."

"I see," Brockton said with a bit of relief. His shoulders relaxed. "Help me place Kyle on a gurney. With the Meltdown activated, wheeling him out will be the fastest route. But first, I need to go to my office."

Lucian nodded. "Lead the way."

CHAPTER 76

*L*ydia stepped into the hall with her gun held ahead of her. She half expected to get another shot at Lucian, but if she revealed the truth, she *hoped* the chance to kill him came soon, before he escaped TransGenCorp. Lucas followed her but kept his attention behind them so no one attacked from the rear. Rex padded along the floor beside them. He was too much a pup to be expected to track an enemy, much less protect them, but his keen sense of hearing and smell might alert them to other lesser dangers.

Midway down the hall, the main lights flickered. A buzzing sounded from breaker boxes. A few seconds later, the overhead lights shut off. Darkness filled the halls and rooms. Emergency lights popped on at various intervals in the halls but hardly bright enough to drive away the darkness.

Lydia looked at Lucas with concern in her eyes. "You don't think Idris told us the truth, do you?"

"About what?"

"Destroying one thing unleashes others?"

"The truth seldom fell from his lips."

"Maybe, but," she said, peering down the dark corridor. "Perhaps it was his little safeguard all along."

Lucas released his gun's safety. "Meaning?"

"Maybe he feared Helmsby would discover a way to do what you just did and afterwards, the process reset the program to release other shifters, or more soldiers."

"I never estimated that he'd be that smart, but I could be wrong. We have little time, so we have to hope we don't encounter anything unusual."

The dull alarm moaned endlessly through the intercom speakers in each room and hall. The annoyance was more disturbing than the shadowy darkness looming around them.

A door swung open at the end of the hall. A man-like creature stepped through the door. In the dim lighting, all they could really see of the strange, slender form was its glowing yellow eyes. It moved closer to the emergency light. The light washed over it, making it more recognizable. Its arms hung down like an ape's, but it didn't possess the mass or width of a massive primate. Its furless body was muscled with thick sinewy cords weaved around its bulging biceps and chest. The glowing eyes peered in their direction. The sudden grunt it gave indicated it could see them.

Lucas watched its slim figure in the hallway, and he suddenly recalled the creature Daniel had seen on the outskirts of Pittsburgh when scavenging the area for food. The eerie beast had followed Daniel into an alley, but eventually Daniel lost sight of it. Morton had somehow killed it in the alley, out of Daniel's view. Morton, however, never discussed *how* he had killed it. Lucas always assumed Morton knew a lot more than the rest of them, and the cat enjoyed having his secrets.

Lydia backed against the wall and aimed, squeezing off two rounds. The first shot threw the creature's left shoulder back. The second shot caught it in the chest. It clasped its hands to the chest wound and dropped to its knees. Its swelling body vibrated violently. A pulse of yellow energy flashed and ran through its body. Dark, black eyes stared at them.

Anger consumed it. The beast pushed itself upright and flung its hairless arms above its head and roared. Its mouth stretched wider. Jagged teeth gnashed together. The gunshots had not done any obvious damage. No blood or liquid gushed from it, only pain-filled outrage. It lunged and ran straight at them. Lydia's weapon didn't frighten it.

Lucas grabbed Lydia's hand and tugged. She started to resist, but she sensed how fast the creature approached.

"Which rounds did you use?" he asked, pulling her through the door and slamming it shut. He turned the deadbolt.

"The denaturers your clone left us," she said, expelling the clip and exposing one round.

Fists pounded the metal door. The creature snarled and growled, pressing its weight against the door. The thudding became louder, harder, and small dents protruded through the metal. Its maddened determination sought to find a way through the thick barrier eventually. It had one need.

Revenge.

Lucas frowned. "The denaturers didn't faze it at all."

"No."

"You only pissed it off. Let's hope that there aren't more of them nearby."

"Indeed."

Lucas scrambled through the room, which now he discovered, was only an office for one of the scientists employed by TransGenCorp. The faint light on the other side of the office was bright enough to reveal another door. He hurried to it and flung it open to find a small laboratory. Two cages with open doors set against the far wall.

The pounding on the metal door never ceased. It intensified with unrelenting violence.

"It's going to eventually get through that door," she said. "We need to find a way to kill it."

"I know," Lucas said. "But by the time it gets through, we'll be in the next hall."

She grabbed his arm and pointed. She placed her index finger to her lips. A set of hollow, glowing golden eyes met his from the open door on the far side of the laboratory. Crouched lower was a second set of eyes, green like emeralds. These eyes belonged to a different kind of furry creature. The two creatures blocked their only escape route. The metal door behind them rattled. Loosened screws fell from the hinges. In minutes, or maybe less, that door was going to fall.

Lucas' eyebrows rose in question. He glanced at Lydia.

She shrugged. "I don't have any ideas different than yours," she said. "Let's just see how this plays out."

The small shifter growled and leapt at them. Outside, an alarm sounded. Time was running out. They went for their guns. The emergency lights dimmed. Everything around them suddenly became darker.

THE CORRIDOR FILLED with the smell of burnt rubber and melted plastic. Electrical wires burned in the ceilings and the walls. The Meltdown was true to its name.

The air in the dark room of winged shifters—like the one that had killed

Randy three years earlier—was sucked out through the ventilation duct. The creatures convulsed, staggered, and fought to breathe. Their tiny lungs compressed. Their iridescent eyes slowly closed and their bodies collapsed onto the litter-covered floor.

The genetic soldiers in the liquid-filled tanks shook. The Meltdown shut off the oxygen supply and the heart monitors became inactive. The genetic creatures' eyes popped open, and for a brief few minutes, they struggled. Their muscles tightened. Their tongues shoved the oxygen plugs from their mouths. They inhaled thick liquid into their lungs. They doubled over and their hearts stopped beating.

Further down the corridor, behind the sealed door with the biohazard warning sign, electronics locks clicked. The main door opened, followed by smaller cage doors.

Voices chattered with excitement.

"Humans are here. In the halls. Humans."

"Kill them," another high-pitched voice shrieked. "Kill them. Kill them."

"Yes," another whispered. "Let them come. Kill."

Like a frightened flock of blackbirds taking to flight, their piercing voices shrilled. The door opened wider and their hunched little bodies filled the dark hall. Their timid little feet touched the cold tile floor for the first time. There was so much more they wanted to learn.

CHAPTER 77

*L*ucas grabbed a metal chair and flung it upright as the small furry shifter lunged toward him. The chair legs caught its neck and flipped it against the wall. It shuddered from the impact, shook its back, and bared its teeth. It charged.

He pulled his gun, fired, and a denaturer delivered its poison. The bullet ripped through its gut. It chattered and rolled into a ball. He expected it to stretch out and make another attack, but it gurgled. Froth bubbled from its mouth and it stopped breathing.

"At least it's dead," Lydia said.

"Yes, but that leaves these other two."

Lucas aimed his gun out of instinct at the taller creature, the twin to the one beating down the door. Its eyes beamed more from curiosity than fury.

Lydia leaned closer and whispered. "No, don't shoot it. You saw how the other one reacted."

The metal door folded inward and crashed on the floor. The strange shifter wailed with triumph. Its sibling stepped closer but still didn't make any attempt to attack.

"We're trapped," Lucas said.

A warning blared over the intercom system: "Fifteen minutes until Meltdown completes."

"Damn," Lucas said. "Bullets won't work and the Meltdown is underway. Perhaps your assumption was correct. Perhaps Idris did program a protective code to release other creatures if his files were tampered with. Something released these."

Carpenter spoke through Lucian's earpiece. "Are you two about out of there?"

"No. We've run into a problem."

"What?"

"We're trapped by some strange creatures that were released after the Meltdown began."

"How?"

"Idris must have second guessed me. He had a backup plan. If I tampered with the system, the gates and cages to other experiments opened. Since he's dead, I have no way to know how to reverse this. We're surrounded. Make sure everyone else is out of TransGenCorp."

Lucas stood still and the two shifters moved closer. Lydia stood with her back against his. She kept her attention on the one she had shot. She had holstered her weapon and stood with her hands raised to defend herself. When it rushed, she would be ready. Hand to hand combat seemed the only thing she had left to kill it.

Kat said to Lucas, "There has to be a way we can help you."

"Afraid not," he replied. "The denaturers are useless on them."

"We'll come get you," Carpenter said.

"No. You'll never make it in time."

"We can't leave you behind."

"Don't worry," Lucas said. "We'll go out fighting."

Lucas tucked his gun behind his belt and pulled a razor-sharp hunting knife from his boot. "You have your knife?" he asked.

Before the words even came from his mouth, she already held hers. "Yes."

"That's my girl."

Lydia's eyes narrowed. She seethed. "Give them Hell."

She ran straight at the creature without any hesitation. It growled and lunged at her. Lydia screamed.

CHAPTER 78

orton's ears had perked when he heard Gil yelling for help through Daniel's earpiece. Julia and Felicia were in danger, and he was too far away to rescue them.

His cat eyes flared crimson red. Extra teeth lined his mouth and his paws grew larger. He tried to suppress his burning anxiety but found, for the first time, he couldn't control it. What he truly began to surface.

"Get me to them," Morton said to Daniel.

Kat placed a hand over her mouth when she noticed what Morton was turning into.

"Now!" the cat said sternly. "I must protect them."

Daniel scooped Morton into his arms and ran for the door. Johanna stayed with the agents. Neither Kat nor Carpenter made a comment. Nothing they said would help.

∿

JULIA GRABBED Felicia and hugged her tightly. She could hear it breathing heavily against the door. The doorknob rattled. Even though it was capable of splintering the door, it never shoved its weight to smash through.

It was waiting for them to exit. It was patient, she thought. Or, it was feeding on their fear.

She placed her hand on the doorknob that opened to the adjoining

270

room, but it was locked. She fought to hold back her tears, but they escaped anyway. She put the gun on the sink. Bullets wouldn't hurt it. Gil had emptied his gun into the beast, and the monster killed him. The gun proved to be a worthless weapon.

Julia returned to the door that led to the adjoining room. She gently pushed her weight against it. The center of the door was flimsy, and not solid wood. Should she apply more force, it would give way. After all, the door was old and cheaply made.

She took a step back and gave a sharp, violent kick. The door caved through the center. She shoved her shoulder hard against it and burst through. The outer fragments of the door clung to the hinges.

Julia ran with Felicia in her arms toward the door. She turned the bolt lock, and the other bathroom door splintered apart. Whatever had killed Gil was coming after them. She pulled the door open and ran for the concrete stairs that led to the lower level parking lot.

Misty layers of fog crept across the parking lot. For a second she froze, feeling like she had stepped through time to the day when she ventured into the shrouded streets after Daniel. She expected to hear howls of hungry shifters racing toward her. She shook her head and drove the memories from her mind. She had to protect Felicia, and not worry about what happened three years earlier. Besides, this creature was different and perhaps more dangerous than those predatory shifters.

Before she reached the parking lot, the creature leapt over the upstairs banister. He crashed through the roof of a car. His face looked almost human, and his body was muscled. Round eyes peered at her through what looked more like a canine's face than a human's. The facial hair and trimmed beard gave it an almost wolfish face. Many of its facial components were merged between human and wolf. The TGC emblem was stitched on its gray bodysuit. The name, Bane, was stitched in red.

Julia started to run for her van, but a squad car pulled into the lot. She wondered if Carpenter had alerted the police to rescue her. She fought against the idea of warning the officer that Gil's bullets had not killed it. But that required yelling, and doing so, would turn the creature's attention toward her. She kept reminding herself that getting Felicia to safety was the most pressing issue. That meant running and putting a lot of distance between them and the beast. She needed to find a place to hide.

Bane pulled himself out of the car and stepped onto the hood. He turned and faced her. His strange, golden eyes glowed through the thin fog. He didn't notice the squad car until the brakes squealed abruptly. The officer, using his door as a shield, fired at the beast.

Julia wasn't certain, but she could swear that it smiled. The officer unloaded his 9mm into Bane. The wolfish man didn't flinch or howl in pain. He sprang to the pavement and rushed him. The officer turned and pulled a loaded shotgun from the car. He fired, catching the creature dead center in the chest. Bane lurched back from the impact momentarily. The shot pellets shredded his shirt. Oozing blood leaked from the holes, but he healed as fast as he moved. Deep growls escaped his mouth, and he snarled, revealing his fangs and sharp teeth.

Julia ran. She ran into the ally. After the third shotgun blast, the officer screamed in intense agony. And, as quickly, silence won.

Although Julia never pulled Felicia back to see her face, she knew her daughter was terrified and crying. Her sobs beat against Julia's chest. She feared Felicia would be scarred and traumatized for the rest of her life. She had truly believed this was all over, and now, she feared it might never end except with their deaths.

Several rusted dumpsters lined the alleyway. She didn't think those were good hiding places, but she was too tired to keep running and carrying Felicia. Already her arms were tired. She was short of breath, more from fear than fatigue, and should she continue, she might collapse from exhaustive distress.

Her heart hammered inside her chest. The air grew thicker, colder. She took slower breaths to prevent hyperventilating. Felicia's sobs were now audible. Her hot tears wet Julia's shirt collar.

"It's okay, baby," Julia whispered in Felicia's ear. "It's going to be okay. Please don't cry."

"I'm scared, Momma."

"I know, baby. But don't cry. You mustn't. It will hear you."

Felicia's eyes widened. In that instant, she forced her sobs to stop because, Julia reasoned, her daughter understood the danger that any noise placed them in.

"I've got to get you out of here. To somewhere safe."

Felicia nodded.

Julia gave a weak, nervous smile and wiped tears from Felicia's eyes.

The alley was overgrown with drying weeds, empty beer bottles, and lots of scattered paper and debris. The fog was thinner here than at the parking lot, but like an ocean wave crashed on the beach, a tide of heavier fog spilled from the north end of the alley, threatening to swallow them. Being this close to the river when a cold front passed through brought fog, but this fog brought terrifying memories to Julia. Memories she had thought she'd buried. Suddenly, more fears crept into her mind and assaulted her fretfulness.

When she had fought shifters to help protect Daniel, she had been stronger. Now, though, holding her only child, she appeared weaker, because she allowed the fear of losing Felicia to overpower her will to survive. She tried to thrust away the fear and draw on her inner resources to survive, but she found them outside of her reach.

She disappeared into the thicker fog and dry weeds crackled beneath her feet. An angry snarl like a wolf came from behind her. He was just beyond sight but close enough to rush her. Although she couldn't see him, she sensed he was near. She believed for some strange reason that he was tracking her scent. She doubted even he had the ability to see through this dense fog. He relied on his sense of smell.

"Shhh," she whispered. Her daughter's arms tightened around Julia's neck. Julia stepped gently forward, further away from the beast. Not knowing what lay on the ground ahead of her, each step was a gamble that she wouldn't accidentally kick a bottle or can or make some other disruptive sound that pinpointed their location.

The stench of dead fish and sulfur drifted with the fog, which may have been strong enough to temporarily mask their scent. The wolfish man took two deep breaths. He stood closer than she realized and was trying to track her.

Julia dared another step forward. Then another. She did this until she reached a dumpster. The trash inside reeked of rotten food and produce. She peered into the dumpster and the aroma gagged her. Felicia pressed her nose against Julia's shirt.

At first she contemplated sliding Felicia into the dumpster, but she knew her little girl would immediately protest, and she couldn't blame her. The odor was enough to stifle a dead cat. Instead, she carried Felicia between the dumpster and the brick wall. She sat down and loosened Felicia's death grip from around her neck. She was afraid to exhale. Then she noticed golden eyes. Cold, heartless, golden eyes. They stared at her. Just inches away.

～

"*Thirteen minutes until Meltdown*," the cold computerized voice said over the intercom.

Lydia slashed her knife through the creature's chest at least four inches deep. Her blade came away covered with viscous liquid. Just as quickly as the blade passed through, the wound sealed itself shut. The gel-like flesh solidified into something much more durable.

The creature gnashed jagged teeth, released a gurgling howl, and lashed a violent fist into her jaw that sent her tumbling over a lab table. She hit the floor hard.

Little Rex barked before finding a dark corner to cower in. After cowering out of harm's way, the pup whimpered and whined.

"Are you okay?" Lucas asked, looking for her while keeping an eye on the two humanoids.

Lydia didn't reply. She rose to her feet and growled like an animal. She charged across the table and plunged the blade deep into its chest. It grabbed her wrists and using her momentum; it swung her overhead and sent her through the large window.

Showering glass tinkled around her. She closed her eyes, hit the floor, and rolled. Slowly, she staggered to her feet, holding her knife tightly in hand. Piles of glass shards surrounded her feet.

"Dammit!" Lucas yelled. "Stay the hell away from it!"

Lydia leapt back through the shattered window and drove her knife downward, toward its head. It batted her arm away, spiraled, and shoved a flat hand against her chest. The blow lifted her two feet off the floor. She landed in a pile of glass and slid. The creature rushed and bombarded her with blows that should have killed her. Blood dripped from her facial lacerations. Her left eye swelled. Glass fragments were imbedded in her legs.

Lucas kept a table between himself and the other humanoid. His body couldn't withstand a fraction of the damage Lydia had endured. He realized Lydia was in real danger. Without the sensation of pain, she didn't know the severity of her injuries. Lucas wanted to protect her, but he was helpless. She was more powerful than he was. If their battle relied upon guns and knives, they'd win. But at the particular moment, he thought she was going to die. And if it were true that she no longer wanted to live, she'd fight until the creature killed her.

Lydia's rate of recovery was rapid; however, it also demanded time to heal. Severe injuries took longer, but she wasn't going to retreat or stop to catch her breath. Her narrowed eyes indicated she had become what she dreaded. Inside, she did have a demon of sorts that longed for the chance to emerge and inflict pain, to kill.

With its ape-like arms, it lunged at her. Even though the gun was useless, he raised the 9mm to shoot, hoping it distracted the creature long enough for Lydia to get away. But he didn't have a clear shot and might accidentally shoot her instead. He wasn't certain if Lucian's threat about the bullets being able to kill her was true or not. He dared not chance it and lowered the gun with reluctance.

Her blade ripped through its left biceps, flaying open muscle fibers. The creature's eyes widened. She lunged toward it. Its right hand wrapped around her throat and squeezed. She stiffened and brought the knife upward. She drove the blade deep into its gut, but its hold didn't lessen. With both hands, it choked her, trying to break her neck.

She dropped the knife and clutched its muscled wrists, trying to break free of its hold. The growl escaping its lips was more a laugh than anything else. Lifting her off the floor, it shook her. Her face reddened, and Lucas swung the metal chair into the crazed creature's back, knocking it off balance.

Lydia collapsed to the floor and fell forward. Catching herself with her hands, she rolled and sat up. She wheezed, coughed, and fought to breathe. Once her breathing stabilized, she vomited.

"Ten minutes until Meltdown is complete."

"Lydia," Lucas said. "Let's get the hell out of here. There's no way to kill it."

Lydia ignored him. She didn't seem to like the fact that these things couldn't die and that this one had bested her. She wiped blood from her cheek and lips and looked at her bloody hands. Calling upon her mental focus, she forced herself to stand. She braced against a lab table to steady her legs.

The other humanoid remained docile, which made Lucas wonder if the other one was only bent on killing Lydia because she had attacked it first. Its anger fed off hers. And she didn't plan to stop until one of them died. Lucas didn't see how she could possibly win the fight. A part of him believed she no longer cared if she died. She believed she was a monster like the clone and the creature in front of her. Even though Lucas insisted she wasn't, he did somewhat believe her now. And yet, he loved as much as he always had. But he didn't believe he'd be able to rescue her from herself. No words or coaxing could switch off her killing instincts.

"Lydia, please," Lucas said. "Let's go."

"Giving up so soon, brother?"

Lucian stood at the open door with Kyle draped over his shoulder.

Lucas frowned. "Brother?"

"Like it or not, but we're one in the same. Genetically, without my genomic advancements, we're twins. Or, would you prefer me to call you father?"

"Neither."

"Then brother it is," Lucian smiled. "Take Lydia and leave. I'll take care of these things."

Lucas shook his head. "They don't die. We can't kill them with the denaturers and knives do no damage."

"It's because you don't understand how they function."

"And you do?"

"Lydia, go with Lucas. Get out of here."

Lydia dove to the floor, grabbed her knife, and spun a perfect roundhouse kick. The creature's head flung to the side and its body did a half-spiral. She went for its throat with the blade. She shoved the blade through its neck and twisted.

After the humanoid regained balance, it grabbed her wrist with its hands and twisted. She kneed, where its groin should be, hard enough to bring it off the floor. It squealed and released her. She spun three hundred sixty degrees and drove the knife in its back. It didn't cry in pain. Instead, it rounded around, hard and fast, slamming its elbow into her face. She lost balance and dropped across the table, facedown.

The creature was atop her in seconds. It straddled the small of her back and interlocked both hands around her throat. It pulled back on her neck. Her face flushed red, slowly turning purple. A crackling sound ran along her spine.

Lucas watched helplessly.

A crazed look gleamed in its eyes.

A look of triumph.

Victory.

Lucian pushed past Lucas and tackled the creature, knocking it off her. He wrestled it to the floor.

Lydia massaged her throat and stood slowly. She walked to Lucas. The other creature watched with curiosity. It didn't seem to comprehend anything. Since they never attacked it, it never bothered them. Its eyes watched Lucian but never moved.

"Watch and learn, brother," Lucian said.

Lucian's fingers lengthened two phalanges longer. With speed unlike Lucas, Lucian's hands dug into the creature's chest. Sloppy wet sounds came from the opening. Seconds later, Lucian held its pink heart, but not an ordinary heart. This heart had wires and computer chips attached to the cardiac muscle. Lucian tossed the heart to the floor. All the energy drained from the strange being. What mad science was this?

Lucas' mouth opened to ask a question, but Lucian smiled. "I don't have time to explain. Go. I'll take care of the other one."

"What about Kyle?" Lydia asked.

"He goes with me, too," Lucian replied.

Lucas' eyes narrowed.

"No harm will come to him, I promise. In fact, I can help him. Medically. I think the damage he suffers can be reversed."

The want and need to kill his clone returned. But the longer he stared at Lucian, the less he liked the idea. Like Lydia, Lucas understood he wouldn't be killing an enemy. He'd actually kill a part of himself. To accomplish such a morbid act, he'd have to seek his inner rage and cast it on his mirror reflection, but that wouldn't kill the part of himself he sometimes hated. That part remained inside him and continued to live, even if his clone died.

To some degree, Lucian was his own person. Ninety percent of his genetic makeup was Lucas, but the experimentations Idris had forced his clone to undertake made him a different person altogether. He hoped he wouldn't regret allowing his clone to go free, but he protecting Lydia was his top priority. For a bit of irony, he was now indebted to his clone for coming to their aid twice. But now, Lucas needed to save Lydia from herself, if nothing else.

"Nine minutes until Meltdown is complete."

Lucian eyed Lucas. "Kyle's safe with me. Nine minutes might be enough time for you to get out of here. Kyle will only slow you down."

"And he won't you?" Lydia asked.

Lucian smiled. "I know a quicker route out."

Lucas took Lydia's hand and pulled her to him. "Let's go."

"Do you believe him?" she asked.

"What choice do we have?"

"None, I suppose. But it doesn't mean I like it."

"Me, either."

Lucian glanced at Lucas and smiled.

Lucas said, "Thanks … for saving her … us."

Lucian replied with a single nod.

Lydia grabbed Rex. They hurried down the hall, found the room with the hidden stairwell and headed up. The chattering cries and glowing eyes in the catacombs told them they were not alone. The door locked behind them. Darkness shrouded them. Both pulled their guns and paused to listen to fluttering wings, strange cries.

They were not alone.

Daniel drove through a red light, following closely behind a squad car with its lights flashing and siren blaring. His chest was tight from anxiety. He took deep breaths and tried to calm down. Tears burned his eyes because he wasn't driving fast enough. For three years, nightmares had haunted his sleep, but none of them frightened him as badly as the thought of losing Julia and Felicia.

His wife and daughter were supposed to be safe at the hotel. With agents guarding the parking lot and Gil inside the room, his family was assured protection. But hearing Gil's anguished screams quashed any hope that Felicia and Julia would still be alive when they arrived.

What had been able to get past the outside agents, survive Gil's multiple gunshots, and manage to kill the agent?

Morton kept pushing autodial to reach Julia's phone over and over.

"Still no answer?"

The cat shook his head. "It just keeps ringing."

Daniel shook his head. A lump swelled in his throat. He glanced at the speed odometer. They traveled at seventy-five mph in a thirty-five mph zone. Daniel believed that was way too slow. The police car ahead of them hadn't been assigned to lead them. But, for reasons unknown, he believed the officer's destination was to investigate the disturbance at the hotel.

The world outside passed like a blur. Trees, parked cars, and pedestrians melted into abstract objects. He focused on the taillights ahead of him, ignoring everything else.

When they reached the hotel parking lot, the officer stepped from his vehicle and shouted. "What the hell are you doing?"

Daniel swung open his door. Morton jumped out. Daniel pointed at the hotel. "My wife and child are inside."

Morton didn't wait. His paws widened, and he ran upstairs to the second floor.

Carnage filled the parking lot. A shotgun and spent shells lay on the ground beside a police car. The officer's body was thrown over the flashing lights. Blood dripped from his severed throat into a thickening pool that ran down the windshield and hood into small, riveting streams that trickled onto the asphalt.

The officer on the scene reached into his car and retrieved his two-way radio.

"Officer down," he cried, scanning the parking lot. "Send backup and several ambulances. We have a lot of dead bodies here."

Beneath the thin fog, two dead agents slumped in their cars with the side glass shattered and their necks apparently broken. Daniel glanced at them, and then he ran for the stairs. Whatever killed them did so without notice.

Morton met Daniel at the open door of their room.

"They're not here," Morton said.

Daniel ran a hand through his hair. Tears burned his face. "Where could they have gone?"

Morton surveyed the parking lot. "They can't be far. Her vehicle's still here. She fled through the adjoining room."

"That's good."

"Yes, but it followed her. We have to find them."

Exasperated, Daniel said, "I . . . where do we start looking?"

Morton sniffed the air. He turned to the left and glanced at the alleyway. "That way."

Daniel followed him down the stairs and ran down the alley. A small shoe lay on the narrow lane.

It belonged to Felicia.

Morton's eyes blazed red. He looked at Daniel. "Stay here. They're not far. Leave this to me."

Daniel shook his head. "No, I won't let you do this alone."

The cat's paws swelled. Large claws sprouted outward. His teeth grew sharper. He shrugged. "Suit yourself. But this *won't* be pretty."

CHAPTER 80

Yvonne lowered Helmsby when they stepped onto the dock. She contemplated how to get him to the other side of the inlet. Helmsby applied his full weight, and to his surprise, he felt no pain.

"Nancy," he said. "Take your belt off my leg."

"Is something wrong?" Yvonne asked.

Helmsby shook his head. "No. Just inspect it, please."

Nancy untied the belt and removed the cloth bandage she had made. Other than dried blood, nothing else was there. No wound. No trace of the bullet hole at all.

Yvonne and Nancy stared at him. "How?"

He looked at Nancy. "Remember the injection I took after Maria attacked me?"

She nodded and smiled. "You mean?"

Helmsby shrugged. "I guess so. Somehow I must have gained quick tissue regeneration due to it."

Yvonne laughed. "That's good. Now we don't have to lug your ass around anymore."

"Do you know where that stairwell leads?" Helmsby asked.

"Yes, but we can't reach the main entrance in less than ten minutes."

The surviving shifters scurried toward the dock. Yvonne pulled her gun and shot the closest one. It cringed, shuddered, and rolled into a ball, dying.

The other shifters were smarter and didn't feed on the dying shifter. Instead, they pressed closer.

Through the earpieces, Carpenter said, "We have a boat on the way. But there's less than ten minutes before the Meltdown takes effect."

"Where we are the Meltdown isn't going to affect us. But we have a different problem."

"What?"

"A shitload of shifters."

"Any way to kill them?" Carpenter asked.

"Until I run out of bullets, which won't be much longer."

Nancy grabbed her father's arm tightly. She stepped behind him. Shifters chattered and growled. Their sharp teeth grated. Yvonne fired and killed three more. Her gun jammed. Three more stepped closer.

"You two jump to the other dock," Yvonne said. "I'll hold them off."

"We're not leaving you behind," Helmsby said.

"Just do it!"

"Yvonne," Helmsby said.

She eyed him sharply. "Bob."

Helmsby lowered his head like a henpecked rooster. He placed his hands on Nancy's shoulders. "You go first."

Nancy's eyes questioned whether he'd actually jump after her.

He nodded. "Don't worry. I'm right behind you."

"Go, honey," Yvonne said. "I'll be across after your father."

Nancy took a deep breath and made a leap for the other dock. Her right foot hit the dock and slipped. She fell forward, caught herself on her elbows, but knocked the air from her lungs. She winced and quickly stood.

Helmsby looked at Yvonne. "You'd best be straight across or I swear I'll come back."

"Just go. I'm coming."

A sad expression hung on his face, but he didn't argue further. He was concerned that she'd sacrifice herself to protect them. He made the leap more gracefully than Nancy had. He turned to motion Yvonne to cross, but a shifter charged her. Without flinching, she smashed the butt of the gun into its chattering mouth. Sharp teeth spewed from its mouth. It recoiled in pain. Its glowing eyes narrowed and it spat blood.

Instead of running to jump to them, she ran the other direction.

"Yvonne!" Helmsby yelled. "What the hell are you doing?"

She didn't reply. She dove forward, retrieved the dead guard's gun, rolled, and dropped the clip from the gun. She sat up and rammed the clip of denaturing rounds into the gun and fired several shots. The three shifters dropped where they stood. Spasms rippled through their bodies as they died.

Helmsby and Nancy embraced her when she reached the other side of the inlet.

"You had me worried," Helmsby said.

She laughed and winked. "You shouldn't doubt me. I plan to cash in on your promise."

"So do we wait here for them?" Nancy asked. "The water's too cold for us to swim."

"I have an idea," Yvonne said.

"What?"

She pointed. "Let's empty one of those crates. It should be buoyant enough to support us. We don't need to drift out far. Only to the outside of the cave's mouth."

Helmsby frowned. "Why can't we just wait here for the boat?"

"We can't that chance. More guards or shifters come to the docks."

"Ahh, okay."

CHAPTER 81

*K*at and Carpenter returned to TGC's parking lot. The coroner zipped the black body bag over Tyler. Kat wiped away tears. They loaded his body into the rear of the coroner's van.

Carpenter wrapped his arms around her and squeezed. She rested in his arms for several minutes. Hot tears spilled down her cheeks. Her mind replayed Tyler's death, and she pushed Carpenter away.

"Kat, I'm sorry," he said. "We really thought all this mess was over."

"We lost a lot of people here today," she said.

"I know, but I swear—"

She waved a hand and turned away. "Save it! I need a few minutes to myself. Alone."

He nodded. "Take your time."

Kat watched the rear morgue van's doors close. It was so final. Could she ever forgive herself for hurting his feelings? She wished she wasn't so bull-headed about opening her heart to others. To become vulnerable to love was something she avoided. Had it not been for her stubborn thoughts of not dating a coworker, his feelings would have been spared, and rather than him requesting to ride with Denton, he'd have been with her. And now he was gone forever.

For what? The FBI's failure to make certain TGC had been shut down forever.

Inwardly, she battled remorse and rage. Changes would be made, in her life, and in the outcome of TGC. One way or the other, she'd guarantee nothing else emerged from the scientific facility. No, too much death had occurred and the trail of blood led to these doors.

Idris was dead. Lucas' clone had seen to that. After the Meltdown completed, she wondered what else might emerge. It was obvious that the FBI might not ensure the finality that she wished to see.

The van rolled through the parking lot. She walked to Tyler's smoldering car. Seeing his blood sprayed across the upholstery made her turn away. *Dammit!* She wanted to cry, but sudden anger overcame her sorrow.

Fire flickered and smoke drifted through the shadowy fog that slowly dissipated. TGC mercenaries lay crumpled over barrels, Jeeps, and one another. When she came to the body of a National Guardsman, her knees weakened. Facedown, the body appeared so fragile and she now realized that so was life. She placed a hand on his shoulder and turned him over. Tears flooded her eyes when she looked into the young man's frozen eyes. He couldn't have been more than twenty years old. His face was innocent and now eternally silent. His face and Tyler's death would haunt her for years.

Kat glanced back. Carpenter talked to the National Guard Captain.

"How can you ignore all this?" she whispered.

The crimson TGC emblem of one dead mercenary caught her attention. Two soldiers, not like these men, but worse than Lucas' clone, had escaped by boat. Finding these men seemed impossible. But she understood that was now her mission. Too many innocent people would die if these men weren't captured and taken into custody.

Kat doubted the FBI would take the proper initiative to find them. They certainly failed with TGC. Perhaps the file on these soldiers would disappear as easily as they had vanished into society. It might simply fade away to the government agencies, but she'd keep a mental note until they were captured. Even if it meant she hunted until she found them.

Kat wiped away more tears. Near the covered flatbed truck was the stairwell where the mercenaries had emerged. She pulled her gun and approached warily. Perhaps it was because she was a woman, but most of the cleanup crew paid little attention to her while they gathered bodies and extinguished fires. But, like a cat, her curiosity got the better of her. She wanted to know what was in the bunker and where it led. The only way to find out was to go down the stairs.

And down she went.

CHAPTER 82

*L*ucas was concerned about Lydia. After her brutal battle with the strange humanoid, she had grown weaker, making her ability to heal slower. They took the stairs and she leaned against Lucas. The stairs ended in a place Lucas didn't recall seeing.

"I think we've gone a floor too far," he said.

She frowned. "Should we go back down?"

"No. We have to keep moving. There should be an exit around here somewhere."

The corridor narrowed, and the floors changed from tile to smooth concrete. They seemed to be heading into an older section of the cavern where the mining tunnels had over a century before. The construction had long been abandoned, for one reason or another, and therefore, no rooms were here. For several minutes, Lucas wondered if the hall simply dead-ended.

He was surprised that his clone had risked his life to protect and help them get out of TransGenCorp. The selfless act was enough that Lucas planned to look the other way and not hunt Lucian down later. Lucian's participation in destroying the creatures had saved Lydia's life. She wasn't going to back down, even after Lucas pleaded for her to run. For her to continue fighting would have been suicide. Either due to her fatigue, or self-control, she somehow managed to tame the monster that she insisted lived inside her.

Lucas interlocked his fingers with hers. They ducked where the concrete ceiling lowered. They remained crouched for about one hundred feet before the ceiling rose, allowing them to stand again. Lighting was nil. Emergency spotlights flickered but were positioned so far apart that their radiance barely left a dusk-like glow.

Rex had lost any sense of bravery and followed slowly.

Behind them came the chirping and fluttering of what sounded like a swarm of feeding bats, but Lucas expected worse. Idris hadn't lied. Destroying his prized facility opened doors for worse creatures to emerge. He wondered what things might have already escaped.

Lucas leaned forward and prepared to run faster, but he suddenly slowed and pulled Lydia against the wall. He pointed ahead of them. Beneath the faint glow of the emergency exit sign stood two mercenaries. They guarded a door. The only means Lucas and Lydia had left to escape was directly past these men.

"Why would TransGenCorp post guards here?" she asked.

"I don't know."

"Do you think they saw us?"

"No, or they'd have fired at us by now."

The coming cloud of chirping winged beasts echoed down the narrow corridor. Closer. Their high shrills stabbed into their eardrums with a constant ringing sound that forced them to clamp their hands over their ears to lessen the pain. The abrupt movement was enough to reveal their position to the guards.

The two men lifted their rifles and stared through the scopes.

"Damn," Lucas said.

One soldier lowered his gun. "Lucian?"

Lucas sighed with relief and the tension in his chest lessened. He stepped forward, closer, so the men could see them. "Yes?" He turned to Lydia and whispered, "Stay here."

"*Why* are you here?"

"The Meltdown. TGC is collapsing. They haven't warned you?"

"No," the guard said, looking at his partner. "No one's informed us."

Lucas studied the corners of the ceiling above the doorway. No intercoms. These men were expendable pawns for Idris to sacrifice if anything ever went horribly wrong.

These emotionless men looked identical to the others inside the incubation chambers. With so many of the men designed from one template,

Lucas wondered where that original man resided and how dangerous a foe he presented.

Lucas needed to get Lydia through the door and hopefully escape before the oxygen was sucked out of the facility. Knowing what these men were, he had to find a way to get out without allowing them to escape.

"What's behind the door?" Lucas asked.

The guards slung their rifles over their shoulders. "It leads to the old mine shafts and further down, the TGC sewer system."

"Interesting."

The other soldier asked, "The place is really going to shut down?"

Lucas nodded. "You have the key to the door?"

"Yes."

"Unlock the door. It's the only way out." He glanced at his watch. "We have less than five minutes before this place seals shut."

Lydia stepped from the shadows with Rex at her side.

"Who is she?" the guard asked.

While the one guard removed the key from his pocket Lydia rushed the other man and pinned him against the wall. Lucas pulled his gun and took the key.

The beating wings grew louder.

Closer.

Before she noticed any movement, the guard Lydia held kneed her in the stomach and kicked her right leg. She lost her balance, and he reached for his gun. She dropped to her hands and swung her feet around, knocking his legs out from under him. A bullet struck the ceiling and a chunk of concrete thudded onto the floor. Lydia grabbed the gun, twisted it from his grip, and in the process snapped his wrist bones.

Shrieks echoed and fluttering wings darkened the corridor. The cloud of darkness eerily displayed hundreds of slanted green eyes heading toward them. As flying flock nearer, the rolling echoing cries became more understandable.

"Kill them. Kill them. Kill them," they chanted.

Lucas shoved the key into the lock and twisted. He pushed it inward and thrust the guard he held into the maddening flock of winged creatures. Lydia grabbed Rex and hurried through the door. Lucas shut the door and engaged the lock.

The piercing cries forced the two guards to cover their ears and drop to the ground.

Lucas nearly lost his footing. Rex whimpered and his tail curled between his legs. They weren't standing in another hall, but on a six-foot square platform. Wind blew past them, so the Meltdown wouldn't have any effect on them.

A massive crack allowed a long ray of light to filter into the tunnel. When his eyes adjusted to the light, he found a rusted ladder that led downward. At one time the shaft might have been a crude elevator. All that remained now was a ladder.

"Be careful," Lucas said. "This platform is unsteady. We need to descend the ladder, if it's solid enough to support us. Once we reach the sewers we should be able to find a way out."

Lydia didn't reply. She watched through the small square window in the door. A flock of fifteen or more winged creatures hovered and dove like hungry seagulls. Their razor-sharp beaks ripped hair and flesh from the two guards.

One guard hunched on the floor and covered his head with his hands while the other stood and swung his rifle like a club to bat them out of the air. Firing a rifle at close range was useless. It made a more effective club when the swing connected.

He successfully battered three of the creatures to the floor. The dying winged creatures flopped around in circles. The man seemed to be getting an advantage and might have survived had he noticed the two hovering behind him.

The first reared its beak back and shrilled. Lucas and Lydia covered their ears. Even through the thick metal door, the sound was painful. He couldn't imagine how much worse it was on the other side.

The birdlike creature dove and flung its talons, slicing a jagged line across the man's face. He turned to see the hovering beast, which gave the second one an open view of his throat.

Its sharp claws pierced through the softness of the man's neck. Dark blood spilled, flowed. Several of the fliers landed atop his body and sucked the oozing blood.

The other guard crawled toward the door on his elbows. He patted a hand ahead of himself like a blind man. Lucas was horrified to see the man's face. His eyes were gone. Blood leaked from the empty sockets. Shreds of pink flesh hung in ribbons. His lipless mouth opened to speak but four of the creatures pecked and carved the flesh from his bloody face. His pain was too much. He lurched forward once more, and then, he didn't move anymore.

Lucas turned away.

Lydia hugged him tightly.

Rex whimpered with uncertainty.

Lucas tapped his earpiece. "Carpenter?"

"Yes?"

"We're out of the dangerous part of TransGenCorp. I'm not certain where we are. Some kind of mine shaft."

"You have no idea where it comes out?"

"No, but we're close to the sewer system. We should be able to come out somewhere along the river, but I'm not absolutely certain."

"Keep me posted. Once you're where we can get you, we'll pick you up."

"Thanks."

"Don't mention it."

Lucas dared a glimpse through the window again. Both men were dead. The winged little beasts feasted on their bodies. He pulled the door handle. The door didn't budge. It was secure, and he hoped the creatures never found a way out.

∾

MAGNUS DROVE the sleek Jaguar back to the front gate after the battle ended and parked across the street. He and Donovan promptly shut their car doors and walked through the fallen gates. No one questioned them for being there. They looked like they belonged. After walking past several smoldering vehicles, they found the open bunker, pulled their guns, and headed beneath the pavement. They planned to find Dr. Brockton and Lucian and kill them. Anyone else was extra entertainment.

∾

THE MISTY FOG lifted from the river but the overhead sky remained a gloomy gray. Blue lights flashed on a police boat. The boat slowed and turned a sharp semicircle. It coasted alongside the crate that held Helmsby, Nancy, and Yvonne.

The officers tossed ropes with safety rings and pulled them to the boat. After getting them situated, they were covered with heavy, heated blankets. Helmsby flashed a broad smile, sitting between his daughter and Yvonne. He draped an arm across each of their shoulders and squeezed.

He looked into Nancy's eyes. "It's time I took a vacation. A damn, *long* vacation."

Nancy's eyes moistened. "Dad, you've never taken a vacation . . . ever."

A tear escaped his eye. "I've already lost one woman I treasured without ever taking the time to enjoy life with her. I'm not going to make the same mistake twice. I can't lose the two of you."

"New oceans?" Yvonne asked.

Helmsby nodded. "Yes, set sail."

CHAPTER 83

Julia crept slowly away from the golden wolfish eyes. She scooted further behind the dumpster, and it released a low growl. She stopped and clung tighter to Felicia. Her daughter muffled cries against Julia's chest, trying to be quiet.

Bane studied her with strange curiosity as she did him.

Then, his eyes narrowed and he bore his teeth. Although he wore a TransGenCorp uniform, he was far from being a human soldier. She held no doubts that Idris had sent it to kill her and Felicia. He was definitely more animal than human.

Blood dripped from his teeth and claws. He reached for Felicia's hair. Julia pulled her daughter out of his reach. He snarled. Her rejection of his touch brought a grim smile. Again, he reached for Felicia with a timid hand. If his intention was not innocent, all it took was a second for him to crush Felicia with his strength. She didn't trust him. Should anger suddenly consume the beast, there was no way to know *what* he might do. She had seen what he was capable of.

Julia pushed away from him and hurried out from behind the dumpster. He growled and gnashed at her. An orange ball of fur blazed between Julia and the beast. Without looking back, Morton said, "Run to Daniel. Get out of here."

Julia turned to run.

Felicia said, "Cuddles?"

Julia ran into the thick fog and glanced back over her. Morton was no longer a cat. His eyes glowed red and his face was hideous. His jaw was filled with rows of sharp, jagged teeth.

Neither Julia nor Felicia had seen him in his true shifter form. Only Daniel had. Felicia's eyes widened. Her face paled.

A fierce growl roared in the alley. Morton answered with a dark cry of his own.

Julia ran for Daniel, and he shortened the distance between them. He wrapped his arms around them and kissed them.

"Thank God you're safe."

"Where's Cuddles?" Felicia whispered.

"He'll be here soon," Daniel replied.

The dumpster rattled and shook. A few seconds later, Morton's little body rolled beside them. He limped and shook his head. He frowned at Daniel. "Get them out of here. I'm not sure I can stop it."

A laceration along the cat's side mended slowly.

"You come with us then," Daniel said.

"No." Morton shook his head. "It'll catch and kill you. Get them to safety."

"But it may kill you."

"Doubtful," Morton hissed. "Even so, you three will be alive. That's what matters to me."

"You're important to us. Think of Felicia."

Morton's red eyes narrowed. The fierce anger in his eyes pierced into Daniel's soul. The cat seethed through sharp teeth. "I *am* thinking about her. I'll die to protect her, if necessary."

Daniel nodded. He turned and took Julia's hand. They disappeared into the fog, and something dropped on the pavement with a gentle thud. Morton recognized the bag as the one he had given Daniel. The antidote syringes.

A strange idea loomed in the cat's mind. The denaturer bullets didn't harm this creature. Perhaps its strangely created genome protected it from those degradation elements, but his cat curiosity made him wonder if the antidote might counteract those properties.

Morton smiled. "Only one way to find out."

The wolfish man stood over him. With swiftness only a shifter cat possessed, Morton yanked a syringe from the bag, pulled off the cap with his teeth and stabbed the needle into its arm when it reached down for him. No evident pain came from the injection.

The creature grabbed Morton around the throat. Morton noticed the name tag on its uniform.

Bane.

Odd, he thought. It has a name.

"Bane?" Morton said.

Bane grunted.

Morton taunted, "Wow, they didn't bother to teach you how to talk? It must be the weakness of the canine genes. Or simply plain stupidity."

Bane's brow furrowed. He might not be able to talk, but he understood the insult. He gnashed teeth and tightened his hand around the cat's neck. Morton bit into its meaty wrist. Bones cracked. Bane howled and flung the cat against the brick wall.

Morton landed between the two dumpsters. The world blurred around him. He squinted and shook his head. His only danger was losing consciousness. If he did, Bane would track down Daniel and the others.

Morton opened his eyes. Bane came closer.

The cat tried to stand, but his lack of strength prevented him from rising quickly enough. Thick fingers wrapped around his neck and squeezed. Morton's growl was embarrassingly soft and muffled. Bane shook him and flung him further into the fog.

Morton's muscles tightened when he hit the pavement. He rolled into a ball to lessen the impact. His nemesis roared. Morton rose to all fours and then collapsed. His strength was gone. He fell to his side, panting.

Bane advanced, and Morton wondered if the injection had any effect at all. Nothing seemed to change due to the antidote. Morton had never felt weaker. Trying to morph, he discovered his body suddenly denied him the ability. He looked at his forepaw and flexed.

No change.

No huge nails.

Nothing.

"Dammit!" he whispered.

Bane towered over him with eyes blazing victory. Morton made no attempt to flee. He didn't have enough energy. Had the denaturer he'd been shot with caused permanent damage? He didn't know, but his current situation looked bleak. For the second time in less than a day, he believed he was going to die.

Bane's muscled hands reached for Morton.

A gunshot blasted through the silence. Bane clutched at the huge hole in his chest. Blood seeped through his fingers. Morton took a couple steps back.

The massive shotgun blast wasn't healing. Blood spilled freely without any signs of stopping. The antidote must have made the creature weaker, preventing his tissue regeneration.

A second blast echoed. A chunk of Bane's head exploded. He fell forward, dead.

Daniel lowered the shotgun. "You didn't think I'd just leave you, did you?"

Morton smiled. "Where are Felicia and Julia?"

"I sent them in the van to go to the FBI headquarters. We'll be with them soon."

Morton sighed. "I'm sorry."

"For what?"

"Letting Felicia see what I really am."

"She saw you, but I don't think she believes it was really you."

"All the same. I didn't think before I shifted."

Daniel picked Morton up and rubbed the bottom of the cat's chin. "It's okay. You put your own life at risk to save them. That's what matters the most. Felicia will be fine. She's seen worse on television."

Morton closed his eyes but didn't purr. "I have another problem though."

"What?"

"I can't morph anymore."

Daniel frowned. "What?"

"Watch." Morton flexed his paw and again, he failed to alter his claws or digits.

"What caused that?"

Morton shook his head. "I think maybe it was the denaturer I was shot with, or perhaps the antidote itself. Some component of it must have altered my DNA to where I cannot shift my metabolism anymore. That's the only reason you killed Bane with the shotgun. I injected him with antidote."

"So? It's not a big deal. You've never shifted that much around the house anyway."

"Yes, Dan. I know. But, what if I lose my ability to talk? What if I become a … blah … *normal* cat?"

"I hadn't thought about that."

"We need to find Helmsby and get him to examine me."

"We will, but first let's get to Julia and Felicia."

"Yes. They're more important."

Daniel hurried through the alley to their car. He tapped his earpiece. "Carpenter, everything's under control here. We killed the creature that killed your agents."

"Good. Give me the details later. Dr. Helmsby, Nancy, and Yvonne were picked up on the river earlier. Lucas and Lydia are on their way out of TGC as well."

Daniel looked at his watch. "Shouldn't the Meltdown be complete by now?"

"The time is up, but he said that they are in an outer mine shaft that leads to the sewer system. They are no longer in the facility itself. So the Meltdown won't affect them."

"And his clone?"

"No idea. I'll meet you at headquarters soon. We'll discuss further details then."

"Okay."

Morton was reciting poetry as Daniel drove.

"What are you doing?"

"Trying to keep my voice intact. You never know when … *meow*."

Daniel turned toward Morton with a stern look. Morton smiled and stuck out his tongue. "At least I still have my sense of humor."

"God forbid you lose that, you smart ass."

CHAPTER 84

*L*ucian carried Kyle over his shoulder until they reached the corridor that led to the underground bunker from the inside of TGC. He opened the door and set Kyle inside. He reached to shut the door, and Brockton placed a gentle hand on Lucian's shoulder. Lucian turned with his gun.

"Easy, Lucian. It's just me."

Lucian lowered his weapon.

"I brought more injections for you and some I believe might help Kyle heal somewhat, though he may never be what he once was."

Kyle studied Brockton with genuine interest. Kyle's vision grew clearer, and he seemed more alert.

"Thanks," Lucian said. "We need to get out of here unnoticed."

"With all the Guard on the surface? That may be impossible."

"People must believe I died here."

Crashing sounds rattled in the room ahead of them. Lucian clicked off the gun safety.

KAT CRINGED after she knocked over a garbage can near one of the bunks. She held her breath and listened. She didn't know if more soldiers lingered behind, but since they were mercenaries, it was doubtful anymore remained inside the bunker.

She took a deep breath and held her gun to the side of the corridor entrance. The overhead lights flickered and dimmed.

Something more than shifters had kept TransGenCorp alive, she told herself. She wondered what else Carpenter had kept hidden from her. When she returned to headquarters, she planned to dig through files until she discovered what they *hadn't* shown her. Idris must have had partners somewhere, and even though he was dead, TransGenCorp wasn't necessarily dead. The Meltdown had completed but experiments could be moved, or they perhaps some projects had already been shipped elsewhere. Data files were easily transferred or stored at other facilities. Other labs possibly existed elsewhere.

The dim lights faded and emergency lights flipped on approximately every thirty feet down the corridor. She bit her lower lip and stepped into the darker hallway. Some answers might be found further inside.

The eerily, quiet corridor edged her nerves. She expected something to bolt from the shadows and attack. Witnessing Morton's transformation had unnerved her, and had she not seen it, she wouldn't have believed it possible. But being in the darkness now and knowing how quickly shifters transformed made her suddenly uneasy.

Kat turned to head back and thought of Tyler. Her heart grieved. She tried to recall how he looked when they were together, but those memories were overshadowed by his death, the gunshot to his head, and his blood splattered across the interior of the car. Her hand tightened on her gun, and she stormed into the hallway. Midway, a voice from the shadows caused her to raise her gun and aim.

"Who's there?" she asked.

Lucian stepped beneath an emergency light.

"Lucas?" Kat asked.

"No."

Dr. Brockton stepped beside Lucian with Kyle at his side.

She raised her gun. "You're his clone?"

"Lucian will suffice." He aimed his gun at her head.

"What's farther down the hall beyond you?"

Lucian shrugged. "All that's left of TransGenCorp. You do know you can't go in there now? Lucas shut it down."

Sweat beaded Kat's brow. The gun in her hand weighed heavier the longer she trained it on Lucian.

"Where are Lucas and Lydia?"

"I assumed he'd be with you by now. He headed out some time ago."

Kat's eyes darted to Brockton. He looked unarmed, and Kyle looked more curious than dangerous, in spite of his hideous appearance.

"Who's with you?" Kat asked, clearing her throat.

"Dr. Brockton, my physician, and Kyle."

"They're free to leave," she said. "But I'm taking you into custody."

Lucian laughed.

"I'm serious. We have orders to arrest you for the murders of the senators and guards."

"Shoot me if you must, but I'm coming past you."

He took a step toward her and a lump swelled in her throat. "Please, don't make me shoot you."

"Ma'am," Brockton said. "Lucian will die if you take him into custody. Authorities won't administer the medicine he requires to stay alive. He needs me and you need him even more than you can imagine."

Kat frowned. "I *don't* need him. He's a killer."

Brockton nodded. "Yes, but it goes far deeper than you know. Blackmail forced his hand to kill. I've worked with him for the past six years."

"Sorry," she said. "He's coming back with me to face justice."

Lucian shook his head. "I'm not going with you."

He took another step.

She fired.

The bullet struck his left shoulder. He winced and then he smiled.

Kat took a step back.

Lucian shook his head. "Your bullets are useless."

Under the light, he pulled back his shirt. The wound healed and shut.

A hand slipped around Kat's throat while another pressed a gun barrel against her temple.

"Should've taken her up on the offer, Lucian," Magnus said. "She wants you taken alive. We have orders to *kill* you."

"And they sent *you*?"

Donovan grabbed Kat's gun. He smiled, looking her up and down. "We'll have fun with you later."

Magnus' cold, black eyes glistened like polished obsidian when he glared at Lucian. "Your companions are free to go. We don't give a damn about them. The reward is for you. But if you try anything, she's dead, too. Now drop your weapon."

Lucian narrowed his eyes. "Idris hired you to kill me?"

"No, not directly."

"Well, Idris is dead," Lucian said. "I killed him. So if he's to help with your payment, you're out of luck."

"GenTech will honor the kill contract. Just like you proved to be a failure to Idris, Idris became useless to them."

Kat struggled to wiggle free, but Magnus pressed the gun to her temple and clicked off the safety. She stopped moving.

"Another biotech company is involved?" she asked.

Lucian trained his gun for a clean shot at Magnus' head, but Magnus was cautious. He crouched low to keep Kat in the direct line of fire.

"Yes," Lucian said. "But nowhere as big as TransGenCorp."

Lucian glanced at Brockton. "Whatever happens, make certain Kyle gets out alive."

"I will."

Lucian studied Magnus for a moment. "Let the lady go. Then kill me or take me to them. No need to make her suffer, too."

Magnus laughed. "She's FBI. It would be foolish to let her go since she's seen us. She'd hunt us down."

"They don't know who we are or what we look like, but she does," Donovan said. "Now, dammit! Put your gun down!"

Kat's fearful eyes stared at Lucian. With a faint smile, he nodded. Extending his hand outward with his fingers wide apart, Lucian acted as though he'd comply, but instead, with incredible speed; he shot out the emergency light nearest them.

Lucian rolled, grabbed Kyle, and pulled him to the floor. Magnus fired two blind shots where Lucian had been standing. Donovan tried to fire Kat's gun but failed because she had the safety on. Lucian fired and shot Donovan's right knee. He recoiled in pain and fell to the floor. Kat's gun slid across the floor.

"Stay down," Lucian told Kyle.

Brockton was gone.

Kat grabbed Magnus' free hand and twisted. He raised his gun to shoot and she rammed her fist into his sternum. The impact expelled air from his lungs and cracked bone. He lost his balance, and Kat pinned him by pressing her knees into his chest. She grabbed her handcuffs.

Donovan crawled for Kat's gun. Lucian stepped on the man's shattered knee. Donovan wailed. Lucian aimed his 9mm at the man's head.

"No!" Kat screamed. "Enough people have died today."

"There were going to kill you."

"They didn't, though, now did they?"

"No," Lucian said, smiling. "Because I saved your ass. You still want to take me in?"

"I have no choice."

Kat clamped one side of the handcuffs around Magnus' right wrist, and he shoved. Off balance, she lost her hold and flung her arms to catch herself. He swung a swift right, striking her in the face. The free cuff followed the blow and cut her left jaw. She rolled and shielded her face from a second strike. Magnus grabbed her gun off the floor and fumbled to get his finger on the trigger. She swung an elbow and knocked the gun from his grasp. He rolled and slid across the floor toward the 9mm.

Kat tasted blood. She rubbed more blood from her cut cheek with the back of her hand. The cool air made the stinging laceration burn. She tried to ignore it. She pulled herself to her knees and scrambled to stop Magnus. His hand was only inches from the gun when she dove onto his back. She grabbed a fistful of his hair and slammed his face onto the concrete floor several times.

Magnus reached back to pull her off. She caught his wrist and twisted upward. He groaned. She crushed his nose and mouth against the floor again, and then held down his head. A pool of thick blood formed beneath his nostrils. He exhaled and blood bubbles skimmed across the viscous, crimson fluid. She tightened his arm until he cried out and pulled back his other arm and locked the cuffs.

Donovan shifted on the floor. Lucian noticed the bullet wound was meshing closed.

"You do realize they're like me?" he asked. "You can't hold them with normal cuffs. Besides, he's already healing and will be back to full strength in a few minutes."

Brockton rushed into the room and yanked the lid off a syringe. He thrust it into Donovan's shoulder. Then he hurried to Magnus and did the same.

"What did you inject him with?" Kat asked. "Will it kill him?"

Brockton gave Lucian a nervous glance. "It will disable them so we can get out of here safely."

Kat frowned. "A tranquilizer?"

Brockton shrugged. "You could say that."

Lucian helped Kyle to his feet. "Let's get out of here."

Kat picked up her 9mm and pointed at Lucian. "I'm sorry. I know you saved my life, but I have to arrest you for murder."

Lucian smiled. "I can't allow that. Not when there are dozens of other soldiers out there like them. Some are worse. By letting me go, I can do more to help you than anyone else can. That is, if you *want* to stop what Idris created."

Kat lowered the gun. "You're going after them?"

He nodded. "No one else can stop them."

"Where's GenTech located?"

"I don't know. I've never been there. I have met some of the scientists when they came to TransGenCorp to get blood samples from me. I'm the prototype. Well, technically Lucas is, but after my advancements, I've become the new template."

"All of you look the same?" she asked.

"No, thankfully."

Kat holstered her gun. She ran her fingers through her hair. "God, I hope I don't regret this," she said. "But I'll make a deal with you."

Brockton steadied Kyle. Kyle was getting stronger, but his balance remained impaired.

Lucian replied with a look of confusion.

Kat took a deep breath. "You help me stop GenTech, and I'll tell Carpenter that you disappeared."

"What interests do you have with them?"

"It's personal."

"I'd do it anyway," he said, putting out his hand.

She shook it. "Kat. My name is Kat."

"You know mine, but understand that I won't partner with the FBI on this. Only with you."

"They'll know nothing of it. I promise. I've been victim to enough of their lies. This time the projects will end."

"You have my word that we'll stop them," Lucian said. "And after it ends, my life can begin."

They returned to the stairs to the overhead parking lot. Kat peered out. Carpenter was headed toward the bunker.

"Shit," she said. "I don't know how we're going to get you out without him seeing you."

"Let him see me."

Lucian headed up the stairs. She grabbed his arm. He turned and his face was completely different. Her mouth dropped open. He looked nothing like Lucian.

Seeing the surprise in her face, he said, "Details later. Right now, let's get the hell out of here."

Brockton walked Kyle ahead of Kat and Lucian. Carpenter stopped to talk to Kat, but she brushed past him.

"Kat, talk to me. I'm sorry about Tyler's death. We didn't know TGC was this bad."

Kat waved him off. "I need some time to think."

"Okay, but who are these people?"

Kat turned with tears in her eyes. "Survivors, Carpenter. They're survivors. Something I wish I could say about Tyler."

Carpenter dropped his gaze to the pavement and let her walk away.

CHAPTER 85

$\mathcal{A}$ half hour of walking through sewer catacombs, Lucas and Lydia finally found their way to the riverside. Her strength had partially returned, but she remained distant and quiet during their journey out. Lucas wasn't certain if she'd move on with her life or if she still wished to die.

A police boat picked them up. They met Daniel and the others at FBI headquarters. Kat, though, wasn't there, nor did she attend the debriefing later. She refused to answer any calls from Carpenter at all.

Helmsby agreed to surrender all his data files that he had copied and stored at his home laboratory. He also agreed not to do any further research with shifter DNA unless the government requested. They did ask that he do several genetic tests on Idris' remains. Tests proved that it was Idris. Though they could breathe easier knowing Idris was dead, Daniel remained somewhat skeptical, as did Lucas and Morton.

Whatever Brockton had injected into Magnus and Donovan had killed them. The genetic soldiers that fled on the river were never found.

Morton slowly regained his morphing abilities, which still didn't deter his wisecracking demeanor. He was savvier than ever, and to his relief, Felicia never made the connection that he was the shifter that attacked Bane.

(THREE DAYS later)

The small wedding chapel was filled with roses and lilies. Lucas stood before the minister and Daniel was his best man. Julia stood opposite as the Maid of Honor. Johanna and Nancy were bridesmaids. Felicia stepped timidly down the aisle, dropping rose petals onto the carpet while soft music played. Morton followed with rings clenched in his teeth. A cat never walked prouder.

The music ceased and then the wedding march began. Lydia entered the back of the chapel dressed in an elegant wedding gown. Her arm entwined with Dr. Helmsby. When she reached the altar, Lucas smiled broadly. The radiance in her eyes made his heart swell. None of their party had a dry eye. Even Helmsby, who was seated beside Yvonne, wiped away tears. She squeezed his arm, and he patted her knee.

After the vows were exchanged, everyone met in the reception hall and ate cake.

Daniel approached Helmsby and shook his hand. "I'm sorry for my attitude during the past three years. I guess I saw everything all wrong. I misjudged you."

Helmsby squeezed his hand. "No, Dan. I don't blame you for any bitterness. I now see my errors, too. It wasn't right for me to place you into the heart of danger just because I knew that you could survive it. I guess we've both learned a lot."

Daniel nodded. "True, but still, I should have been there for Kyle."

Helmsby smiled. Tears glistened in his eyes. "We learn too late about some things. Had I lost Nancy, I couldn't have gone on. Take care of Julia and little Felicia. Treasure them. I might have found a lot of ways to preserve the longevity of life, but I learned the hard way. There are no guarantees. Take advantage of each day you have with them."

"I know."

"Are you going back to the apartment?"

"No, we can't live there anymore. We hired a moving company to pack up our things. We're buying a house further out in the country for more privacy. What about you?"

Helmsby looked across the room at Yvonne. She talked with Julia and Johanna. Nancy hugged Lydia.

"I promised Nancy I'd take a long vacation." He pulled out plane tickets from his coat pocket. "How's Italy and Germany sound for starters? London after that."

Daniel laughed.

"What's so funny?" Helmsby said. "I've missed so much over the years. My biggest regret is that Margaret didn't get to venture to these places with me."

"She'll be with you in spirit, my friend."

Helmsby squeezed Daniel's shoulder. "You know, I believe you're right."

Julia took dozens of digital photos of Lydia and Lucas. They informed the crowd that they were spending their honeymoon in the Grand Canyon.

Daniel picked Felicia up and held her while watching his friends laugh, drink, and talk. Johanna rolled out the blueprints for her new workout studio.

Daniel smiled. After all, they had faced together three years ago and the past week, they were still alive. The fight for survival was finally over. They could live their lives. He was thankful to have these people as his dearest friends and family.

AT TYLER'S FUNERAL, Carpenter placed a hand on Kat's shoulder when Tyler's casket was lowered into the grave. Lucian, with his newly altered face, stood on the other side of her.

"Kat, we need to talk," Carpenter whispered.

"I quit, Carpenter," she said. "I'm through with this. I can't take anymore lies."

"What will you do?"

"PI work. I'm a good investigator, so that's what I plan to do."

"You don't plan to go after anyone formerly associated with TGC, do you?"

Kat smiled. "I have no idea who my clients will be, or who I'll have to investigate."

"I wish you'd reconsider. I like having you on my team, but I must warn you not to stay involved with any of this. If you leave, you're no longer allowed to work on these cases."

She turned and pointed a finger in his face. "Understand that I'll do whatever it takes to stop those responsible for Tyler's death. I don't give a damn *who* they are, either."

"We're on that. They'll be brought to justice."

Kat leveled a stern glare at him. "One time I truly believed everything that you told me. I placed my full trust and confidence in you."

"I know you're bitter, Kat. I understand that. But, I'm still your friend. It may take you awhile to see that, and if it's time you need, I'll be here. I'll wait. But we are working on it."

She shrugged. "Not fast enough, if you don't mind me sounding disrespectful."

"Okay, Kat. You know how to reach me, if you ever need me."

Carpenter walked away with his hands shoved in his pockets. Kat stood and stared at the grave long after they covered it with soil. Everyone except her and Lucian remained.

Across the cemetery, near a sepulcher, stood two men dressed in dark suits. These men weren't part of a procession. They stood watching Kat and Lucian. They kept their guns visible as a silent threat. The overcast sky warned of darker things to come.

Lucian nudged her. "We have company."

Kat looked across the cemetery. The men got into a red Jaguar and sped off.

"It's not over," she said.

"No, it's just beginning."

Kat nodded and handed him her business card. "I had these printed today. This address is where we'll work. That's my phone number."

Lucian tucked the card into his shirt pocket. "Thanks. I'll head after them, so you can leave without looking over your shoulder."

"Be careful."

"They're more afraid of me than I am of them."

"Maybe," she replied. "But that can make them even more dangerous. Once we get set up, we'll bring them down."

Lucian nodded. "Yes, they'll remain hidden for awhile until they feel more secure about our intentions. Otherwise, these two wouldn't have fled. When we do flush them out, it will be outright war again."

"I'll be ready," she said, checking her gun clip.

"I always am."

AUTHOR'S NOTE

Thank you for purchasing this novel. If you enjoyed this book, please check out my website and join my mailing list at www.leonarddhilleyii.com to receive a free digital copy of Forrest Wollinsky: Vampire Hunter.

If you could also take a moment and leave a review, it is greatly appreciated!

Blessings to you and yours.

ABOUT THE AUTHOR

Leonard D. Hilley II grew up a quiet, shy kid with an inquisitive mind. Learning to read at an early age, he fell in love with books. He read every book he could get his hands on and stacks of dark comics about ghosts, monsters, and creepy things that stalk the night.

Like a lot of boys, he caught beetles, wooly bears, butterflies, and had an ant farm. When he was ten, his interests in science increased even more after seeing a professor's insect collection. Soon he set out on his quest to build his own collection. He also learned to rear butterflies and moths to obtain perfect specimens. He learned botany, gardening, and set his goal to become an entomologist.

At eleven, he saw Star Wars. His imagination soared. Soon after, he discovered Roger Zelazny's Chronicles of Amber. Six months later, he had written the first draft of a novel. A novel he later discarded, but the characters stuck with him. Years later, these characters came to life in Shawndirea, which Hilley intended to be a novella for Devils Den. The characters, however, refused to be ignored and took the opportunity to unveil Aetheaon in their first epic fantasy. Lady Squire: Dawn's Ascension was quick to follow.

Shawndirea was Hilley's farewell to butterfly collecting, and those who have read the novel understand why. He has taken Ray Bradbury's advice to heart: "Follow the characters." He does. He follows, listens, and take notes—often never knowing where they're going to take him, but he's never been disappointed in the results.

Hilley earned a B.S. in Biology and an MFA in Creative Writing to combine his love of science and writing.

Sci-fi Titles: Predators of Darkness: Aftermath, Beyond the Darkness, The Game of Pawns, Death's Valley, The Deimos Virus.

Epic Fantasy: Shawndirea (Aetheaon Chronicles: Book One), Lady Squire (Aetheaon Chronicles: Book Two), Frosthammer (Aetheaon Chronicles: Book Three), Shadowfae (Aetheaon Chronicles: Book Four), and Devils Den.

UF/PR: Succubus: Shadows of the Beast (Nocturnal Trinity Series: Book One), Raven (Nocturnal Trinity Series: Book Two), A Touch of the Familiar (Nocturnal Trinity Series: Book Three)

YA UF/Paranormal: Forrest Wollinsky Vampire Hunter; Forrest Wollinsky: Blood Mists of London; Forrest Wollinsky: Predestined Crossroads.